The BRILLIANT DARK

THE REALMS OF ANCIENT TRILOGY:

Scion of the Fox
Children of the Bloodlands
The Brilliant Dark

S.M. BEIKO

THE
BRILLIANT
DARK

THE REALMS OF ANCIENT
BOOK III

Published by ECW Press
665 Gerrard Street East, Toronto, ON M4M 1Y2
416-694-3348 / info@ecwpress.com

Editor for the press: Jen Hale
Cover design: Erik Mohr / Made by Emblem
Interior illustration: S.M. Beiko
Author photo: Teri Hofford Photography

This is a work of fiction. Names, characters,
places, and incidents either are the product of
the author's imagination or are used fictitiously,
and any resemblance to actual persons, living or
dead, business establishments, events, or locales
is entirely coincidental.

LIBRARY AND ARCHIVES CANADA
CATALOGUING IN PUBLICATION

Title: The brilliant dark / S.M. Beiko.

Names: Beiko, S. M., author.

Series: Beiko, S. M. Realms of ancient ; bk. 3.

Description: Series statement: The realms of
ancient ; book III

Identifiers: Canadiana (print) 20190109998
Canadiana (ebook) 20190110619

ISBN 9781770413597 (hardcover)
ISBN 9781773054162 (PDF)
ISBN 9781773054155 (ePUB)

CLASSIFICATION: LCC PS8603.E428444 B75 2019
DDC JC813/.6—DC23

The publication of *The Brilliant Dark* has been generously supported by the Canada Council for the
Arts which last year invested $153 million to bring the arts to Canadians throughout the country and is
funded in part by the Government of Canada. *Nous remercions le Conseil des arts du Canada de son sout-
ien. L'an dernier, le Conseil a investi 153 millions de dollars pour mettre de l'art dans la vie des Canadiennes et
des Canadiens de tout le pays. Ce livre est financé en partie par le gouvernement du Canada.* We acknowledge
the support of the Ontario Arts Council (OAC), an agency of the Government of Ontario, which last
year funded 1,737 individual artists and 1,095 organizations in 223 communities across Ontario for a
total of $52.1 million. We also acknowledge the contribution of the Government of Ontario through
the Ontario Book Publishing Tax Credit, and through Ontario Creates for the marketing of this book.

ONTARIO CREATES

ONTARIO ARTS COUNCIL
CONSEIL DES ARTS DE L'ONTARIO
an Ontario government agency
un organisme du gouvernement de l'Ontario

Canada Council
for the Arts

Conseil des Arts
du Canada

Canadä

PRINTED AND BOUND IN CANADA   PRINTING: FRIESENS   5 4 3 2 1

MIX
Paper from
responsible sources
FSC
www.fsc.org   FSC® C016245

For all of you — the darkness doesn't last.
We cast our own light. Tomorrow is a golden sliver that,
once slipped through, leads into a brighter country.

Part I
FLICKER

WE ARE *the* FLAME

S tick the landing.

That's the only phrase — a dumb one, a desperate one — that clung to Saskia's brain. She didn't know who exactly she was talking to in her head, since only stupid people gave themselves advice (so said Phae). But what she was doing tonight was plenty stupid, so she'd take what she could get.

And no one knew she was out here, either. Not the curfew wardens. Not the neighbours. Not even Phae. Saskia was quiet, knew when to watch, when to listen. And you had to be stupid not to know that any authority would be otherwise occupied with what was going down at the Old Legislature. They wouldn't be for long, and the time to hesitate was over.

Ultimately, Saskia didn't trust that she'd stick the landing, but as she scampered between buildings up Broadway, under flickering street lights, her canvas bag smashing heavily across her chest, she figured she had nothing else to do but jump.

It was dark. But the dark wasn't much of a threat to her — and hadn't been for a long time. Sometimes it felt safer in the dark, considering what the world looked like during the day. Saskia kept her hood up. It wasn't the dark that worried her, but the cameras. The constant feeds. In the 4,067 scenarios she'd run in her stress-addled brain, she didn't dare consider anything other than success. There was no alternative.

Saskia flattened against the wall and turned her face away, stiffening — members of the Elemental Task Guard rushed past, grunting under their heavy packs, faceless under their full-helm visors. Her heart sped up when she flicked her head back to see where they'd gone — towards Memorial, which was now called Reclamation Street. She focused on her breath, forcing her pulse to slow, but those cracks of burning doubt crept in. *This is so stupid. Why are you out here risking your neck for them, anyway? They wouldn't do the same for you.*

She shook her head, hands diving into her pack at the hip and pulling out the battered tablet. Plastic and steel, the weight of it slightly more reassuring. It made her feel in control. Stick to the facts — and the facts were that she was already out here. If she went back now, she'd just pace in her room until sunrise, knowing she could've done something and that she'd chosen to be afraid. No more of that, no matter what they said.

Saskia pressed the power button, checked the time against her wristwatch. Fifteen minutes. A few keystrokes and swipes and the app was up. So were her firewalls, old code that would do better in a pinch than nothing. Her pulse was back up, eyes darting, and when she zeroed in on exactly where she had to go to make this work, it played out in her head as cinematically as it had when she'd programmed this weeks ago.

Now all she had to do was not get caught.

⁓⁓

"I don't know why you think this is, like, the best idea you could possibly come up with to *pass the time*."

Ella's bottom lip curled at Saskia's comment, but she still kept stuffing her bag. "This isn't some game, Saskia. You wouldn't understand. You're not one of us."

Saskia felt the stab between her ribs just as acutely as she always had over the last seven years. Anger roiled up in place of the shame, no matter how she tried to shove it down. "I think I know more about any of this shit than you do!"

"Shut up!" Ella whirled, but this time Saskia could see on her best friend's face how torn she was. "You don't get it, do you? You can leave this crummy apartment and be, like, normal. Have a future. You can have all those things that Mundanes want. But I can't. My Family *can't*."

The two girls jerked at the sound of something crashing in the apartment hallway, as Ella's bedroom was close to the fire escape and the walls were so thin. A woman yelling. A baby crying. The electricity flickered and went out, but it wasn't dark for long. The palm of Ella's hand lit her stricken brown eyes with bright Denizen flame.

"I just . . ." Saskia's jaw was tight, eyes bone dry. She was upset, but she hadn't cried in years, not really. "I don't want anything to happen to you. I don't want to lose you."

Once, Ella might have put her arms around Saskia, and they would have hugged fiercely, feeling each other's bones move with their love, but they were older now and knew better, and these days, Denizens should stick together, trust only each other. Mundanes were the enemy.

"If you want to help me," Ella said, focusing now on her little flame, which was growing wider and wider, "you won't get in my way."

⁓⤳

Instead of heading back out into the street, Saskia shuffled along the building she'd hidden against, farther into the back lanes of houses and small apartment buildings crushed against Young Street. Even before the Restoration Project, coming down here after midnight would have been dangerous, but with the Task Guard posted everywhere, especially downtown, *especially* by the Old Leg, no one dared. Not even errant, Mundane drug dealers. A cat yowled, darting out of the shadows. Saskia froze when it threw her a withering stare before scampering back to the much-safer hole from whence it had come.

It's just a cat, she told herself, twice for good measure. It wasn't a f— well. It couldn't have been *that*. Not anymore.

But the line from the story leapt up like a familiar friend whispering in her ear. *Once upon a time, a girl was followed home by a fox . . .*

Saskia shook it off. *Pull it together.* Across the back lane, she rushed a collapsing fence and vaulted over it, landing shy of one of many huge piles of trash crammed between houses, against chain-link. A quick survey with her watch's flashlight showed it to be more of the same — charred old tech, probably seized from a Denizen house, decommissioned and flung out here to be collected for precious metals and scrapped. The Task Guard didn't want Denizens to be connected in the ways the Mundanes got to enjoy. Wouldn't want them to assemble. To think twice about putting their powers to use. Saskia scavenged these junk piles often, their contents filled her bedroom nearly floor-to-ceiling. It kept the quickly tumbling world on some kind of keel.

It kept the shadows quiet.

. . . and after the fox followed the girl home, Death came for the both of them . . .

Saskia bent over, digging the heels of her hands — callused from soldering wires and pinching receivers — into her eyes. *Stop. Not now.* Her heartbeat was picking up. This was what she wanted, she reminded herself. To be the damned hero for a change. She wasn't going to freeze up. Not this time.

She took a breath. She counted. She straightened her spine and dropped her shoulders. *Not this time.*

The cat was long gone, and Saskia was alone in the back alleys of a city she'd never known except under the rule of anxiety. Of caution. Of an undercurrent of fear that she carried everywhere with her. She took another sharp breath and darted from light post to light post, feet quick and legs strong. Just like Barton had taught her, each stride like she was pulling against a current, and somehow, the stronger the bursts, the more her heart evened out. It was in running that she felt him most with her, and though she desperately wished he were here now, wishes were no good to the logical mind even at the best of times.

She'd have to cross Reclamation Street eventually, be out in the open with little protection. Saskia had known the risks, made all the calculations. But she was still more human than all the half-finished devices strewn across her workbench. Machines that had been her closest friends . . . apart from the one she was stupidly trying to save tonight.

Saskia dashed up another side street when she heard nearby bootfalls, more shouts. She crouched, gripping her black hood tight in one hand. She squinted at her watch and then at the app. Not yet. She still had time to stop this.

Saskia's head jerked up. Quick-checking the map, she was ten feet from the outskirts of the building's side lanes, the perimeter of cameras waiting for any opportunity to catch her. She ran through probabilities. Getting caught was becoming the likeliest. *Stupid brain.* She didn't condemn it long — she'd need every neuron to make this work.

Keystroke. Flick. She realized she was close enough to deploy the code. A sudden rush — she could pull this off from the *shadows*, be home quick before Phae noticed she was gone. A flush of premature triumph. She —

The explosion rattled the windows of the rundown apartment block she hid beside, hammered the ground. Saskia went flying into a dumpster at her back, though she didn't land hard enough to do more than knock the wind out of her. Screams and shouting, the heavy, horrible noise of weapons charging up to fire the first sonic salvo. Saskia winced, looking up at the wall emblazoned with an icon that was seared into her eyelids whenever she tried to sleep.

The fox head wreathed in flame, the red spray paint shining bloody in the luminous dark. The face of a girl. A face Saskia knew once, though briefly.

ozone before it was slammed into the belly of anyone not cooperating, shocking them to a crumpled pile. *Set phasers to stun*. Except Saskia's version put out a high-pitched sonic wave that temporarily shorted out the electricity on the perimeter fence, including all spotlights directed on camera blind spots, and the sirens.

It also left a gap in their digital fence, something Saskia was about to burst through.

Body low, she rushed towards the part of the fence that had been taken out in the blast. The Task Guard soldiers were otherwise occupied at the front steps of the building, and she'd have the element of surprise on her side now that they were shouting, scrambling. She took out the VR visor, slid her finger across the banged-up tablet, and shoved it into the back of her jeans. The firewall was down. Her code was doing its parasitic work in their periphery system and would provide ample distraction for those in the Old Leg's control centre in the massive dome Saskia stared up at.

The Dome was once the eye of the Owl's authority, but no longer, the story went on. A lot had changed. But that wasn't going to stop her now.

Saskia dropped the VR visor over her eyes, slid on her micro-sensored gloves, and lowered into the stance she'd seen her real hero, first-hand, drop into before rushing in.

"Showtime," she muttered.

⁓⁓

"Get away!" Ella screamed, arms and fists flaring bright with fire, and every time she lobbed a flaming shot at an advancing guard, her elbow felt the kickback of a sawed-off shotgun.

She wasn't the only Fox still standing, but there weren't many left after the first bluff. The Guard had known they were coming. That was the risk they always took. She hadn't wanted it to escalate like this, or so quickly. They hadn't even gotten inside, to the chancellor. They were still within the main courtyard. They hadn't made it very far before the sonic clubs were out, before Denizens had gone down.

Now Ella was trapped, cornered on the huge limestone steps she'd only ever seen through industrial fencing. She'd gone on a tour of the building, once when she was very small and the world had been different. Damien was on her right, but he was coughing up blood, and Ella wasn't exactly the strongest of the lot of those who had rushed in here in the first place. Clare, on her left, was cradling her shoulder, and when her crisp eyes met Ella's, they were wet with tears. Ella had never felt more like a kid than at this moment. And she was definitely no Roan Harken.

She wished Saskia were here. To tell Ella one more time that she was an idiot, so that Ella could tell her she was right. And though she knew it would fall on deaf ears, Ella prayed, stupidly, to anyone who would hear: To Deon. To Ancient. To Roan Harken herself. Prayer was futile: the guards charged up their weapons and advanced.

Then the sirens and the lights died. And the Task Guard wasn't looking at Ella anymore. There were surprised shouts, the blue sparking light of the sonic batons fizzling along with the certainty of their trigger-happy owners.

"What the hell is that?" she heard a guard cry, pointing towards the ruined fence in the murky dark. He dropped his weapon and fled, screaming.

Ella lowered her fists, squinted. They were all looking

towards the gates, the ones she'd blown apart to barely make it past the first wave, and the guards were scattering now, terrified. Some staggered, as if struck, and with each blow of this invisible monster chasing them out of their own turf, there was an awful roar, like a house fire, like a howl, and Damien nearly fell down the stairs when they all glimpsed what was on one fleeing guard's visor monitor.

"Deon?" Clare hissed. Ella caught Damien, and the three of them decided that, divine intervention or not, it was time to go.

≈

The problem with any bit of tech that is worn to augment reality is that *anyone* can augment it. So reality itself is easily manipulated. Saskia knew that better than anyone, code or not.

She'd spent foundational weeks, probably more like months, sculpting and designing and building the enormous image of Deon now burned into the retinas of the fleeing guards. Her research had been thorough. She'd interviewed a lot of older Foxes who had been more than happy to describe the god their Family had taught them to revere. An enormous warrior woman, with a head — or a helm, some people said — of a fox, with a mantle of white flames on her wide shoulders, nine tails, like the Japanese myth, wagging behind her, arms and legs braced in the leathery hide of primordial beasts she'd slaughtered with her blade of flickering purple garnet.

A world like this could still use a few heroes. And Saskia was more than happy to provide one.

The second problem with tech wired into an optic nerve is that seeing was believing. Whatever the poor viewer was seeing, their brain registered it as real. Corporeal. So if that manufactured semi-hologram took a swipe at you, your eyes told your brain which told your body that you were, in pointed terms, screwed.

These were problems Saskia had planned for. But she had her own crosses to bear. To get the best range, she had to move in order to make her digital Deon maquette move. She picked up an errant bit of fence from what was probably Ella's first foray into criminal terrorism, and that bit of fence became Deon's garnet blade. Many of the Task Guard weren't sticking around long enough to figure out they were being bested by a ghost in their well-oiled machine.

It was anarchy, to say the least. And those without the faux–Spirit Eye tech could only catch the fleeing guards' hysteria. She hoped Ella had dropped the stupid risk-taking bravado and seen this turn for what it was — a way out. Saskia lifted her visor, and her enormous, flickering mirage of Deon stood over her body like a skin, waiting for her next physical command. There was a flare of fire somewhere near the huge stone steps of the legislature, and in that flash Saskia swore she saw a girl, grinning, as she ushered two others past the still-dead fence and into the safety of the dark.

Saskia laughed out loud, pumped her tense fist. She imagined that her VR Deon cracked its wide fox jaws in an unsettling smirk of its own.

Then her chest tightened, because in that same dark she'd just thought safe, something else climbed out into the gloaming and was staring right at Saskia.

She stopped breathing. *No. Not now. Not again.*

There was a second of pregnant silence, then a bang like a thunderclap in her skull, and the lights and the sirens were back on, the doors of the Old Leg bursting open before her, with the Task Guard in their cruel grey service-issue uniforms pouring out.

"No," she hissed. She slammed the visor down, ripped the tablet from her pants as she backed up towards the busted fence she'd just so brazenly come through, certain and unafraid. But when she whirled, she was knocked over by the butt of something made of steel, and the tablet and the visor went flying. They didn't matter now. Both were dead. Her head rang with pain, and she tried to get up, to run like Barton had taught her, but her hands were being pinned behind her, a zip tie tightening as a knee pressed her into the cold pavement.

She didn't close her eyes, though, still staring at the place where Ella had gotten away. Where the Moth Queen stood, as she had moments ago, clear as the illusion of Deon Saskia had conjured. She knew this was no illusion. Death's many eyes were full of their terrible knowing. Her enormous wings gaped wide, her many needle fingers folded, patient.

"Follow the moth," the great old Mother Death whispered. "The choice must be yours."

The words cut the last shrinking bit of fight out of her. As Saskia was hauled to her feet like a quivering fawn in a sprung snare, and she was taken up the steps and inside, all that was left behind were a few brown moths, fluttering around the floodlights of the city's Denizen prison.

Primer

*F*rom the manifesto of Chancellor Lochlan Grant, formerly
of the White Militia, now chancellor of the independent
U.N.-overseen Elemental Task Guard:

Their book of faith was printed on scrap paper, trash, using
old binding methods. Methods that couldn't be tracked,
everything done and copied by hand. Sometimes the paper
was handmade, the covers stitched to the block. Handwritten,
like it was just another one of their rituals, another way of
staying separate from us.

So much has changed in the intervening seven years,
and the removal of the last copy of this book from the streets
has me thinking of the propaganda of wars gone by. Wars
to come. Strange to think that all it took was for these
enemies to throw another moon into the sky and reveal that

yes — magic is real. If you want to call it that. A genetic anomaly, more like. People casting out evil frequencies.

But magic is here. It's always been here. Hidden from us. Denied us. That book, that primer, it mocked us, those of us who were born normal, but what they *call "mundane." The book is gone now, but its memory endures.*

The books littered the streets in the beginning, though you won't find them now, except in our military archives. Know thine enemy. *Back then, when the dark moon showed up, you could find the books, sometimes mere* zines, *washing up in gutters, on people's doorsteps, thrust into mailboxes.* Yes, we exist, *they tried to say with these gestures.* We mean you no harm. Read our parables, our myths and legends. Know that they are real. Understand that they are true. The world may be coming down on top of us because of them — but we mean you no harm.

A book has never been a more dangerous weapon.

We all found ourselves living inside a strange fable, even as we tried to resume our normal lives. Where were you when the world cracked open? Was anyone close to you found out to be one of those hex-slinging psychopaths? Didn't your uncle get turned into a nightmare tree? So I guess the world is tired of humans, eh, if these god-things have anything to say about it?

It's an international crisis. But the sun keeps rising and we have to keep going. Schools closed for a while. Some people didn't leave their houses. If you found out your neighbour could drown your family or scorch them to dust or obliterate everything you owned in a hurricane — it's not even a question of what would *you do. It's what* did *you do? There was a lot of violence and chaos that came out of*

23

*it, despite how these Ancient-followers tried to reassure us
they meant us no harm. They hide behind friendly animal
faces. And we all watched them, I'm sure — the U.N. trials
were televised as the leaders of this cult came forward of
their own free wills. Pious martyrs, hands held open. Their
demonstrations of power were proved legitimate. We were
living in Fantasyland, population seven billion.* They
mean us no harm.

*They call themselves Denizens. I will continue to call
them monsters until we can truly say we've achieved peace.
They are, at their hearts, extremists. Conjuring arcane
powers that shouldn't have been only theirs to command.
Powers tracing back to* gods. *Real ones. And further back
to one godhead: Ancient. The name is burned behind my
eyes. It should be in yours, too. I've asked myself every day
— why is such a force, with such power,* sleeping *as this
all happens to the world it apparently "made"? Where is
their god now? Then I look up at that dark moon above and
wonder,* Is it coming for us after all?

*You don't remotely want to entertain these questions
sometimes, I know. Because a part of you always believed
that the world wasn't as pedestrian as we imagined. Now
you hear about these grand battles and a secret war and you
think,* There's no place for me in this magical world. I'm
only human. Mundane.

*We look to the sky every day, though, and no matter
how closely the story touched us, we're all part of it now.*

*The Denizen extremists called it "The Darkling Moon."
They were all about using figures of speech that evoked their
mythological brainwashing. As if it would make the reality
a bit easier to choke down. It isn't really a moon, anyway,*

not by science's estimation. It has no mass; it doesn't affect tides. It's just a shadow hanging above the world, one we can all see, no matter the time of day. It doesn't abide physics or reason. We didn't deem it a threat, just a smudge. The real threat was walking among us. Had been for longer than anyone cared to find out.

But the book tried to prove otherwise.

It was destroyed. And that defense was a reactionary one, for all of you who think us *the extremists. The Task Guard is a force guided, in principle, by the nations of the world. A conflict beyond any of us had hurt defenseless people. You can't blame anyone for the reaction that made the Task Guard a means of survival, of inevitability. We've all seen the groves of the twisted dead. Monsters creep around in broad daylight. Tar sands and reserves of precious industrial resources and whole economies have been ransacked and collapsed because of this Ancient, because of its* people. *This is our new reality. We didn't shape it,* they *did.*

Their book outlines the basics of this parallel world. They try to paint themselves as our allies. Forget that now. It has and always will be us against them. Otherwise we wouldn't have been in the dark all this time, would we? Nor would we be in this new dark now.

When I first saw the book it was early days, when the curtain had just been lifted, back in 2013. Denizens were trying to regroup, trying to pull themselves together to win sympathy from the rest of us sorry sods. We mean you no harm.

But we all have to look at that savage smudge in the sky. That's the evidence of harm yet to come.

The book outlines the basics. There are five arcane powers: Fire. Water. Wind. Earth. Spirit.

Each of these powers is governed by a god — a First Matriarch. That's your next problem: a religion steered by women. Each of these matriarchs has an animal totem: fox for fire, seal for water, owl for wind, rabbit for earth, deer for spirit. There's more. It goes on and on. Stones. Prophecies. Darkness. Good and evil. And death. Always *death.*

All you need to know is that it's dangerous. I've seen these people in action when they're desperate. No better than the witches of a bygone era, trying to control us. Maybe they have always been controlling us. After all, those Owls, the ones who have cooperated with us since Dark Day — when that moon showed up and started driving everyone to lunacy — they were the ones keeping all this hidden. They were the old authority. Mind control. What else could they control?

But no longer. This is the new age. The new authority. The world has seen its share of growing pains already. I'll be the first to admit that. But you have to make the tough calls for the greater good. In order for certain ways of life to survive. For the right way. The Mundane *way.*

The Denizen way was not meant to survive. They had to come to an end eventually. I am hoping that, together, we can take them into that good night, and we can all be back on an even playing field. We have yet to open the right door and see them out of it.

Magic — it's something that needs to stay where it was born. In a book. In the dark. Out of our hands.

And out of theirs.

Task Guard Teeth

The aide found him at the window, staring down into the square below the building's Tyndall stone steps. Where it all had unfolded, hours ago, where patrol had since been doubled, where clean-up was ongoing. Where the evidence of the attack had been cleared, but the memory of the threat lingered over heavily edited broadcasts. The Owl Unit had been dispatched to do the dirty work on most of that. *They have their uses*, the chancellor had said.

Mi-ja had knocked demurely on his office door, but the chancellor hadn't answered right away. Now she knew why.

"Sir?"

He was so still that, for a moment, he didn't look real, mannequin-rigid on the other side of his desk, staring out the window, a book in his hand. The cover was hunter green, a colour that made Mi-ja think of home, which made her think of her mother, a Rabbit in disguise from even her own daughter, and the day she was dragged away by the Task Guard. Her mother's betrayal had shattered everything she'd held dear about who she was, about what her family was. It had been the reason Mi-ja joined up in the first place: Denizens in secret could only cause harm. She wouldn't see that happen to anyone else, and so, like many others, she'd joined the Task Guard as soon as it formed, to do her part.

But she knew the book. It was the chancellor's account of the Restoration Project. Part of the Task Guard training syllabus, the book contained tales of the front line when the moon appeared, when the global threat of Denizens hit them all over the head. Mi-ja had found the book slightly manic, and so had few expectations for its author, a man she had only just met after being assigned to him on this diplomatic mission.

Mania didn't quite cover it.

The chancellor still hadn't turned, and the rise of his starched back was so minute she couldn't tell if he was breathing or not.

"Clever, wasn't it?"

His remark cut the silence suddenly, and, hating herself for it, Mi-ja faltered. She wasn't one to be flustered, not with her training. Not with her loyalties already tested.

"Sir, I don't —"

"The trick," he replied, and she heard the frown in his sharp words before he finally turned, and she saw the proof of it.

Mi-ja loosened her clenched jaw. "Sir. The hacker has been detained in the isolation block. Her file and detailed background check have been processed. We have not yet contacted her guardian, as per your request, though the time frame for questioning a minor without guardian contact is narrowing."

No response but a slow exhalation. He turned away again, and she could see his face in profile; his eyes were dark, dark as the city skyline beyond the caustic floodlights of the Task Guard compound.

"A Denizen?"

Mi-ja shook her head, though he didn't look over to see the gesture. "No, sir. A Mundane. Cohabitates with Denizens and has quite a history with them." Out from under her arm she pulled the thin screen she'd carried in with her, the one with the prisoner's information. She should have read the file with her usual detachment, but she couldn't help feel a pang of pity for the girl. "The insurgents —"

"Got away. Of course they did. That was the point of the ruse."

The chancellor finally gave up the window and turned. Mi-ja had only seen him at a distance when he'd arrived earlier that morning from Ottawa, and seeing him close up now she was shocked by his youth, knowing the things he'd done, the things he'd said, and his deeply rooted beliefs that had basically formed the core of the Elemental Task Guard in the first place.

"It won't be the last attack, for well and certain. If they're Cluster-initiated, or independent rebels, it smacks of knowing how close we are. I'd get used to it, if I were you."

Mi-ja narrowed her eyes, found it odd that he sounded so flippant about the Fox terrorists who had just blasted through their security gate.

"The hacker, though," he went on, now standing in front

of her, expectant, his neat desk between them. He put the book in a drawer at his hand, locked it. "A girl, you said?"

She did not like the dangerous spike of light in his eyes, but she met them all the same and nodded. "First-time offender, lives in the neighbourhood —"

He made a noise of impatience, signalling she hand over her screen to him. Like beckoning a terrier. Too many in her unit and in this facility were falling over themselves for this man. She'd forgotten to be unsettled and swung to annoyance.

But he was her superior. With a plastic smile, she passed him the device, which he snatched and dove into, flicking his fingers across the screen, his glare flying as he absorbed the file.

"First time," the chancellor scoffed. It wasn't a question. "An incredible feat of digital terrorism on a military organization for a *first-timer*. And she's how old?"

He was already turning away from her again, so Mi-ja wasn't even sure the question was directed at her. "Sixteen," she said.

Pity for the girl welled up again. Maybe it was because the girl was alone, or because Mi-ja had seen how terrified she was when the cell door had slammed shut. She hadn't even whimpered, but Mi-ja had seen the girl's eyes.

So she couldn't help but blurt, "Surely she was just protecting her friends. And since she wasn't the one directly responsible for the damage, or capable of it —"

The chancellor swung around the desk and to her side like a man who had learned to be fast as a means to strike first. Mi-ja took a step backward but met that unforgiving glare, this man whose "study" of Denizens and their lore had been a keystone of Restoration, and for ETG trainees. Especially those in Winnipeg, which was deemed ground zero to a lot of what had shaped the new world.

"Do you know why I'm here?" He searched her uniform for rank. "Lieutenant?"

Oh, she knew. But she'd said too much already, so she only replied, "The Zabor Incident."

His shined shoes audibly creaked as he leaned back, his smile cutting lines in his too-young-for-what-he'd-done face. "This city," he started, canting his head back towards the window, and the pockmarked urbania beyond. "It's nowhere. Winnipeg has never been on the global radar. But we should have been looking closer. That was our first lesson. Because this is where it all started. Where it all *keeps* starting." The smile splintered into a sneer. "A teen hacker, a Mundane, one of *us*, no less, went to such lengths to protect her Denizen friends? Loyalty is no longer innocuous, Lieutenant. Nothing is a coincidence. So don't get precious with me, especially now. Especially *today*."

He lifted the screen as if it were a menu, a list of information to be digested into ammunition. The image of the girl flickered on the LED, and Mi-ja felt her stomach tighten. As terrified as the girl had been during processing, she was about to be at Chancellor Grant's mercy. And Mi-ja didn't imagine such a thing existed.

"Another orphan," Grant snorted. "That's what Roan Harken was. That's how this all began. Orphans. And fire." He tucked the screen into his breast pocket, then thrust a sheaf of papers into Mi-ja's surprised hands. "This report is your only concern now. It will be public knowledge in a matter of hours, as well as all these shenanigans that went on tonight. We try to leave nothing to chance, but from chance comes opportunity. We must forget pity. Remember why you joined up, Lieutenant."

Mi-ja's eyes skittered across the internal memo, originating from NASA, and her mouth dropped open in disbelief as she slowed down to re-read it.

"Tell me how precious you're going to be now towards Denizens and their willing protectors," the chancellor said as he left the room, swift as a snake, and Mi-ja was glad for it when she leaned against the desk, hand at her mouth.

⁓҈⁓

Oh gods oh gods oh gods.

Saskia clenched and unclenched her hands, trying to get the feeling back in them. The hands that had brought her here in the first place. A hysterical idea came to her mind: if she cut them off, they couldn't prove anything. Maybe she really was going crazy.

Her calves ached, and she didn't know why. Ached to run the hell away from here, maybe. Ached with the memory of how close she'd come to making an escape. Instead she'd stood there, like an idiot, probably hallucinating. *Oh gods.*

She slammed her bound hands into her forehead, trying to get her heart rate down. She was terrified. She was ten years old again, in a distant forest, feeding her brother's dead body into a monster's furnace, hoping to be the hero then as much as now. For a while she tried to convince herself that memory was all some terrible nightmare. That she hadn't really done any of those things. But the evidence was in the sky, every day, just as there was evidence now that she'd made the wrong decision all over again tonight.

She slid to the cell floor, scuffing her Keds, her jeans. A hero she'd never be.

But this is what you wanted, she thought, on repeat, like a corrupted MP3. *Not like this*, she snapped back. *Really did not anticipate the imprisonment.*

The walls were thick stone, black and cold and sealed tight. No windows. *The isolation unit*, she'd heard one of the guards say. Saskia wondered what this room had been before the Elemental Task Guard had taken it over, turning the parliamentary building into a compound-cum-prison — what some claimed was a secret experimental lab. Who knew how far underground she was, how wide the compound stretched? Maybe they were watching her now through secret cameras. Or maybe they had thrown her down here, oubliette-style, and were intending to forget all about her.

You knew a pit like this one once. Beneath a castle made of ash, with a new father who loved only his daughter wreathed in fire . . .

She rested her head on her knees. The dark fairy tale of how she got here. Sometimes telling it to herself made her feel at least somewhat special, or touched, in a world of people with powers. Sometimes it helped. Right now it was just making her nauseated.

And then, when the little girl became a tree to split the rock monster in half, she thought, This dark place is at least mine. *But then a little flutter still inside her. A light, reminding her she felt regret. Love. And a Rabbit saw this light and pulled the tree apart with the roots of his hands, and the burning sickness inside her stayed in the tree as she was pulled out of it. Maybe a scar inside of her remained, as a reminder, but when she woke to thank the Rabbit, she was whole. She was healed . . .*

The cell door was steel, its locks crushed hard into place behind her — but she'd memorized the code on the digital glass panel in the seconds before she was locked up. A lot of good it did her on the inside. But despite the digitization, the door was still tangible metal, and Saskia was convinced it was closer, closer, every time she looked up.

Now she looked at her hands, the zip tie removed and replaced with a heavy magnetic cuff. She didn't regret any of it. Not really. And she smiled because Ella was safe, hopefully had taken the hint to lie low. Ella wouldn't go home. She was stupid, but not that stupid.

Home. The joy of knowing her friend was free instantly withered when she thought of home. Of what Phae would say. *Never thought I'd be longing for Phae to yell at me,* Saskia thought. After all, maybe Saskia wasn't going to see home ever again. No government would be happy to find out their sophisticated defenses had been crushed by an eleventh grader.

Saskia let herself breathe, and her chest felt a little lighter as she looked at the cell walls again. Just walls. She touched the concrete and wondered if Barton had been in a cell like this. She closed her eyes, feeling him there with her, even though he had been lost and probably would be forever.

Barton had been the one to teach Saskia about regret. He'd begged her not to feel it, especially in the wake of doing what was right. Maybe she was still hero material, after all.

The locks in the steel slid inward, and she jumped to her feet as the door slammed open.

And then Saskia forgot all about bravery and heroics, pressing her quivering spine into the back of the cell before the guards reached in and dragged her out again.

Grant's mind was a burdened thing. Writing in these note-books helped to calm him, though he had not felt a state of calm, or anything remotely close to it, in too long to remember.

While he waited in the interview room for the prisoner to be brought up, he wrote feverishly.

Bloodbeast activity was our first priority, he wrote in his care-ful printing, which he would type up later, rather than sleeping, because he felt such a vicious urgency to get this information to people before it was too late. *They burst out of the earth like weeds, with teeth in unthinkable places aimed directly for us. The Denizens I talked to, back when I was young and naïve and I believed they had anything useful, let alone true, to say, said that Bloodbeasts were caused by the corrupted, restless Denizen dead. Or else other entities brought up from environmental destruction. The reasons all read like fantasy dogma. But we didn't need the reasons. Denizens wreaking havoc, alive or dead. Something had to be done. At first, Denizens were trying to put out these fires, but innocent folk were getting hurt. Intentionally or otherwise.*

This was our bread and butter in the beginning. You could call us a militia — many did — but we got the job done when the Denizens couldn't. We made it our responsibility to annihi-late the bogey-creatures plaguing more than just children. This was key to rebuilding the trust that the Denizens had broken with everyone. The bad guys were not going to win. We would not allow it. In a way, we were protecting Denizens, too. That's all we ever wanted. To protect. To preserve.

Now we must be prepared again. The Darkling Moon has sent us a message, and we must interpret it quickly to use it to our advantage, to end this conflict, once and for all . . .

Grant laid down the pen, flexed his left hand, knuckles grinding. Remembering those early halcyon days, he allowed himself a grin. Bloodbeasts from the Bloodlands. Apt names for bloody business. Grant often dreamed of the Bloodlands, that weird underworld of ash and wreckage from which the Darkling Moon had sprung, like its progeny still creeping up in the cracks it'd left behind. He dreamed of the place vividly and often imagined he'd conquer it, given the chance. Maybe that chance would be soon. Maybe everything *did* happen for a reason, despite what he'd just thrown at that simpering lieutenant. Project Crossover might be inevitable after all. And he imagined he'd be the first to plunge through into that scarred otherworld and claim it for himself.

He would make all of this right again.

He put the pen back to the paper. *We* will *master the realms and send these monsters back into the hellmouth they came from. And I'm not talking about the Bloodbeasts this time.*

His pen faltered. He had already divulged, in one of the earlier published volumes, what had led him to this path in the first place, yet it always came right back each time Grant sat down to write at all. He'd been a writer first, a twenty-five-year-old journalist, looking at this freshly darkened world through an investigative if naïve lens. If history taught him anything, it was what would happen next: fear prevailed the moment an *alien* group with firepower showed up. Grant had tried to hear the aliens' side of the story. Learn about them. *Know thy enemy.* He'd been younger, after all. But that hadn't saved Kelly, or the other Mundane protesters his sister rallied with, from that Rabbit dropping a building on them. It had been the last straw not only for Grant, but for the world. Five years later, seeing the work it had all led to, it wasn't a terrible legacy; Kelly was never going to amount to much more than a martyr, anyway.

And that suited Grant just fine.

Footsteps approached and Grant closed the journal. The room, made entirely of plexiglass panels, lit up with a message scrolling in front of him — a rotating image of the prisoner, the statistics from the report he'd practically memorized. He tapped in his security code on the console to his right, and all the panels turned black. With his confirmation, the door at the far end of the room opened, and two guards, each with a light hand on the prisoner's elbows, guided her in.

He did not stand.

"In unity." He nodded to the two female guards, their faces stoic. They brought the stunned girl in by the cuff on her wrists and attached it to its magnetic pad on the table opposite Grant. They nodded back to him and retreated to the door. When the door slid back into place, locking behind the guards, Grant dropped his gaze to the girl.

She was still staring at the table, mouth closed tight as a fist.

Grant cleared his throat and she flinched, looking at him as if she'd only just realized he was there.

"Saskia Allen Das." Saying her name seemed like an invocation, but Grant was no fool. In most mythologies, names had power, and if you knew a demon's name, you had power over it. Not that this girl looked like a demon, or remotely dangerous. But Denizens used to call down their gods to *put their power onto their names*. This girl didn't look like she could pull power out of a light bulb.

Grant felt a pang of disappointment as his finger flicked across his console. "There's no need to look like I just shot your mother, Bambi," he snipped, unconcerned about the barb in his throwaway comment — Saskia's mother had died when she was quite young. "You're underage. Which means the crime you committed can't be considered a federal offense. Yet. Laws dealing with these things are put into practice rather rapidly these days." The girl swallowed. She looked younger than sixteen. He really had no idea how to talk to kids.

Grant shut his eyes, folded his hands in front of him, and tried to recalibrate. When he opened his eyes, he said, "Let's start over. I wanted to tell you that I'm impressed."

Saskia worked her jaw, leaned back in her chair as far as the mag-cuff would allow. "Impressed?"

Grant felt the tremor start at the corner of his eye. "You're in trouble, sure, but what you did out there . . . Let's just say that when a person your age is able to override some of our best tech, you've done well." He smiled. It wasn't a lie. He *was* impressed. Maybe even grateful.

"Your friends," he went on, and their faces flashed on the screens around them, with rap sheets eclipsing Saskia's footnote of a file, "if you can call them that, anyway, got away. But it's only a matter of time. You went to some lengths to protect them, and they destroyed government property . . . probably could have done more damage than that. We're lucky they didn't take any lives." He leaned in. "But you let them escape. That might be the thing that troubles me the most, Miss Das."

He watched her look around at the faces of the Denizens — kids, like her — and linger over one girl, a blond with a deviant stare. Grant knew immediately what lay beneath that lingering look. "Love?" The word felt cheap in his mouth. Saskia's gaze whipped away.

"I understand," Grant went on. "Love isn't the crime here. But we're at war. There are plenty of crimes to go around."

"I thought we were at peace," the girl muttered, though she tensed as if she hadn't meant to say it out loud.

Grant waited. His finger shifted to the console. "Peace. Well. I wouldn't expect you to have a solid grasp of global conflict. Or perhaps I'm underestimating you."

When she tensed further, he knew that he was right.

"Can you tell me about yourself, Miss Das? That accent seems a little off."

She shut her eyes. Obviously this was painful for her. Grant was glad. He had it all in her file, of course, but he needed her to say it. It would make her weaker.

"I was born in Scotland," she answered miserably.

Grant flicked another key, and her file scrolled around the blank screens flanking the interview table, like a shocking merry-go-round of things better left unsaid. She watched it all, expression doleful.

"Go on," he said.

"My mother was from Japan. My father was a lorry driver from Durness. We lived in the country. The hills. My aunt helped out."

Another handful of keystrokes. "And are you an only child?"

Her jaw tightened. "I am now."

On the screens around them shone images of children covered in black marks with red-ringed eyes, as if they were on fire from the inside. Overlapping these were more photos of black twisted trees whose bark gave the impression of grim faces, reaching dead branches skyward from roads, hospitals, shopping malls. The Cinder Plague in newsprint, sightings of a grim monster made of rock drilling a road beneath continents to let more monsters, more children, in.

"They say that's where it all started. Scotland." Grant smirked. "The thing about peace, Miss Das, is that it's hard won after a period of absolute chaos. We've all seen too much. Some more than others."

The screens around them seemed bloated now with the news stories, the images, the running footage scrolling.

The girl's eyes glistened, but her face was hard when she finally met Grant's taunting stare. "We all lost something because of this."

For a moment, Grant felt a chill, and he shook it off like a wood tick before it could stick its head in. He thought of his sister, of words he couldn't take back, a partially finished condo building and the protestors that Rabbit had crushed . . .

Without looking away, he swiped a hand again, and the screens went dark, save for a single file behind his head. "Many people went missing in those early days. That's inevitable when monsters are let loose. And with those *awful* Cinder Kids turning all kinds of innocent folks into nightmare trees . . . it's hard to keep track of them all."

He knew that the image behind him was of a toppled truck with a jagged black tree trunk speared through the driver's side, the door and aluminum crumpled like a toy.

Saskia's hand was tight and shaking in her cuff.

"It was all catalogued eventually: every attack. Every victim. Every roadside accident. Every parent desperately looking for their disappeared children in the Highlands, only to meet their own grisly ends." Saskia was crying openly now, chin tucked to her chest. "It's any wonder that those children even turn up at all. Some might call it a miracle."

"Stop it!" the girl sobbed.

Grant hadn't realized how close he was leaning towards her, as if he wanted to crush her with more than the sad truth of a world gone mad, and her loss in it. He settled back into his chair, adjusted his suit, and stood. She seemed surprised when he flicked a code into her cuff, and it sprang open.

He passed her a handkerchief, wordless, and gave her a moment to regain what little composure she'd had.

"You've been able to build a new life here. Luckier than others, I imagine. But paperwork is paperwork, and not even with magic powers on the loose can a child emigrate from a war zone unchecked." He grimaced. "I'm not sure your guardians would appreciate your behaviour tonight."

She stiffened, and then he added, "But I do."

Saskia didn't have a chance to do more than cover her noise of shock with the handkerchief as Grant picked up the device from under the table and slammed it down in front of her. The bent plastic and cobbled metal clattered. He assumed it was entirely garbage-salvaged, but it had done the job of locking into their network, and locking everyone out, for more time than could be mentioned out loud. *Such technology could be useful — refined, of course — if in the right hands*, he thought.

So could those inventing and operating it.

He leaned over and pressed another key, and the images that this hacker's nimbly coded mind had broadcast across the optical devices of the Task Guard's best and brightest appeared on the screens.

Grant folded his arms, the flaming illusions flickering. "I knew your other guardian, you know. The one who went around, mopping up as many of those nightmare trees as he could after Dark Day. Barton Allen. One of the few Denizens I grudgingly respected."

"What?" she growled. Grant felt a bit surprised at the fury in her voice, given she'd done little more than quiver since she sat down.

Another tender spot, then.

"He was a noble guy, I'll give him that. For all his later . . . transgressions." He watched her eyes narrow. "He could have done so much more, however, if he'd cooperated with us instead of pitting himself against us. And it's because I can see his defiance in you that I'm making you the same job offer."

Her eyes widened. "What job offer?"

Grant looked momentarily to the screens, to the image of the enormous Fox god, wreathed in unholy flame, tearing through the ranks of men and women who should know better. There was a frightening realism to the movements, to the shape of Deon. For a moment, he was mesmerized by the power there, even if it was just a projection. Even if it wasn't real. That power felt closer every second. It was happening, at last.

The silence stretched long. "You're not one of them, Miss Das. Though perhaps you wish to be. At least, you wish to help Denizens, don't you?"

"I guess so."

Grant could see that latent anger was still threaded there amidst her confusion. He flicked the console, and the raging fire god faded to black. Recalling how close he'd already come once before, he frowned. "Barton Allen wanted to help Denizens, too. But he wouldn't listen to reason."

Saskia grit her teeth. "So you executed him for it?"

His head swivelled towards her like a bird of prey's. "Executed? Is *that* what you think happened?"

She was shaking. "All I know is . . . is that he came into this compound willingly and never came out again."

"Hm." Grant made his face blank. "And perhaps that is all you'll know. Unless you consider my offer."

The scared girl was wiped away. Saskia Allen Das looked ready to leap up from the table and put her hands around his throat. The tension in her legs was visible.

Then she froze. She was still looking at him, but her eyes went wide, mouth parted slightly. No, not at him — *past* him. The back of his neck prickled, and he whipped around, but there was nothing there save black, empty screens, and his and Saskia's reflections.

When he looked back, her body had gone slack in her chair, her gaze inward, the moment gone. She whispered something.

He leaned in, perhaps too close. "What was that?"

"I'll consider your offer," she said, only slightly louder. Whatever she had seen just then, it had prevented her from immediately rejecting him.

For what he planned, what he needed, he'd take it.

He tapped in his security code, and the door in the back of the room opened. The original escort guards came back in, and Saskia stood, head bowed. She was just a scared kid again.

"See that she makes it home safely," Grant said with a smile. "You're free to go, but I'll check in. Don't worry about your friends. We have it well in hand. We'll talk more soon, Miss Das."

When the girl and the guards were gone, Grant hesitated only a moment before turning the screens back on, replaying the image of the great god on its rampage, bringing down a garnet blade with the force of everything Grant had always wanted.

His hand flexed, as though the blade was in it, and it felt closer than it ever had.

The DARK EYE

"It was as you predicted," the woman at the head of the gathering said, head lowered. "The attack failed."

They were gathered in a dark place, as had become their custom. They had waited all this time, and so long, but it had been worth it. The beginning of the end. The moon had moved.

Beyond the woman who had spoken stood the man they called the priest. A man once shamed, brought now to the forefront of their movement. One who inspired hope in the hopeless, Denizen and Mundane alike.

The priest folded his hands, contemplating. "Nothing is certain," he said, after a pause, considering things long behind him, and the undetermined ahead.

Murmuring amongst the gathering. Dissent and hesitation and fear, always fear. But a pulse, subtle and electric. He spoke over it. "Soon, the darkness will speak. The signal will come. It is the *receiver* for which we must be vigilant. We must still wait, yes, but not too much longer. I have a feeling it will come to us, and our way into the compound will be clear." He turned, jerked his head, and two men came forward.

No matter what they did now, it was in motion. The moon would track towards the sun. The eclipse would come. And soon, the final act.

"Bring me the Fox girl, Ella," he said. The men nodded and left.

The man leaned forward on the table and contemplated what was spread out before him. Scriptures in various languages. Pictograms. Semiotics to describe the indescribable.

A red ring around the dark moon. A moth. And rising beneath them, the godhead they'd all been waiting for.

"The door will be opened," the man muttered to himself, "and we will all have to make our choices."

⌇⌇

Saskia perched at the edge of her bed, watching the faint line of dawn breaking over Winnipeg through the high-rise window. She'd heard Phae get up. She turned down the analog radio that went on at seven a.m. every morning in lieu of an alarm, even though the broadcast had made her unable to move at all — until Phae had stirred in the hallway.

The scent of incense was bright in Saskia's nose as her guardian lit the taper, muttering the proper prayers as if there were anyone in the void still listening. Saskia turned her head, saw the flicker of blue beneath her door. Smiled a bit, imagining Phae's glowing antlers woven from her long black hair. The image made the radio's message dull for just a second.

They weren't afforded much privacy in the cramped, hastily rebuilt building, but Saskia was always mindful of Phae's need for it. She was an inward person. Had always been that way since Saskia had known her, and before that, Barton had told her. But Phae had become even more stoic, probably because of the things she'd seen in another world. These things had made it harder to penetrate the heart that Barton had fallen in love with — he remained the only one who could.

That last part he hadn't told her. Saskia had just felt it, observed it, from the first time she'd seen them together, in a faraway hospital in Newfoundland.

"That's your gift," Phae had said to Saskia once. "You can know people before even they do. You're a bit like an Owl that way. You just need to remember to keep certain things to yourself."

But Saskia wasn't an Owl. She was nothing.

Your gift. It was a backhanded compliment, even back then. Saskia would never be one of *them*, and Phae knew it. And it certainly didn't stop her arguing with Phae about it constantly. Like last night, which had been particularly bad, given the circumstances. At least the others hadn't been up, though likely they'd been woken, for all the yelling and sharp barbs that Saskia couldn't take back, even though all of this was her fault. She'd barely slept afterwards. With the radio's grim newscast about the world Saskia was waking up to, she didn't know if she'd sleep again for a long while.

She heard the front door click as Phae made her way out to do her rounds. Off to visit with the neighbours, who gratefully accepted her into their apartments, like she was some kind of prophet. The last prophet.

Saskia shuffled into the kitchen, filled the kettle, turned on the electric stove. She timed it on her watch. Resources were already scarce and highly regulated in the city; electricity had been switched mostly to solar and water, what with the Pipeline Disturbances. *They'd dug too greedily and too deep.* Saskia grinned. She used to read *The Lord of the Rings* and wonder if they weren't living it now. When Canada built those oil lines, they probably hadn't factored in possible underground monster attacks that would bottom out the economy. Denizens, most of all, were afforded less and less of what was left to go around. Generator time was the least of it.

The kettle boiled and she snatched it from the element before it could squeal. She shut off the stove, checked her watch. Good — Miyala would have enough electricity to heat up breakfast for the others later. If they ran out of generator time by day's end, she was sure Ella would do them a good turn and cook something for the kids come dinner. They always loved her trick of cooking an egg in her bare hand —

Saskia's whole body tightened and she closed her eyes. The thought about Ella had been so automatic, like she'd woken up and everything that had happened last night was just a terrible dream. Saskia would get ready, like she always did, and she and Ella would walk the first leg to school together, before splitting up to be with their own "kind." They'd go into their separate school buildings. They'd learn two distinctly different curriculums, the Denizens learning how grateful they should be that they're allowed to participate in society, separated by a concrete partition, while Saskia's side was taught that the kids on the other side weren't to be trusted. Then, when it was all over, the girls would meet by the Maryland Bridge and walk the mile or so back to One Evergreen together, reliving all the stories of Roan Harken they'd grown up on. It made the wall more bearable.

But today was not yesterday.

Saskia pulled out a rag, absently running it over the countertop. The only reason she and Ella had become friends, so long ago, was because Phae had healed Ella's mother when she'd taken a tumble down the stairs that the building super-intendent had refused to fix. And anyone in this apartment complex would do anything for Phae, knowing her rare power, knowing the deep places she'd been and had come back from. Saskia grimaced, wondering what that was like, that reverence.

She felt a prickle at the back of her neck and turned, push-ing away the strange message she'd had thrust at her last night. Pushing it deep down so no one, not even her little broken family, would know. Maybe she'd get some real answers today. Until then, she'd smile like nothing was wrong.

"Hey, Brain," she said to the little presence behind her. "You want some tea?"

Saskia poured it into her Thermos, waited a beat. Then the little boy came sauntering out from hiding, accepting he'd been discovered. "Okay," he said.

Saskia poured him half into a chipped mug, filled the rest with a bit of milk. Damn, they were getting low on milk. She'd have to trade a laundry token for a dairy card . . .

The little boy that she called Brain — but who was really named Jet — took the tea, inhaled. "It's your birthday today."

Saskia had connected with Jet pretty quickly when he'd come to live in their apartment at One Evergreen, overlook-ing the Osborne Bridge. He reminded her of herself — an impression of who she'd been, all those years ago, when all this first started. Touched by something that she didn't quite understand but was paying for now.

"That's right," she said. "Just another day, though. Gotta go to school then take care of you guys."

"Too early for school . . ." Jet muttered, but he didn't challenge Saskia further, staring into his mug. *He never misses a thing*, she thought. She was giving herself extra time so she could go to the Old Leg grounds, see what the radio had promised with her own eyes, even though she'd only just escaped from there last night.

It was daylight she needed to see it by.

"School," Jet went on. "I wish I could go to school."

Jet, like all the other Owl kids, wouldn't be allowed to go to a regular school until he'd reached the age of fourteen, when he could register and take the Complicity Exam, which had recently been revised under the updated Canadian Charter of Rights and Freedoms. Complicity meant either employing their telepathy for the Task Guard, or . . .

Saskia bent down, zipped up Brain's hoodie, passed him a Kleenex. "Wipe your nose," she said. "Phae teaches you lots. Believe me, you wouldn't want to go to school anyway. It's pretty boring." And dangerous, in its own way.

He narrowed his pale eyes up at her over his tea, shuffling into a chair at the kitchen table. "You're just saying that so I don't feel bad. About being different."

"Stop that," Saskia said. "You can't go reading people's minds without their permission, remember?"

His eyes fell. "Sorry."

She tousled his hair, picked up her bag, and stuffed the Thermos into it. "See you after, Brain. Be good."

"You, too," he said. He must have heard everything last night. She felt a pang of regret in her chest at his too-young, seen-too-much eyes, red-rimmed with sleeplessness. She thought of Chancellor Grant, everything she held dear that he threatened, and the pang became protective anger.

She kissed Brain on the top of his head, hugged him tightly, and went out the door, the smell of incense clinging to her denim jacket. She'd press her nose into her collar, later, inhaling deeply, taking strength from Phae, despite their many arguments.

Nothing could ever be the same after last night, so she'd hold onto what she still had.

⋙⋘

One Evergreen was a high-rise overlooking the Assiniboine River and Osborne Village. Once upon a time, the entire thing had been knocked down in a cataclysm caused by a river demon — long story. It had been hastily rebuilt in the aftermath. But Saskia thought about it every day, how when they rebuilt it, they couldn't have predicted it'd be deemed Denizen Housing within a couple of years — part of the Restoration Project after Dark Day. Denizens had to live together, separate from everyone else, pushed out of their homes and corralled into apartment blocks like this one.

That was just the beginning.

From the wide window in the third-floor stairwell of her building, she squinted up at the smudge in the sky, like someone had put a cigarette out in the lightening grey. Even when it was overcast, and the sun vanished behind the clouds, the Darkling Moon was still there. Waiting.

Had the world really changed that much? Saskia now lived amongst Denizens, had grown into herself with them. Their struggles had been her own, but she was outside, always. She'd been touched by something else but it wasn't Ancient. And it wasn't their mystical gods or the enchanted thing that bound them together. Truth was, she hadn't felt connected to anything for a long time, no matter how hard she'd tried, or how Phae had included her in her patchwork family of lost children. Even Saskia's privilege of staying with Denizens, and not being put into the foster system to grow up with other Mundanes, was because of Barton's contribution to saving Mundane lives from all the Hope Trees he'd undone. Even if, in the end, he couldn't save his own.

But the one word to describe Saskia was *disconnected*. Except, maybe, from that smudge above her head, and everyone else's heads, which had sat in the same place in the sky for seven years. Saskia had been a fundamental part of hanging that darkness in the sky. Very few people knew about that who were still around to tell the story.

But Chancellor Lochlan Grant knew something, and that had scared her.

The building was coming alive with smells and noises and voices. Sometimes the busyness was unbearable, but leaving this early often helped. She didn't run into Phae after all; that was just as well. Saskia seemed unable to keep what was on her mind off her face the older she got. And she didn't want anyone wishing her a happy birthday. She didn't want to fake-smile at them like she was happy to be seventeen.

She walked up Osborne through the neighbourhood. This city had never been home to that many Denizens, even before Zabor. But now they'd all been squeezed into close quarters — those who didn't disappear for months at a time for government inquiries. It was early in the day yet, and the only people on the streets were the Elemental Task Guards, keeping watch for dissension. For Denizens without their registration cards. Their eyes skated over Saskia as she passed. They weren't interested in her this morning. After last night, she felt like she'd painted a target on her own back, but one conflict must have blended into another. Besides, she'd heard the reports. They had bigger fish to fry.

It had been a slow transition in the beginning of all this; when it all came out that, yes, there were people who could manipulate the elements — an entire culture of magic users living alongside regular folk — it was chaos. And not only that, but actual *monsters* were popping out of the woodwork, too. Not from one source, but all over. Denizens were blamed for making these monsters, for calling them up, even though it was Denizens who, in the beginning, were the ones fighting the monsters. Saving people.

It didn't matter. Bloodbeasts were a Denizen problem. And when Mundanes got hurt by Denizens who were tired of shouldering the blame, Denizens became the real monsters.

As for who was to blame, you could lay that on only a handful of Denizens, really. Maybe only a red-haired girl Saskia had known for the briefest time, and the man who walked with her, the one with dark wings . . . but they'd been gone as long as that moon had hung in the sky. They were just legends now.

And they'd *failed*.

Saskia bit her lip. Didn't want to think about it. Yes, things had changed. People lost their jobs. Denizen licensing became mandatory in Canada and the rest of the world

— now that the Moonstone wasn't hiding them any longer, they were unmasked. Seen by all since Seela corrupted the stone, then Roan and Eli took it with them on their nether-realm dive. What they left behind was a world of element-manipulators who were punished if they didn't comply. *Register yourself like registering a firearm.* Except the weapons were people. And humans didn't trust *other* humans on the basis of faith alone at the best of times. How were they ever going to cope with people who had *powers?*

The back of her neck prickled as it had with Jet, and she stood aside on the sidewalk, a contingent of the Task Guard coming by in their grey and white uniforms, scrutinizing her, but she met their eyes, each of them, and they looked away. She had nothing to hide.

One guard kicked the last one in line and the girl staggered. She had a mark on the front of her uniform — a pair of wings. She was an Owl, then. And she looked miserable. Saskia threw up her mental walls, just as one of Phae's friends, Jordan Seneca, had taught her.

The Owl ignored Saskia. She was obviously too concerned with trying to keep up with her unit, anyway. They passed, and Saskia crossed the road, continuing on to the Old Legislative Building, heart in her throat.

Saskia always thought about Jet on her morning walks, because he got up every morning, no matter how early, to say goodbye to her on her way to school. And that was all well and good, but Saskia didn't want him poking around in her head and picking up things he couldn't understand. Things she was about to get herself into if she went along with Grant's offer. Or, if she didn't, Jet might get hurt. They all might. Saskia had put them in that position. She had to make it right.

She shook her head. It wasn't fair that a smart kid like Jet was being denied a proper education. The prime minister, much aged from Dark Day but voted in consistently since he'd steered the ship through the crisis, had paid lip service to *acceptance* and *understanding* and *fellowship*, but Denizens, particularly Owls, were considered a threat. Not all of them were good people. Lots of them were fed up with being treated like criminals for their gifts, their birthrights. Their penchant for control. So regulation was needed. Especially those who could not only read minds, but make people do things against their will. So safer to be cooperative, and perhaps use those gifts for the sake of "the greater good."

Otherwise you were "processed." Saskia had never met a Denizen who had survived having their inherent powers removed, but the government insisted they'd gone on to live better, productive lives.

Registration. Processing. Othering. None of these practices had ever served any society well. She sat in a classroom day after day, forced to memorize histories bloody with these things, but all she had to do was look out the window, watching history repeat itself.

Before she knew it, Saskia had passed the point where she and Ella would usually part ways, and for a second she hesitated, looking around, hoping Ella would be there, hidden somewhere, and Saskia could stop worrying for once . . .

"Saskatchewan!"

Saskia flinched and turned. A chubby boy with dirty blond, barely combed hair jogged towards her, grinning. He was yanking his jacket on.

"Cam," she answered, trying to smile back at him over her

rising panic. "Didn't know you were physically capable of getting up this early."

"Oh c'mon," Cameron panted, catching her up easily. "Don't act like you haven't heard it all over the news."

Saskia swallowed, wincing. "I was going to see for myself."

"Me, too!" He threw an arm around her shoulder, and for a second Saskia forgot how tense she was. "It's crazy that we're alive when this is happening. What's your guess, then? You've got a lot of insight into this stuff, with your foster sister and all."

She knew he meant well, and there was a lot he couldn't know about Saskia at all despite their long friendship, but she prickled all the same. "And what, you think that makes me an expert on the end of the world?"

Cam did up his jacket clumsily, considering. "So you think that's it, eh?" He grinned again. "Sweet."

"Everything's a joke to you," Saskia muttered.

He punched her affably in the shoulder. "And your problem is you can't ever take one."

Cameron Vadaboncoeur was a Mundane, like Saskia. They'd gone to the same school since she'd moved here with Phae and Barton, hung around in the same circles when she wasn't sneaking off to spend time with Ella. He was friendly but stupid, with delusions of grandeur, and easily led. Saskia never understood why he wasted any time with her — after all, she was aloof and an outcast despite her own brightness. She didn't fit in anywhere: not a Denizen, despite childish wishes on stars and black moons and birthday candles, and not quite Mundane, either, considering she was raised by, and lived with, Denizens.

Cameron was obsessed with the Realms of Ancient, which meant he dumped his naïve questions all over her like she was the resident Wikipedia of Ancient. Saskia put up with it to fill the silence . . . that's what she told herself, anyway, when she had a short fuse, like right now. Really, he was as good a friend to her as Ella. She needed to rein it in.

"Hey," he nudged her. "What's up?"

She scoffed. "Really, Cam?"

"I mean aside from the *usual*." He rolled his eyes skyward. "We're all a bit screwed up but you always seemed to be ahead of even me on that curve."

Saskia needed to change the subject. She'd wanted to be alone, really *see* if she could tell the difference in the Darkling Moon's location in the sky — that's what the radio had said, that it'd moved, but she'd need more proof than a panicked broadcast. Of course, she didn't need to go to the Old Leg to see it . . . but a part of her hoped beyond hope that maybe Ella might be there. Instead, here was Cam.

"It's my birthday," Saskia blurted, tucking her short dark hair behind her ear. It was a better save than what really was crowding her tongue, the desire to tell someone, anyone, what had happened last night at the Old Leg, and later beneath it. About what she'd seen in that interrogation room behind the chancellor. What he'd said to her. What he'd offered.

Instead she upped her pace, cramming those thoughts down deep with the others, but stopped when she realized Cam wasn't following. She looked back at him on the sidewalk with a raised eyebrow. "What?"

"Saskatchewan, why didn't you tell me earlier?" Cam raced back up to her, shaking her bodily like she was an

Etch A Sketch; he was big as a bear and Saskia wasn't exactly sturdy. "Happy birthday, you giant weirdo!"

Saskia sighed. "Right back at you, nutbar."

"This is great, though! I mean, I can't believe all this is happening on your *birthday* of all days. You sure you aren't some kind of Chosen One?"

Saskia felt like she'd been punched in the gut. "Not me, nope."

His dopey grin was quickly eroding her fatalistic thoughts, but she'd have to shake him after they made it to the Leg. Though, maybe she was better off sticking with Mundane company when she was out in broad daylight — she felt like there were eyes on her everywhere.

"There'll probably be a lot of people there — maybe I can get them all to *sing for you.*"

Saskia rolled her eyes at him, smiled in spite of herself.

They were getting closer to the Legislative grounds now — the bridge was just ahead, and the Golden Boy statue winked in the rising sun. The Darkling Moon framed it moodily, and Saskia felt a painful squeeze around her ribcage. The building looked so different in the daylight, yet unchanged, as if last night hadn't made a dent in the regime at all. She hoped she wouldn't see anything freaky again. Not with Cam here.

Follow the moth. You must choose. Red sigils cut into the air, their runes a message she couldn't read, and a sharp sound exploded in her inner ear. Fire and dark wings. She looked away quickly, back to the sidewalk.

Cam popped his lips. "Don't tell me you think this is somehow your fault."

Saskia whipped her head towards him, feeling sicker. "Why would you say that?"

He shrugged his big shoulders. "You look more morose than usual, that's all. Cheer up! Take some excitement when it comes. Besides, you're seventeen now. I know exactly what I'm gonna do now that I'm seventeen."

Saskia frowned. "So you're in?"

"Hells yeah!" He pumped his fists. "Mom got the confirmation package in the mail yesterday. I start this week."

"Right." Cameron's greatest dream was to join the Elemental Task Guard. He'd probably lose it if he found out she'd been offered a *job* with them only last night, by the chancellor himself. "So you're going off to fight monsters even before you graduate."

"This is the time to sign up, Sask. You really should consider it, what with all that's going on." They had a much clearer view of the Darkling Moon now, not obstructed by buildings, the autumn-ravaged trees offering a screen of leafless branches. "I heard someone on the radio say it's because of these weird cults that have sprung up. The ones worshipping it — you know, the Cluster? So sinister, but also so lame. Then there's those Denizen extremists making those public political statements. Like those Foxes at the Leg last night, blowing stuff up, did you hear about that?"

She shrugged. "Whatever. It's just people acting out. Scared people. Stupid teenagers like us. None of it's got anything to do with *you and me*, right?"

But Cam went on. "Adam Dean saw another one of those river things the other day, when it frosted overnight — you said they came out when it got cold, right? When the river starts to freeze? And it would've got Adam, too —"

"Yeah," Saskia cut him off bitterly, "if that Seal guy hadn't stopped it. I heard all about it. So where was the Task

Guard then? I'm sure they swept in and arrested the Seal the minute *they* heard about it."

Cameron just sighed. "You're always on *their* side, no matter what you say."

"I'm not on anyone's side!" Saskia snapped, but she could see his neck colouring like it did when they got into these spats. "The world is crazy, and everything can't be painted in black and white, good versus evil. Sure the Task Guard sounds like it's all victory and virtue, but you know less than dick, Cam."

They went on in silence after that. Saskia's temper had gotten touchier recently. They turned onto Broadway after crossing the bridge. "I'm sorry," she said after a while. "It's just . . . I'm stressed out." She wouldn't say anything more. She was dangerously close to spilling her guts. And for a second, Cam's face had been the chancellor's, and all the things she'd wanted to say to that lunatic threatened to burst out. But he'd offered her a *job* . . .

"We all are," Cameron retorted. There *were* a lot of people there, standing on the open public lawns, amid bronze statues, just outside the perimeter fence, staring up. The crowd was likely still lingering from the press conference on the lawn in front of the Leg, led by the chancellor himself. Saskia was glad she'd missed it. But the rubberneckers were still here, long after the camera crews had left. Staring at the black moon that wasn't really a moon, just a shadow, hanging over them all.

Saskia and Cameron stopped, looking up with everyone else. It was a shadow that hadn't moved in seven years, had stayed fixed in the sky, vigilantly observed by governments and Denizens alike since it'd rocketed out of the Atlantic sea and stayed there.

But last night it had definitely moved.

Saskia couldn't stare at it for long, so she shut her eyes. Felt the pressure around her ribs again and tried to calm herself down. *Listen to the signal*, the voice had whispered. *You must choose whether you answer or not.*

Saskia lurched, and Cam looked away from the sky. "What's the matter?"

"I've got to go," Saskia said roughly, heading back for Broadway.

"I'll see you at school later?" Cam called.

Saskia was tired of lying, especially to Cam. He meant well. And she didn't want him involved. So she sped up.

Follow the moth, Saskia . . .

She shook her head. No matter where she went, the dark moon was an eye on her back. The eye of death.

The WAY AHEAD

Solomon Rathgar stared at the open palm of his hand, tracing the lines in it. Lines that had split and creased more in these seven years than all the time before that. He had observed, too, lines cutting his drawn face, as the months crept by. The shadows in it tightening.

You've a long lifeline. Her voice tinkled merrily in faraway memory, mocking laughter in it. *I'll grow mine to match, so you don't get too ahead of me.*

"Demelza," he said her name under his breath because it wasn't enough to think it, anymore. He needed to say it for it to be tangible. For the memory of her to remain.

"Sir?"

He started. At his shoulder was the chancellor's new aide, Mi-ja — how long she'd been there, he couldn't say. "Nothing," he answered. "Just an old man, rambling, you see."

She gave him a weak smile. An apology. "The chancellor has asked to see you. Shall I help you down there?"

He'd already known Mi-ja's reason for coming, but he didn't say as much. Just smiled back, nodded, and followed her down the long compound corridor, one stiff step at a time. The use of his powers was highly regulated, but he would need to keep them sharp. Especially now that things had been changed drastically overnight. Testing them on the unwitting aide outside of the control zones — really a kind girl, all told — would hurt no one.

He had hidden the shard of surprise when he'd sifted through what she knew about this summons, and had seen, amongst the cacophony of psychic sensation, mention of Saskia Allen Das — the last person to have seen his son.

He winced, as he often did, thinking of Eli. When the aide looked up in apparent worry, he shrugged it off and leaned heavier on his cane.

The corridor was long, lined with vexing, bleach-bright lights reflected back on white and glass the deeper it went. Finally they reached the elevator, climbed in, and it moved quietly lower, lower still, and Solomon stared at the ceiling of the compartment, imagining the shaft above them, feeling the weight of the earth and the distance of the sky.

He closed his eyes and for a moment he could smell the sea, the salt in the corners of his eyes, the wind a flirtatious punch to the lungs. And he could hear her voice calling above the noise, "*. . . and the, what do you call it? 'The Tube'? How can you stand it? Owls aren't meant to go underground!*"

Solomon smiled. "And what about your hiding place, in the Fairy Glen? Stuffed into that tiny cave, the size of you."

"Fair." *Demelza paused, the wild air playing with her hair as she stared out to the water. She hugged herself tighter, and all Solomon wanted was to reach for her.*

"*It feels safe in there,*" *she said at last, her voice growing more and more distant. "I suppose I feel like the earth can keep a secret the way the sky cannot.*"

Solomon felt a hand on his arm, and he startled.

"Sir?"

He shook himself and strode ahead of Mi-ja, through the open elevator door, as if he hadn't had the wind knocked out of him. "Let's get to work," he said evenly, as the aide caught him up.

The floor was a steep concrete ramp encircling the chamber. It stretched before them, taking up not only this level but the five levels above. Every time Solomon was summoned down here, it was too familiar. It was all a circle, the walls a silo of cables and channels and fuses and all manner of mess. But the irony of it — that the Elemental Task Guard had practically built themselves a summoning chamber — had not been lost on him, nor on the other Denizens trapped in servitude to this mad caper.

"Rathgar!" bellowed a voice.

The man himself, Chancellor Grant, was standing on the topmost platform, encircling what was undulating in the core of the chamber, that great turbine, that menace. Where he stood was the bridge, main control, but he was already starting towards a scaffold. "I'll come down to you."

How thoughtful. Solomon smiled briefly, and as Grant made his way towards him, the brittle smile crumbled. "Is there any change after the last power transfer?" he muttered to Mi-ja.

"Not in the device, no," she replied. He glanced at her; her mouth was a flat line, face vacant.

"But something *has* changed," he insisted.

She only swallowed, looking straight ahead. Solomon's guts twisted, and though he didn't lean on it entirely, he clenched his cherrywood cane all the harder.

Grant was a sharp Mundane, and light on his feet. He was down far quicker than Solomon anticipated and was striding towards them. Solomon hadn't any time for further clandestine questions, so he extended his hand and shook Mi-ja's. She looked mildly disgruntled.

"Change is a good thing," was all he managed to say to her mystified expression before Grant descended on them and extended his hand to Solomon.

"Thank you, Lieutenant," Grant said to Mi-ja, dismissing her. The crisp lines of his face stood out as much as his teeth.

Mi-ja saluted and stiffly left. Solomon tried to put her out of his mind — and what he'd surreptitiously snatched from hers while she'd been distracted by the handshake.

A signal had come through from the other side.

He turned to Grant. "How goes the good fight?"

Grant's smile seemed to deepen. "We're still fighting, which is still good."

Solomon hemmed his eyes in, not quite a smile in return. This was their usual repartee, but there seemed to be an edge to Grant's mania today. "I trust that the rest of your stay here has been uneventful?" Solomon asked.

They headed towards the bridge above. Solomon assumed they'd take the lift that Grant had come down in, given that Solomon was missing a leg, and the control panel was on the third concentric level. But they passed the lift, the ramp leading them up and around, Grant moving more like an overexcited child than a seasoned militiaman.

After a beat, Grant answered, "It's been educational, to say the least, but not without its benefits."

Solomon knew about the infiltration. The hack. Knew that Security Control had been "sorted" recently, and those who had been on shift when it happened summarily canned. Apparently an entirely new engineering staff was being brought in, the current one thinned due to lack of results.

Word was Grant had found someone who could make this horror show of his come to fruition.

"And you're sure?" Solomon asked, though it was pretense; he had known Grant for too many years and had been a part of this particular circus since it pulled into Winnipeg, but he wanted to hear it himself. "You think you can do what Allen stopped us from doing?"

"Better," Grant replied. Solomon had never seen his eyes shine that way, with more than excitement. Fever. "I *know* we can. All the work we've done, what we've sacrificed. It won't be for nothing, old friend. A message has come through from the other side. The key to opening the door. We're close now."

The confirmation was one thing, but the honorific was what Solomon clapped to — *friend*. Solomon tried to focus on his breathing and not on the pain shooting up into what remained of his thigh as they climbed. This time he *did* lean on the cane. Gods, he was getting old. And if Grant was any friend, he wouldn't make him scale this bloody monstrosity. But deep down, Solomon knew it was some kind of test. So he soldiered on.

"With that godawful moon above us, and traitors all around us, we need to work twice as hard in half as much time," Grant went on. "When the world's about to end, you always need a foxhole to jump into."

Solomon paused only a step, and, though he hadn't thought of her as often as he thought of Eli, Roan Harken's face flashed before him. The girl who had started all of this, and she wasn't even here to end it.

But maybe, on the other side, she was doing her job after all.

They'd come to the top, at last. Solomon caught his breath, wiped his brow with his pocket square. Grant was quite a ways ahead, chatting in low tones to the men and women in the fore — Mundane engineers, physicists, *soothsayers*, for all Solomon knew. He glanced about the ever-stretching space below, filled with rushing personnel. An anthill about to be hit by the lawnmower.

Then Solomon looked over into the core of the chamber, and for an instant he was back there, back *then*, standing over the Pool of the Black Star. Years ago now, staring uselessly into a crackling abyss into which his son — and Roan Harken — had dove. At least, back then, there had been a lifeline ensuring they'd come back out. *Where are our lifelines now?*

This abyss, however, was a complete fabrication. *An abomination!* he snarled inwardly. At least a Bloodgate was something of Ancient, something pure and aligned with the balance of which he'd once been a custodian. This was metal and terror and technology soldered together, boiled down, and poured into the mould of frenzy. The hole of the core descended at least a mile farther underground, so looking into it one had the impression of falling into nothing. And some subjects had. They'd needed the space to calculate something ridiculous, like *dimensional drag*, some made-up term used to describe the goal of Project Crossover: to build their own Bloodgate. To open the way to the other side, whether that be the Realms of Ancient or the void. A contingency, a *foxhole*, Grant had called it. Not for Mundanes to be dropped into.

Solomon had another word for it: a Denizen death sentence.

"Allen got us far, though he didn't leave us with the means to follow. Ironically, it turns out someone close to him may be able to get us that bare inch standing between us and final peace."

Grant's words were acid. Solomon nodded as though they were manna. "Indeed. Everything we've wanted is within our grasp now." He turned his face, slack with the years of all his mistakes, directly to Grant. "What would you have me do?"

Grant sneered. "Make sure your unit is ready. I want to double down on Denizen screening. Rake the traitor ideas out of their heads before they form. I won't have them ganging up on us like they did last night, trying to scare us or stop us. I want the troublemakers' powers yanked out of them, and the suspicious locked up — until their *pen* is ready for them."

Solomon looked down again into the core of the machine. The walls of the chamber sparked, electricity arcing across like ropes at intervals. Suspended in the core was an empty, circular metal frame, and the bolts slithered into it, the first vestigial promise of a vortex.

It had only worked once, and they'd needed a living Rabbit neutralizer to do it. One who had experience with Bloodgates. Nothing had worked since.

"And then?" Solomon asked. But he didn't need to be told.

"Then," Grant confirmed, the smile all gone, replaced only with desperate hunger. "The world will be *ours* again."

They stood like that awhile, looking down into the nothing they'd built together, the possibility that it promised. Then both Solomon and Grant pulled the twin reactor keys up from beneath their shirts, the chains coming over their heads.

Grant, as was his custom, toasted Solomon's key with his own. As if each test were a celebration.

"Thank you for your contribution, as always," Grant was saying, moving to the Apex's bridge, waiting for Solomon to join him. "Though if this batch doesn't prove rewarding, we can move on the Seals. Their retreating to the North always unnerved me. Better to put them to use."

Your contribution. Solomon knew what he meant; of course he did. Solomon supervised the removal of Denizen powers, taken from those who wouldn't comply with the ETG, and they'd discovered that these removed powers could be used like a power source.

Solomon refused to look down into the reactor that time. All those people. Begging to be spared. To not be parted from their silent gods. At least most of them survived the process. Though cut off from Ancient, it wasn't much of a life afterwards. Solomon knew what he'd do if the roles had been reversed.

So much suffering, all for this. All for nothing. But maybe soon it would prove to have been worth something after all.

Solomon slid his key into the slot beside Grant's. In seconds they'd do a single quarter turn counter-clockwise, then another. Then the Apex would hum to life, the Denizen power source would move through it, and they'd get a reading. See how much closer they were to the other side. A smooth mechanical voice began a countdown.

In that second before, the only prayer Solomon had the

strength left to send into the ether was to Eli. It didn't matter if he heard it or not.

May your mother protect you where I have failed.

The keys turned.

～≈

The national anthem played. Everyone in the classroom took their seats when the last note faded over the intercom.

". . . and, as always, we remind you all to remain vigilant in times such as these. Task Guard escorts are available if you feel at all unsafe in your neighbourhood. If you see anything out of the ordinary, remember that saying something could save a life."

Everyone whispered about the assault on the Old Leg. Saskia had expected an assembly about it, but nothing came. This school was one that filtered directly into the ETG programs now, and every teacher was, really, a soldier in their own right. Saskia and Ella used to delight in finding out — or, at least, dramatically fictionalizing — the lives of their teachers. The ones on the Denizen school side were Mundanes, too, and harsh, strict, mean. Denizens were lucky they were getting an education, they were made to believe through the snickers, the punishments for nothing. Denizens should be shipped off to do free labour on the struggling farms or collapsed mines, put their curses to good use.

That's what they called their powers, their gifts. Ella said they'd pay for that someday. Now look where she was. Meanwhile, the teachers on Saskia's side patted her classmates on the head for outing their neighbours, who were never seen again. Everything was wrong, every day, and Saskia had somehow thought for a second she could stop it.

The teacher droned on about some assignment regarding the Dark Day Treaty. This woman, with her severe hair pulled tight to her skull, her smile that was trying to be a comfort but came off like a car accident . . . wasn't she supposed to be distracting them? All anyone wanted to talk about was the moon moving, the attack on the Old Leg, and all the reports swirling. Instead, she was riling them all up, hands shooting into the air, her smile's wreckage twisting wider with every gesture.

This is what a heart attack must feel like, Saskia thought as her classmates volleyed rumours like crumpled paper, the teacher doing everything to keep the ball in play.

"I hear they captured the terrorists already."

"I hear they're going to have their powers taken away."

"I hear they're going to execute them."

Saskia didn't bother trying to set the record straight with any of them. *If those Foxes lost their powers*, she thought, *it would be death. No one survives that.* Saskia knew a lot of things that her classmates would be stunned to hear — but she could never share them or she'd be a sympathizer. No. Better to keep her stories to herself.

"Never let them doubt your loyalty," Barton used to tell her, "even if it's bullshit."

She always liked it when he cussed.

So Saskia just stared straight ahead, as she had, every day, so no one would ask her a thing, or question her quiet, code-nerd exterior. Code was boring to them, but to her it was something she could always turn to, get lost in, imagine scrolling endlessly across the back of that classroom. She could code herself to be a completely different person and no one could crack the truth: that overnight, she'd become a rebel. A disloyal dissenter. She was a former Cinder Kid. Definitely not one of them.

In AP Math, her best subject, she glanced at Cam, who was surrounded by jockeying bro-buds congratulating him on joining up. Everyone at school seemed psyched to drop out and drop into the fray. They all wanted to be damn heroes.

So did you, Saskia chided herself.

But Cam had kept his word and said nothing about Saskia's birthday, and when he caught her eye he gave her a thumbs-up. She looked away quickly. What would Cam do if he ever found out the things that Chancellor Grant had thrown in her face last night?

What would he say if he found out Saskia was seriously considering joining the Task Guard, too?

She'd been trying to push it away all day, but she was still inside that interrogation room, frozen with panic in a way she'd promised herself she'd never be. "If it were me, I'd be out there doing something!" Saskia had often spat at Phae during their petty arguments. "Roan always did something, but you were always too scared!"

How easily the words had come out, but they'd cut Saskia twice as deep for saying them. The truth was, she'd been running scared ever since Phae and Barton took her in and brought her here, tried so hard to give her a slice of the normal no one remembered.

A former Cinder Kid. Maybe the last person to see Roan Harken alive. But certainly the person who had killed the monster that had taken her brother from her. Urka.

Barton did try to do something, she reminded herself. *And look what happened to him. Once upon a time a Rabbit thought himself above the wolf, until he was dragged deep down into their lair, and not even his bones were found.* That the chancellor had known Barton, that maybe he'd been the one who took him away, made it so much worse. Was history going to repeat itself through her? Or was this her chance to change everything?

Last night, Saskia had felt for a moment that she could call some power to her, something pushed down deep, and make Grant pay. Make them all pay for what they'd done to her and the family she'd chosen. Even now, in this classroom, Saskia wanted desperately to go back to last night and change how everything went down . . .

Saskia clenched her pen so hard it snapped, sending ink splattering on her white shirt. She groaned audibly, and the teacher noticed, sending her out to get cleaned up.

In the washroom, in front of the bank of mirrors, Saskia threw water on her face, knowing there wasn't much to do about the ink except button up her denim jacket and sigh.

When she wiped her cheeks and stared back at the huge dark circles under her sleepless eyes, she thought back to the night before, in the chancellor's presence . . . when another face had been unexpectedly staring back at hers.

The Moth Queen had been there in the interrogation room, behind the Chancellor. Time had frozen. Mother Death, as she was known, flexed her enormous wings, which curled into the edges of the room, as if she'd break through those screens before anything might break her.

Eternal, inevitable, Ancient's grim reaper. Saskia was not supposed to be able to see her — after all, she wasn't a Denizen. She thought her stomach would collapse in on itself like a black hole.

"Calm your heart, now," the voice urged through a mouth that was not really one beneath a hundred onyx eyes. Her thorax crackled, and her many hands folded.

Saskia took a breath. The Moth Queen leaned in, leaf-antennae twitching as she inspected the chancellor, though he made no move or paid no mind. Perhaps Saskia had slid sideways into a plane of existence only she could notice. Or, more likely, she'd finally gone off her nut.

"This man courts death," the Moth Queen said, rearing back to her mighty height after her appraisal. She turned again to Saskia. "Consider his offer. Let him think you his ally, for it might allow us an opportunity. I will come to you again, at the creek where the river goes by. It will become clearer in the way you've always wished it to be."

It was less a prophecy and more a debriefing. Saskia had been shocked, then, wondering, specifically, if she'd snapped from the stress.

But now she blinked . . . and was suddenly back in the girls washroom at school in the present. When she looked back into the mirror, that's all it was. No black screen. No bug queen.

Until she noticed a flicker underneath the fluorescent light, and she whipped around, took a tentative step, and reached.

A tiny brown moth, triangular wings flexing as it landed on her finger. She watched it carefully, measured her heart-beat, and thought, *Follow the moth? Does this mean I'm being chosen —*

Until the moth exploded in a spark of flame and ash, and Saskia screamed and lurched out of the bathroom, clutching her chest.

Follow the moth, she thought bitingly, *at your own risk.*

The LAST DEER LEFT BEHIND

Phae had gone about her rounds in the apartment complex, much more aloof than even her baseline. She always had so much on her mind, and really no one to talk to about it. She'd done that to herself — both the isolation and this pile-on of obligation. So many relied on her. And still the one person she kept coming back to this morning was Saskia.

Of course it was. She'd been sick with grief and worry last night, especially when Ella's Aunt Cassandra had told Phae, sobbing, where Ella had gone. And Phae knew that wherever Ella went, Saskia would inevitably follow.

It was around one in the morning when Saskia was escorted back to the apartment, and as the Elemental Task Guards explained the situation, their words crushed Phae like the walls of an ocean seven years back, in a confrontation that shouldn't have led to this life she was now forced to live.

A life without Barton.

"Do you have *anything* to say for yourself?" Phae seethed when the guards left.

Whenever Phae and Saskia got into it, which was often, since Saskia had gone from a quiet child to a preteen with heroic notions to a *suspiciously* quiet teenager — Phae admitted it made her feel like she was young again. Like she was arguing with Roan, trying to talk sense into her, to keep her from rushing headlong into every bizarre cause. Who knew she'd be effectively raising Roan's doppelgänger, who had a similar penchant for never asking anyone for help.

As usual, Saskia clammed up, and Phae had wanted to shake her, but instead she decided it was *her* turn to storm to her room first. All their unsaid words filled the apartment like a toxic gas, clinging to Phae still when she knocked on the Morenos' door on the eleventh floor. It was time to put all of that away and do what she could for those who depended on her.

After a few seconds of Phae gathering herself, Elena Moreno answered, and Phae's pain was once again crowded out by someone else's.

That's what she'd wanted, after all. She'd seen this scenario too many times. All she could do was try to offer comfort. Even if no one could offer the same to her.

"We took her to the hospital," Elena said, eyes red-rimmed from crying. "But she didn't want to die there. She wanted to see you."

Phae steeled herself. "I'm sorry, Elena," she said, taking both of the woman's hands. There usually wasn't much else to say.

She sniffed but shook her head. "No. You've done so much for my family. For *everyone's* families." Her eyes were hard. "You've given us strength when we all forgot it."

They treated Phae like she was an elder, but most of the people in One Evergreen, or any of the other Denizen housing projects, were so much older than her. Phae was barely twenty-five, after all. Yet the weight of all their pain added at least eighty years to her weakening spirit. She'd been forced to grow up too quickly. Having Saskia in her life made her feel older still.

Phae smiled thinly. "I'll go and sit with her now. You get some rest." Elena let go of her hands, nodding tiredly, and moved away from the bedroom door. Phae went inside and shut it behind her.

The old woman in the bed tilted her head, breathing ragged. She still managed a smile. "You came, *sacerdotisa*."

Priestess. "Of course, Isela." Phae went into the chair beside the bed. She took the old woman's hand. "I'm here."

Isela's eyes squeezed shut. Phae sent a tendril of flickering blue from her fingers into Isela's. "Is that better?"

The old woman nodded. "Don't waste your strength on me," she croaked. "A Rabbit always knows when the hunter's come."

Phae smiled at the old proverb. She could still heal things. Small things. But her powers had limits. She did what little she could, but it did tire her out fiercely. "Just rest," she said, as if she was begging it of herself.

"What was it like? For the others?"

Phae squeezed the old woman's hand. She knew that relating the stories of other Denizen deathbed scenes she'd witnessed would not remotely help in this situation. "It's different for everyone."

Isela's mouth twisted. "Death is still a certainty. The Moth Queen doesn't stop for anyone. But what's the point of dying once you know your soul isn't going where it was promised?"

Phae sighed. "There's still a lot we don't understand. Nothing is certain."

"It used to be," the old woman argued. Phae smiled; she still had spunk, all things considered.

Phae relaxed her tense shoulders. "You all know so much more about Ancient than I do," she replied. "You've just got to trust your faith."

"But you've *been there*," Isela urged. "You've seen the realms. So they must still be there. Yes?"

This is usually how the conversation went, before the end. Everyone wanted at least some reassurance that there'd be something waiting for them on the other side. In Isela's case, it was the Warren she dreamed of, just like all the other Rabbits. The final resting place of their souls, in the comforting embrace of their First Matriarch, Heen.

But Phae had only ever seen the Glen. Watched the flicking soul-shadows of Deer racing around the silent mountain. Walked with her own adopted god with three faces and a terrible fatalistic attitude towards the world. That hadn't given her comfort. Especially since Phae wasn't born a Denizen — she was made one. She chose this path, and it'd led her here.

And the last time she'd seen the Glen, it had been completely destroyed.

But she didn't tell Isela any of that. She smiled again. "The Matriarchs are with us, even when we don't feel it as much as we used to."

Isela relaxed into her pillow, shut her eyes. "Ancient may be silent, the Matriarchs' influence waning, the Calamity

Stones lost, but I still dream of running through wide open thickets. I still believe it's there."

"That's all you need," Phae said. Isela spoke no more, breath coming unevenly as she relaxed, as Phae helped steer her towards the end. "May Heen be with you."

One of Phae's hands went up to the chain around her neck, to the stone hanging from it and hidden in her shirt. She smoothed a thumb over the locket that contained the stone she'd thought would save everything. Yet so long ago, at the edge of a cataclysm, that moment had never come, and the stone had gone silent. Still, silent or not, it was Phae's only comfort now.

Isela's hand loosened. Phae didn't hear the sound of fluttering moth wings like she did in her dreams, but she could imagine them clearly enough. She sat back in the chair as another soul fled to another plane, or maybe it remained floating around this room. But whatever the place, she had no proof it existed.

Phae looked out the window to the dark smudge hanging over them all and felt, as she had for many years, the crushing weight of her failure.

❧

Seven years ago, in St. John's, Newfoundland, Phae had woken suddenly with a weight pressing on her legs. At first she thought she was being crushed, until she looked down and saw it was someone else's body lying across hers.

Phae reached down and laid a hand on Barton's fuzzy head. His hair was soft like a cottontail, amusing given his

Family. She hadn't thought she'd actually, really touch him ever again.

He jerked awake and slammed back into his chair. "Phae!" And his strong arms were around her neck, hugging her fiercely.

She touched him tentatively at first, then squeezed back just as hard. "I'm not dreaming."

"Nope," he pulled away, face broken by his exhausted grin as he took off his glasses and rubbed his eyes. "Though it doesn't mean the world's any less of a nightmare."

It was morning and light slanted across Phae's hospital bed from the window. There was something dark hanging in the overcast sky. "What's —"

"We don't know yet." Barton shook his head, glancing at the thing once and looking right back at Phae, laying his palms on her face. "But you're okay, and that's good enough for me right now."

Everything came crashing down on her like a nauseating tidal wave. "Wait — what happened?" Frantic, she looked around. "Where's Roan? Eli?"

Barton sat back stiffly in the chair, massaging his legs. His running blades were propped up against the laminate bedside table. The grave look on his face made Phae's stomach knot up like scar tissue.

"Don't know that, either," he said, voice quiet. "They had a plan. We all did. God knows we sacrificed enough to see it through." His mouth twisted. "But we obviously couldn't make the winning goal."

Phae shut her eyes and pressed her fingers into her temples. The last things she remembered came to her in snatches: the wide and raging sea. Natti had been there — and Roan.

Roan was changed into something terrible — then all at once she'd overcome it. Her body was a vessel for the stones that they'd all been desperate to bring together in the first place, the fifth of which Phae had carried with her from one crumbling realm into this one. A last bid: wake Ancient. Save everyone. Stop the Darklings from breaking through.

Her eyes flashed open and she whipped off the bed covers, as if the dazzling trinket was lost amongst them. "The Quartz," she hissed, frantically searching, nearly yanking out her IV line. "Where is it?"

Barton had been fastening his blades on and caught her before she tumbled out of bed. "Easy, Phae, relax."

"Relax?" she whirled on him, dark hair in her eyes. "How can you say that? How can you say we failed? *Where is Roan?*"

There was a knock on the door so quiet they barely heard it.

"You can come in, Saskia," Barton said to the little face pressed into the gap in the doorway.

The girl was skinny, small. Her black hair was cut in a ragged bob around her chin, freshly combed. She wore a hospital gown underneath a terry cloth robe, and though she looked tired, her big round eyes never left Phae as she came around the bed, hands twisting in front of her. She couldn't be any older than ten.

"You're awake," she said to Phae.

Phae's glance darted quickly to Barton and back to the girl. "Hello," she said uncertainly.

"This is Saskia," Barton said, settling back into his chair. Saskia climbed into the chair next to him. "She was the one who found you."

Phae blinked at the girl slowly, trying to master her thudding heart. "Oh." She swallowed, not sure how to ask. "Is she —"

"No," Barton answered right away. "But she knows about us. She knows quite a lot, actually." He smiled at Saskia, who looked away, chewing on her fingernails. "You can talk to Phae. She's —"

"A Deer. I know," the girl huffed. "And you're a Rabbit. And I'm no one."

Barton raised an eyebrow. "Believe me, Saskia. Being a Denizen isn't all it's cracked up to be. And Phae and I are still pretty new at it." He tried to smile at Phae, but she was staring at the round dark shadow in the sky behind her visitors.

"That's them, isn't it?" Phae said. "The Darklings."

"Yes." She was surprised it was Saskia who answered. "They're free now. They're together."

Phae looked at her oddly. "How do you know that?"

Saskia had been kicking her feet in the chair. They went still. "I saw it when I killed Urka."

"Urka?" Phae's heart sped up again. "How?"

"We can go over that later," Barton said, standing carefully and using the bed rail for support. "As for me, I need at least three gallons of coffee. And to check in with my unit."

Phae blinked, trying to comprehend what he'd said. That's right — Barton was wearing a sort of green linen uniform. That was why they'd separated months ago: he'd joined a coalition that had formed between Families to fight the threat, called Seela, that was after the Calamity Stones.

Barton still hadn't answered Phae's most burning questions, though. He must have known it, which was why he was trying to make his escape. Phae tried a different question. "Is Natti all right?"

Barton turned back. "She's down the hall. You can ask her yourself. She's a bit more battered than us. But it'll take more than the end of the world to knock her down, I think." He squeezed Phae's shoulder, and she held his hand, kissed it, before he left the room.

Saskia remained. "The Quartz sang," she said after a while. "Roan went through the song, and away."

Phae sat up a little straighter. A snatch of hazy memory confirmed it. So that part had worked, at least. "She got into the Brilliant Dark?"

Saskia lifted her shoulder. For someone so young, she looked like she'd seen too much. *Haven't we all?* "Eli went with her."

That offered Phae some comfort. At least her best friend wasn't alone. "There's hope then." She couldn't help it — she turned her head, looked out the window one more time. That thing hanging in the sky seemed to command her attention. She knew there might not be any looking away for a long time.

She felt a solid, smooth weight pressed into her hand and looked down.

"I don't know about that," Saskia said, taking her hand away and revealing the winking surface of the Horned Quartz. "It washed up on the beach with you. But it's quiet. It's not saying anything anymore. Not since the others cracked."

Phae stared at the stone, the gift with which Fia, a god whose own faith in humanity had barely hung on at the end, had entrusted her. The key to the last Realm of Ancient, where Ancient itself slept. If they'd opened the door and done everything right, it should have woken the slumbering godhead. Should have stopped this.

But it hadn't. The Horned Quartz just looked like a dull piece of glass now, nothing like the mystical gem imbued with any of the grace Phae had felt when it was given to her.

Phae felt like she was falling. "But Roan —"

"I'm sorry," Saskia said, and when Phae looked up she realized the little girl was crying. "Roan's gone. And I dunno if there's any way for her to come back."

～＊～

Natti often thought about waking up in that hospital in St. John's, these days. She replayed everything, tried to change those memories, but always awoke to the same outcome. She'd known the consequences, of the words she couldn't take back. Seven years later, there was nothing much she could do with these regrets except offer them up to the snow.

Natti peered out into the tundra, scanning. Snow upon snow. White shore, white sea. She narrowed her eyes towards the south and pulled the crossbow off her back.

"What is it?" her mother asked. She had been on the shore, where the water lapped against the crusted rock, praying. It brought her comfort, even if no one was likely listening. Not even the sea.

Natti didn't reply, just aimed, let a bolt of ice fly, and they both watched the object in the sky hurtle landward. "Third one this week," she said.

They made their way across the tundra towards the crash site. It didn't take long for them to come upon the drone with black curls of smoke peeling into the frigid air.

The wind sliced past, but their faces were well bundled against it. Natti pulled down her mouthguard. "They just won't quit," she muttered. The drone was just another warning.

Her mother shook her head, toed the wreckage. "Not until they have what they want."

"I know what they want," Natti grunted, scooping up the drone. She often brought them back to town, displayed the crushed plastic and steel on a shelf like a trophy. It raised everyone's spirits, though it always darkened hers. "Maybe I should surprise them and give them *exactly* what they're looking for."

When they made it back to the cabin in the village, remote and removed and barely connected, as had been the deal, her mother bent to unlace her boots indoors. "Are you seriously considering going back to Winnipeg? To meet with the chancellor?"

"The moon moved," Natti replied. "Not even *we* can ignore that. If things are shifting, our help might be needed."

Her mother peered hard at the daughter she'd gotten to know only these past few years through uneasy silences and difficult times. "It was your call to keep us Seals separate, all those years ago. You yourself said it was the only way to keep this Family safe."

Natti didn't disagree. She had been right; they'd been safe. But at a cost that had been weighing on her as each day passed, looking out into nothing but a wide, empty sea melting at a rate it never should have. She had no compass to follow. No confidence to keep for anyone. She'd trusted people before, and for years she believed they'd let her down.

"So what if there are more of those river hunter things popping up?" Her mother waved her hand. "Isn't that why the Task Guard formed? If you ask me, him wanting you to go there and start some kind of Seal Unit is the most obvious trap I've heard of. All those Rabbits disappearing last spring, no cause or reason, but probably for processing. We're next."

Natti scoffed. "Of course it's a trap. But something else is going on. Reminds me of what Barton tried to do. Reminds me that once upon a time, there were some of us who had a plan to fight back, if the fighting was good."

"You'll remember, then," her mother said darkly, moving into the kitchen, "what happened to that boy because of what he *tried* to do."

She passed Natti then and squeezed her shoulder, probably as much to reassure herself as her daughter. Natti turned to close the interior cabin door, but happened to squint skyward, that black smudge sharp and clear even against the midnight sun.

"Hmph, well," she said, shutting the door with a slam. "Maybe I'd like a front seat to this impending doom we've all been going on about for so long."

Maybe, she thought, *I'd like to see what remains of my friends, one last time, before the end.*

"Aivik?" Natti called down the hall. "Have you seen my bag?"

MARKED *by the* DARK

S askia stood now in front of the house where it all began.
It was like all the other houses on Wellington Crescent.
Big, old, grand. Many of these houses had been seized for the
Restoration Project, lived in or run by the Elemental Task
Guard and supplied with government funding; it was the
same in other cities. Larger houses acted as central dormito-
ries for the Task Guard who were integrated into neighbour-
hoods, in this case, houses specifically near the Old Leg and
the Law Courts. It made dealing with conflicts easier, they'd
said. What it really did was remind people, Denizens in particular, that they were being watched by their neighbours.

But Cecelia Bettincourt's house — long taken over, semi-
rebuilt, and its infamous summoning chamber beneath it
likely filled in — housed more than just the enemy. It housed
a history. Saskia didn't know why she'd come here, but
she'd wanted to see it. She thought, maybe, if she was seeing

Death, she'd see something else in the place Death set this all in motion, with Roan Harken.

Saskia and Ella had spent maybe too much time here, daring one another to get close to the house. After scaring themselves giddy, Ella would regale Saskia with everything she'd been told had happened in this house, filling in the gaps and strengthening the legend of Roan, her family, and their quest for justice in the face of authority's version of the greater good. Roan had been a Fox, after all. Last scion of a family that had sacrificed so much to change the unchangeable Narrative. It was a good story. Saskia never got tired of hearing Ella tell it with such passion. Such fire.

The corners of Saskia's eyes burned.

Whether the stories were true or not, whether any of it mattered now, Cecelia's house always made Saskia feel like she was a part of that story, even though she'd been relegated mostly to the margins. And this house was still here, and that meant something.

Saskia's heart caught when the front door opened, and a stream of cadets came out into the street, likely to relieve other street guards. Gods only knew what went on in these satellite houses. Some of the officers loaded into a dark van and pulled away. Neighbours didn't seem to mind or do more than glance up from their yardwork. Just a normal civic routine, like a garbage truck making its rounds.

You could be one of them, Saskia thought, watching the van disappear up Lanark. *You could learn all their secrets and undo them from the inside.*

Yeah, right. More hero stuff to fail at. Saskia turned the other way, towards the open waters of the Assiniboine River across the road. She played a game in her head that she often did, staring stalwartly ahead. *Don't look up*. She knew the moon would be there. A permanent immovable (until today) fixture in the sky, watched diligently by every international government space program. After the first couple of years, the world let its guard down and tried to resume the day-to-day in their new normal.

But when it'd landed up there, it took out satellites. Didn't just obliterate them — it *sucked them in*. And it did the same to anything the world tried to launch near it. Some people theorized the black mass-less ball had some kind of sentience. That it didn't want people to be so connected anymore. So there went the internet, cellphones.

Why did Mundanes bother with theories? All they had to do was turn to the Denizen lore, to actually listen when the last Family leaders urged Mundanes, *begged* them, to ally with Denizens to fight whatever the moon was.

But that conversation was over before it could start.

Saskia did finally look up. *I lose again*. The Denizens had a name for it: the Darkling Moon. Because that's what it was — an amalgam of the three darkest souls in the Realms of Ancient, monsters who wanted nothing more than to snuff out Ancient's creation and leave behind only shadow.

Three entities that Saskia had known, in one form or another, a little too intimately.

She looked around, hands thrust into her pockets, kicking the sandy path, deflated. What was she doing out here? She'd get a citation for skipping school, and if she was already on the ETG radar, she could be arrested again. She realized, like last night, she didn't care. She'd reached the height of terror and survived. What did school matter when the world was coming to an end, as Cam had predicted?

Saskia had come to Cecelia's house on the way to Omand's Creek — *where the river goes by*. She'd hoped, somehow, Ella might be there. That they could go back to the way things were. That had been childish. Even though, technically, she still *was* a child . . . she couldn't remember what it felt like to be one.

Saskia should have talked to Phae first thing this morning, instead of hiding in her bedroom like a moody goddamn teenager. She should have told her everything.

She raked her hands through her hair, ready to move on with one last look at the house. "This is so stupid."

Then she felt it again, that pull she always felt mid-dream, except this time it was like being yanked through a hole beneath her, despite standing perfectly still. Down a dark chasm, falling through a bank of fluttering wings that got in her mouth, her eyes. *Follow the moth*, the voice like a house fire whispered, screamed. She covered her ears, but the sound jackknifed through. A high-pitched whine, a chord, singing. It scraped the inside of her head but couldn't resolve.

And even though her eyes were closed, something was bursting like fireworks against her dark eyelids. Something red. Something shivering. She felt her hand come up against her command, and she was tracing the air, tracing out the red.

Sigils. She couldn't read them, but she recognized them — from once upon a time when darkness was eating her up inside, eating every bit of hope she had left. *A Cinder Kid*.

Her heart felt like it was enlarged, too big for her too-human body. She yanked her hand down with the other one, staggered. *I need to find Ella*, she thought, in her own mental voice, her own mind. She just needed to stay in control. She just needed to talk to her friend. To someone. Anyone.

She bolted and paid attention to every breath, just like Barton taught her. The red in her vision was fading, blurred by the tears she'd been saving, but the echo of the sound followed her. Like a broken frequency, like bad static. It followed but faded as she kept running until she was over the train bridge towards Omand's Creek.

∾≋≺

Sometimes Phae would sit quietly for a long time, holding the empty stone in her both her hands, pressing her palms together as if she could crush it. But it was like a diamond, *like Barton's resolve*, she thought — it wouldn't crack.

She'd inhale a shaking breath and think of him. Think back to being lost on a strange and uncanny shore, yet across the void there was a red tether of fate binding them. Even separated by a metaphysical barrier, a distance that couldn't be counted, they had found one another. Felt one another.

It had been five years since that tether had snapped.

"Is it time for lessons now, Phae?"

Phae opened her eyes. "Yes, Jet. Sorry. Lost track of time." She closed the clamshell locket that held the Quartz, put the chain over her head, and tucked it back under her shirt. Getting up stiffly from her place in front of the small makeshift altar, she covered it with its black sheet.

Jet looked up at her expectantly with unblinking eyes. He was rather intense for a ten-year-old. *Saskia's age when* —

"It's Math now, though, Jet. Not Lore." She recognized the book in his hand — spine cracked, worn well. It wasn't one of the old Primers that Denizens passed around urgently when they were being hunted by the new regime — it was a book that had belonged to Barton, one that everyone in the apartment shared.

Speaking of . . . "And where's Lily? And Victor?"

Jet's eyes went to the floor. "I don't know."

"Jet." Phae's tone was firm. "Where are they?"

The hand not clutching the book was in his pocket. Phae gently pulled on his arm to free Jet's hand and look at his palm. It had been burned. "I'm going to guess you didn't get this from the stove," Phae sighed as Jet took it back, rubbing it.

"Victor is studying for Complicity. They're in their rooms," Jet finally said gloomily. "Lily went to Cara's."

Phae heaved a sigh. Victor was a Fox, and at fourteen he had it as bad as any other Denizen teenager — his powers were volatile during puberty. But he'd grown weary of wearing a target on his back. He was going to take the "exam," and be faced with the choice: give up his powers and try to reintegrate into the society that distrusted him for his birthright . . . or keep them and become an instrument of the regime.

Lily and Cara were another matter. The Rabbits, those who were vocal about it, anyway, had always regretted giving up on the hard-won Coalition that had formed between Families to fight the creature Seela all those years ago. Phae understood — she as much as anyone grieved the losses suffered. The Rabbit Family had suffered more lately. Many of them had gone missing in the spring after a surprise "search," since there had been talk of bringing the Coalition back. Nothing got past the Task Guard.

But everyone's minds weren't on such distant things today, probably glued to the radio since that thing in the sky had moved a fraction. What did it mean? Were the Darklings going to enact their final waking? What could the human forces do against it that the Denizens couldn't? And if the Elemental Task Guard intervened, would it only make it worse? *Let them try*, Phae knew some would remark. *Let them get burned for what they've done to us.*

The image graffitied on the wall of the Law Courts that had caused such a stir a week ago was like a brand in Phae's memory — her lost best friend's face, the red dripping flames a bloody reminder. *JOIN THE FIRE FIGHT*.

Phae had smiled, even then. For a second, she'd wanted to join whatever fight there would be. But looking down at Jet now, she knew that wouldn't be possible. She was needed here.

The desire for rebellion could be seen a mile away. And any Denizen who'd had enough of being crushed under the boot of the strange new world order would use Task Guard strong-arming as an excuse to fight back. It was already happening — had been happening.

But with these new cultists springing up, and violence in the streets, Phae didn't doubt that the ETG would soon be knocking on everyone's doors, Rabbit or otherwise, and Complicity would be less a suggestion. That Saskia was now involved in all of it brought her heart to a boiling point.

"Give me your hand," she said to Jet suddenly. Without looking at her, he gave it over. She pressed her own palm over it, and he hissed as if it stung. The blue light sparking off her hair-antlers flashed on his pale face.

"Better?" she asked. He nodded. "Just ignore Victor. I'm sorry he burned you. I'll talk to him later." She inhaled and tried to smile. "Come on. Lore is fine. The others can do math on their own time today."

Phae was tired. The morning had started early and since

Saskia, then Isela, Phae was feeling weighed down. Too many people panicking. Too many people stuck to their windows, looking out, watching and waiting.

"They're all just scared it's going to end," Jet said.

Phae sat next to him on the sofa. "Jet . . ."

"I didn't read your mind that time, honest!" He was earnest. "I heard it on the radio, too. I can see it on your face. The way you keep touching the stone around around your neck."

She flattened her mouth. "I guess being observant isn't a crime."

The book in his lap looked huge. He wasn't a big boy — he was twiggy, hair floppy and in his eyes, and he didn't like going out much. He stuck by Saskia, but he needed other Owls. *His own Family*, Phae thought, her mental walls firmly in place. Jet didn't need to read it from her mind — she was sure he thought about it enough. Jordan came, when he could . . . but he'd been arrested one too many times, and Phae was afraid they'd locked him up for good.

If only Eli were here. He'd had his flaws, and a titanic ego, but he'd been a leader. That's what they needed now. And he had willingly leapt into the great beyond with Roan (or so the story went). Besides, Phae had a fatal flaw of her own — trying to see the good in people long before it'd run out.

But with no Calamity Stones, there were no Paramounts, and with no Denizen gatherings legally sanctioned, any new leaders that *did* appear would be firmly underground, anyway. Or complicit with the Task Guard.

And if a war was coming — it would be no place for children.

All Phae could hear was the sharp bark of Saskia's desperate plea. *Don't you want to do something?*

Jet had the huge book tented in his lap. "What happens if the Darklings *do* wake up and come back down here?" he asked. The page he'd turned to was part of the section specifically devoted to the Darklings' part in the Narrative — Ancient's *great plan* for Denizens and the world they were sworn to protect. A plan that even the godhead had forsaken, slumbering for an age without a care for what happened to its creation, now in the hands of its godchildren, the First Matriarchs, and those in their divided Families.

Even the images painted in the book did no justice to the creatures as Phae had seen them — up close or in Fia's great pool, far away in the now-shattered Glen.

She didn't answer Jet directly. "Can you tell me the Darklings' names?"

Jet pointed to the images, reciting. To the half-woman, half-snake: "Zabor." To the multi-armed supplicant, grinning: "Kirkald." To the horse-like creature without a mouth: "Balaghast."

"That's right," Phae nodded. "And what do they represent?"

He pointed to each again. "Chaos. Harm. Silence."

She didn't want to scare him. She should be going over the good parts of Ancient and Denizenship. Things like how a Denizen's core purpose was to protect life in this world with their gifts and powers. That the Families were meant to work together in concert to maintain the balance that the First Matriarchs set out in Ancient's name. But her heart just wasn't in it. It was all flowery sentiment, after all. She'd seen Denizens in practice, the Families divided and fighting for authority. Look where division had brought them. Look what all their good intentions had wrought.

Phae had tried to stay neutral in the years since Barton

left. Tried not to steer the children she cared for in any one direction. But after all, how safe was it for them, as Denizens? Would they need their powers now, more than ever, to fight?

But Jet flipped the pages. "And what about her?"

Phae blinked down at the image, feeling the hair on her arms rise. Hadn't she just wondered about this, at the bedside of a dying woman? "The Moth Queen? What would you like to know about her?"

Jet wrinkled his nose. "The Moth Queen used to mark Denizens to sacrifice to Zabor, right? But Roan Harken stopped all that, because Death made a deal so it could be impartial again. Right?"

Who was the teacher now? Phae felt her heart catch, thinking of Roan. "What are you getting at, Jet?"

He tilted his head up, eyes round, as if the answer were obvious. "Saskia has been marked by the Moth Queen, hasn't she?"

Phae was utterly still. "What?"

"She's *seen* her," he pressed. As if he wanted Phae to explain how the Moth Queen could have come to Saskia if Saskia wasn't a Denizen.

She laid her hand over the inked image of the moth woman with her manifold hands, piercing eyes, and wide wings that promised, apparently, absolution.

"How do you know that, Jet?"

His eyes fell. "I couldn't help it, that time."

⁓

Saskia had stopped herself before she came around the corner that would overlook Omand's Creek. She wasn't holding out hope that Ella would be there, but if she wasn't, at least the others would be — those burnouts wouldn't be anywhere else at this time of day. Especially today, when the Darkling Moon they loved had given everyone a show.

Would the Moth Queen be there, if these Cluster-wannabes were? But maybe they'd seen Ella. If the Moth Queen didn't show, and was, really, just a figment of Saskia's oversaturated imagination, at least she could gather some intel on her best friend . . . really girlfriend. So Saskia inhaled and went sharply around the corner.

She could smell their cigarettes as she picked her way down the hill. One of them hissed, pointed at her. They all watched her approach, sneering with their teeth out. Saskia didn't have any way of defending herself if things got nasty against these teen-extremist Denizen dropouts, but she kept thinking of Ella, and took some strength from that.

"Well looky who it is," said the girl in front. Her hair was a bad black dye-job. *At least mine's natural*, Saskia thought. But she kept her face calm.

"Dannika." She nodded. "Josh. Amanda." She made a point of naming them all.

Josh leapt up, all skinny jeans and DIY piercings. "Heard you were there last night. With Ella and the others. What happened?"

Saskia hesitated. Amanda, Josh's girlfriend, laughed. "Look at her face, Josh. Scaredy Sask wasn't anywhere near the Old Leg last night. She'd have pissed herself for sure."

"I was there." Saskia confirmed, and the way Amanda's face dropped with shock gladdened Saskia's racing heart. "Where'd you hear that?"

Dannika flicked her cigarette out. "Doesn't matter," she

snapped. "The Dark Moon has willed all of this into motion. Whatever happens, it's meant to be."

The others nodded gravely, as if they really believed their culty crap meant anything. Saskia shut her eyes as they rolled back into her head.

Dannika and Josh were Denizens. But Amanda was a Mundane, like Saskia. The Cluster said everyone was welcome. More than once, they'd tried to rope Saskia into their group. There wasn't much to it: you just had to worship a triple demon-amalgam in the sky, praying for the end times.

They were stupid poseurs. If they'd seen what Saskia had, with Seela, they'd be the ones pissing themselves for sure.

"I even got up close and personal with Chancellor Grant himself," Saskia said coolly. She needed to up her cred, and fast, if she was going to get anything out of them.

Josh's red-rimmed eyes bugged. "Whoa. And that fascist Task Guard asshole didn't throw you underground with the other experiments?"

Dannika openly slapped him on the arm, and the skinny bundle of sticks nearly tripped over himself. "Shut up. She's lying. She wants something."

Saskia swallowed. "Grant offered me a job. On the inside. I figured that'd be of interest to your . . . priest."

Dannika had been watching Saskia closely. She leaned back, arms folded. "A job?"

Saskia was already losing her patience. She gestured at the other side of Omand's Creek, towards Wolseley. "Maybe I should head up there and ask the priest myself. After all, the 'Dark Moon wills it.' Probably. I doubt it could will the three of *you* to change a tire."

"Hey now." Amanda got between them, even though Dannika's smirk had turned into a threatening snarl. "It's broad daylight, and there are a ton of ETG pricks sniffing around." She swung on Saskia, jabbing herself in the chest. "*We* deal with the priest. No one else. What do you want, Das?"

Saskia heard Dannika's boot crunch in the dirt. Felt the warning tremor in the ground. Dannika was a Rabbit with an axe to grind at the best of times.

"I'm looking for Ella. I know she and Clare and Damien didn't just come up with the idea to attack the Old Leg, or the chancellor, on their own. I figured it was either you or the priest, given how the Darkling Moon just *happened* to have moved that same night. All told, I'd say that even if you don't know where Ella is now, you're responsible if anything happened to her."

A rock shot up from the ground and into Dannika's open palm. Josh whipped his head between the two of them.

"We don't know anything about Ella or the others," he said. "The priest told them to wait, that it was too risky, with the chancellor-twat newly arrived and probably more ETG with him. And as usual, he was right."

Dannika sniffed. "Whatever that dumb Fox gets into now doesn't involve us. We all want to finish what Roan Harken started and be the hero, Das, but you have to be smart about it." Her smirk climbed. "Tell us about this job, and maybe we'll see if we can scrounge up whatever remains of your girlfriend."

Saskia stared at the rock, Dannika tossing it up and down like a baseball in her fingerless-gloved hand. Whether they worshipped the Darkling Moon, or figured themselves vigilantes, or had some Hallmark creed sewn in ironic patches on their denim vests, these kids were still just kids.

Saskia squinted. This had been pointless. "Maybe I'll just keep it to myself. Maybe I'll sic the Chancellor on *you* instead."

Suddenly the rock was singing past Saskia's ear towards the river. She grunted and twisted, clapped her hand to her ear, as she heard the screech of a river hunter, hit by the rock but still crawling along the mud towards them like an oil-slicked eel.

Saskia scrambled back, tripped. Hadn't Cam mentioned something about these freaky things showing up recently? She looked to the others, but they seemed more stupidly awe-struck than afraid.

"It's a sign," Josh breathed. "They can sense their mother coming back for them."

Then there were two river hunters, hissing and clicking in their alien monster tongue, mouths vertical gashes. A third hunter cut through the water, scrambling to follow its fellows. *Great.* Sure, there had been monsters creeping around Winnipeg, and any other corner of the planet, since the Moon showed up. But these were Zabor's direct spawn, and they hadn't been seen since she had been sent back to her hole, when even Roan Harken assumed prematurely it was all over. Once, Mundanes wouldn't have been able to see them, but that was over now.

"This isn't funny," Saskia said, jaw set. "Don't provoke them. We have to get out of here."

Amanda hollered, almost cheering. She shook Josh. "Isn't this amazing?" He was smiling, too. Like it was Christmas.

"You're all crazy," Saskia said, eyes watching the third hunter. This had been a terrible idea, Moth Queen or not. "I'm out of here. Enjoy blackhole gazing till your eyes fall out."

Josh leapt forward and snatched a fistful of Saskia's jacket. Dannika took the other side, dragging her closer to the river-bank and holding her there.

"Guys . . . you shouldn't," Amanda hazarded. Amanda was a Mundane, too, after all. Self-preservation was kicking in. Maybe she'd be next.

Saskia dug her heels into river muck, the hunters getting closer.

"Let me go!" she yelled, smashed the back of her head into Josh's face and heard a satisfying crunch, but with that he dropped Saskia onto the bank in a heap. She cracked her forehead on a rock, stars blooming in her vision.

"Shit!" Josh said. "Let's get out of here, Mandy."

Saskia raised her head, vision bleary. A river hunter was nose to nose with her. It smelled like rotting fish. Its toxic teeth, cracking jaws, and claws were an inch-away promise.

She didn't move. The red eyes were locked on her. She had nothing to fight back with.

A twig snapped. Saskia whipped up to her knees, then her weak legs, because the river hunters perked at Dannika, who had stepped forward with a hand out.

"Don't be stupid," Saskia hissed. "Either earthquake these things into oblivion or *run*."

"C'mon, Danni!" Josh was a Fox, at least, but he looked like the only thing he'd ever set on fire were his pants when he fell asleep smoking. "Let's *go*!"

Dannika crept closer, lip quirking. "They won't attack us. We're true believers. The Dark Moon sent them to *test us*."

Now Dannika was beside Saskia. Saskia's head throbbed, and those blooming stars in her vision popped, fizzled. A buzzing in her ear, like a mosquito hovering when she was half-asleep. She twitched. *Not now*. The stars in her vision were turning pink. Turning red.

The nearest river hunter had reared up slowly, as if it was sniffing in Dannika's direction.

Then it was suddenly on her face, shrieking and writhing and biting, and Dannika was screaming, and Josh and Amanda were already running away as fast as they could. Reflexively, Saskia dove, grabbing the thing, throwing herself on top of it till she wrenched it off Dannika and hurled it back to the riverbank with what little strength she had.

The two other river hunters watched the first one splash and disappear. But they turned back to Saskia. The sparks in her dotted vision suddenly resolved.

The sigils, this time, were clear, and lined up over the river hunters, like a label. Saskia could understand them.

Mother, they said.

A river hunter surged forward and Saskia braced herself for the attack, but its slick arms went around her, protective and pleading, travelling up her body and twisting about her outstretched arm like a contented snake.

It looked down at Dannika, terror-stricken and bleeding by Saskia's feet, and *roared*.

Dannika finally managed to get her legs back under her, tearing off after Josh and Amanda, who had been watching from the crest of the hill.

"You freak!" Dannika wasn't dead yet if she was still hurling insults — but with the bite Saskia had witnessed, she might not be too far off once the river hunter infection took hold.

The river hunter wrapped around Saskia's arm hissed, but loosened, calm. Then it clicked at Saskia disapprovingly, a purple tongue flicking out to the blood coming down the side of her head, her ear.

The sigils were flexing, but fading, and Saskia tried to blink them away. *Protect our own*, the sigils said, or had the *hunter* said it?

It slid away, then, back into the river with its sibling as if it had never been there at all. The sigils were gone completely when the creature disappeared.

Omand's Creek was silent but for the roar in Saskia's ears and her ringing skull. She staggered and turned, because there was another sound. The flutter of wings.

She was wider than the bridge's struts, and her uncountable hands were folded in front of her beneath a cloak hewn from dried leaves, the husks of departed creatures. The Moth Queen was as horribly tangible now as she'd been last night in the interrogation room. She was here. She was real.

"So now you see," the Moth Queen said, her cloud of children hovering about her twitching leaf-antennae.

Saskia swallowed, swiping the blood mixed with river hunter saliva from her ear and wiping it on her jeans — she hoped she wasn't infected now, too.

"At the risk of sounding dumb," she said, "I don't know exactly *what* I saw." Did she *want* to know?

One needle-tipped finger stretched, and though she was far away, it was still within reach of Saskia's forehead. "You saw the sigils. You bear a darkness within you, child. One you cannot escape. But one that might yet save us all."

Saskia wanted to collapse, or run. She could do neither.

"No. Whatever that plague was, I was healed. I survived. I'm not a Cinder Kid anymore." But she had seen those red sigils, letters or runes that told their own story, even before

103

today. She'd draw them in the dirt, in the air, to calm herself down. Since Barton pulled her out of that tree, she never saw them again. Until the last couple of days. Saskia didn't like what the sigils could mean or what they were telling her. *Mother*, the river hunters had called her. That's what they'd called Zabor.

The Moth Queen couldn't smile — there was barely a mouth there, pinched and small, even with her enormous, hissing groan of a voice. But she sounded pleased. "You destroyed the Gardener when you were but a girl. Not an easy feat to come back from. Not without help."

Then Saskia felt it — like a smudge on her skin, where the Moth Queen pointed. It felt impossibly cold, like an ice pack had been pressed there. When she glanced into the brown water of the creek by the little footbridge, she saw the dark thing there. A black circle with wings in the negative space.

"You marked me?" she croaked, turning back, expecting the Moth Queen to never have been there at all. But now the Moth Queen was close, towering over Saskia. Now Saskia felt a new sensation — one that begged her to close her eyes, to embrace eternity.

"Not just me. Something else marked you. And your time is not yet come." The Moth Queen was reassuring, running a sharp and delicate hand tenderly over Saskia's head. "There is a war happening alongside the one in your world. One I can see but can do nothing about. But you? Child of the Bloodlands, aided by Death. Perhaps you can go where I cannot."

Saskia cringed, had to move away as far as she could. "I'm tired of all these riddles and prophecies. You made it sound like I should take what Chancellor Grant offered me. And these sigils, and that *noise*, and now river hunters are acting like obedient guard dogs around me? It doesn't make sense. It can't. So I need you tell me straight — what do you *want*?"

The Moth Queen hadn't moved. Saskia thought she saw a tremble of something beneath her many gaping eyes. Uncertainty?

"No one has asked me what I want, before," Death finally admitted, head tilted.

"Oh," Saskia said, clever retorts all dried up. She looked down again at her reflection in the water and heard, felt, the Moth Queen draw up next to her and look down into the water, too.

"I want to return to where I am of use," the Moth Queen went on. "I have been barred from going back to the Realms of Ancient. To do what I am made for. Even Death can grieve for all the Denizen souls left wandering, away from their ancestors and their due, these seven dreadful years. I am a mother in my own way. It is unbearable to me."

Saskia was surprised to hear the fatigue in the Moth Queen's voice, the raw, almost-human regret tinging the painful-to-hear voice. "Am I being chosen now? Like Roan was?"

The Moth Queen turned so quickly the sound was like a massive tree collapsing into a ravine. Saskia flinched.

"Chosen?"

"Well!" Saskia threw her arms up. "The dreams! The messages! You *need* me, don't you?"

The Moth Queen turned and dragged her massive thorax to the rock that Dannika had only just vacated and sat down, folding her twiggy hands beneath her sharp chin. "Do you remember me, child? From before? From inside the tree?"

Saskia had expected more riddles, not direct questions, or even a conversation, from what had to have been the most complex creature out of Ancient's legendarium. She knew immediately what the Moth Queen meant, though, and her memory of Urka — of the blow Saskia herself had delivered that ended it — rose quickly before her like an auto-accessed video file.

"Sort of," Saskia said.

The Moth Queen nodded, to herself. "I wove your very cocoon. But you, like the Fox kit Roan, slipped it. Ancient chose Roan, yes. For what reason now, I cannot surmise. So much is wrong. So much is uncertain. Why would Ancient wish Death to be parted from Ancient's own creation? Why would the gods now be silent?"

Her shoulders fell, just a little, her wings shivering. "But just as Roan carried death inside her after escaping it, so have you. And much more than that, you carry the Darkling mark. Their creatures see you as one of them — you were, once, carrying Seela's plague as a child of the Bloodlands. And part of their song has been left inside you."

Saskia's head swam— and not from hitting that rock. She stepped away from the water and stood in front of the Moth Queen, squeezing her arms into her body. "What do you want me to do?"

The Moth Queen looked directly at Saskia, as if her body was going to open up and devour her. Instead she sighed, the sound of a house fire going out.

"What I want, in the end, doesn't matter," she said. Saskia felt the tears come fierce and sudden, and the Moth Queen held up her hand. "Listen carefully. Your capabilities could be of use. But the choice isn't mine. It never has been. That is what is at stake here. There are no chosen ones. Only the choices that you make. The world will turn, and things can happen with or without you. You must decide your place in that. *You* must choose. The Narrative was only one plan. But the story has already been rewritten."

Saskia cast her eyes on her feet and realized her nails were biting into her forearms. "I want to help, though. I want to fight."

"So do I." The Moth Queen's voice echoed across the small creek, and when Saskia looked up, there was just a single moth, fluttering in her face and landing on her forehead. But the moth seemed to sink into her skin and vanish, and Saskia knew that the smudge had vanished with it. Not gone, just quiet. Waiting.

"Take comfort from your family," came the last whisper inside Saskia's head. "Whatever you choose, they will need you before this is over."

Family. Now Saskia sank to her knees, looking over to the train bridge and back to Wellington Crescent as the sun crept higher, the dark moon following. Death was a neutral aspect of Ancient.

She was more naïve than she thought.

Ella wasn't coming back, and even if she was, what would Saskia say to her? *Turns out maybe I'm a Denizen after all. But my Family is Darkling. My Family is going to end everything.*

What did any of it mean? And if Roan Harken were here, wouldn't she just rush into the fray, consequences be damned?

Saskia got to her feet after a while, cold and sore, head throbbing. She wasn't Roan Harken, no matter how much she wished it. No. This was so much bigger than Saskia, than her fear, than all of it. She had to be smart, like she knew she could be.

She had to talk to the chancellor. Then she had to talk to Phae. And maybe, now that destiny was no longer a factor, they could make their own choices about where they would end up.

Saskia ran, fast as Barton, for home.

SIGNAL ACROSS *the* VOID

"What sort of signal?" the priest asked.

The other man shifted on his feet, staring at the black granite of the floor. It was speckled with silver veins, catching the odd light of the LED lamps brought down to illuminate the space. Once, golden circles may have shone there. Or the reflection of fire. Deon's fire. Now it was cold and dark, the hearth at the back of the room empty. Same with the alcove hidden beneath it, where the Dragon Opal had been stashed. But that was a long time ago.

The man stared upward, where the sky was, somehow feeling it was very far away. "They don't know yet. It came through when the moon began tracking, through Project Crossover's great machine. There's part of it missing, it seems, and no instrument can interpret it. Yet." His chin tucked. "The Task Guard will move on this quickly. We will have to be quicker." The visitor tensed. "Grant believes it is something that will turn the tide. Open his Bloodgate. Win his war."

The priest was in the centre of the room, his back to the visitor, as he worked at something on the floor. He nodded. "And Grant believes that the key lies with someone he recently arrested. A girl, to whom he's just offered a job."

The visitor had come thinking that all his intel was new, but the priest had his little followers everywhere.

"History does have a habit of repeating itself," the priest muttered bitterly, flushing out the lines, the shapes, with a lump of red pastel clutched in his tight fist. He stopped suddenly and glanced about the chamber. "If this house were alive, it could tell you." It sounded as if he believed it was.

Then the priest sighed and leaned back on his thighs, surveying the work on the floor. Sigils fanned out before him. The knees of his pants were coated in red, as if he'd been praying in an abattoir.

No golden circles here. But red ones. Even in the semi-dark, that much was clear.

"We all have our parts to play," the priest said. "Keep an eye on the girl. And when the time is right, she will come to us. Then we can test whether or not she has her part, too."

Then he looked upward as the visitor had, to the ceiling of the basement, imagining that, above him, the Darkling Moon moved. Scrutinizing his work. Approving it.

The visitor clenched his cherrywood cane, caught up in his own mire of thoughts, and gladly left the priest to himself.

"Surely this isn't necessary, Chancellor."

Phae stood tall in the spartan living room. The children were crowded in the kitchen. She was trying her best to be a shield, as always. Saskia knew that she'd put up an actual shield, if she had to.

From Saskia's hiding place in the apartment's interior entryway, her fists shook. When she'd come to her front door, which was flanked by two ETG personnel she'd never seen before, she'd had enough sense to come inside quietly, though she couldn't hide here forever. In the kitchen, Victor was standing in front of Jet, who was shivering behind his legs. Lily clutched Victor's hand. They were all confused, terrified. Saskia didn't blame them, and the look on Jet's face was like a frozen knife in her side.

"Saskia Allen Das is your charge, is she not?" the chancellor asked Phae.

Phae kept her face impassive. "You wouldn't be here if she wasn't. I'm already well aware of her transgressions. And I didn't think I'd have the honour of you gracing us with your presence." She folded her arms. "I would have catered."

Saskia bit back a snicker.

The chancellor, though, let out a low, forced laugh. "I can see why Barton was fond of you."

Phae's dropped, pained gaze made Saskia's skin burn. The chancellor smiled stiffly, making the sharp lines along his cheeks look like incised scars. "In any case, I'm not here to speak to you this time, Ms. Das. Though if you'll find your way to putting me in touch with your friend Nattiq Fontaine, I'd be more than obliged."

Phae raised an eyebrow at his changing tack. "I haven't

heard from Natti in years, Chancellor. No one really has. I'm not sure exactly what you want from her. Or from Saskia."

He shrugged. "These are troubling times. The more allies we have for order, the better off we'll all fare."

Grant turned towards the kitchen. Jet tried to make himself smaller. "There's no need to be afraid," the chancellor reassured, holding out his hands. "I'm not the one who wants to hurt you. But you can help me, if you're so inclined, by telling me where your foster sister is."

Phae slid in front of him. "What do you want here? I thought you cleared Saskia of any wrongdoing last night. Has she committed some crime in the interim?" She couldn't keep the edge out of her voice, especially when she lowered it. "The last time you showed up here, I never saw Barton again."

That raised a chuckle from the chancellor's austere, thin mouth. "Come now, Phae. Barton came willingly, after all. And accidents do happen. Even he accepted the risks."

The colour draining from Phae's face. Saskia's was at critical mass.

"I just wanted to check in," the chancellor said, withdrawing. "There's so much going on these days. Once upon a time, you worked alongside us to mitigate these threats that you and your *friends* invited into everyone's lives. I'm just a glorified janitor for the last messes left behind." He strode from the kitchen, scrutinizing the photos on the walls, gaze lingering on Phae's small altar in the living room with its extinguished incense. "I have a feeling that the Darkling Moon hasn't moved of its own accord. We're all doing what we can to minimize . . . the consequences."

Saskia grabbed for the doorknob. Running now would do eff all, and Saskia couldn't just rush off to her room, undetected, like she usually did when confrontation hovered. So she screwed her eyes shut and slammed the door behind her, hard.

Someone in the kitchen shrieked — probably Lily, she was easily startled. But Phae was likely the most shocked when Saskia marched stiffly into the room. The chancellor seemed cheered by this development.

"Speak of the devil and she shall appear." The chancellor reached out a hand to Saskia. "Just the girl I wanted to see."

Phae recovered quickly and stepped closer to Saskia, eyeing the chancellor but leaving the question for her ward. "Saskia . . . what's going on?" Her eyes went right to Saskia's bleeding ear, and Saskia saw her guardian's fingers itch to seize her face and get a better look.

The chancellor looked between them, smirking as his hand dropped. "I'd expect better communication, but I can see there's been a breakdown under your roof, Ms. Das." He turned to Saskia, as if Phae was no longer there. "Have you given any further thought to my offer?"

Saskia didn't look at Phae either, now. She stepped farther away, face flushed, jaw tight.

"Yes," she said to the chancellor. "I have. And I'll do it."

The chancellor laughed. "Grand. In the interest of time, I'd like to have you picked up tomorrow morning, then, for Basic. If that's agreeable to your guardian."

"It is *not* agreeable!" Phae snapped. She grabbed Saskia by the forearm, wrenching her close. "Saskia, what's going on? What have you just agreed to?"

"It's my choice to make," Saskia snapped. "I'm seventeen now. I can apply for the Task Guard with or without your permission." Her eyes were fierce and wet and pleading, and

Phae let her go and backed away, as if she wasn't sure who she was looking at.

"That's right!" The chancellor clapped. Phae started. "I'd seen your birthdate on your file last night. But with so much going on . . . Happy birthday, Saskia. We'll try to turn this experience into a gift for you. For all of us." His hand landed heavily on Saskia's shoulder as he passed, and he glanced smugly at Phae.

Before he went he turned, jerking his head at Phae's altar. "You could learn something from Saskia. Best to put your trust into something real and reliable, like the Task Guard. Something that will actually answer your prayers."

After the chancellor was gone, Phae leaned heavily into the wall, as if she could barely stand. Saskia wanted to go to her, to try to explain, but Victor, Lily, and Jet came rushing out, swarming Saskia before she could move.

"What did you *do*?" Victor asked. "C'mon, Sask, spill it!"

"Are you okay?" Jet asked, pulling on Saskia's jacket, insistent, still shivering.

Their chattering was too much to bear, and Phae surged at them. "Everyone. Out. *Now*."

Saskia hadn't moved, hadn't raised her head from staring at the ground. The others backed away. "Brain," Saskia said, and his head snapped up quickly. "Go next door, okay? Take the others."

Jet nodded and grabbed Lily's and Victor's hands. Though the two were much older, they seemed too stunned to do anything more than follow him.

When the door clicked behind them, Phae was on Saskia, shaking her by the forearms. "Are you all right? Are you crazy?"

Saskia finally looked up at her, and though her eyes had been wet before, the tears were long dry now. "No. And yes."

Phae looked like she wanted to yell and scream and tell her she was too young to know what she had done. But then something else crossed her face, and she gathered Saskia in tight instead.

"Talk to me," she whispered into her charge's wind-messed hair, trying to do what Barton might have.

Saskia stiffened, but she didn't move away. Phae led her to the sofa, and Saskia perched at the edge of it, staring numbly at the living room carpet, not sure where to start.

Phae sighed above her. "I'll make us some tea." She went into the kitchen, and Saskia watched her go before turning back to the carpet. It was scuffed, cheap, and Phae tried to keep it clean. So did Saskia, when homework needed doing and she needed to avoid it. The truth of it was she had traced every synthetic strand in that floor, memorized like threads of infinite code, because this is usually where Phae did her major lectures, and Saskia had never been one for eye contact when she'd screwed up.

Which she had again, royally.

"There's something I want to show you," Phae said suddenly, crossing the living room and leaving behind their tea, as if it'd only been an excuse to collect herself in another room.

Saskia snapped out of her daze, frowning. "But don't you want —"

Phae lifted a hand. "There'll be time for that."

Phae bent over her altar — a low table Saskia had pulled from a back lane during her many garbage-dives. The surface was incised with the face of a woman — *Mucha style*, Ella had said of it, though Saskia didn't know much about art. Resting atop it was a slender bone of antler from the Assiniboine Forest. Then the incense. A lumpy candle. From her place on the couch, Saskia saw the chain around Phae's neck, the pendant hanging heavy. Phae hesitated over the drawer under the table, touched the locket under her shirt, and smiled faintly.

"Here," she said, turning to Saskia, offering her a folded slip of paper.

Saskia got up, approached cautiously, as if it were a trap, but Phae aimed the smile at her — a worn-out facsimile that was supposed to reassure her — and Saskia took the paper, unfolded it.

It was a photo that Saskia hadn't seen before. "Is this . . . ?"

Phae's finger hovered over each person as she named them: "Me, Roan, Barton, Natti. And the scowler back there is Eli, obviously."

Saskia's heart, already overwrought from the day's mis- adventures, took an excited misstep. The picture was taken sometime in the spring, on the grounds of the legislative building, before there were perimeter fences and prison cells beneath it. The river was behind the group, the trees bloom- ing. It was a picture from another world, almost.

At the forefront of the shot was Roan, a companionable arm around a Phae who seemed so different than the one now kneeling on the carpet at Saskia's shoulder. Hopeful. The Phae in the photo was half-bowled over by her friend's embrace, while Barton, smiling from his wheelchair, held Phae in his lap with one strong arm and looked at risk of falling over himself.

Saskia's chest squeezed.

On Roan's other side was an Inuit girl, one elbow up on Roan's shoulder, while the other hand was clenched in a superhero fist under a wink. She looked powerful, as if she had swagger to match Roan's. Saskia had only met Natti Fontaine once, before she'd retreated North, and it hadn't exactly been under good circumstances.

Slightly apart from the group was a taller guy, dark hair, furious grey eyes that would make you regret crossing him. Saskia knew that look well, despite only having spent a couple of days under its scrutiny. Eli Rathgar had saved her life, too, in his way.

Here he seemed tense, arms crossed, not looking directly at the camera, head tilted at the other four, as if he couldn't figure out how to join them — or if he wanted to.

"This was right after Zabor," Phae said after a while. "There was a sort of commemoration for us held by the Owl Council, when it was still here. A begrudging thanks." She shook her head at the memory, half amused, half grieving for days long gone.

Saskia hadn't looked up, trying to memorize their faces. Trying to understand all of them and what led them to each other, these disparate strangers and the new family they'd made.

"I think this is the only picture of all five of us," Phae said, her eyes pinching. "I think it's the last time we were all truly together."

That's not true, Saskia wanted to say, but she kept her mouth shut, nodded. These five *had* all been in the same place seven years ago, when the monster Seela brought everything to bear over the Atlantic coast of Newfoundland. Phae had just emerged from another world, and everything had seemed like it must have after the battle of Zabor — victory assured, the big boss brought down with their united wills alone.

But fairy tales only got them so far.

"When I look at this picture, I see a group of kids who didn't have a hot clue what they were doing. Yet they succeeded. Mostly by fluke." Her smile was utterly gone, as if her face hadn't been built to hold it. Saskia knew *that* look all too well. "I see a bunch of kids who had potential. And it's gone now."

Phae got up stiffly but left the picture with Saskia. "I see five heroes," Saskia mumbled, smoothing the creases.

That's when Phae spun. "There's nothing heroic about reckless decisions," she snapped. "That's what gets people killed these days. This isn't a comic book. It never was."

Saskia felt the anger inside her rising. "You don't know —"

"But I *do* know. Better than you ever will." Phae continued to pace, her expression a rictus of shifting despair, anger, exhaustion. "What you did at the Old Leg. That's definitely something Roan would have done. And she would've been proud. But I'm *not* Roan. Even she recognized that. I was always her sober second thought." She stopped, twisted. "What did you think you'd achieve, aligning yourself with that *reptile* Chancellor Grant?"

Saskia's fists were bunched on her knees, so much she wanted to say piling up in her mouth, but she just couldn't hit the release valve. "I don't know."

"Have you seen the Moth Queen? Don't lie to me, Saskia."

Saskia's eyes ripped up from the carpet. "What?"

Phae folded her arms. "Jet told me. He's worried about you, too. We all are. But if the Moth Queen is coming to you . . . why didn't you tell *me*?"

Saskia felt sicker with every breath. "That's just it. I don't *want* you to worry about me! I can handle this! I can *fix this*."

"Fix *what*?" Now Phae was shouting; Saskia was glad she'd sent the others next door. "You think getting involved with the *Task Guard* is going to help you? Is the Moth Queen *making you* do these stupid things?"

"No one's making me do anything!" Saskia leapt up, nerves burning. "What can I do? I'm not a Denizen! I can't fight like any of you! But I . . . I can make things. I can sneak around, gather information. I can find out what they did to Barton, I can —"

"That's enough!" Phae cut in, expression dark. "This isn't a game, Saskia. Look what happened to Ella. She's still missing, but Clare and Damien were found. Their families were also detained, and Ella's aunt has been frantic all day, with the Task Guard coming and going in this building. That's why Grant was here, checking in on her, on *you*. He is *not* your friend and he is not your ticket to saving the day. He's dangerous. And the Moth Queen? She is literally death itself. Is that what you want?" She was closer suddenly and pointing at the photo. "I had friends once. But we all made impulsive choices we can't take back. And I'm so tired of . . ." Her voice hitched. "I'm tired of losing the people I love."

Saskia had been ready to defend herself with cutting rage, but it emptied out of her as if a cork had been pulled from her back. Phae was a lot of things, but she was not vulnerable in front of anyone, least of all Saskia.

"I can't make any choices for you," Phae said finally, and her cool hand was on Saskia's cheek. "You're your own person. But if you want to make adult choices, then you have to stop being so childish. There are consequences. Not just for you, but the people who care about you."

Saskia's gaze fell. "I loved Barton, too, you know." Phae's eyes swam, and Saskia stepped out of her guardian's grasp. "Even a bad decision," she said, "is better than making no decision at all."

Once upon a time, those words had been Barton's. Some of his last. Phae was a brick wall. "Saskia —"

"I'm tired," she said, and she made for her room. Once inside, she held tightly onto the doorknob until she knew Phae wasn't going to come in after her. Then she took one more look at the photo still clutched in her hand.

I had friends once, Phae had said.

Sidestepping her cache of old laptops, milk crates of abandoned motherboards, and full functioning monitors streaming C-DOS code, Saskia tipped into her bed, curling up around the photo. Her mind raced, and she needed to be alone.

Most of all, she didn't want Phae to see her cry.

꧁꧂

Saskia didn't dream — not really — because she couldn't sleep. Instead, she sunk deep down into a numb sort of blankness, and let it pull her away, for a little while, from the pain her pounding heart had pulsed into her whole body. Ella, Phae, even Barton. All the people she'd let down. She was just trying to do what she figured was right, or good. Why did it always have to be so hard? And what if she just kept letting everyone down until she had no one left?

She had grown accustomed to spending sleepless nights with the blue glare of her monitors on her face, some of them spooling neon-coloured code as she ran little program experiments, self-made modules, or went about defragging systems as if raking a Zen garden. Comfort in patterns. The screens often lulled her into some kind of slumber that was, absolutely and blissfully, dreamless.

But Saskia's mind had slipped in a few bits of key binary lines that allowed her to function without falling apart. Stress can do that, she'd be the first to admit, especially since so much had been compressed into less than twenty-four hours and was crushing her even now.

When she was younger, every night for so many years seemed consumed by nonstop nightmares. She had her means of coping, getting through the days, pressing onwards, trying not to dread the nighttime. She sought respite in logic, in numbers that allowed her to slip past nightly horrors. It was rooting herself to reason that had allowed her to survive this long.

And it was Barton who had given her her first computer.

"Happy birthday, kiddo," he'd grunted, hefting a heavy-backed monitor onto Saskia's desk in her room. This was when they'd started their uneasy life together at Barton's parents' house, in Wolseley, a few months after the hospital in Newfoundland. Winnipeg was as foreign a place to Saskia as any, since she'd barely left Scotland her short life. The Allens had been kind to take them all in, especially since Phae's parents weren't exactly interested in welcoming her back with open arms.

It was supposed to be a new beginning for all of them, and for a while it was, before all the houses that had bore summoning chambers were seized, before the Allens had to go away for their own protection.

The monitor rattled the collection of odd rocks and sticks

and slices of bark Saskia had picked up in her wanderings around the neighbourhood.

"I'd forgotten," she'd said to Barton at the time, about her birthday. A lie, for sure. She figured Phae and Barton had enough to worry about. She didn't want to burden them, and she didn't want to be disappointed, either. But she couldn't help feeling just a little bit excited now, so she pinched her mouth to hide it.

Barton had crawled under the desk, connecting a huge CPU tower, rummaging for cords. When he started to stand up, he misjudged where the table was and cracked his head.

Saskia muffled her snicker in her sleeve.

"Yeah, yeah, I'm a chucklefest," Barton mumbled, coming back up for air. "I want to show you something."

He pulled out a keyboard, blew on it aggressively to dislodge the dust caught between the blocky squares. "This was my old computer from middle school. It's pretty basic, but I had fun with it. I figured we could, too."

Saskia was skeptical.

"It's okay," she lied again. "You didn't have to get me anything. I don't need it."

"Nice try," Barton replied, patting the desk chair. "C'mere, kiddo."

Saskia watched Barton's fingers fly across the keyboard, text showing up on the black field in pixellated green. This computer wasn't at all like the one her brother, Albert, had had — even recalling their old room in Durness made her feel queasy, with the outdated pink-coloured iMac they often fought over. For one, there were no program icons on Barton's computer, no regular desktop to see anywhere. In order to do things, Barton had to type out commands.

"I used to have nightmares, too, Saskia. They scared me, mostly because I couldn't control them. At least, I thought I couldn't." He was looking squarely at her, as he always did. He always made her feel seen.

Barton tapped the monitor. "Sometimes, we have to treat our brains like computers, because that's what they are." He smiled, his teeth pearly. "I used to stay up late, messing around with this computer, when the nightmares would get bad. And I used to think, *I'm going to type a command in my head to make myself sleep*, or *I'm going to write out code in the air like counting sheep*, or *I'll order my thoughts like files on a floppy drive*. I don't know if it'll work for you, too, but it's worth a try."

Code? Floppy drive? Saskia's hands twisted in her lap; she didn't want to have the nightmares anymore, didn't want to see Albert's bedsheet-wrapped face dragged through a shadowy forest, or a megalith monster with axes for arms chasing her.

Most of all, she didn't want to see Barton, who, then, was tangible and real right in front of her, falling down into a pit that she could never quite pull him out of. That nightmare was new, and it scared her the most.

In that moment, all Saskia wanted was to make *Barton* happy, because that's all he'd ever done for her. "Okay," she said. "I'll try it."

Soon after that birthday, Saskia clung to HTML, C+, and basic C-DOS prompts like a security blanket. At night, the territory behind her eyelids became a formless static void, comfortable. Reliable as the code.

But tonight, that same monitor Barton had given Saskia years ago, dormant in the sentimental-but-strip-for-parts pile, flashed on without prompting. It chirped, a sonic canary in the mineshaft. Behind it, a whining chord that was already becoming too familiar.

Saskia's eyes fluttered open, groggy from floating between sleep and memory, and she felt the monitor's light strobing against her vision.

"What?" She sat up, rubbed her face. The monitor was blocked by a few other machines, and she crawled down to the floor under her desk to reach it, pulling it to her lap.

The screen flickered, scrolling green text, symbols, and wingdings that meant virtually nothing. "How is . . ." She hefted the yellowed box, turning it over, fingers going for the power port.

It was plugged in, somewhere, in the sea of wires and cables under her desk, but to what?

Then the screen went black, and the text had turned, somehow, red. A cursor blinked, straight, threatening. Then, letter by letter —

S A S K I A

Her fingers gripped the monitor. Maybe she was still asleep.

R

U

THERE

She involuntarily reached for a keyboard, but there wasn't one. "Dammit," she muttered, trying to find one in the clutter.

S A S K I A, the text went on,

I

CAN

HEAR U HOW

CAN

I

HEAR U

This was crazy. Was this computer hooked up to some network? But these models didn't come with built-in microphones, let alone serviceable speakers, so how was she supposed to respond? She didn't have any keyboards nearby . . .

"I . . . hello?"

The cursor flickered. The screen, for a microsecond, looked fragmented, then more text.

HELL O

Saskia swallowed, trying to slow her breathing down. "Who are you?"

THE

SIGNAL

IS

FOR

U

Ice clamped her veins. The possibilities flooded through her, their relative chance variable attached to them like a toe-tag. A prank? An ETG trap? Some kind of system failure? Or, likeliest, just another nightmare.

It could be another message from the Moth Queen. But then why would she bother with old garbage tech?

You have heard the signal. Take comfort in your family, they will need you before the end.

"Tell me your name," Saskia said, voice shaking.

There was almost a smile beneath the words:

MISSED

U

KIDDO

Saskia let out a strangled noise. "Barton?"

There was no way. She should've pushed the monitor off her immediately, thrown it out the window into the parking lot below, but instead she held it closer to her face. "Where are you?" she asked frantically. "What happened to you?"

The cursor blinked, then shivered like it was alive. The screen flickered again and shattered 8-bit afterimages flashed with it. Those same red sigils, becoming three-dimensional impressions in her mind's eye, twisting around one another like burning snakes, stamping themselves in her vision. A red ring, a black smudge intercepting a disc of light, a flame going out, broken wings, roots going deeper than they should, but holding on, holding on so tight.

Barton at the bottom of a chasm, bound and a part of it, and beneath him, a darkness that moved.

S A S K I A, the text shivered, then the letters changed, folding on top of one another. The monitor was hot, sparking, but Saskia wouldn't let it go.

"I'll find you," she promised. "I'll save you!"

D O N T, the last word shivered, before the monitor went black, and suddenly very cold, in Saskia's shaking hands.

Part II
FLASH

These Many Broken Realms

SEVEN YEARS AGO

I woke up choking on cloistered, stale air in the dark.

I rolled over, wretched. Pulled that air into my lungs desperately and tried to piece together that I had still had a body I could control. I felt like I'd been struck back to life by lightning, and probably wasn't too far off.

Which meant I was alive. *Third time's . . . wait, fourth? Ugh. Definitely lost count now.*

And this waking was way too similar to the last time I'd been in the Bloodlands, barf and all. I scrambled to my feet, but I was alone this time, and my hand, which had just been holding someone else's, was empty.

"Eli!" I shouted. There was only darkness and ash, and coming for me from the splintered black — teeth.

"Shit!"

I spun quickly and the snapping jaws missed my face. I put up my fists, readying for the next blow I couldn't see.

The landscape on all sides was cloaked in grey and shadow, and the thing that had come after me had slipped back into the nothing. I jerked my hand out, automatically trying to summon the fire. For light. For protection. Anything.

But nothing came. Just an empty palm. A *human* palm. Nothing inside me, either, but the cold.

I didn't have time to feel anything other than panic before the shade launched at me again. It snarled and yipped, and it didn't move like anything corporeal. It was translucent, just a shadow, but when my hand came up to block it, sharp teeth sank into my skin, making my panicked cry echo harshly in the grey.

The creature landed in front of me, still snarling, and as we stood like that awhile, me hissing and clenching my hand, the déjà vu hurt more than the fading pain.

The thing in front of me was a Fox. A Fox with eyes like little coins that assessed me before it turned tail and bounded off. I shook out my hand, confused. I was alive, and I could still feel pain. Give and take, I guess. But that shadows here had teeth? At least that problem was delayed — for now.

The mist whipped up — if that's what it was. The place reeked of sulphur and burning, as it did the last time I was in the underworld, and I covered my nose when the smell went down my throat. I knew I wasn't going to get anywhere by just standing here like an idiot, so I wracked my brain, tried to remember . . . what happened? How the hell did I get down here? Where was Eli?

This had to be the Bloodlands. But that felt wrong — hadn't we been trying to get somewhere else? Somewhere more important? I reflexively touched the back of my head to make sure there wasn't some slimy sucking worm mouth feeding off it, but no. I'd just hit my head — hard. What had we been trying to do . . .

We. I clung to that. I hadn't come down here alone.

"Eli?"

We'd done this song and dance before: a burnt place filled with shadows, me a dumb kid fighting monsters I didn't understand.

That seemed years ago. The dumb kid part was still pretty much the same.

The images came flooding back into my skull, furious and insistent. A churning sea. A resonating chasm in the middle of it. Five stones brought together, and us leaping into the unknown, because it was the Brilliant Dark we were going to. The dwelling of Ancient, the godhead who could get us out of the mess I'd caused in the first place.

Had we somehow fallen down the wrong rabbit hole? And if this was the Bloodlands, what the hell had a Fox been doing down here? There was something strange about it, too — it had been tangible, but it seemed like it'd popped right out of the landscape, a shade of a Fox. Real and unreal.

I wasn't going to get answers here, in the silent dark. And when the echo of my voice died in the silence, I did the only thing I could think to. Put one foot in front of the other and walked.

Eli's wings were gone. And it was dark. He had no idea where he could be now — or how he could be here in the first place.

He touched the space between his shoulders, and was, for a second, glad he was alone, because the tears came up unbidden, and Harken would make it more awkward if she saw him lose his preciously cultivated control. It wasn't that the wings were a part of him; it was that their loss just pressed all his other losses down on him, hard, crushing him further into the rock beneath his wincing face. Then he realized what it really meant, not having them, and he dragged himself up to sitting and touched his chest.

The Moonstone was gone. Then he realized he'd given it to Roan, who had acquired four Calamity Stones, and the loss of her now meant that both of them were in even deeper trouble than before.

Eli wiped his eyes, then tried to get his bearings as he stood shakily. *We came down here together*, he thought. But Roan was definitely not with him now. He didn't bother calling out in case something *else* was here with him, listening, and he took a step forward only to feel the other foot come down on empty air. He jerked backward quickly to avoid slipping over the edge.

The wind was bitter and the air was thin, and as he crawled back to that cliffside and looked down, he confirmed his current reality.

The Owls who trained him — *in another life*, he added bitterly — had painted the picture of the Roost in a way that Eli, even back then, couldn't fathom. He'd had his own visions of the place. Of course he had — he'd borne the Tradewind Moonstone long enough, had one of the strongest connections to his Family's realm than anyone before him.

But the visions he'd had were impressions of someone else's story: a vast starlit sky, the only surfaces ones to perch from — trees, boulders, all floating in seamless harmony between ledges of white stone. Phyr's perch was the highest: a rock carved from the moon's shadow, where she could observe all below with her austere judgment from the top of the universe. The last way station at the edge of time.

But the sky of this place had been shattered. There was no moon in sight. And the rock Eli had ended up on hung in that broken sky above what he knew *had* to be the other Realms of Ancient below: the split mountain of the Glen, the caved-in underbelly of the Den, the ruptured woods of the Warren. The waters of the Abyss clung around them all, endless, maybe empty. No more divinity. Only hell.

"Shit."

Without wings he was paralyzed, trapped up here with no recourse but to go from rock to rock — if he could see more than a foot in front of him. The black below was fathomless, so there was no telling how truly far that drop was. And here he was, in his body with all its limitations and fragility that would certainly kill him the longer he stayed here.

Something fluttered in his periphery and he jerked his head towards it, getting up clumsily and backing from the ledge. Shadows and sparks. The impression of wings in a dark that was slowly lightening. Dawn? The rock beneath his feet felt hard, tangible. The air he sucked into his pain-wracked lungs wasn't poison. This place was real, not a Veil-tripping fever dream. Which meant it had its rules, and Eli just had to learn them to survive.

Even in the passing moments of taking careful steps around his newfound prison, the light increased by degrees, revealing a pale, dusty fog purling around his ankles. But finally, before him, it revealed a platform ahead, slightly higher than the one he was on, and another beyond that, and another.

A staircase. He tipped his head back, trying to see where it led, but the fog gave up little more than that.

Without looking back, he climbed.

⤙⤚

It took me a bit longer than it should have to realize the Calamity Stones were gone.

The minute I did, my hand flew to my sternum where the cursed weight of the Dragon Opal had been stuck, boring into more than my spirit and burning me from the inside out. But there was nothing there now. I should have been relieved, but all I felt was emptiness. I checked the rest of my body — one shoulder, which, only temporarily, bore the Sapphire when the *thing* that had taken over my body took it from Natti's aunt. I checked the other shoulder for the Emerald, which I'd torn off my own father. Then my forehead, where Eli had given me the Moonstone in the last bid to end this before —

I staggered and caught myself on a wall. It was warm, despite that it was made of rock. Everything was still dark; I had the distinct impression I was underground, that the earth was suspended above and all around me, because the air was moist and close. But ahead of me there was a light. I headed for it, punch-drunk and desperate for the hope that light promised.

We'd come to this place for a reason, and we'd failed. We brought all the stones together, wagered everything. This wasn't how it was supposed to turn out. *You checked off all the boxes and you still managed to fuck this one up, Harken.*

So no Calamity Stones. No Opal. And no firepower. After everything I'd had shoved down my throat, the losses and the spent legacies — here I was, back at the beginning. Roan Bloody Harken, powerless, useless. Alone.

Human.

The light was still a ways off. I stuck to the wall to guide me, sniffed. This wasn't the Bloodlands, but it smelled like burning and blood all the same. Eli would know. He always had the answers. *If he's still in one piece*, I thought again. *He's alive!* I retorted internally, trying to stab that first snatch of doubt.

Whatever alive *means down here.*

"Okay," I said aloud, "think. We brought the stones together. They cracked. The Darklings got out of their hidey-holes. I can remember that thing hanging in the sky before Eli and I took the plunge: Zabor, Kirkald, Balaghast." *See? I know some things!* But how the hell was that gonna help me now?

A snarl in the dark, the scampering of paws. I flattened back against the wall, reined in my breathing and remembered the teeth. More shades like the one that had attacked me earlier passed me by, not even sparing me a glance. Their eyes were little mirror chips, flashing as they dashed towards the light. Obviously they knew something I didn't. *Which could fill forty-two encyclopedias.*

"Well, it's a better sign than none," I said under my breath, because talking to myself had provided at least minor reassurance. Even if it was also a sign I was losing my mind.

The shades faded, and with no answers of my own, I followed.

❧

Eli tripped over an errant stone. He felt off-balance, like a piston had been taken out of his legs. He touched the space between his shoulders instinctively, as if expecting the feathered limbs to still be where his torn shirt and jacket promised they could be.

His hand fell back to his side, then to his eyes, pressing, kneading. He'd been climbing this path for days, this floating staircase of fog, rock, ruin. Hadn't he? The decimated Roost, deadland of his forebears, high above the other realms of the four Families below. And if the lands below were anything like this one, he didn't have much hope for finding answers . . . especially if it was he and Roan who had shattered them all in the first place.

Eli didn't yet look down to judge the damage. He couldn't bear it. He could only look up and ahead and keep climbing.

But even he couldn't argue against exhaustion. He eventually collapsed in a brace of calcified roots.

His head went into his palms. *Think!* After all, he did that well enough *without* the stone, before . . . when he was young. When he didn't know any better. When he was ready to be reckless and to rush in the very way Roan had, when he'd first taken the Moonstone. Her recklessness is what he resented most about her, because it was his same sin. But that felt like — and was — another life. Another Eli Rathgar.

He had to reason this out, but the gears in his skull ground to a halt. Why was his head as foggy as the soupy air? There was no playbook for what happened when you took your own body into the Realms of Ancient, though he and Roan had done it before, in the Bloodlands. This was different. This felt permanent.

A shuffle nearby. A shiver.

Eli leapt to his aching feet, tense, primed. He twisted as the fluttering came close, a shadow in the ash-air. A body was a liability — especially a weak, power-stripped body — but he couldn't rely on his mind just now, so his body was better than nothing.

He gasped, spinning with the impact of the heavy shade when it caught him in the face. He tried to pivot but was broadsided from behind by another dark weight. Wings slamming against him, a screech. Eli remembered then that he'd fought bigger, worse things, and muscle memory was an asset. He stepped to, knocked the next three blows aside, but in the fluttering greyness he hadn't taken stock of where his feet were, and he slipped over the edge of the floating rock.

With a scrambling reach. Eli caught the underside of a root knot, howling when his shoulder made a sickening pop under the pull of his body weight. Despite all that, he held on, grimacing he swung his other hand up to grip the dead wood. His legs kicked out, but there was nothing beneath him. He had to pull himself up.

Let go, Eli.

He tried to tune out the pounding in his head, straining to hear the voice between the beats. *Let go*, it urged again. *Fall. It's what you want. It's so much easier than climbing.*

A vicious indignance swelled in Eli's chest like molten lava. "Don't tell me what to do," he seethed. He had become sloppy, letting down the walls around his senses and allowing this intruder in.

You're tired. The voice inside was at once calming and a sneer. It was not Eli's inner voice. Accustomed as he was to the voices of the Moonstone whispering to him, making their demands, overlapping one another and jockeying for supremacy, he knew this was different. It was one voice. A female one. And in his panic there was no placing it.

He wouldn't hang around here any longer, vulnerable to ghosts. Eli's arms lit up with pain when he tried to hoist himself up, and he dropped back, vision swimming.

He screamed as knife-sharp talons raked down his back, the blood spilling out of his aching flesh.

"Alive!" he heard, screeched on the low wind. "Alive!" Then there were more claws, this time going for his eyes. "Traitor! Stonebreaker! God killer!"

Eli fought to find a foothold again, but it was increasingly seeming like the cratered deadlands below were the only ground he could count on. Maybe sooner than he thought.

Let go, the voice whispered. Sobbed. Or was that Eli now? His lips parted. He did not remember the last time he'd been afraid. Even when Roan had gone deep inside herself to battle the demon in her Calamity Stone. Even when he'd faced down death when she took the Moonstone from him. There had been no fear because he trusted, for the first time in a long time. And when she'd taken his hand and they'd stepped off the precipice together . . .

This fear was a foreign sensation in his mouth. He was a little boy again in a croft by the devastating sea. Fear had been so far away for a long time, because what had you to fear when you had wings? But they were gone now. And so was Roan.

That's it, the voice coaxed, and Eli could clearly picture the owner of the voice nodding with encouragement. *You're almost there. You've done enough. You've been through enough. Do something for yourself for once. Haven't you earned your rest?*

Eli felt his fingers slipping on the root, his lifeline. The attacking wings and the screeching were farther away now, but not far enough that their echoes weren't still a threat. The blood trickled down his back like tapped syrup.

"Only the dead!" A shriek nearby. A warning. "Life cannot live here!" *They must be the spirits of Owls long past,* Eli thought, *looking to make me one of them.*

Eli gulped a breath, shut his eyes, loosened his grip.

Then he howled.

The cries were cut off as, adrenaline pumping, he threw himself up and over the ledge like a great gust had given him a leg up.

Blood roaring in his ears, he slid shaking to his hands and knees, parting his dark, filthy hair out of his face.

Before him was a tree. In every branch were white eyes in black, translucent heads, bodies feathery bodies puffed and agitated from their hunt. Their wings fluttered, claws catching in the dead, bent bark. They were certainly the shades of the dead — incorporeal, nearly see-through, but from the blood trickling between his shoulders they had some form, and fight, left in them. And they were all staring into what was left of Eli's living spirit.

They opened their beaks as one and let out a cry, shattering the air. Eli threw himself down, cradling his skull.

He didn't know how long he stayed like that, ears ringing, but when he finally looked up, there was silence again, and only the throbbing of his shoulder, his bleeding back. No more shrieking. No more homicidal voice in his head.

He sat up, examining the ashy air, the empty tree, the path ahead in the curling murk that went ever upward. Though he was alone again, and somehow alive, he was aware he had been tested. But for what purpose, he couldn't yet know. Not unless he got to his feet and climbed on.

And so he did.

The wind's echo followed with each painful step up this cracked staircase. He was less and less certain why he hadn't let go, knowing absolutely that he wanted to. So badly. But for one memory. One insistent idea. One hope that hadn't yet faded.

He stopped a moment, pulled back his sleeve, and touched the chain-shaped scar on his arm before going on. *Maybe she's up there. At the end of this. Maybe I don't have to fall alone.*

God killer, the wind hissed at his heels. *You have cursed us all.*

⇜⇝

When I got to the place of light all the other shades were headed to, I realized what it was. I'd seen something like it — a proxy, a man-made structure in one of Cecelia's many memories shown to me by the Opal before everything went wrong.

A hazy beam of light illuminated a round amphitheatre whose steps headed down to a central platform. There weren't any gold rings or acolytes, no Denizens standing around, waiting to be shown a vision of a great and powerful Fox warrior god. I'd only lately seen Deon herself, desperate and begging me for help. A lot of good that'd done her. Or me.

There was no Cecelia here, either. Or Ruo. Just me, and hundreds of small Fox shades with their coin eyes shining above their bared, alarming teeth.

"Stonebreaker," I heard one say. Great — more talking Foxes. That always led to solid results.

I swallowed. "Not on purpose," I answered. I glanced up; that weird slanted light filtered through a giant hole in the ceiling. It wasn't natural in the way I understood light. From where I stood I couldn't make anything out, and I wasn't about to make any sudden moves to investigate.

One Fox, its dark hackles raised, opaque shadow body translucent in the uncanny light, came closer to me. "You are not dead."

I let out the breath I was holding. "Not yet."

Some of the Fox shades' lips loosed over their teeth. Some of the hackles went down. A murmur. "You are from the Uplands?"

I narrowed my eyes. I had to tread carefully here. After all, if my last brush with these things proved anything, they could hurt me. "I guess you could say that." But I had questions of my own. "And what are . . . you?"

"We are the dead," they answered in unison, like a piercing alarm.

"Makes sense." I looked down again to that central platform. Shimmering in the light, on a high spike of stone, there it was.

The Opal.

As if they'd all collectively perceived my shock, the throng of shades parted, an invitation to walk down between them. They still kept their sharp gazes trained on me, a few snapping at my ankles with each of my careful steps down the stone staircase. An invitation with a warning.

So — this must be the Den. Deon's territory, resting place of the Foxes. *No one's doing much resting*, I thought. I couldn't rightly count how many faces were watching me. If this was supposedly their afterlife, their underworld, there would be untold billions here, right?

I stopped at the level just above the dais. I may have felt panic just a few minutes ago when I realized I didn't have the Opal and that the connection to the fire that defined me was gone . . . but the Opal had caused me a fair share of grief. I felt like I was back in Cecelia's summoning chamber, left with nothing, grasping at what was in front of me that could promise a way out. This felt just like another trap. I needed to be smart. I needed to think like Eli.

I'd reached the dais. The Opal, on its own finger of rock, was about three feet above me. If I jumped, I could snatch it, make a run for it. But I had to be honest with myself. *Do you really want to?*

"What happened?" I asked the silent gathering, turning momentarily away from the Opal. They all seemed to be waiting. "Where's Deon?"

"You tell us," said a Fox nearby.

"Chaos. Harm. Silence," said another. "You were a stone-bearer. You broke your sacred trust with Deon. You broke her trust with all of us."

Their voices were all strange and harsh — it was difficult to keep track of them. "I didn't do it on purpose!" I shouted over them. "We were trying to wake Ancient, to open the way to the Brilliant Dark —"

"Naïve pup," said another. For a second my heart leapt, and I thought it was Sil. Could she actually be down here? But again, I couldn't tell who had spoken.

"The Darklings have slipped their prisons," volleyed another Fox. "They're loose in the Uplands. Meanwhile, Deon is gone, the Opal is ruined, and the realms are connected now. Connected as they were never meant to be."

That one was more than a criticism, pure blame. I glanced

up over my shoulder, noticed then that there was a wild split through the Calamity Stone and that it didn't shine at all.

I turned back. "Look, Deon herself was behind me on this. On stopping the Darklings. We had *done it*. *We'd won*." Now I was bordering on hysterical, begging myself, as much as them, for it to be true when I knew better.

"Don't you understand?" This was the Fox closest to my feet; this voice was full of despair. "You cut us off. All of us. The Matriarchs are missing. Not even the Moth Queen can ferry the Denizen dead to their promised homelands. You did this."

"Lost." The word echoed around the chamber, barked in uneven, angry, miserable tones. "All is lost."

The Opal above me made my hairline bristle. What the hell were they all expecting me to do now?

"You must finish what you started."

I froze. The Fox was sitting directly in front of me, surveying me with its singed eyes. I had definitely recognized that voice.

The shade stepped forward, and its small fox body rose, shifted, grew. It was the shadow of a man, the outlines faint. The other Foxes changed all around me, too, taking the shapes of the people they'd once been. Details in faces were difficult to discern; they were still just spirit shadows. Their hollow pinprick eyes were still the same, boring into me. But this close, I could see the features of this fox shift: the outline of a beard, of a mouth twisted in aggravation. Jacob Reinhardt, one of the Foxes from the Conclave of Fire, the one who'd challenged me at every turn — who'd nearly killed me once. It looked like he hadn't been so lucky in the intervening weeks since I'd seen him last.

I backed up, tripped, and landed hard beneath the Opal. I looked up in time to see something spun in the air at me, and I opened my hands to catch it.

A sword hilt. Bladeless, but heavy all the same.

"Finish what you started," Reinhardt's shade repeated.

I didn't have time to answer, because a horrible tremor went through the ground, tilting the world outside the chamber violently and sending the dead and me reeling. The ground cracked. The fissure roared. The shades fled and I staggered, twisting to see the Opal shivering on its dais. *There are some things I keep circling back to, hoping blindly for the same results.* So I reached out for the Opal, desperate, even as the world around me shattered and tried to crush me into nothing.

I jumped.

Training Day

The uniform was freshly starched and pressed. Grey, white, black. Even the Elemental Task Guard had colours, like a sports team . . . one that always won the tournament because the game was rigged. And now Saskia had cheated her way onto the winning side.

She ran her finger around the collar, trying to swallow but also trying not to choke, mostly on her own dismay. Saskia didn't bother looking at herself in the mirror, either. She knew what she looked like as she smoothed her hair down, bit her lip, and she wanted to preserve how she saw herself outside this alien outfit.

She didn't want to see the mistake reflected in her eyes.

"You're one of *them* now."

Saskia turned towards the voice at her door. Jet was staring at her, and his eyes were wet with unspilled tears.

Saskia had been fiddling with the hem of her jacket, the belt at her waist. She ran a hand over the solitary patch on her shoulder, signifying her low rank. At her collar, an enamel pin represented her position in the engineering department.

At her breast, the ETG crest: a white starburst.

"I'm sorry I can't explain it to you properly, Brain," Saskia said, trying to smile. "But it's not forever. It's like . . . playing pretend. Like playing Roan Harken. You liked that game, remember? When we played it before?"

Jet wiped his nose on his sleeve, still clutching the doorway. "For how long, though?"

Beside Saskia was the now-silent computer monitor she'd stayed up all night with. It hadn't yet turned on again, but she was sure, so sure, it could. She just needed to find the right parts, to catch the signal . . .

"As long as it takes," she declared — to Jet, to herself. She moved towards him, hands stretched out for reassurance.

Jet shivered and leapt into the hall.

"Can't," he said, shaking his head, the tears finally coming. "I don't want to be taken away. Not now. Phae needs me."

A lance of glass went through Saskia. "Brain, it's still me. I'm not —"

His fists were tight at his sides. "Just don't get us into trouble, Saskia," he said, his voice getting higher. "Just do what you're supposed to, then stop playing and come home, okay?"

Saskia's hands fell. She didn't reach for Jet again. "Okay. I will."

He didn't look up, just took off down the hall, likely to Phae's room. For once, Saskia hoped Jet *had* taken a peek inside her mind, so he could understand. She hoped he'd found the truth in there, that she was doing this for all of them, to help the Denizens who had saved her, to prevent worse still from happening to them at the hands of the ETG. To save Barton. To save everyone.

To save myself.

She hoped that, whatever he'd seen in her mind, it had given him the comfort Saskia just couldn't feel. She hoped he hadn't seen the darkling inside that she was going to have to become.

⁓⁓

The black car that had picked her up in front of One Evergreen was not standard, nor was it necessary. New recruits reported to the Judiciary in the Law Courts on their own steam, and had to go through hours of screening, paperwork, processing, and tests of loyalty before they were admitted to the Old Leg for assignments and training. They were not chauffeured there like a celebrity.

Cam had spent so many years pining for the ETG that he'd studied every which way to get into their ranks, had counted down the days to his turn, and blabbed the whole process to Saskia. Now that it was somehow happening to her, she had the steps memorized. She hoped the rumours weren't true, the ones about them sticking a tracking chip under every soldier's skin, erasing your autonomy to serve this magic-monster-fighting militia. Saskia hoped for a lot of things, though she knew her hope might not hold out.

The cutting feeling Saskia had felt talking to Jet stayed with her, inching through her organs and slicing away everything but her compliance. This car could take her to the Law

Courts, the Old Leg, or to another cell where she'd rot forever and the chancellor would have a good laugh. A place where they hid the bodies of the non-complicit, the traitors.

She could be going anywhere. She had known that the second she'd slid into the back seat, the windows tinted, the leather pristine. But if she was going to the brig, the means of getting there was all wrong. The passenger window of the car was marked with the ETG insignia, true, but in the centre of this white starburst was a golden cross. The chancellor's mark. She was valued cargo.

So she guessed it would be a short ride to Broadway, where all the ETG buildings huddled, but long enough to imagine exactly where she was going, and for what purpose.

Saskia had a feeling there would be little room for ceremony or paperwork today. She was likely to get straight down to business as the chancellor's new pet. She pressed her fingers into her exhausted eyes. The chancellor was probably desperate then, for what she tried not to imagine, because whatever it was, he was willing to bend the sacred rules on which the very ETG was founded — order, loyalty, absolution — bend them to admit her into some dark inner sanctum, where she could be of *use* to him.

That's what the Moth Queen had wanted, after all. For Saskia to be of use. For her to get inside, use the regime somehow to save the Realms of Ancient. Would it be today? Tomorrow? Would it be too late already?

She folded her hands, took a breath, and leaned back in her seat. There were still many rules, bent or not, and Saskia would need to adhere closely to them if she was going to play this game.

If she was going to win it.

In the end, she was right; she wasn't about to go through basic training, indoctrination, or conditioning. They didn't go in the same door she had been taken through when she'd been discharged from interrogation. Instead, the car slid into an underground garage, going far too deep for comfort, and came to a stop at a shining aluminum-panelled door, where someone had been waiting for her.

"Hello, Miss Das. I'm Mi-ja," the young woman said, beaming at Saskia with a curt bow. The smile even looked real. These people were good.

Saskia gave a stiff bow in return, noting that Mi-ja's starburst also bore the gold cross. She was the chancellor's aide, then. Mi-ja turned smartly, and Saskia followed obediently down brightly lit halls, past rooms with more walls made of glass, like her interrogation room.

At one room she'd paused, all the walls glittering with flashing imprints of rabbits, deer, foxes, owls, and seals.

"To master your enemy, you must first know exactly who they are," said a short man with a lantern jaw, gesturing at the images whose light reflected off the faces of attentive would-be soldiers. They were as young as Saskia. Too young. "The Denizen religion is comprised of five animal families, each worshipping their own powersake's god. It may all sound whimsical as you study their origins. A flight of fancy. But remember: these people might look like us, act like us, but they are not us. They are dangerous."

The alluring, almost hypnotizing plays of light flicked suddenly to loud, shaky-cam footage of Denizens being captured by the first iteration of the ETG, the White Militia. The Restoration Project. Saskia tensed; it was footage every child in her class had grown up seeing in school, but it still made her dizzy. A woman punching the ground, making a seismic wave that knocked out the cameraman. A boy freezing a militiaman mid-step using rainwater in a parking lot. A building coming down on Mundane protestors . . .

A girl with a flaming arm, standing on the roof of a car, facing down a man with golden eyes; behind them, innocent bystanders, Mundanes and Denizens alike, frozen against their wills — this footage was marked *Recovered from Owl tampering*. In the residual fire of the girl bringing her fist up, Saskia saw red —

A hand on Saskia's arm made her jump. "This way, Miss Das," Mi-ja said. Her tone was friendly. But Saskia didn't trust anything she heard or saw in this place.

The words of the lecturer followed her down the hall: ". . . Roan Harken, the girl who painted a target on this fair city, has become the symbol of the Denizen uprising, which is why we need you now, more than ever . . ."

Saskia strained her hearing, trying to listen further, but they had taken a corner and were climbing a flight of suspended steel stairs. "Where are we going, if I may ask?" Then Saskia quickly added, "Ma'am."

Mi-ja gave Saskia a wry look. "You will be debriefed after routine consultation. Your mental health profile will be evaluated by the Owl Unit to determine your viability for service."

The cold lance of glass became a bomb detonating inside Saskia. "The Owl Unit?"

Mi-ja patted Saskia on the arm again. "Don't worry. You're not on trial. If you're not deemed fit, you won't be arrested again — just sent home. But it is the most efficient way, and quite painless. The Owls under our jurisdiction have a lot of restrictions on their power usage, so you needn't worry about your mind being tampered with."

Yeah. Nothing to worry about. Just, like, my very real plans of sedition. "Better than being microchipped, I guess," Saskia couldn't help but blurt, nails digging into her palms. Mi-ja narrowed her eyes but didn't ask.

Coming down from the other end of the hall was a procession of even more teenaged would-be soldiers. *Just how many new recruits have been signing up, lately?* Saskia thought, counting twelve in the double lines coming towards her. Maybe the Darkling Moon had Mundanes scared. Maybe that was enough to convince everyone something bad was going to happen and anyone had the power to stop it.

Isn't that what I'm here to do? The answer didn't come, though, because picked out from the second line was a familiar face that Saskia couldn't hide from: Cam.

His eyes widened when he saw her, mouth slightly parted, but then he clamped it shut and stared straight ahead. When they got close enough to pass each other, his face broke into an excited smile Saskia couldn't help but return, despite the circumstances.

Weirdo, she thought at him, but then suddenly Mi-ja stopped walking.

"Through here," she said, and the doors split open with an unsettling pneumatic hiss. Saskia's smile dropped off her face like dead skin.

The room on the other side of the doors was bathed in complete, blank white. The lights were recessed in such a way that Saskia couldn't tell, exactly, where they were. Medical instruments and blank monitors were flush against the walls, small retractable tables set up at intervals along the room's edges. She was surprised to feel her fingers itching to turn those monitors on, see how they worked.

Sitting with his back to the room was a man in a black suit, a stark contrast to the ETG standard issue uniform. When he turned to face her, Saskia felt for a moment that she recognized something in the sharp creases of age at the brow, the angular jaw.

Mi-ja led Saskia inside towards a chair opposite the man. He adjusted his tie, and Saskia noticed the Owl Unit insignia on the breast of his blazer — the set of white wings, but in the centre of it, that same gold cross she was starting to get tired of seeing. The chancellor really wasn't taking any chances with her.

"Saskia, this is Solomon. He will be performing your assessment today."

Saskia stared at him, still feeling that familiar twinge. The man stared back through light eyes framed by well-kept grey hair, giving him the impression of a faded lion. The corners of his eyes creased and Saskia lifted her outstretched hand.

"Miss Das," Solomon said regally, the corner of his mouth twitching as he shook it. "A pleasure."

She let his hand go and worked very hard not to wipe it on her pants. His accent was strange, like maybe it once had been British, but had been beaten into all flat vowels and carefully enunciated consonants. A pretender recognizing a peer.

Mi-ja motioned to the empty chair, and Saskia lowered herself onto it. It dug into the backs of her legs and was set so she was eye level with Solomon. He had bent himself slightly away from her to fiddle with an instrument on a tray, a slender crown of metal with a read-out receiver, likely wireless, blinking beneath its surface. Solomon lifted it to his eye, squinting between it and a panel set into the table.

"That should do it," he said, more to himself than Saskia. She glanced at Mi-ja, who was hovering at a console near the back of the room, tapping something into the tablet she'd been carrying with her. Behind her, the wall was dark. Saskia imagined, for a moment, that the chancellor was standing behind that unreadable wall, watching her. It was absolutely likely. She stared at it, counting to five. She saw only her reflection but still felt strengthened by the small act of defiance she was displaying, no matter who was on the other side of the glass.

"Can you walk me through the assessment, sir?" Saskia asked, her voice much more even than her racing thoughts — thoughts that were suddenly more dangerous than the Denizens she'd seen in the video room.

Solomon looked up at her, then placed the steel ring back down. She noticed that his fingers were long, stiff-knuckled. *Piano player's hands*, she thought absently, before that was railroaded by *I wonder if that crown will electrocute me the second it lands on my head.*

Solomon folded his hands in his lap. Saskia noticed then he had a prosthetic leg, the edge of it making an odd crease in the black trousers.

"Can you tell me what the powers of the Owl Family are, Miss Das?"

Saskia frowned at his evasion. "Owls can harness the air and thus the wind."

Was it a trick question? Was he reading her thoughts right now? *Build a wall, brick by brick.* Jordan Seneca had taught

Saskia this, had taught all the kids in One Evergreen, when he wasn't hiding from his own many Denizen infractions. Saskia had her mind-wall thrown up as solid as she could manage the minute she'd walked through the pneumatic doors, but she wasn't an Owl, not even a Denizen. It was only a matter of time.

"And mind-reading," she quickly added. "Telepathy. Suggestion. Owls could make themselves virtually invisible if they wanted to."

Solomon nodded, seeming neither pleased nor fazed by the bitterness her answer. "It was because of this that they were the authority of the Five Families. Tremendous gifts with tremendous burden. They exercised these powers carefully, because I'm sure you can see how easily mind control could get out of hand."

"Not anymore," Saskia said immediately, reciting what had been hammered into her and her peers during her forced ETG education. "Not since the Task Guard regulated them."

Solomon's expression was blank. "For the greater good. Of course."

He tapped a few keys into his console, likely an access code, because the screen flashed green. Saskia stored that code in her head for safe keeping, behind her many bricks.

"You enjoy coding, I hear," Solomon remarked, still typing.

Every remark, every throwaway, was not casual conversation. It was an opportunity. Saskia had to take each of them in stride and not let her temper or her fear get the best of her. He still hadn't explained this test.

"I enjoy working with machines. Code is its own type of magical power."

Solomon smiled at that, glancing up. "Then you'll be interested to know that the Elemental Task Guard did studies on an Owl's telepathic acuity, namely on the output, and have discovered that it can be translated, and thus measured, as a type of code — more accurately, a frequency." The corner of one eye winced as he resumed typing. "Similar to how the Task Guard's ocular devices can detect general Denizen individuals in plain sight."

Unsure what kind of response he wanted from that, Saskia remained neutral. Had his voice risen with slight sarcasm on the word *discovered*? This man was at least in his sixties but looked much older and was obviously an Owl. Complicity or not, it mustn't exactly be a point of pride to admit to her, a Mundane, that his own people had been dissected like biology class toads.

"A frequency," Saskia repeated. "Like a radio wave. And my mind is the receiver."

"In simple terms, yes," he replied. "But in this case, no one is here to feed a code into your brain to control you. I will ask you questions and translate the answers as they rise to your surface thoughts. I've no need to go any deeper. Or any ability to. The Task Guard have thought of everything. For your safety."

Saskia opened her mouth to ask another question but was stopped as Solomon raised the crown and placed it on his own head. He looked, for a moment, like a doomed king in a play Saskia was not at all interested in studying.

She couldn't believe she was protesting. "But I thought —"

"This device was for you?" Solomon's smile was somewhat dark. "You're not the dangerous one in this room, Miss Das."

Not that you know, she carelessly let bob to the surface before slamming it back behind those bricks whose mortar was barely dry.

"Calibration set on Fractal 032," Mi-ja said from her console, her pleasant features now sharpened to get down to work. Her fingers were poised to tap out everything that would soon unfold. "You may proceed."

Solomon nodded, then looked directly to Saskia. He did not blink. Neither did she. "Let's begin."

She let the air out of her lungs, inhaled, and readied herself.

"What is your name?"

"Saskia Allen Das."

"Where were you born?"

"At a hospital in Thurso, Scotland."

Solomon's cheek twitched ever so slightly, but he went on.

"Good," he said. "Now, verbal communication will cease, and I will speak to you in your mind. If you have not experienced this before, it may be jarring at first. You may respond verbally if you are unable to mentally. Before I do so, I will ask you to think your intentions for coming here, to join the Elemental Task Guard, clearly and precisely, that they may be at the forefront of your thoughts."

His voice, though flat, was melodic. Persuasive. Was he hypnotizing her? No, whatever the device was, the *Fractal*, it would not allow him to do anything more than what his stated intentions had been. There were still rules.

Saskia nodded.

Hello, Miss Das. Can you hear me?

Solomon's voice was different in her head. Far more musical, like the undertones she'd picked up.

Yes.

She wondered briefly what her mental voice sounded like, but then quickly realized it didn't matter. She needed to focus.

As I said, I cannot go deeper than your surface thoughts. I am sorry for the intrusive nature of this test. Sadly, I was the one who invented it.

It was an odd feeling, having this conversation in her head, while still staring directly at the man speaking into it. His expression was completely blank. She had to make hers blank, too.

Why are you sorry, if the test is necessary to weed out possible traitors?

The question elicited a flash of something on that blank face. *You are very canny, aren't you?*

She shrugged mentally — if there was such a way to do that.

Do you understand what you will be doing here, as part of the engineering team?

No, she answered at once. She pushed everything away as if it was an enemy. As if she didn't have her own plan.

There is a project you will soon become privy to. A project that requires building something and managing frequencies as codes, like we talked about. Is that something you'd be interested in undertaking?

I do enjoy building and programming, as I said, she answered. A flicker of memory seeped under her wall of the giant Deon she'd conjured out of code. A bit of pride.

Canny, as I said, Solomon replied.

Saskia refrained from saying *shit*, either verbally or mentally. For a moment, Solomon's eyes cast to the floor, then flicked back up quickly, as if something had jarred his thoughts. His *frequency*.

Does it hurt? Saskia asked, meaning the Fractal crown.

Solomon did not smile outwardly, but she had the strange sense he was inside. *Everything hurts, but nothing more than grief. I think you understand what I mean.*

Saskia felt her heart speed up, thinking of her father. Her brother. Suddenly she was back in those woods, dragging rope, then lunging at the creature that took them both.

Saskia's fists tightened. She needed focus. Control. Then she thought of Barton. *Just breathe*, he said.

Don't worry, Solomon's voice was almost tender, in her head. *This isn't part of the test. I've lost someone, too. When you are briefed on Project Crossover, you'll understand that many of us have an interest in seeing it succeed. We all have our reasons as to why. You will find your own reasons, very quickly. If you don't have them already.*

He winced again, as if fighting against the machine. Saskia dared not turn away, or even move, to see what Mi-ja was doing. From her peripheral vision, all she could tell was that the chancellor's aide hadn't moved from her spot. Mi-ja hadn't noticed these subtle betrayals.

Then the high-pitched whine started up in Saskia's right ear, and in her vision, flecks of red light.

No, Saskia cringed mentally, trying to shy away from it, trying to stay still. *Not now.*

What is that? Solomon asked. Saskia watched his jaw clench, like he was trying to balance what the machine attached to him read, and sort what chaos was taking over Saskia's surface thoughts.

The signal, her brain blurted, too late.

Solomon's eyes widened, but before they could go further, Mi-ja piped up. "Test duration complete. You can remove the Fractal now, Sergeant Rathgar."

Saskia's hands crumpled her jacket, but she didn't care. *Rathgar?*

"Scanning for anomalies," Mi-ja went on, like she, herself, was a program. The room was utterly silent. There had certainly been more than one blip on this radar, and Saskia waited for the hammer to drop, as her brick wall had exploded, leaking every precious lie for the entire Task Guard to see.

Solomon was staring at the ground, waiting. Then Saskia felt a pressure on her shoulder. She looked into Mi-ja's moving mouth but didn't hear the words coming out of it.

"— clear," she said. "I can take you through to engineering now."

Saskia looked numbly to Solomon. His already pale face looked mottled, exhausted. Had he . . . rigged the test, somehow?

Sadly, I did invent it.

"It was a pleasure to meet you, Miss Das," he said in his flat, calculated voice. He did not shake her hand again. Both of them rested in his lap, the one on the bottom releasing its fierce grip on the fabric of his trousers.

Saskia just slid stiffly from the chair, following Mi-ja out of the room without a backward glance. She was all clear. She'd passed the test.

Whatever the cost of passing the test had been, she would have to pass the next one to discover what it was.

GRIEF IS ALWAYS HUNGRY

Days progressed. Or at least, Eli imagined they did. There was light, then there was darkness.

And when the light improved, and after Eli ate what little he could find (and barely trusted) he'd crawl to the edge of the rock and look down to the realms below.

As he thought, they looked just as bad as this one.

Huge black plinths stabbed upward through thick canopies. Beyond the forest of the Warren, still inland, was a great, empty desert, the cracked steppes of the Den, all rock and ruin and silence. Something terrible had happened in this world.

A calamity, came the voice in his head, which had dogged Eli all this time. It didn't need to say much to get him riled. But it also wasn't wrong.

He rose, wondering how much longer he might go on with such little food as dried roots, errant shrivelled nuts, and barely any water. He was so thirsty that the endless waters beyond the shores of the realms below — the Abyss — looked inviting, and drowning seemed as good an option as any at this point.

Eyes to the ground as he climbed onto another crumbling, uneven surface, Eli saw, beneath a fallen tree, a shape wink across the dark surface of something in the knots.

Water.

He threw himself face first into it, drank greedily. He didn't care if this was some sacred pool, or that he'd get sick from contamination (if there were parasites in the underworld), and he scooped more into his mouth until he caught sight of the shade he'd seen in the water's reflection, landing on a branch above his meagre puddle.

The bright eyes took Eli's measure. He tensed, ready to run if it dove for him.

"You're him," the shade said. "The last Paramount."

Eli stared at the shade with open curiosity — at least this was a distraction. He leaned back, still kneeling, hands spread on his thighs. This shade, like Eli, wanted answers. "What of it?" Eli snapped.

The shade took a quick step to the side, closer, head bobbing. "Everything is changed. The pillars of the Glen came down. The Quartz is gone. It was like a keystone — without it, the structure has collapsed around us. Something dark from below rose to take its place."

The voice coming from the shade was a man's. A worn-out croak. "I know," Eli said, looking back towards the edge of this rock, towards what he'd thought was the Glen's great mountain. "The whole place has rather gone to pot."

He shouldn't have looked away or been so cocky, because

buffeting wings smashed into his temple. Eli swung, missed, and the shade landed on a spiked outcrop just out of reach.

"Even the wind has died," the shade admonished. "You did this. You and that *Fox*. This is what happens when you forsake your authority for a rat."

Now Eli realized he'd recognized the voice. Not specifically — it was the voice of one of many that had plagued him for too many years. A voice that had been mercifully silent when the Moonstone had become corrupted.

"You're one of the ancestors, one of the previous Paramounts," Eli sneered. "What do you want?"

"To show you what your arrogance has wrought," it barked back at him. Eli noticed then that other shades were circling. "The stones are shattered and we are unmoored. The dead are restless, and we can't even reincarnate. Phyr is gone, the wind is gone, even Death cannot come here with our brothers and sisters to deliver them their rest. All is lost because you didn't kill that Fox when you had the chance."

That Fox — Roan. He didn't dare say her name. "You've seen her. Where is she?"

But the shade was done talking. It swooped back in, sharp beak aiming at him. Eli staggered, but more wings were coming for him. They were trying to push him over the edge again.

Let go, the voice howled.

Crossing his arms over himself, summoning the unspooling thread of his will, Eli cried out and cracked them back. "This is getting *old*," he bawled. "We did this. We know. We came here to make it right. To wake Ancient. We thought we were going into the Brilliant Dark. Please." And Eli hadn't expected the words to come out, but he let them: "Help me."

The shades, in their mad circling, seemed to slow, to look at each other, and as if they'd collectively decided something in their silence, they banked up and away, and they left Eli alone once again.

He'd call that a semi-win, at least.

God killer. Phyr was gone? The Moth Queen shut out? It was worse than he'd thought.

For the first time since he'd woken up in this place, Eli felt certain the answers would be at the top, even if Roan wasn't, though he childishly hoped for both. He climbed desperately, tripping over himself, blood rushing behind his eyes. Roan would be there, and they would fix this.

Let go. The voice had folded back into the corner of Eli's mind, momentarily defeated.

"Not yet," Eli hissed.

⤞⤝

For a while, I was happy to let the dark take me. I deserved it. I'd jumped at the chance for the Opal, just like I had in Cecelia's summoning chamber, hoping for a different outcome. Wasn't that the definition of insanity, or something?

Buried alive. Just barely alive, though. Intermittent tremors from beneath the Den squeezed me and pushed me up closer to the surface. And as if I were some demented plant that the soft soil rejected, I burst back out into the ashy air, half-buried, half-cocked.

And still alive, to my infinite surprise.

I stayed there for a while, hefting handfuls of crumbling tan dust into my empty palms. My head rang and my stomach burned with hunger. I didn't know how long I'd been underground, crushed. It didn't matter. Now I was back in a world of pain and confusion with nothing beyond the ringing in my head.

Eventually, I kicked my way to flat, solid ground. Behind me was a recent heave in the surface pierced by an enormous black plinth. Behind it another, and another, onwards into the murky distance like drills, not shining or glinting like glass in the grey light but devouring it. I knew something so evil-looking had to be from the Bloodlands. But how it got into the Den, I had no clue. And none, either, about where I'd ended up now.

I touched the pocket of my hoodie but didn't put my hand into it. I needed to think.

I'd come back up to the edge of a forest. Trees toppled and wrecked, but their boles enormous, blocking out the sky above me (if that's what it was) I didn't know where the fissures had carried me. I didn't know if I was above the Den, or miles from it, or if there was even a Den left. I wondered if my legs would even work if I tried to get up.

Why bother, I thought. *You're going to die of thirst or starvation soon anyway.*

So I was pretty surprised when my inner voice became Eli's — not him, not really, just the memory of his complete lack of pity: *Stop being a bloody baby, Harken, and get the hell up.*

Like it was someone else's body obeying a command, I rolled aside, putting one leg up and the other under me. I caught myself staggering against a tree and put my forehead to my clenched fist against the severe bark. I had to find Eli. I'd brought him into this mess. Maybe together we could stumble our way out of it.

Find Eli. It was enough to buoy me forward, one painful step at a time.

It took awhile, but as I trekked further through the weird wilderness, I found the light above breaking through what I thought was just an endless dusk. I'd walked far enough, it seemed, to find day.

The light was not the sun, though — it couldn't be, could it? It was, instead, a red disc wreathed in acrid yellow. It reminded me of when forest fire smoke from B.C. floated eastward over Manitoba, casting everything in its dystopian fume. There really was no place like home, Dorothy.

This place was trying hard to be real; it felt like it was breathing, calculating. It was tangible, like me. Grass and dirt and rock and tree. Most of it upended, the aftermath of a prehistoric meteor. Huge cracks in the ground that'd shattered, like the tectonic plates of one realm crashed up against another.

I touched the vegetation. Things growing. We'd learned about this type of thing in geography; I glanced at the sky again, took a breath of what had to be air, and assumed this biome was new but functioning. Living within the limitations of a natural cycle. But I thought of Sil then, of her original lessons, painfully not that long ago: the realms were eternal. Real and not real. Lands of the dead, of the ones who came before.

But this was different. Had what we'd done above made this place explode with real life? Dead life?

My head hurt.

I didn't register stopping, hunkering down in a twisted bed of roots, too tired to go on, to guess. This was Eli's department, not mine.

My eyes stung, but I closed them. I missed that giant asshole.

I slept a little. The dome above dimmed. Darkness settled in. Hours later, it lightened again. I scratched the movement of this night and day into the ground. When I got up to try to find water, I found a lake and drank from my shaking hands, desperate to quench my thirst. Eli would've hesitated. *Why didn't you boil it?* he'd scowl at me. I watched the water bead off my skin. I was so cold. Inside and out.

The landscape beyond the lake spread into a type of badlands, a middle ground between the woods and rocky steppes. There was very little shade activity in that place, and though rough and sandy hard-packed ground, my little square of land was sheltered by a bank of weird gnarled trees, growing sideways out of a rock face at the edge of it.

If I walked far enough, would I come to the edge of everything, and maybe even the Abyss, the realm of the Seals? Or had that, too, dried up entirely, and were the dead souls of that place refugees on this hateful shore? Maybe I'd walk right off the edge into nothing. Maybe that's where Ancient was.

I went back to my root-bed in the woods, paralyzed by not knowing. I drew my knees up to my chin and shut my eyes.

I needed to go back to how we'd got here.

We'd started by dropping blindly into the portal the five Calamity Stones had made, stupidly thinking Eli and I would land on the final boss level, do what we came to do, and leap back out again. Instead I'd woken up alone, without a clue. No powers. No gods. No Fox familiar on my shoulder barking directions. Not even Eli, always mocking me. Sometimes

I squeezed my hand open and closed, already forgetting his in it. We were supposed to be here together.

He was probably dead, too. Like everyone else here. I began to truly believe I, too, was turning into a ghost.

"Maybe you are."

When I looked up, I had already tensed, no time to move if a blow was coming. But it wasn't — this was just an echo of something I didn't think could have followed me down here.

Myself. My dark self. The passenger riding coach in my body, in my head, that had tried to make me into a darkling. The thing I had sacrificed everything to eject. And she was standing right in front of me.

I tripped to my feet, cold sweat burning. "It's not possible."

The other me just grinned, spreading her hands. "Of course it is. I'm still a part of you. Maybe a little subdued. But at least I still have a voice."

"Shut up." I snapped my hands to my ears, wrenched my eyes closed. "You're not real."

"I'm more substantial than you, right now," she said, moving past me to survey the trees, frowning at the dark plinths jutting out of the ground. She pointed. "These things have to be from the Bloodlands. But you knew that already. At least it's familiar territory." She folded her arms. "How are you going to get out of this one, Harken?"

What, my shadow id was a motivational coach now? "Mind your own fucking business and go back to the hole I put you in."

This other me's eyes were black, blank, but not threatening. "We all have our darkness. Some manage it better than others. But if I'm here," and she laid a hand across her heart, like a pledge, "it's because you *need* me."

"You're lying!" I shouted, but I held my ground, however shaky it was. I remembered this me in dreams, pulling me in, and I wondered for the briefest flash if she was keeping the fire from me. I still hadn't been able to conjure even a spark.

Nega-Roan looked disgusted. "That one's on you. So is all this. But you can work with it. You always do." She opened her arms. "You've heard the noises at night. Animals, monsters, call them what you will. This place has rules, like your own world. Things here hunt and feed. You'll need to do the same if you're not going to be the hunted or the starved."

I'd had enough of this. I brushed past this flimsy hallucination and hiked deeper into the trees — to where, I didn't know. Anywhere but here.

"I don't intend to stick around," I muttered to myself. "I'm finding Eli, and we're going to get Ancient, and we're getting out of here."

I looked over my shoulder and the vision was gone, but when I came up a rise I nearly staggered backward down it; other me was standing in the tree just off my path, arms crossed and casual. She looked bored. "And how long do you think you've been here, already? A day? A week? A year? A hundred?"

I ground my teeth. "You're just trying to fuck with me."

"Why would I? If you die, I die. I'm not exactly transferrable."

I looked above me. The light had moved, it'd been a day and night. But suddenly my head felt light, my throat thick, breathing windless air in a wild deadland I could never hope to understand. Shadows shifted in the middle distance, and already the light seemed like it was fading.

"How are you going to make up for all the mistakes that brought you here?" other me asked, sinister surround sound in both ears. I couldn't move. "Eli could be anywhere. Time works on fairy-tale logic. The princess gets trapped under the hill for a day, and when she returns a hundred years have passed and her loved ones are long dead." I felt her teeth at my throat, her presence a cold spot at my side. "You could walk for miles and come back to this tree. The woods could just be changing around you. Nothing here wants to see you survive."

I closed my eyes, pulse racing. "You can't hurt me. You're not real."

Her hands felt very real, suddenly cupping my neck with absolute tenderness. "You'll need me soon," she said, "if you're going to make it. No one can live with so much regret eating them up inside."

I crumpled to my knees, weakened and resigned to the kill, but she was gone. If she'd ever been there at all.

But the cold she left behind lingered inside me, and I rubbed my chest, that absent space where the Opal once burned. Everything had happened so fast. It had been cinematic, heroic. There hadn't been time to breathe, let alone think. Back in Cecelia's summoning chamber, I'd taken the stone because of what having it had promised. I'd taken everything it came with and had become a willing prisoner in my own body, blindly assuming it would all work out without really knowing how.

I curled up on the ground, cradling my head. Eli was right all along. I was — am — stupid. I never thought ahead.

I never thought about what could happen to me if I failed. Happen to everyone around me. Happen to the fucking *world*, the one above and this one below. I'd never once imagined failure as a possibility if I just kept going.

I stared at my hands. My palms were stained purple from the ripe berries I'd snagged hours earlier. These hands weren't good for much now. I'd thought, without the stone, I'd still be as I was before it. I'd had power even back then. And I'd brought it out myself. Now I was keeping it *from* myself.

That just made me think of Sil again, and Winnipeg, two more things that made my head hurt more. It had been all so easy. *The Chosen One*. What a joke. Now look where my gods-damned choices had brought me. Sil should have let the Moth Queen take me when we'd all had the chance. Zabor would still be in play, but it would have been someone else's problem.

I didn't need a shadow-me telling me any of this.

I pulled my damp, grimy hoodie closer to my unwashed body. The truth was, I'd made every stupid choice that had led me here, to this miserable, cursed place. I'd brought my body and all its limitations with me into a plane I'd broken. And if I didn't get my shit together, I was going to die down here for nothing.

And so was Eli. If he wasn't dead already.

☙❧

Eli was not much of a camper in recent years, not after ambition had given him access to the finer things. But he wasn't an idiot. He knew he couldn't go on much longer like this.

He kept looking over the edge. He kept considering it, adding his own ruin to the one below.

Then he'd find something inside himself, something so small but still there, and he'd turn away. A little fire.

The voice in his head had turned oddly conversational.

What will you do when you get to the top?

"Ask questions."

And what if there is no one there to answer?

"Then I'll find the answers for myself. Like I've always done."

Not lately, the voice corrected. *You've had help. From more than one person. From her.*

Eli felt the migraine at the back of his skull throb forward into his temples, like a crown. "Then I'll find her."

And what if she's gone? What if she left without you? What if she's dead?

Without thinking, Eli reeled back and smashed his fist into a tree. He choked on his own cut-off scream, cradling his mangled hand. Certainly bashed, luckily not broken. Still, a stupid thing to do.

The last barrage of questions had been thrown back at him in his own voice. His own thoughts. His own fear.

Why do you care so much for that girl? the voice asked, and it was with a tenderness Eli nearly trusted. He shook his bloody hand after test-flexing the joints, then straightened his spine.

"What do *you* care?" he shot back. "Are you bored? Are you unaware that the last ten years of my life have been infected with voices thinking they could command me? I'm a prodigy for insanity-deflection. You're wasting your time."

The silence was so heavy that Eli held his breath, waiting.

The answer came with the sigh of the wind, which startled him. After all, the wind had died, hadn't it?

I know what you've gone through, it said, and if Eli were in any shape to empathize, he'd have thought it was tinged with regret. *I know what you gave up to take that stone.*

"Oh, do you?" He scowled, heaving himself up the next platform of rock. His injured shoulder sang with the effort, his bruised hand throbbed. The rocks were getting farther apart, the higher he went, the gaps between them wider and more treacherous. "Is this the part where you renew your encouragement that I've 'done enough' so I can fling myself overboard?"

No, the voice replied, after a moment's consideration. *Though I'm not sure what you're persisting for. Not yet.*

That made Eli stop, look around, because the voice, however faint, seemed less in his head now, and more in his ears. He peered ahead, the fog peeling back momentarily to show that his next ledge would require a jump. A narrow grab of sure fingers on rock — fingers he'd just stupidly smashed out of childish angst. He needed peak skills and reflexes, but they were likely operating at about five percent.

Eli stared as the fog seeped back in. "What do you want from me?"

The voice crept across his awareness like a many-legged insect, and Eli knew these words were spoken with a smile. *For you to jump.*

Foolishly, he looked down. Nothing much to see, obscured as things were, but he could guess. The Roost was the realm above all things. If Eli did fall, he'd die before he hit anything. Or he'd fall for a hundred years or longer, and by the time he did crash, it would be far too late to find Roan. To fix what they'd broken. To finish what they started.

Maybe months ago — years? — before any of this had happened, before he'd woken in the Bloodlands with a better grip on himself despite being chained to another person, he would have just done it on his own. After all, everyone else he'd ever trusted had left him. His mother. His father. He only had himself to rely on.

Roan was the only person who hadn't let him down.

Stop being such a dick! Roan's voice was a sonar ping in his chest.

At that he grinned, took it at a run, and jumped.

Ah, the voice said just as Eli's fingertips caught the ledge. *I see now.*

With that small kernel of what he had left, he pulled himself over, legs lead, head rushing and empty all at once, his many injuries from his shoulder, to his fingers, to his back roaring with white hot pain. Everything hurt, every sense, and suddenly the wind rose and he felt like he was being ripped apart.

The air around him cleared. The fog had dropped, and above him, Eli saw a sky of impossible stars in an inky void.

"I didn't *want* to leave you," the voice said, and the words were clear, harsh, no longer in his head. Eli jerked up, despite the pain it caused him.

There was a shade a few feet away, its feathered back to him. Eli rolled to his knees and dipped his head.

"Phyr," he said. "Great Mother of Owls."

The shade rose, taller, but not as huge as a god. Its owl wings, pinned to its side, did not divide into nine. There was no Pendulum Rod, the sacred item the First Matriarch used to manage time. And when the shade turned, striding for him, Eli put one leg up, unable to stand, numb. This was not Phyr.

The features clarified. The face looked at him with the sorrow he'd seen so often in his waking nightmares. The face he could never save.

"There is nothing great about me," the woman said, her form still dark, opaque, but unmistakable.

"No," Eli croaked, "no." The woman knelt before him, her hands cold on his stunned face. "It's not you. It's not real."

His mother's face was a knot of grief. "Now we might both begin to know," she whispered, "what is on the other side when we jump."

She grabbed hold of his skull like she would twist it off, pressing her insubstantial thumbs into his temples, and everything went dark.

⁓⧉

Endless days of nothing. Dark Me followed at a distance, but she didn't confront me. I knew that I was doing her work for her, wandering, stiffly, getting lost in strange landscapes, pressing myself into small corners to avoid shades, hiding from screams that may or may not have been my own. I didn't go far from the lake, from the gnarled trees, looking out into the steppes and saying, "Maybe tomorrow," every day. But I never went any farther. I walked in circles. I was losing it. Dark Me came closer. Day and night passed. It was always so cold.

There was no sign of Eli. No sign of anyone. Shades circled above me like vultures, but I knew they were Owls. Same difference. It seemed like everything was just waiting until I gave up. Life must be so tempting to the dead. I hadn't seen any Fox shades in a while. I was alone. And I would stay that way.

I lay down in the dirt one night, and I dreamed of a golden tether around me, tugging.

I could feel Eli close by, his own fear drawn to mine. I tried to take comfort in that, sent reassurance back across the line. "The thing about grief," Eli's voice said, "is it never really leaves you. We heal around it. We have to. The dark feeds on it. Don't let it. We're stronger than that."

Images. Shapes in the void. Memory crowding me but kept at bay by the gold, the warmth. My scarred arm tingled. "It feels safer in the dark," I said.

I still couldn't see him. But I felt him across the tether. "I know," he said. He felt it, too. He was struggling, same as me, wherever he was. "But we have work to do."

When I woke up, my mind felt a bit clearer, but I was still stuck here. Dark Me was huddled nearby, black eyes assessing.

"Eli is alive," I told her, triumphant, buzzing with it.

She lifted a shoulder, neither agreeing nor disagreeing.

But it was enough for me, and I got up, dusted off my jeans. "Every choice that led me here was mine. Fine." I started walking, waking up with every step. "Then I have to choose to keep wandering this blistering, monster-infested cesspit just to punish myself — or find some purpose to wake up for beyond peeing behind a bush."

I glanced over my shoulder. Dark Me's eyes narrowed.

"I won't let grief win," I said to her. To me.

"I don't want that, either."

I couldn't wipe the confusion off my face quick enough.

She moved closer too quickly. "If you want the fire back, you'll need to put away what's stopping it. I can help you forget."

My fist tightened. This time I grabbed *her* by the throat, squeezing lightly. A promise.

She vanished in black smoke. Gone, but not forever. It was fine. I was still strong somehow.

I needed to move on from this place by the dead lake and the crooked trees and the hole in the roots over which I'd become landlord. So as dawn gave way into the red day, I picked a different direction, and marched. I had to choose to survive. Mostly out of spite. Eli would've liked that. Maybe.

I had a weapon at least. I'd kept the bladeless hilt of Sil's garnet sword close, even though I couldn't summon any fire or any power to me. It was still a comfort. A tangible reminder of where I'd come from. As it was, I could use it as a bludgeon. *On ghosts? Sure, great.* If I wanted a blade for it, though, I was going to have to find fire some other way.

I'd tried the two rocks thing. A childhood of Scouts (which I loathed at the time) had taught me enough to keep me going so far. Second Wolseley, that was our group's name. MacGyver a stove out of a soda can. Chop wood properly with a child's axe. Orienteer with nothing but the sun to guide you.

Build a fire so you don't die.

But I was impatient, exhausted. I swore. I alternated the rocks and the two sticks. *Fuck.* I threw them both aside, kicking a tree and smashing my blistered fists into the ground. *If you have enough energy for a tantrum then you can do a thing you thought was easy in seconds*, Eli's voice taunted. I was finding too much comfort in pretending he was here, talking to his ghost. *I'm not dead yet*, he replied. I replied. Yikes.

"Shut up," I sighed. I hunkered back down, picked up the rocks, and went at it above a small bundle of dried grass. I kept glancing at the empty hilt of the sword I'd come to rely on. *Remember where you came from.* It was proof I could survive.

Finally some smoke, sparks. When I at last managed a small, withering flame, I became aware I was sobbing only when the flame bowed backward with my shaking breath.

It was the brightest, warmest thing I'd seen or felt for days. It was more than beautiful. I banked up the kindling. I reached for the fire with my bare shaking hand, knowing I had to take this test, and when I threaded my fingers through the flames unharmed, I finally felt like I was going to be okay.

But when I looked up, I wasn't alone anymore.

They had crept up, making no sound in the bleak under-brush of the ridge where I'd taken refuge tonight. Their fox bodies were dark, near-silent, and their empty eyes seemed golden as they stared into the fire. Huge dark tails switched.

Had they been following me all this time, since they'd first come after me in the Den? My hilt wasn't even in reach. And what could I do to the already-dead, who seemed to be doing better than I was?

I calmed down, finally realizing they weren't even look-ing at me at all. The fire was all they focused on. So I did the same.

My body relaxed in the halo of the warmth, and my mind went back to a time, in a hidden chamber beneath Cecelia's house, when the fire danced alive in a circle around me, and

I felt like I belonged somewhere for the first time. I'd known so little, but gods, had I ever needed that warmth.

I glanced from the fire to the Fox shades. They all looked so similar, as if their souls had been cast from the same mould. Maybe that's what my spirit looked like when my body's shell had been sloughed off. The thought was less morbid than it sounded.

A voice from amongst them hissed, "Deon."

"Deon," answered another, with a baleful moan.

I steeled myself, became rigid again. I'd been alone so long, talking to invisible friends and enemies. I needed to talk, to ask.

"What happened to her?"

My pulse quickened as they flicked their piercing gazes upon me.

"You should know," answered the one nearest the fire, directly across from me. It wasn't a threat or an accusation even. Maybe they wanted answers as much as I did.

I gazed into the flames, recalled the last time I had seen Deon herself. Deep in the Opal, partway in my own mind. She was weak and desperate and had asked *me* for help.

The Opal cracked so loudly in my memory it jolted me, and the shades yipped as if they'd heard it, too, scattering back into the shadows they'd crawled out of. I was alone again with only their sorrow left in their wake. One shade paused, though, turned and looked at me straight on — or at the fire, it was hard to tell. It looked for a long moment before it vanished with the others.

I shut my eyes and let the fire warm me while I still had a body to appreciate it.

A River Frozen Still

The problem with using the Cold Road, a path Natti hadn't taken in years, was that it would be almost *too* expedient. Sure, it was a means of travel that even the Elemental Task Guard or the traitorous Owls couldn't detect. Yet for all the years she'd delayed going back to Winnipeg, going *home*, she thought bitterly, she was still in no rush.

But she'd have to be. Time was running out. The Darkling Moon had moved two weeks ago. She'd dragged her feet long enough and had carried so much guilt for it even longer.

She thought of the two bears, Siku and Maujaq. Messengers of Ryk, the First Matriarch of all Seals, Empress of the Sea. She went over those myths a lot lately, trying to find either truth or comfort in them. Natti's own life had become a myth, a weird story. But she still couldn't figure out how it'd end.

The bear claw around her neck hung on a strand of leather, which she tugged at now, the cord snapping. She grasped it tensely in her large mitten, standing on the precipice overlooking the icy sea, a landscape that brought her something separate from comfort — a blithe emptiness, a knowledge that she could step into freezing endless waves and disappear for a while.

Going away had always been tempting, but she felt most herself when she turned away from that impulse. This was the place where the glacier had risen. Where the Sapphire had revealed itself. *If we'd left it down at the bottom of the sea, this wouldn't have happened.* But that wasn't true, either. Seela would've found a way. She was comforted that they'd fought on their own terms, even though it hadn't gone the way she'd hoped.

Siku, before he had given up his spirit power, had passed it along to Natti. Had promised that he wasn't really gone — something of the Inua was inside her now. Even something of Maujaq, who had fallen in the fight against Seela. Natti felt like it was time she took up the mantle they'd left her, not only bridging the gap between worlds but leading the fight for what their Matriarch had believed in.

Life. The inevitability of the sea. And Natti had to admit that she didn't want to leap into the fray again alone.

You are made strong by the love of your friends, Siku had said. She hoped she still had that love, because she had pushed it away with a rage that had consumed her deeper these seven years. She'd buried it under a placid face, unreadable beneath brown skin and blue tattoos lining her eyes, cheeks, mouth.

She figured now was the time to make it right. *Say your goodbyes while you've got someone you can say goodbye to.*

"Feh," she said aloud. She wasn't usually so maudlin. She'd say goodbye when it came to that, but until then, she'd make damn sure she'd fight. To the bitter end.

So Natti turned the bear claw over and over in her hand, until the world changed around her into a deep blizzard rushing past, aurora spooling out bright and alive above her, blocking the black moon that always seemed to watch her. The Cold Road opened at her feet, and she stepped onto it. Alone, but not for much longer.

～≈

It took no time at all. When the snow parted, the Seal's air of the Veil faded. The aurora dimmed, and Natti was standing in the Forks Market, where the two rivers met. A homeless man startled, squinted at her, then went back to muttering to himself.

She took off her mitts, stuffed them in her pack. She had shed more than her heavy-duty winter gear when she left the other Seals behind, in Aivik's hands. *Take care of them*, she'd said, *and by the time you hear from me again, be ready*.

Her mother had hugged her closely and fiercely. "Whatever you decide to do," she said, "we will follow you. We will still fight in Ryk's name, though she can no longer hear our prayers."

Natti had prayed anyway.

She started walking, heading for Main, then Broadway, and squinting up at the tall buildings of the downtown core. The overcast autumn sky roared with air traffic, making her wince. The sidewalks were still busy, but the usual urban crowds seemed thin in comparison to the uniformed guards patrolling beyond Waterfront Drive. Everything was bizarre.

Bizarre, but that was home. Point Douglas, where she was born and raised, likely had crumbled even further under the boot of the Elemental Task Guard. The situation now had less to do with race, and yet more to do with it than ever before, but regardless the poor always suffered more. Everyone was scared, as they should be. But Natti couldn't help anyone in the North End if the world was going to hell first.

The chancellor wouldn't know yet that she was here, though it was only a matter of time. He had summoned her enough times, tried to make inroads with Natti and the Seals as a political move, tried to do it in the name of sense and reason, the benefits to all involved. But the messages had moved beyond cordiality. If she refused again, she assumed he'd come for the whole Seal Family. He'd call them impertinent. He'd nuke the ice cap right out from under them — though the rest of the planet was already destroying the permafrost quickly enough on its own.

Best Natti confront the chancellor now, when his guard was down. But she had to gather some intel first. She might need someone to have her back . . . even though she really didn't deserve that. If she had to go against the entire ETG alone, so be it.

Crossing Main, she moved towards Assiniboine, as if her thick boots couldn't be guided any other way. It had less to do with her feet, and more with her blood, coursing red rivers beneath flesh. There was another river she needed to see.

Needed to find out if it, too, had changed.

The walkway curved downward, beneath the steps of the Old Leg, beneath the statue of Louis Riel, whose Tyndall stone podium had a sheet draped over it. Glancing about,

Natti pulled the moisture from the cool air, casting a layer of mist that lasted long enough for her to lift the corner of the sheet, unseen.

She dropped it just as quickly and stalked away. Underneath it was a graffitied symbol, much debated amongst Seals, but likely somewhat of a call to arms here. It made her chest burn all over again with the same anger, the old bruise. Roan Harken's face. *JOIN THE FIRE FIGHT*. Other iterations had *We Are the Flame*. Not everyone had the whole story. Not everyone understood the cost of good intentions. Natti, for one, still battled with them.

An exhale to let it go, as her mother and the other ice summoners had tried to teach her. Send it to the sea, where it will sink, where it will become food. Don't let it become an angry spirit inside you.

She then went down to the river.

She could only go so far. The river had once been an open promenade, inviting to tourists and urban daytrippers, but no longer. A black fence had been erected on either bank, preventing people from going too close. Criss-crossing gates rose out of the water, like sewer traps. The water moved around it, leaving detritus behind — trash, Coke bottles, pamphlets. She saw a flyer encouraging ETG sign-up. She saw a poster with *MISSING* typed across the top in bulging letters. And another one. And another. Pleas for help.

She thought for a moment she saw the flash of red eyes above a clicking gash mouth, but when she looked again, it was gone.

Her head tilted west, towards the source of this brown and green and unknowable river. It had its own voice like all bodies of water, but it carried the same despair Natti did.

If she spoke, the river would reply. But Natti was never one for talk.

A cold wind flung her hair about her mouth and shattered the river's surface until it looked like scales. A serpent's tail. But that serpent was long gone, cast into the sky with its siblings. Natti didn't need to look up to feel the Darkling Moon; she saw its reflection in the water. The Earth's moon affected tides, though it was part of the Owls' power and purview. So Natti imagined the dark moon must be hers, her curse, her burden to bear. And it was. And it wasn't. It was all of theirs. Roan's, Eli's, Barton's, Phae's. All the Denizens who had let this happen. All the Mundanes who hurt Denizens. All the people who hurt each other.

The Darklings were the inevitable consequence of any of them thinking this world was a thing to be possessed.

Natti didn't know how long she stayed there, staring at the river, even when it began to rain. She could have redirected it off her easily, subtly, even though the Old Leg grounds were crawling with ETG guards. But she let it soak her to the bone to feel the knife of the cold, because though they had failed, at least they'd done it together. At least they'd had each other.

Until Natti had pushed them all away.

꿈꿈

SEVEN YEARS AGO

Phae knocked lightly on the hospital door with a knuckle. She didn't wait long before pushing in, startled when she saw Natti racing around the room, gathering up her belongings, hospital gown covered partially with a too-big sweatshirt likely yanked from the lost and found.

Aivik held his hands up, his face a mosaic rainbow of bruises. "Natti, just stop, okay? Neither of us is ready to travel." He twisted when he saw Phae. "Talk some sense into her, eh?"

Natti froze, hands clutching the bedrail. "Phae," she croaked. Even with the room between them, Phae could see how tiny Natti's pupils were.

Phae went immediately to her friend and put her arms gently around her. Natti was shaking. "Let's sit down a second, okay?"

Natti gruffly pushed her off. "Can't. We're getting out of here."

Phae's hands felt numb, and she was at a loss for what to do with them. "But you're hurt. Barton said you fractured a lot of things pretty badly. I thought I could —"

"*Don't* think about it," Natti snapped. "I don't want you touching me. I *want* to feel the pain. I deserve it. We all do. None of you *get it*."

Phae moved back to the other side of the room, looking pleadingly at Aivik, who shrugged. "You can heal me up, Phae. I'm not too proud to admit I'm a wuss."

She smiled at him, patting his arm. "I will in a bit. Why don't you go find Barton for me, okay?"

He nodded, taking one last pitying look at his sister before lumbering out of the room on his crutch. Phae would've healed Aivik right then, but she'd barely been able to get out of bed herself. Offering to heal either of them had been mostly a bluff to get Natti to calm down.

She'd stuffed the cracked Quartz in the pocket of her hospital robe, put a hand protectively around it as she watched

Natti, unsure what she could possibly do or say. It had dawned on her suddenly that this was the last Calamity Stone left in the world, and Phae kept thinking, *Maybe if I squeeze it hard enough, maybe if I push and push, I'll feel what I did when I came out of the Glen . . .*

Back then she'd felt the Matriarch, Fia, resonating inside her. She'd felt beyond death. She'd felt that she was only made of Spirit, and that it was enough, and it was good.

She had emerged as not a woman, but a song, and it had been sung back to her by the sister stones. Phae had felt so much, *too* much, and it had been more than beautiful, more than healing. She had felt what Spirit truly meant, the last unabashed hope of a god who didn't believe in it.

Now that hope was as cracked as the lump of glass in her pocket.

"No one can go anywhere right now," Phae said to Natti, shutting the hospital door and lowering her voice. "Barton's been speaking with his unit. The whole Coalition. We're all playing this day by day now. The world's militaries are on high alert for anything remotely pointing to Denizen activity. The last elders are all going underground, because we expect a United Nations tribunal any day now. We all can't go around like we used to. We have to plan this carefully, and —"

"Exactly," Natti replied, holding a pair of jeans against her hip-to-toe cast. She threw them away, and instead reached for a long, flowing hippie skirt from a stockpile under the bed. "Of course I'm going to be careful. There's too much at stake. I have to go back to my mom. To my Family. I'm needed with the Seals now. And it's best to do it when everyone's got their heads up their asses. They won't be able to stop me even if they try."

Phae couldn't help but suddenly feel petulant. "But *we* need you. Barton, me, Aivik. We're all connected to Roan. To Eli. It's our responsibility to —"

"Responsibility to what?" Natti shouted, moving far quicker than she should with that broken leg. Adrenaline was a hell of a drug, but it'd wear off soon. "Don't you talk to me about Roan." Natti's finger was in Phae's face, backing her into a food tray. "This is all her fault. She killed Aunty. She's the one who fucked up everything. She was on Seela's side this whole time."

Phae took Natti's hand, but she ripped it away. "It wasn't like that, and you know it. Her stone was corrupted. She *did* manage to fight it off —"

"Too late," Natti was muttering, "we were all too late."

It was like she was in a panicked fever. Phae tried to call up the power, her fingertips sparking blue, but it was harder than it ever had been. With the stones gone, would Denizen power wane? Would she lose what precious grace she'd taken for granted? Natti turned her back on Phae, squared her shoulders, and shivered.

"I need to be with my *true* Family," Natti said at last, her voice hard as an ice floe. "The one I chose is broken. That's on me." When she turned back, her face, though slightly ashen, was utterly calm. "You weren't there, Phae. You didn't see it. I thought it was going to be the end. I sort of wish it had been. How screwed up is that? We all survived, and look at the world we have ahead of us. They're going to hunt us down, all the Mundanes who will blame us. And they'd be right for it. We risked everything, and we lost." She licked her dry lips. "Best not to meddle any more than we already have."

The door opened behind them. Barton had arrived, and Phae and Natti both glared at him.

"Natti," Barton said, passing Phae with a perfunctory squeeze to her arm. "I've talked to Commander Zhao. There's a transport ship we can put you and Aivik on to take you to the North. It leaves in a few hours, though."

Phae felt twenty protests seizing her jaw. "Barton, no —"

Natti snatched her crutches and was basically bounding out of the room. "Fine," she said roughly, "I'm ready now. Let's go."

Phae gave Barton a look to melt steel before she rushed after her, down the hall. "Natti, please wait!"

"I'm done waiting," she snarled. Aivik came around the corner, nearly knocking Natti over, and Phae caught up.

"I may not have been there," she fumed, voice growing as feverish as Natti's, "but I was in another *realm*. One *your* god sent me to. You don't know what it took to convince Fia to give me the Quartz, to even get back here alive! We've all done things, taken the risks, but we did it *together*. We have to *stay* together."

Natti would not turn around, not this time. "Maybe you should've stayed in the Glen," she said. "At least we both got to see our gods before we killed them."

A woman with a shaved head and wearing green Coalition linen had come down the hall and looked questioningly from Barton to Natti and Aivik. She seemed to survey the gathering with too much grave understanding.

"This is them, Kita," Barton said. "They're ready."

"I hope so," she said to Natti and Aivik. "This way. We have a ground vehicle waiting in the back. Hurry, if you can."

"With pleasure," Natti uttered, face even whiter now, and she took one last look at Barton, at Phae, and at the little girl clinging to Barton's leg. The one who had found Phae washed up on the seashore, who had convinced Natti to come out of the hole beneath Seela's compound and survive another day.

Natti looked at them all with mean, disappointed eyes and left. She didn't dare say goodbye.

RED SONG

S askia remained cautiously hopeful after falling into a sickly
sort of routine. At least now she had a plan.

After the first week she still hadn't discovered quite what
she was working with the ETG for, or what good she could
do there. One week and Ella was still missing. One week
and the Moth Queen hadn't bothered to show up again, even
when Saskia begged her to.

One week, and she still couldn't get that old computer in
her room to turn on.

While the lab was separate from the recruit intake, or even
the classroom training barracks, the place seemed to swell with
activity every day. In that first week, Saskia hadn't seen nor
heard from the chancellor, and she was grateful for it. "Every
day brings a new urgent matter," Mi-ja had said after those first
couple of days, beaming her plastic smile. Saskia didn't buy it.
Every day she steeled herself when taking sharp corners down

sterile white corridors, expecting the chancellor's sick, sharp-faced smirk on the other side. She was absolutely convinced he was just waiting for her to slip up.

Not much room to slip up when you're doing nothing, Saskia had sulked. She asked herself over and over if her infiltration had just been a pointless risk.

She saw Cam now and then. Combat training was not done on site, though, so these instances weren't predictable. Trainees billeted outside of the city, in a community of co-opted farms in nearby Steinbach, which had virtually become its own military town. New recruits still had to come in for classes, however, since they were underage and the ETG had its own propaganda-filled "education" program. Saskia had mercifully skipped that part.

Saskia's work was more important than socializing, anyway. That's what Mi-ja had told her during the daily debriefings with Saskia and the rest of the engineering team — meetings that just seemed to reinforce how "important" their work was without actually making them do anything.

The rest of the team were all much older than Saskia, and intolerably suspicious of her. While they were all new hires like her, anytime Mi-ja left the room they became a hive of nervous bees. They complained about the impossibility of working under such conditions, since they were given only breadcrumbs: papers on theoretical physics, folding dimensions, the transmission of frequencies from deep space . . . and a firm encouragement to re-read the chancellor's memoirs about the White Militia. What did all these things have in common?

Some guessed this mystery gauntlet was a test of loyalty and threw themselves into playing along. Others were terrified, looking for someone to blame. Then they'd look at Saskia disapprovingly. She was young and no one knew her story, but they all seemed to know the chancellor had hitched his star to her. She was nervous, too, but she was willing to wait. The others didn't know a thing about waiting.

It came down to this: her team was tasked with building something that would be implemented into the ETG's greatest asset, one that had a lot of time and money and brilliant minds sunk into it already, but was giving them . . . trouble. Word from on high was they were waiting for clearance on a new development that would make their jobs much clearer. "Read the papers you're given about Project Crossover," they were told. "Prepare yourself."

Project Crossover itself was not revealed to them in anything but vague promises: *this will change the tide of our current circumstances*. And *Project Crossover will allow humans to take back their broken authority over this world*. These documents, with official Canadian government letterhead, were rife with black marker streaks: *REDACTED. RESTRICTED. FEDERAL CLEARANCE ONLY*.

On her second day, Saskia was given a tour of the asset in question. The rest of the team had been working with it before she got there, had already developed a hands-on approach to it. But still, none of them could see what Saskia did the second she walked up the concrete ramp and to the steel railing that stopped her from disappearing into the Earth's core.

Yet for all the holes in their instructions, the pieces of everything slid neatly together when Saskia looked down into that oblivion machine. The Task Guard called the machine "The Apex." Saskia had another name for it.

A Bloodgate.

"It worked once, god knows how," one of the engineering team members had said offhandedly when they thought Saskia was out of earshot. They were as bad as her classmates, these grown astrophysicists, most of them doctors six times over. "I hear they got a Rabbit neutralizer in to do it. Except now they have no idea how to make it work without him, or what he did to wreck it."

Saskia knew. Because she knew what type of person Barton was, if that's who they meant. He'd go along with what the ETG wanted — seeing that their machine could work. But he'd do whatever it took to make sure they couldn't do it again.

When she first saw the machine, Saskia thought of the Large Hadron Collider, a marvel, a true invention engineered into being to explore the frontiers of possibility. This thing that the Task Guard had built . . . all Saskia could see was a loaded gun.

It descended miles into the ground, a tube of steel panels, electricity arcing off it. Somewhere, there would have been a reactor to turn it on, which meant there was an enormous turbine, coils of wire the circumference of her body, and on and on. This had been a huge undertaking, something the Task Guard would have had to hide for years. Saskia drowned in questions — they had been testing the machine, but for what purpose? Who had built it? What had they tested it on?

Or who?

When it came down to it, it was just a dark hole. But how had they managed to dig such a hole in the first place? There were some questions Saskia could answer for herself, the longer she stared at this thing, tuning the chatter, the grinding, the general noise out. She remembered what Rabbits could do. They could dig and dig and dig. But they could also open doors that no one else could see.

In the scant two years Saskia had become close to Barton, relying on him to occupy the space of father and brother at the same time, she had sat at his prosthetic legs, begging to know everything. Whatever slip of magic he could spare. He was generous with that knowledge. People liked that about him. He told a story, and it made you feel like it was yours.

Bloodgates, he'd said, were tricky things. Just like Owls had the augmented skill of telepathic manipulation besides their wind-harnessing, Rabbits could part dimensional space — *That's how I understand it, anyway*, he'd say, pushing his glasses up his nose. They could feel for a crease, and open a way to the Bloodlands, because, as the roundabout story went, Heen was the one who dug the Darkling Hold to put away the three beings of destruction, and her descendants inherited this ability to feel the way there.

Bloodgates were easier to open in certain locations. Once closed, they could not be opened a second time. Bloodgates could not be created, either. When it came down to it, not all Rabbits were able to open or shut these doors, and no one had really discovered a pattern in determining who could. What was the purpose of knowing how to do this dire thing, anyway? The Bloodlands weren't necessarily the promised land. If anything, it was Denizen Hell. Going down there was a last resort. But it was a good place to put things you didn't want to see again.

They called the Rabbits who could perform this feat neutralizers. Someone who managed a balance between creation and destruction, if only rarely and for a moment.

There was some overall Denizen suspicion towards neutralizers, too, because they were, in this minor way, connected to the dark. And they could use this connection to enact a ritual that could remove a Rabbit's power, given to them by the god Heen.

Owls could take away powers, too — anyone's powers. Maybe they resented that they weren't in total control.

Barton had had to become a neutralizer himself, after being mutilated by one in order to save his life. He wasn't bitter about the fact he had been severed. If he carried any ill feelings about it all, he'd long ago learned to let it go. *Doesn't get you anywhere*, he'd say to Saskia, when she was experiencing her own bad taste of the world. After he disappeared, Saskia often wondered what sort of things he may have grown capable of doing, if the world had allowed him.

Now she knew.

The engineering team were the only ones allowed in for the daily tests run through the machine. But then the first week had ended and, surprising everyone, Chancellor Grant showed up himself to provide the marching orders. As much as Saskia had dreaded his appearance, his presence made her hope that her luck was about to improve.

"I know it's been difficult working on this project with little to go on. You, with all your . . . many gifts." He'd been addressing the whole team, but his glance lingered over Saskia, and she met it. "It took some time to secure the highest government clearance on this, so know that if any of you were to speak of this, to anyone, including your deaf cat, there would be consequences."

Saskia rolled her eyes to overcome the anxiety growing in her.

"There's something you will now listen to. It'll be your first time hearing it, but soon you'll have every tonal shift memorized. Your task will be to build a receiver that can not only fill in the missing gaps of this transmission but lock on to its location."

The room had been silent. Somewhere, someone flicked a switch, and Saskia's guts twisted so hard, she collapsed.

She came to seconds later, with one of the team members, Beth, holding her up.

"Keep it together or you'll be out of here," she growled. Saskia snapped her head up, finding her feet, head throbbing. Beth shoved her aside, giving her a look that said *Don't screw this up for the rest of us.* Luckily the chancellor wasn't looking at Saskia anymore.

The recording stretched on. Saskia was already ten steps ahead; it was the same warped, sonic sound that seemed stuck inside the winding canals of her ear and brain. The sound she heard when Barton — or a good trickster — had sent her a message. It was the cracked music box of an evil carousel, and she couldn't get off.

"We are calling this the signal," the chancellor said over the noise, which was making most of the team wince. Some held their ears but kept their faces blank. Which, Saskia thought, seemed the best response to most of what went on in this place. "It came through this very machine, recently. So here is your task: you will interpret it. You will locate it. And once that location is determined, in this dimension or another, I believe we can direct what we've already worked so hard for, and open the door at the time we need it most. You will be the ones to carry Project Crossover over the finish line, and end any notion of war consuming this planet."

Open the gate. Win the war. Now get to work.

"He's batshit insane," another tech, Jonathan, had said, in a quiet lab at the end of a hall where Saskia was scanning through the first 0.23 seconds of the signal's readout, to the part where there seemed to be a gap of silence, part of the chain of code deleted. The team had been divided into little clusters like this, to dig through wavelengths till their eyes and ears and brains hurt. They had to apply the science they already knew to an illogical plane.

Saskia was game. Because that missing piece was inside her head.

But she darted Jonathan a skittish glance from her screen. "Maybe keep comments like that to yourself." *Unless he's just trying to bait me so I say what I'm really thinking and get kicked out . . .*

He groaned in his seat, cracking his back. "Grant knows exactly what he is. It's how he gets results. But please. A signal that'll lead us to . . . another dimension? We have a real theatre of war here, not in la-la land. This isn't what my Ph.D. is for."

Saskia put her headphones back on. "If you're living in a world where people with powers are the living breathing bogeymen, and you can't cope with the possibility of another dimension, you should throw your degree in the trash."

She turned the recording up to drown out Jonathan's answer, and despite how painful it was, she listened hard. Listened to see if anyone was talking back.

Saskia felt, finally, like she was in control. It was only a matter of time before she did exactly what she was told . . . and got through to the other side first.

Now, at the close of the second week in those labs deep underground, Saskia finally felt like she'd made actual progress.

Phae kept the Horned Quartz, the hollow, lightless shell of it, inside another shell. She'd put it in a locket, where she couldn't touch it with her skin, because it was a painful empty hope that it would reflect its unique warmth into her. It wouldn't ever again.

While Saskia didn't pretend to have a window into Phae's mind, or her secret pains, she knew that Phae didn't open up the locket often, and that she took it off when she showered in the mornings. Saskia had been careful, when she was finally allowed the privilege to walk to and from the Old Leg facility on her own, to test the weight of rocks and rubble she picked up on sidewalks, on boulevards, at abandoned construction sites. Eventually, she found one similar to the size and weight of a triple-god's heart.

She held the Horned Quartz now on her walk home, pulling it free from her ETG uniform pocket. Since it was made of material not of this *dimension* — she scoffed out the chancellor's word — it wasn't detected by any of the body scanners during her daily searches. She'd become good at taking risks.

Finding the dummy rock to be the Quartz's stand-in had been easy. But lying to Phae had been even easier than that, and that unnerved Saskia most.

This job seemed tailored just for her: part of the wretched signal filtering unchecked in her head; Barton's message coming through just to her; the Moth Queen's mission. All of it converged with Saskia. She didn't want to think about the implications of that just now and had successfully plunged through her second week, thinking of nothing other than the work at hand, all of it, even this dead Calamity Stone she'd borrowed from the woman who'd taken her in. The deeper she went, the more determined she was to succeed, and the more alone she felt.

All the lying made her feel like Ella. She'd barely thought of the girl she'd lamely thought she loved. There was barely any room for her right now. She spared her one thought, even if it felt inauthentic right now — *When this is all done, I'll do everything I can to save her.* This was quickly overridden by that storyteller's voice: *Maybe she doesn't want to be saved.*

Saskia stopped, running a finger over the crack in the Quartz. *It sang*, Phae told her. *It harmonized with the voices of all the sister stones forming a chorus. And there was another song, too, one that came from the answering dark. It was like no music you could ever hope to remember.*

During the day, in the labs, Saskia was only focused on the signal. Parsing it. What she found or thought about it, she kept to herself. It's not like the other techs were sharing their findings just yet, either; they pettily wanted a reward, a pat on the head, and everyone was racing for that praise. Saskia had already found all she needed, and if she was lucky she could test her theory as soon as tomorrow, before the chancellor forced her to share what she'd discovered. After he'd dropped the signal on the engineering team a week ago, Grant had flown away again halfway across the world for some dire meeting at the United Nations. He would be back at HQ within the next day or two, in fact, so she'd have to be quick about it. Now that she knew she could sneak the Quartz in, undetected, it was just a matter of willing herself to carry out her plan.

Beneath the signal's wavelength, and in the back of her own head, it wasn't just broken static. It was a song. It could be plotted on a staff, like music on a sheet, but there were a few bars missing, overlapping notes that were too faint to pick up. If Saskia could run the signal *through* the Quartz . . . the schematic for building a device that could do this had come so easily, and now it was close to being finished. This was the only superpower of hers that she could possibly believe in.

She'd brought the Quartz today to test it, but that was all. Before she did anything too drastic, Saskia needed to talk to someone. Anyone. Out here in the overcast, the biting cold, she was tired of being alone. She thrust the stone back in her pocket, then pressed her thumb hard enough into her forehead to start a headache.

"I know you're watching me," she said, standing there on the boulevard on Broadway. There were ETG guards everywhere, but what did she have to worry about them for? She was one of them now. If they saw her talking to herself, they'd maybe think her crazy, but they wouldn't question the uniform. No one did.

She pressed harder, never closing her eyes. The place where she'd seen the mark, back at Omand's Creek. She'd tried all this before, and only felt stupid afterwards, but there was nothing lost in trying again.

"You're not one of them," the Moth Queen said. She hadn't been there, then all at once she was everywhere, flickering like a candle about to gutter out in an autumn windstorm. Those weren't leaves filling the air.

"I'm not a Denizen. Not loyal to the ETG. I'm no one, just doing what you told me to do."

Saskia folded her arms, looking out into the traffic-heavy streets, thinking about how every person in every car passing by had a story, had their own precious world, influenced by and influencing all the worlds of everyone else around them. Saskia's life had become about slipping into another world — but whose?

"I've been thinking. About why I was marked." She toed the dirt with her regulation boots. "I'm a Mundane. We can't see the Moth Queen, can we? You're just a projection, in a way. The shepherd of death appears differently to everyone else, but the Moth Queen is only visible to descendants of Ancient. You told me your reasons for needing me, but I still —"

"Question them?" The Moth Queen had risen and seemed to be expanding, the needle fingers working in a way that suddenly made Saskia feel like she was weaving someone else's cocoon, right there in front of her. "You are right to. And, you are *right*." The fingers stalled, tented. "I appear to those touched by Ancient, and its many tendrils. You were touched by one of them."

A needle finger pointed upward. Saskia didn't look; she didn't want to hear that horrible noise again, to see red. Her inner ear itched with the promise of it.

"The Darklings? But they're not descended from Ancient. They're Ancient's cosmic enemies. Destruction versus Creation. The inverse. Ancient didn't *make them*." The Moth Queen's small mouth closed, and nothing moved in her large eyes.

Saskia corrected herself. "Okay. Fia did, I guess."

Saskia couldn't help frowning, then she turned and started towards the back of the Old Leg, towards the river, where she could walk under the bridge to get to the other side.

"You are afraid of the signal and what it means that you

have the missing piece of it," the Moth Queen said, following her in a riptide of little wings. "You are right to be."

"I'm always right, huh?" Saskia retorted, feeling her temper rising. "You said the choice was mine, but you lied. Everything is predetermined. The Narrative. That horror moon. Roan and Eli thought they were doing the right thing. So did Barton. What if I do everything the way I'm supposed to, and it all goes wrong anyway?"

"That's life," the Moth Queen answered. "That's not my area of expertise, alas."

Saskia snorted. "Right."

A moth big as Saskia's hand brushed against her face, and Saskia's vision went out just before she crossed the back lane behind the compound and into the path of a Hummer. It jackknifed onto Reclamation without a backward glance.

"It's not your time yet," the Moth Queen said now as she had earlier, extending one of her countless palms to the great Atlas moth that had stopped Saskia mid-step. "If only you could see with my eyes. But I can only see with one."

The moth on her hand turned over, revealing two eyes on its wings — one hazel, one amber.

Saskia nearly swallowed her tongue. She had seen those eyes before.

"Roan?" she asked. "You can . . . see what Roan does, through her spirit eye, in the realms?" Then the Moth Queen knew so much more than she was letting on. And this meant that Roan was *alive*, whatever that meant now.

The Atlas moth fluttered off, devoured by the ongoing hurricane of wings that seemed to both follow, consume, and comprise the Queen when she manifested. "Roan was marked by me. So were many others before her. Was that also part of the plan, or the result of a choice? Was stopping that plan Roan's idea, her grandmother's, or mine? If Zabor still lived in this river, would darkness have still found a way into the sky above? These are the questions that even an eternity can't answer. All the world's a prism, and there are too many ways we can be refracted through it."

Saskia grabbed a fistful of her shirt, as if she were going to rip it clean off. She crossed the street, walked past the Moth Queen, and paused at the top of the stairs leading down to the river path.

She turned to the great, hulking creature that had come to her, of all people, for help. Death herself with her own desires. "And what if you can't shine a dark thing through a prism?"

Suddenly, the Moth Queen's face was in Saskia's. There were many eyes there, changing, pulsing. It was terrible. It was beautiful. She could see inside Saskia in a way that Solomon Rathgar couldn't. Saskia had been lying to everyone so much, and to herself, that she was afraid the Moth Queen would eventually see that anything good in her had been swallowed, so long ago, in a forest in the Highlands.

"At least," the Moth Queen said, "darkness is consistent."

Just as soon as the Moth Queen had appeared, she was gone. Saskia sighed, then turned, determined to at least get home and replace the Quartz before Phae noticed.

In the path in front of her, under the bridge, stood Ella.

"Saskia," she croaked, a painful whisper.

Saskia was already running three steps down at a time, but she came up short when another figure materialized from the musty shadows of the bridge's recess.

Tears ran down Ella's face. "I'm sorry," she said. Even with the tears, she didn't look sorry.

"Miss Das." This voice Saskia snapped to immediately: Solomon Rathgar. "We need to speak with you."

Her fists shook. "I've heard the stories about you," Saskia said. "You hurt her, didn't you?"

Solomon glanced at Ella, then back to Saskia. "What stories might those be?" he asked, hands folded behind his back. "There were always too many to catalogue."

Ella moved towards Solomon, as if seeking comfort. He did not touch her, but she looked terrified, despite that. "That you're a traitor!" Saskia shouted. "Leave Ella alone! What do you want from me?"

"Traitor." Solomon seemed to be tasting the word. His wavy, iron-grey hair still made him appear like a diminished circus lion, his strength long fled but still with all his teeth. "I'm sure when the stories about you are told, they'll say the same thing. Traitor to Denizens. Traitor to Mundanes. Traitor to your family."

Saskia was still looking at Ella and hissed, "Why don't you fight him? Are they controlling you?"

Ella's face hardened. "No," she said. "But someone's been controlling *you*."

Saskia glanced down, realizing she was still wearing her ETG uniform. She slapped a hand over the starburst crest too late. "I can explain. I can explain all of it. I'm doing it for — I'm trying to —"

"Save the world?" Solomon sighed. "That platitude does get rather old. But then I remember how *young* you are."

There were only the two of them. Saskia could run, but he could stop her, mid-step, if he wanted to. Solomon Rathgar was the most powerful Owl still allowed to move around by day. And Ella was Saskia's girlfriend. Ella wouldn't —

They'd been apart so long Saskia had forgotten that Ella was fast, a holdover from dance class, while Saskia's sport was cross-country running. Ella had grabbed Saskia's forearm tightly before she could think of doing anything else.

She tried to shove her off without hurting her, but Ella wasn't so cautious. She landed a blow directly to Saskia's stomach, knocking the air right out of her, and when she crumpled, Ella pivoted behind her, wrapping her arms around her waist, holding her up and keeping her from falling.

Saskia gasped, coughed. Ella had put her arms around Saskia so many times since they'd known each other. Some rebelling neurons overrode her fight impulse.

Saskia choked, "Ella — stop."

Solomon strode forward, leaning on a cherrywood cane. He lifted his fine-boned hands and pressed his thumbs gently to Saskia's temples.

Saskia tried reason. "You said you wanted . . . to talk . . ."

"More accurately," Solomon cut in, "I need you to sing."

Solomon's gaze darted over Saskia's shoulder to Ella. She let Saskia go abruptly, stepping aside so quickly Saskia nearly fell over, but the power of Solomon's suggestion kept her upright. Solomon was only grazing her with the barest touch, his mind gentle. He was not there to control it, Saskia suddenly felt, but that was no comfort. Not after Ella.

"I'm going to help you," she heard him say, "and when I do, you'll surely help the rest of us. I just want to make sure what I heard when we first met is still there."

But Saskia could barely hear him. She stared straight ahead, Ella on the edge of her sight. She tried to hold on to her, but she was getting farther and farther away. Saskia didn't understand, but Ella was alive, and she smiled, like she was dreaming.

Solomon threw his mind into the painful knot inside Saskia's. His face contorted wretchedly as it hadn't during his assessment in the lab.

"Ella," Saskia heard him grunt, "cover your ears."

Saskia opened her mouth.

That horrible, high-pitched whine in her head, the red strobing in her eyes. She wanted it both to stop and to slow down so she could read the message. It was too fast. It was so loud. *The stones sang to each other*, Phae said, *but something from the dark answered . . .*

The red song filled her every sense. It was far more terrifying than the Moth Queen could ever promise. The blanks of the ETG's signal filled in. The sigils formed its message.

Saskia felt herself scream somewhere inside, then felt herself fall.

Zephyr Rising

D emelza was a fair-haired beauty on the island, as wild as the sea and the wind that stirred it. She clung close to family, minded her god, and dreamed, most highly, of love.

"Be careful," Agathe warned. Agathe was old even when she was really Demelza's age, always ready with a warning or a proverb or an extra scarf against the chill. Demelza wouldn't trade Agathe for anyone, not even a lover.

"I'll be fine." Demelza waved Agathe off now, but she was already staring across the meeting hall, unable to keep from smiling at the man who'd glanced at her from the corner of his eye.

Those eyes were fierce, almost calculating, and definitely troubled. Demelza had, of course, heard of Solomon Rathgar, knew exactly what he was about. Who didn't? A progressive, forthright man, older than her but likely no wiser, and keen to upend the Council of Owls with his radical ideas. Others feared what he would do with his new seat as their de facto leader, feared it would change everything.

She was predisposed to like him already.

This was likely because Demelza feared little. Least of all this Denizen man with his night-black city suit and chestnut locks. He looked too well groomed for the fishing village of Uig, far too controlled for the wild sea that had rocked the Isle of Skye for thousands of years. If he was a Son of the Wind, it was the kind that felt like a clean papercut on your cheek. Like a reprimand.

So she savoured the look of real shock on his face when she opened up her mental wall and fired a psychic spark at him, mental contact static. "Knock, knock," the spark said.

Rathgar smiled at her. Maybe against his better judgment, Demelza imagined.

But he didn't approach her. He was engaged in conversation with Uig's councilman, also an Owl, and the room was buzzing with still-capped anticipation for the ritual and revels ahead. He turned away, then, and left a telepathic message in his wake that only confirmed he'd pursue what she'd just instigated: "Later."

The gathering went as it always did, in Demelza's twenty-some years of knowing it: they met within the central meeting hall beneath the kirk, then went out together while there was still daylight, trekking towards the Fairy Glen like any herd of single-minded sheep. Down the highway, left on the unmarked dirt road, and into the roaring windy field and hills. This place had been Demelza's beloved playground and a sacred place to the Owls of the Highlands.

It was the annual celebration of the summer solstice, a marking of time past and things to come — the Owls of the area called the gathering the Zephyr Pull. Demelza had grown up amid these seasonal events, had marked her life by them as so many had in their own parts of the world, but now that the Owl Council had come to Skye, with their brimstone-enigma leader in tow, she was more than curious.

After the long walk, they gathered beneath the caer, a twenty-foot crest of red rock nestled in the conical hills that could be climbed from behind if you were young and foolish. Rathgar took his place in front of the crowd, to deliver what Demelza imagined would be the usual opening message of Family unity, of loyalty to the burden the Owls carried in shielding all Denizens from those who would do them harm. Rathgar waited as the assembled crowd adjusted their psychic barriers to let his message in, rather than waiting for him to shout above the high gales rippling through the hills.

But when the words and images fed into Demelza's mind, her lowered guard made it feel more like a sucker punch than a reassurance. Her breath hitched as Rathgar revealed his true reason for coming.

She had heard the rumours, of course, long before this day. At first, with her usual cynical scoffing, the whole thing had sounded like a bold lark. Now that it was confirmed by Rathgar himself, by the plan he unfolded before them as a carefully drawn blueprint, there was nothing remotely amusing about it.

He was after the Moonstone.

Demelza gripped Agathe's wrist. Her cousin was controlled enough to stifle a yelp, the corner of her mouth pulling back.

"What is it?" Agathe asked, but when she took in Demelza's ashen face after Rathgar's message, she didn't need telepathy. With a quick glance at the crowd, most of whom had their eyes closed to better focus on Rathgar's broadcast, she steered Demelza towards the rock cleft just beyond the last person gathered. It was a place Demelza had often hid as a child, and when she staggered for it, Agathe said, "Go inside, calm down, put up the wall."

Demelza may have been brash and foolish, but it was a clever cover-up for the panic she sometimes felt, lying awake at night, replaying the vivid dreams she'd had ever since she was old enough to remember them. That same panic gripped her now as she crawled inside the cleft, shaking all over, pulling her long legs up to her mouth. She counted her heartbeats, built the wall around her mind brick by precious brick.

Rathgar's words echoed in her head:

The world is changing. Denizens are changing. With threats of Mundanes discovering us, with Zabor's presence still being managed in this world, and even the very cracks between Ancient's Families, we must secure the Moonstone. There are those who would wish to see it destroyed. The Stonebreakers — lawless, godless Denizens who worship the Darklings — would crack the protection that Phyr herself gave us. We must take back the control and authority that has been our duty. This Council's chief task now, and the task before this whole Family, is to find our Calamity Stone before anyone else does. To re-institute a Paramount with the control and dedication willing to lead us into the new age. It is only with the Moonstone that we might endure. That this world might endure.

Demelza had been more than foolish this day. Her bricks were steel now. Not even a flirtation could penetrate them

— especially one with a man who could undo everything. Her carefully built peace. Her outrunning of her nightmares. Because she knew where the Moonstone was, knew the cost of claiming it — on herself, and on the world. Such a blessing also provided Phyr's foresight. That stone was better off hidden, because she knew, too, exactly who it would hurt if it was unearthed.

No one must know. This had been Demelza's burden. She would bear it alone. She would endure any pain or torment, but she would never give up the stone's whereabouts. She would die first.

How had Rathgar found out about her? Maybe he hadn't — maybe he was going from enclave to enclave, personally putting out the word. Maybe she was still safe. Demelza hadn't even told her parents, no matter how many times she had screamed in her sleep and they had tried to comfort her. She couldn't risk them. Agathe was the only person she had revealed her secret to, because she was steadfast, more a sister than a cousin, and agreed that only sorrow came from becoming a stonebearer. A fate not even an enemy deserved.

He wants it for himself, Demelza thought. *He seeks power.* She didn't know anything about Rathgar, but she couldn't trust him. Or anyone. The stone had called for her and only her, this white rock that looked as though it were made of glass, with golden flecks that sparked from somewhere deep and sure.

A place only she knew. A place she would never dare go. That stone could call her all it wanted. She would not answer. And she would live as long as possible so that no one else had to.

"Hello?"

Demelza whipped her head up so fast it smashed into rock, and she groaned.

"Oh dear," said the voice, and next Demelza saw a hand reach close to her in the space. She took it, unfolding to her feet, and Solomon Rathgar smiled at her, showing no hint of discomfort at the fact they were eye level. Her considerable height had been a gawky feature she'd only just grown into, and when she straightened her back, she had a few inches to spare on him.

It made her feel slightly better about the pounding in her chest.

"Sorry to have frightened you," Rathgar said, bowing, still lightly holding her fingers. "Solomon."

Demelza reined her heart in with the sudden violence of a startled rider. Her mind, and the secrets it held, was encased in granite.

"Demelza." Her smile felt a bit wicked. Playing with this man who could be her enemy might improve her mood, at least. "And you didn't frighten me. Luckily there isn't much that does." If she told the lie convincingly enough, maybe she'd believe it herself.

She reclaimed her hand, rested both on her hips. "Thank you for deigning to come all the way up from London to our humble place of worship. I trust the accommodations aren't too rustic?"

His eyebrow quirked. Good; she wasn't going to make this easy on him. "Not at all. I come where I'm needed, and the community in Uig has been most welcoming."

Demelza's mouth pinched. "Lovely." She stepped away from him, walking back towards the crowd milling about the valley. The ice in her stomach was heavy. Agathe caught her eye, glancing frantically from Demelza to, she soon discovered, Solomon Rathgar, who was following inches at her elbow.

"I'm sorry —" he said again, and Demelza whirled when he touched her, which made him recoil. She should nip this now; flirting with him earlier had been a mistake. She couldn't afford to let her guard down, to let anything slip.

But he looked so utterly, wonderfully pathetic, less a brimstone-and-gall high priest and more a floundering moon-struck boy.

"You do apologize a lot," she remarked. "Perhaps I'm the one who's frightened you."

"Petrified, in fact," he confirmed. "But you were the one who pinged *me*, if I recall."

Damn it. "Perhaps I was aiming for the fellow behind you at the time."

He let out a sudden laugh. "Not bloody likely."

A man who knew exactly how good-looking he was, and likely accustomed to getting what he wanted. He would be difficult to shake, unless Demelza lied more sharply, said she wasn't available or interested, and that wasn't her game, either. Her face flushed, and she turned away.

"This quest of yours," she said abruptly, looking out into the gathering, which was a merry thing with music, drink starting to flow. It felt all so faraway, this peaceful life, and Demelza felt like there was no longer a time when her heart would be light. Not after tonight. "When you find the Moonstone, what will you do with it?"

Silence. Then he exhaled like he'd been holding his breath for months. "Whatever happens, Phyr will guide us. And at the very least, we will endure. The Narrative will endure."

His words were too certain. She smiled tightly as a grandmother approached, bearing whisky, and passed Demelza a tumbler and Solomon one as well before moving on.

Their eyes met. "*Sláinte*," they said in unison, and shot the lot.

The night was young and so was Demelza. Laughter floated in the air with the music, and she realized she ought to snag whatever flirtation she might have, with the time left. The moon rose. A drink and a dance, she promised herself. That would be her limit, and then she would never see this man again.

But by morning her own resolve and Agathe's warning were long faded as Demelza studied the sleeping planes of Solomon's face in the daylight streaming through her cottage window.

She knew now what had frightened her so. It was that this man, or a man so very much like him, was also in her dreams. A man, a boy, she loved more than herself though he wasn't born yet.

That boy would find the Moonstone. And it would destroy him.

❧≈

Saskia was still falling. She'd had this dream before.

A great dark hole. Barton was at the bottom of it. The hole was like a well. Now the well's walls were steel panels. Electricity arced between them. Saskia was plunging through the Apex. Someone was singing. She didn't want to hear it. She turned end over end and felt the tendons in her legs ache for solid ground, tasted acid behind her tongue.

The panels in the endless Apex's reactor flashed. Red words cascaded, following Saskia down.

Help. Help. Help us.

The walls were red. The well was full of blood. Saskia kept falling.

Then her brain kicked in, and she woke up, jolting, but her shoulders were held firmly down, and for a second it was like fighting against internal electrocution.

"Just breathe," the voice above her dictated. "You're awake. It's not real. It's just a nightmare."

But it is real, Saskia wanted to say. Knew it for a fact. But she'd have to quiet her heartbeat first before words could happen.

Saskia sat up, shoved the hands off her. She was on a bed, and she quickly got off it. "What . . . you brought me —" The single bed she'd vacated sat loose on a steel frame, pushed against a wall. Saskia backed into a curtain and yanked it down, the fight response she'd been unable to summon before surging in her blood.

"Saskia, wait," Ella said, even as Saskia found more identical beds, more curtains, ripping them all down, until she burst out into the main space of what seemed more like a dormitory than a prison. A set of stairs led up from the dark into a floor of wood beams above. There was no door in or out that she could see.

"Help!" Saskia screamed at the ceiling, but Ella was on her, hand slammed over her mouth, trying to suffocate her. This time, Saskia fought back, grabbed the hand, and twisted it backward. Ella screamed.

Saskia let go, put a few feet between them, body buzzing as she pointed. "Where am I? Why did you bring me here?"

The questions came out through her teeth as she tried to stop herself from crying. She didn't want to feel weak, but she was feeling too many things. "Maybe you don't remember I *saved* your stupid life, and this is how you . . ." She took a breath, swiped a hand over her eyes. "Just tell me the truth, Ella. Tell me *why*."

Ella cradled her hand. She was wearing different clothes, but besides the injury Saskia just gave her, she looked fine. Healthy. Not at all in danger or a participant in every awful outcome Saskia had imagined.

"I wanted to get in touch with you. Tell you everything. You know I wouldn't lie to you —"

"There's a lot of things I never thought you'd do to me. Aiding in kidnapping was pretty much the top of that list. And yet." Saskia stepped towards her, and Ella went backward. "Your aunt's pretty much had a funeral for you, you know. But I forgot how good you were at hiding. As usual, you weren't thinking of anyone but yourself."

"You should talk!" Ella barked back, and sparks came off her eyelashes. It was a semi-nervous tic that Saskia had once catalogued as precious. Now she scoffed at it. "You did everything to try to stop me. And I'm grateful. Except you went into the rat's nest and came out a rat."

"You don't know a damn thing about anything, and you never did. You're a spoiled poseur, like Dannika and those Clusterfucks —"

"Good one!" Ella snapped. Then they both stopped, Saskia remembering the way they'd been before in their relationship. That hurt more than Ella's fist in Saskia's stomach.

Ella's coiled hands at her sides loosened. "You've had all this intel about the Task Guard. Not only what they're doing, but how to stop them. And you didn't tell anyone. Scaredy Sask wants to be the hero now." Her soft expression tightened again. "You're a hypocrite."

After all this, Saskia couldn't help but laugh. "And who could I tell? Who can I trust? You're the only one I could have. And you *ran away*."

"I didn't run! The Cluster was protecting me —"

"Oh, I get it." Hands on her hips, Saskia glanced around. "We're in some Cluster safe house, right? They finally convinced you they're the rogue 'good guys' in all this." She dipped her head, squeezed her eyes with thumb and forefinger, and looked back up with solid resolve. "I'm not joining them. Or you. Whatever kind of mind-raking trick Rathgar did, he doesn't know a thing about me."

Ella didn't come any closer. "But I do," she said. "You're connected to the dark, whether you like it or not. And you can't do this alone, Sask. I came here *because* of you."

Saskia wanted to believe it. It hurt so much to look into Ella's unwavering stare and want what was once between them to still exist. Saskia had shared every secret with her. Ella had done the same. Doomed lovers from opposite sides. But no matter how much it ached, it wasn't going to go back to the way it was.

Saskia wrapped her arms around herself and stared at the ground. At least she could trust concrete. "You still haven't told me why."

This was as good a lifeline as Ella was going to get. She took it. "Open your eyes, Sask. Where do you think we are?"

A quick glance, a brief inhale. Damp, cold. "Underground. A basement. So?"

"Come on," Ella sighed, impatient. "You were literally

just here two weeks ago, snooping around. You got yourself on the Cluster's radar in the first place when you confronted Dannika and the others."

Two weeks ago? Even as Saskia squinted, trying to take a better look, the basement, illuminated by flickering light bulbs lining solid wood but worse-for-wear crossbeams, just looked like a rebel foxhole would —

Wait.

Saskia frowned as it dawned on her. "We can't be," she started. "If this is Cecelia Bettincourt's house, it'd be swarming with —"

Above, bootfalls, muffled speech, from multiple parties. Dust floated down from the loosened floorboards. Saskia jerked and nearly backed into Ella.

"Shit! We have to —"

As the footsteps came closer overhead, the room . . . changed, as if something had been tripped, like a defense mechanism. The beds disappeared. Over them, flickering like a mirage, were shelves, lockers. The makeshift dormitory faltered under the overlaid image of a massive storage room, as if the room itself had flipped over like a Prohibition speakeasy. The bootfalls lingered, the muffled voices rising and falling. Then they moved away, and when they did, the storage room faded.

Saskia was getting tired of the intimate sensation of her chest pre-explosion. She dashed away from Ella, swiping a hand through one of the last flickering stand of lockers where the bed should be. Then, like footsteps above them, it disappeared.

"It's an Owl feedback loop," she breathed, turned back to Ella. "How long has this been down here?"

Ella lifted a shoulder. "Ever since Roan left. Someone figured it might be of use, someday, so the Owls cloaked it up. This part of it, at least."

Someone. "Solomon Rathgar, then. King Backstabber himself."

Ella was never one to wait around for Saskia to get to the point. She walked past her, to the back wall of the basement. "This isn't about the good guys or the bad guys. Though the ETG is pretty bad. But there can't be sides if there's no world to fight for. The Cluster isn't really the name of some Darkling-worshipping death cult."

Saskia was about to ask the obvious, but Ella put her hand against the dirt wall, rubbing a half circle in it with a palm bordered in flame. The wall lit up. The dirt shivered and hissed away. Another hidden door.

It opened inward and down, to the dark.

"Come on," Ella beckoned, her hand still alight. "This is the place where it all started. And now, thanks to you, it's where we can all decide how it's going to end."

Ella started down, because she knew Saskia better than anyone.

And Saskia, silently cursing herself, followed.

ALL OUR PRECIOUS UNDOING

Eli sprang up with the last of his strength, nearly falling backward as the rush of this shade's — his mother's — memory left him gasping for air, drowned in her life.

She drew away, as if ashamed. "You look so much like your father," she said. "You always did."

"No." Eli shook his head, as if trying to get water out of his ears. "Stop. I can't —" Now that he had his breath back, the questions crowded his mouth. "I was a ritual conception. That's why it was just us. Solomon was never . . ." *Around. In my life. Interested in me. Wanted me.*

Or so he'd thought. But what he'd seen had been genuine attraction between his parents, organically sparked. *Love.* The word was a bitter pill.

The shade whirled and nearly broadsided Eli. "There's so much you couldn't know about me. About him. But now is my chance to fix it. I've waited here all this time. Please let me show you." She reached for him again, and that time he stood his ground, as if mid-battle.

"Don't touch me!" Confusion boiled in his chest. And terror. He hadn't had a panic attack in years, but he recognized it like a loyal dog, straining against its chain. "And you," Eli panted, the pain of the words bloody in his mouth. "*You* left, too."

She had been close, but she faltered as if he'd struck her. Her shade flickered, a strange fading luminous glow at her centre. All the shades he'd seen had never taken the shape of who they were in life. Eli couldn't trust that this was even really happening.

"I left to save you." Her voice was small. "If I was gone, then my dream couldn't infect you. Then the Moonstone would stay lost, as it deserved, and none of this would have happened."

Eli stared long and hard at the shape that had been Demelza. Tall, regal, drained, and monochrome. It had been a very long time since he'd seen her as anything but a sad memory. And at the end of her life she was as fragile as glass, her mind splintered by the very stone she refused to claim. She'd barely recognized Eli before she died.

She was the last true Paramount of the Owls. The only one in centuries who had denied a god's will. And she'd paid with her mind, her life.

"I'd have paid any price for you." Her voice was suddenly inside of him again, reading his thoughts and responding. "But you're wrong. Even at the end, *especially* then, I always knew you. I fought hard to keep the stone away and keep you close to me. Solomon begged me to tell him where the Moonstone was. It wanted to be found. It wanted it so much more when you were born, because it wanted me, it wanted *you*. I sent Solomon away. I couldn't let the Moonstone win."

Eli stood firm despite his weak, shaking legs, and stepped towards the shade. He stood eye-to-eye with her, though his head swam and blood roared in his ears.

"It won anyway. The gods always do. And whatever you have to say to me — it's too late."

Eli spun, retreating, knowing she wouldn't follow. Even his synapses burned. He hunkered down, shaking, until he let his head fall into his hands. What the hell was he supposed to do now? He had to get out of here before everything he'd shoved deep inside himself rose up, teeth snapping.

❧

Failure breeds success, I kept telling myself. I undid the sling I'd made from huge palm leaves and stiff vines I'd ripped away from willing trees. My arm was still sore, but I could extend it now at least. My first real brush with one of those monsters, about the size of a Rottweiler, and I'd lost.

Bloodbeast, the shades had called it. One shade now came up to sniff my injury, then balked. A group of Fox shades had chased the beast off; all those roars and rumbles that I'd only heard in the distance seemed less ominous the farther I trekked across the Deadland landscape. But what happened the next time, when the shades weren't there? There were stakes now. I couldn't get to Eli if I'd been ripped to pieces first.

"I'm still alive, I guess," I said out loud, rubbing my arm, more out of hope than certainty. The flesh wasn't broken but the bruise was nasty. I glanced at the movement in my peripheral and bit the inside of my cheek. Dark Me was agitated today. I hadn't seen her in a few days — what I thought were days — and had thought she'd given up on me. But she was another beast at the edge of my mind, prowling.

"You nearly got us killed," she snapped. "If you'd let me help you, this wouldn't happen. You need the garnet blade. You can't make it work without the fire. Without *me*."

I wasn't about to answer her. I looked over at the Fox shades tailing me like an entourage. I wondered if they could see or hear my id lashing out.

Then a Fox shade snapped at my heels. "Alive, yes. But barely," it said. Everyone was a critic.

"You're one to talk," I grumbled.

"You need to be faster," another yipped, bounding off before I could kick it away. I'd gotten used to them following me, creeping up to my nightly fires, lying down around the crackling light with the tensed readiness of guard dogs.

What did they have to gain from my survival? *The fire, probably*, I guessed. They wanted it back as much as I did. But as wary as I was of the Foxes, I couldn't ignore that they were right.

"I know," I conceded, looking around again for threats — for the other me. She had wandered off somewhere down a bluff, though I could still faintly hear her muttering.

I pulled the bone hilt from my back, where I'd made a strap for it. I ran my thumb over the grooves, the round-ring pommel. The sword, when it was whole, which it wasn't now, reflected me. When Sil gave it to me, it had been a short knife. When I needed to be strong, it became a sword. When I'd been infected by Seela, it turned black. And when I landed down here, it had gone cold. Maybe that was the end of it.

I inspected the empty slot, considering. When it had been a dagger, I'd cut away a part of myself, giving it to the fire, in order to learn what I was up against. Would I have to cut something else out to take my power back?

Another hand slid over mine on the sword. Dark Me had no expression on her face as she spoke. "Regret. Grief. Your mistakes. You can cut any of those out and let the fire through. Let me show you."

Then she was gone, and only my hand held the bladeless hilt in front of me.

"I don't want to pay the price of that," I said to myself.

I let my bad arm with the useless weapon go limp at my side, then snapped it up, a forward lunge. Left foot ahead, right knee bent, body tight. I know what I needed to be, but it was just out of reach.

Cut, came her voice.

"No," I said.

I held onto myself, my footing. I thought of a time when I knew even less than now, when I had someone to guide me. Sil — Cecelia — told me to listen for the drums. To dance. To use the movements of my body to balance and temper my fire, because if I couldn't control it, it could destroy everything.

I listened for the drums now, even if they were just my heartbeat. I slid my feet, turned. The sword hilt may have been empty, but I wasn't. I swung down, thrust out, wheeled. Dancing like this made me warmer. Made me feel like coming home, to a home I'd never had.

The other me said no more. I thought I'd tuned her out. I felt her smile when I thought of Sil, but something was happening, exploring these sensations attached to Sil. We were in the summoning chamber, training. Then there she was, fox warrior form punctured by Zabor's thrashing tail. Then she was leaving me the Opal, and all her mistakes to clean up.

I did feel warm then. Warm and angry. I couldn't help it. My movements became tighter, more erratic, and I sliced downward as I remembered myself taking that bloody stone, thinking I could solve everything, save everyone, and all I wanted to do was go back, and tell them all *no* —

Something inside me snapped.

A flash at the edge of the hilt. A little fire. I tripped over myself and dropped it, staring at my hands.

The Fox shades yipped, bounding and sniffing the empty hilt in the ferns just crushed by my feet. They looked up at me, and I was alarmed at the expectant wonder in their dead eyes.

I raised my hand. Warmth flickered inside my wrist, then wound around my index finger as a flame the size of a leaf. At the edge of the firelight, before it went out, was the other me. She was still smiling.

Then she was gone, and I knew, and somehow was afraid, that I wasn't going to see her again.

I picked up the hilt in the ferns. It was warm. I frowned at it, then at the shades.

"What was I saying?" I asked them. They cocked their heads, as if listening for some truth I'd let go of.

Orange light crept up through the cracks in the hilt, and flashing at the end of it was a purple blade, as long as my arm. A deadly shard of garnet.

"I'm still alive," I repeated. The ground heaved, the shades hunkering down around me, snarling, protective. The fire was there inside me, and it felt closer to the surface.

Whatever drums I'd heard had faded but weren't gone. I felt renewed.

"What are you looking for out here?" one of the shades asked, looking for direction. They all were now.

"My friend," I said, though I was mesmerized by my reflection in the blade. The absence of drums left words pounding in my skull.

Home. *Home.*

Stay focused, Harken, a voice said. A man's voice. Someone I knew once . . . I took a long breath, standing tall, tightened, ready.

"Let's go," I said to the shades, breaking through them and knowing they would follow.

Find Eli, something weak inside ordered me.

The trouble was, even as I put one foot in front of the other, I was having a hard time holding onto who that was, exactly.

❧

Eli went inside his own head but didn't sleep. He wanted to understand.

There wasn't peace there. He was skittering across time, leaping in and out of his memories in much the same way he had with Roan inside the Dragon Opal. He was a boy on a Scottish shore, screaming with grief into an empty horizon. The storm his grief had caused had nearly taken apart coastal villages. That was when Solomon arrived. That was when he'd been tricked.

"You're special, Eli." Suddenly Solomon was behind him in a mirror, his hands on Eli's small shoulders, awkward in the uniform of the Rookery, the Owl boarding school and training grounds in the remote Eurasian mountains. Eli was nine. He'd barely said a word since he'd left Aunt Agathe, and Skye, long behind.

"Together we will do great things. We will find the Moonstone. We will change the world. That is your mother's legacy."

Eli looked up at his father's face. Really studied it at the mention of Demelza. When he looked back in the mirror, Eli was twenty-five, haggard, inches from death, and still reeling from the memory of his parents' meeting. Bludgeoned by that force of their instant love.

He knew he'd never see his father again, the proud force of nature he'd always resented. Now he couldn't even hold on to that rage, despite everything. Maybe his father had believed all along that finding the Moonstone would save them. Maybe he thought he could protect Demelza, too, before she took her own life.

"We did change the world," Eli said to his father's sad reflection, but now he was back within his present body, blinking up into the paralyzed sky.

He was stiff, aching, but he didn't want to stand just yet. The rustle of wings confirmed the air was full of shades, wheeling here and there, but they didn't attack him. Instead he watched as their spectral talons released berries and foreign-looking plants, wizened roots, beside him in a veritable cornucopia. A few whacked him in the face, probably on purpose, and he scowled.

Then they swooped away, towards a flickering out-stretched hand. Demelza had her back to Eli, seated at the edge of the rock on the other side of their remote island in the sky. The shades seemed intent on paying her a gentle, respectful homage before vanishing to their hiding places.

She'd led him here for a reason. Neither of them was going anywhere anytime soon. They might as well talk.

"You control them," Eli said, voice so gravelly he barely heard it himself. He nudged the shades' leavings with his knuckle — food, he surmised — and plucked a berry to examine it, stomach tightening apprehensively at the prospect. Something about Persephone twigged at the place his education was stored, but he was already long doomed. He'd been eating whatever he could find already.

"There's no control involved," Demelza corrected. "Only respect. I'm a shade, just like them. But I refused the stone. They still remember that."

Eli snorted, chewing the strange fruit carefully. "A feat indeed."

His cruel words, unlike the fruit, were bitter, but he didn't retract them. Demelza wasn't better than him, or a saint, it turned out. When he swallowed, he noticed she had turned in profile, patting the space beside her.

Eli scooped up some roots, stood stiffly, and joined her.

"This world *has* changed," Demelza said, as if picking up the threads of an abandoned conversation. "They all did. You succeeded, in a way."

Eli's forehead knit mid-chew on a root that was more like jerky. "This world isn't exactly the one we were aiming for."

"No," she answered. "I'm not sure you can find what you're looking for here, or go back to where you came from. There's an imbalance now. Down there" — she pointed — "those realms haven't been one since the world was young. This new world you've made is your only concern now. As for the Uplands, they're lost to me, to all of the dead. Which means it's lost to you."

Eli stilled. "Define *lost*."

She tilted her head at him, more Owl than woman. "You've seen it, below. The realms have shattered from the inside out. Remember how the realms work. What is the Veil?"

Eli rolled his eyes; as if he needed the lesson. "The Veil is the in-between. A threshold. You can access it through visions, through Paramount connections. But ultimately, it's like a hallway between the living world and a Denizen's ancestral resting place. If a spirit wishes to return to the Uplands for another life, they can use the same channel."

He felt her nod. "Now take away the Veil. What happens?"

Eli looked out past the brink. Into nothing. There was no wind. "The dead can't get here or reincarnate," he said quietly, remembering the former Paramount who had confronted him on the way up here. "So not even the Moth Queen can do anything about this?"

"No." Demelza spread her hand over the ruined, faraway land beneath them. "When the Bloodlands rose and the Darklings broke free, they cauterized the world behind them. It happened when the stones came together. When they broke. And with the gods gone, it's anyone's country."

The root Eli had chewed went down like a piece of glass. No way out. A wrench shoved in the spokes of what all the lore called "the wheel." The Narrative. The unmoving stars above made some sense now. Eli slid a star-shaped leaf between his teeth and tried to silence the inner screaming.

"Well," he said. "Sometimes the only way out is through."

Demelza smiled. "You may look like Solomon, but you're as reckless as I was."

"I was never a patient person." Eli swung his legs over the ledge, admiring the thrill of the emptiness flaring into his knees. He wondered if Roan had figured out any of this yet. He'd have to bother her about it, when he found her. "It's a long way down."

"Without wings, it's an eternity," she agreed, glancing sidelong at him. "I know you're worried about the girl. And you should be."

Eli curled his lip. "Stay out of my head. You're still a stranger."

"Proving my point." Demelza lifted a shoulder. "The dead have very little power left to them. If *I* can easily read you, you'll be dead, too, before you jump."

Eli's temper rose, and he fought to keep his hand clenched beside him; it still hurt. "The Moonstone is gone. It took my power with it."

The cool touch of Demelza's spectral hand made him flinch, but it freed him from the mental briar in which he was tangled. "You had power before the stone," she reminded him. "So did she, your Fox friend. And she's down there now, fighting with what she has at hand to survive." Demelza's face lacked true clarity, though Eli couldn't help but think she looked perplexed. "Finding you is the singular purpose keeping her going, but she's . . . slipping."

Eli's eyes stung, but he wouldn't look at her. "Then I can't stay here any longer."

Demelza peered at him, into him, and he couldn't keep her out. "How will you help her like this? How will you help anyone? A lifetime of grief and guilt is preventing both of you from moving forward. You'll have to meet your mistakes head on if you're going to finish what you started. I can show you how. You remember what I showed you once?"

Eli looked down below again. Her hand had reached for him again, then dropped.

"I remember," he admitted after a while. Before Demelza had become so ill, she'd go into Eli's mind as a child, when he was frightened, when he was unsure, and she would send him a thread of golden reassurance. He'd shown Roan this. She was the only one he'd shown.

He felt Demelza smile, and it annoyed him like she'd invaded his room. "You're partway there. But there's more to healing than a Band-Aid solution."

"I don't have time for faux soul-searching." Eli stood up abruptly, no matter that it pained him, and felt his vertebrae pop like corn kernels. "I've been accused of killing gods and making that mess down there. And I'm tired of this view."

Demelza became blurry around the edges. "Fine."

"Fine what?"

Suddenly she was flickering, then beside him, her voice biting. "Jump then. If you're so sure you'll make it."

Eli glanced down, took a step to prove he was serious. But he scrambled for purchase when Demelza's frigid hand found the back of his neck, clamped tight and pushing.

"Go on," she said.

Eli's feet caught, and he pushed back against her. "What are you —"

"It's easy," she said in his ear, a calming hiss. "Just jump, and you can forget everything that brought you here. You'll be free from your obligations, your failures. Your guilt."

Just as he felt his feet slip over the edge, his heart plummeting in near-death panic, she yanked him back and threw him skidding to level ground.

"What the hell do you want from me!" Eli screamed, staggering to stand, to charge, but her shade was fierce and slammed into him like a battering ram.

"The only person holding you back is yourself," she roared, and Eli pressed his hands to his ears, crying out. "You have to clear it all away. It's the only way ahead for both of you. If you deny yourself peace, you have none for anyone else."

Demelza's voice was a gale, and a rush of sensations, images, flashed in front of Eli like warning lights — the storm on Skye, his inability to save his mother, the Zephyr Trials where he first learned how to betray anyone in his way to power. The finding of the Moonstone. The battle of Zabor. The shattering of the Calamity Stones.

And his hand, on the back of Roan Harken's neck, holding her defeated body over the Assiniboine River.

It was too much. He had ruined too many things. Eli shook his head violently, refusing to fall again, solid on his feet. He willed the images to go away, because he knew he couldn't change them, that they never would truly be gone. And with that recognition, they folded themselves up neatly, sliding into drawers that had their locks busted off. Drawers that were meant, sometimes, to be opened.

His vision cleared. He took a breath. Something wet was on the front of his face, getting into his mouth. His fingers came away red, and he scowled.

"Good," Demelza said, and Eli turned. She was smiling, tapping her temple, and sitting cross-legged with her back to the great emptiness. "You have the insight, Eli. You don't want grief to hunt you. But you have to do the work."

Eli wiped his nose on his sleeve, partially heartened that he still had blood inside him. "And then what?"

Demelza tipped her face towards the sky. "Who can say? You can't build peace outside without finding it in yourself first."

It was painfully saccharine. Everything in him tensed against it. *Peace*. Maybe not outside. Not yet. But inside. *Clear it all away*, she'd said. It had felt so seductive, so many times, when he'd been offered his out. Had Roan been offered the same? Whatever help she needed, he couldn't give it to her in his present state.

But first he would have to sort those drawers. To break off the rest of the locks and carefully consider the contents. He had to be all right with outcomes he would never be able to change and things he couldn't just cut away.

After a while, Eli sat down in front of his mother, carefully crossing his legs. "How long will this take?"

She stared pointedly back at him. Her eyes were the same shimmering coins of the other shaded dead. He had a feeling the time to talk was over.

Eli's mind was weak. Demelza could send hers out and watch Roan's progress, but he couldn't. Not yet. In the meantime, he just had to trust Roan would be all right for a little while longer. She'd have to be. *Just hold on*, he sent the thought away on a line, cast into the gloom. *Don't bloody give in*.

To Demelza, he thought, *Let's begin*, and went into the first drawer.

Another night, another fire. I had taken off my hoodie, tearing it up into strips. I'd been warmer lately, now that the fire was coming back. I wouldn't need the hoodie as it was, even in the night-cold. It needed to serve a new purpose. Making it smaller, into shreds, each one suited to a better use, was like making a new skin. Like moving laterally into an actual tomorrow.

I laid each strip beside me in a pile. I would use them to bind my feet up, bloody and blistered since my shoes had finally worn through. I would build calluses. I wouldn't need these makeshift shoes soon, either.

I stopped, mid-tear, the fire bending towards me, magnetic. I suddenly felt like I'd forgotten something very important. Like something, other than my clothes, had left me. I saw a flash of gold in my memory, but it winked out.

Don't bloody —

The fire crackled. Just embers then.

The night air filled with snarls and yips. The garnet blade reflected the fire's light in elegant crimson beside me. Today the blade had been smeared with black blood, but I'd burned it away. Things came out of this country with teeth snapping, like today's beast — six legs. Jagged antlers like spears. Its guts were a halo on the ground, the drumbeats a stampede, and by the time I was through dancing, I was elbow deep in gore. I'd washed it from my hoodie's sleeves, but it wasn't enough. That's when I knew my hoodie had to become something different.

I'd gladly use the blade tonight, and every night, if I had to.

The snarling persisted and I got up. I didn't have to go far. Even in the dark I could pick out the shapes of shades, the way they rippled as real dark didn't. Their pinprick eyes made them obvious.

Target practice would be good. I threw my hand up and threw down a lob of fire, sending the shades scattering.

"Hunt quieter and somewhere else," I barked at them.

Four Fox shades levelled their heads and snarled at me, but they didn't advance. Where they had been, there was still one shade left behind, cowering. It didn't flee either when I approached it, but it raised its shivering head, huge ears unfurling. A Rabbit.

"So the dead hunt the dead now?" I asked, not much expecting an answer. The Rabbit leapt up and shimmered behind my ankles. The Foxes' mouths were open, chirping from the backs of their throats.

"They do it only for sport, mistress," said the cowering Rabbit, as if defending its attackers. Then its shadow-fur stood on end. "But sometimes, hunted shades become corrupted Bloodbeasts."

"This one has been following us for days," said a Fox, head bobbing.

"If you do turn, then our mistress can burn you in half!" brayed another. The others laughed like their distant cousins, hyenas. I shot another handful of flame, rained cinders on them, and they scattered.

"Idiots," I muttered. Then I turned, noticing the Rabbit was up on its dark haunches, peering up at me. "I'm sorry about them. Everything's messed up around here."

The Rabbit tilted its head, almost shrugging. "It is in their nature to chase. It is in mine to run. We like to adhere to the memory of a natural order."

I sniffed. Not knowing what else to do, I started walking back to the fire. By the time I sat back down to finish dismantling my clothes, the Rabbit was at the edge of the light, pressed between a rock and a tree.

I didn't look up. "Do you have a name?"

I saw the shadow of a giant ear flop, then snap back. "Baskar." A log collapsed inside the fire and crackled. Sparks filled the air. "They were right. I have been following. But I follow for the same reason they do. You have a touch of death about you."

I glanced over at the shade. They were looking right at me. "I've avoided it a few times."

They shook their head. "Not that. You carry it, like a mark. It is in your way of seeing." They looked back in the direction the Foxes had fled. "It is what draws us to you. Makes us trust you as one of us."

A mark. I touched my left cheekbone. *Spirit eye*. The name lingered like déjà vu. I shrugged, slipped my shoes off, and took a good look at my ruined, blistered feet. "You know a lot, don't you, Baskar?"

The Rabbit crept closer, keeping their distance from the flame. I admired the care they took. "Don't worry," I said. "I won't let the fire hurt you. It's a part of me."

Baskar pressed against my leg; I felt a faint coolness from their body, but it was welcome. Companionable.

"Many of us have been here a long time. Many of us find that the things we already knew aren't worth knowing any longer." Baskar tipped their head up to me. "You carry death, but you're not dead. Can you tell me . . . a story from your living world?"

I looked from Baskar into the fire. I squinted. The words

were ready, my mouth was open, but nothing came out. Inside my head, I heard someone laugh, felt that absence like a continental shift, but thought, *Sometimes, it's better to burn the grief away. Remember it, then let it go.*

"I think I can tell you something," I said, unsure. "A story about a girl I once knew."

The Foxes that had chased Baskar had returned, drawn to the fire. Blank but loyal, attentive. I felt like one of them.

"Once upon a time, a fox followed a girl home. The girl was marked by Death. Death gave the girl to the fox, on one condition: she must banish a snake. To do this, she needed a rabbit, a deer, an owl, and a seal. They all did this thing, and they won. The snake wasn't satisfied with its prison and sent its child to get revenge. The child infected other children. All this child wanted was a family. The fox girl was separated from her friends. They all went on a journey. They needed the hearts of the ones all the animals came from. If they couldn't do this, the snake, and its siblings, would take the world away. When they gathered the hearts, it would wake up a sleeping giant, and the giant would save them all."

I stopped. I hadn't realized that there were tears on my face, until my fingers came away wet. I didn't feel sad. I didn't feel anything.

"What happened then?" Baskar breathed, little paws cool on my knee. "Did they wake the giant? Is the world still there?"

I looked at the tears, heard my own voice echoing the story I'd just told as I thought it through. I knew it was my story. I knew . . . I thought . . . I felt suddenly like I was weakly grasping for something, and its trailing threads were slipping through my fingers. That story. The certainty of it. Where had I heard it before? It couldn't be mine. My story . . . what was it, again?

"I don't remember," I said, the moisture on my fingertips hissing away into hot mist. Then I shrugged, because I didn't feel anything but calm. "I guess it doesn't matter if I do. It's just a story."

I looked out into the bleak black woods, feeling as blank as a clean slate inside. "I think I'll write a story of my own."

The UNSEALED CHAMBER

After she had stepped off the Cold Road and back into Winnipeg, Natti spent the night in the basement of an old North End subdivision, a place she'd been pointed to for unregistered Denizens. From what she'd gathered from the other squatters sharing the dank, ETG-defiant accommodations, things in Winnipeg were worse off than she thought.

The chancellor was in and out of the city, but he always came back like a bat to roost. It seemed he'd set up shop in the Old Leg and wasn't intent on going away long without finishing his work here. Whatever that was. There was word that some machine had picked something up from the Darkling Moon. Or was it from the place where the Darklings came from? It didn't matter. Truth was thinner on the ground than the people Natti could trust. Everyone was scared, though, Mundanes and Denizens alike. The ETG presence had swollen. Natti had originally thought to go

239

looking for Seneca, an Owl who usually had some answers. But he was nowhere; either gone to ground or arrested. The chancellor had left town for some United Nations briefings, according to local news, so now would be her chance to act.

There was one last person she could go to, though she'd put it off all this time.

Natti wasn't kidding herself anymore. She couldn't do anything alone. She was barely convinced of this as she walked closer to One Evergreen, looming desolate on the other side of the bridge. She never answered Phae's only letter from years ago — better late than never.

⁀⋙⋘⁀

"She's just doing it to piss me off," Phae said, pacing the living room. Jet watched her progress, and she felt each step dig a trench into the carpet, one they were all about to fall into. Phae's arms were crushed into her body, jaw rigid. She was a fuse ready to go off with no flame.

"But what if she's not?" Jet said quietly. "What if the Moth Queen led her somewhere and she can't come home?"

Phae stopped at that, considering the little boy seriously. "Jet," she said gently. He wasn't old enough yet to know how to be direct, but he clearly wanted to help. And he knew something she didn't. "Do you know where Saskia is?"

He screwed his eyes shut, mouth twisted. Then his face loosened, and he sighed. "I dunno. I'd have to go out and look properly. Who's that man that Saskia talked about? Mr. Rath? He'd know."

Jordan *had* said Jet had much more potential than anyone would have the time to wrangle. Phae always worried she was doing him a disservice with no good Owl role models around. Though those had always been few and far between . . .

"Solomon Rathgar," she said, keeping her voice even. When Saskia had come home from her first day, she was obviously shaken but too proud to admit that anything was under her skin. Not to the other kids. Victor and Cara and Lily ate up her quietly told accounts of her new job. Saskia wasn't exactly pushing their praise away, either.

"You're just full of surprises, Scaredy Sask," Victor had grinned. "First you get arrested, then you take this job. You must really be crazy."

"If I was," she'd said curtly, "they would've known immediately. They screen your thoughts and intentions. With an Owl." She'd spread her arms like a showman, the better to get a look at her uniform. "Guess I passed."

Lily and Cara had *ooh*ed. Phae had just come in from the fifth floor, where Mr. Cole, a Rabbit, was in shambles after his daughter, Dannika, had disappeared. How many more house calls like this was Phae going to make before she snapped? She was already tightly strung, and Saskia's attitude had been the last straw.

"What was the Owl's name?" Phae asked, the little gathering whipping their heads guiltily towards her. "It wasn't Solomon Rathgar, by any chance?"

Saskia didn't blink, just bit her lip and stood up. Classic escape procedure.

"If you've got any brains left, you'll at least stay out of his way," Phae warned. "He's powerful, and a Denizen traitor. He'll try to get into your head and convince you of things you'd never agree to in your right mind." Her mouth twisted.

"Barton could tell you all about *that*. But your employers took him away. You already knew that, though."

The air of whimsy and espionage in the room died before Saskia had left it. Phae was still so angry at her. But who was to blame for the way things had turned out?

Now Phae realized she had been so busy helping everyone else that in her grief she'd let Saskia suffer, calling it collateral for her own ill choices. *If I have to live with my mistakes, she should, too.* But blame wasn't in a guardian's wheelhouse. Barton wouldn't have blamed Saskia. Neither would Roan, for all her extremes.

Phae hoped it wasn't too late.

She slipped on her coat then grabbed Jet's and held it out for him. "If Solomon's involved, then Saskia may be in trouble. And we had better start looking."

Jet's face lit up with something Phae hadn't seen in it before. "Really? Me?"

Her hand was on the door handle, and despite the urgency, she couldn't help grin. "Yes, you. C'mon."

She opened the door and nearly walked into a brick wall. Well. Just a person who'd always seemed as solid as one, hand poised to knock, and just as surprised as Phae.

"Ah," Natti said. "Good, uh, timing."

Phae stared. The dark blue shapes of the tattoos arced over Natti's stern brow, the double lines from chin to mouth. The tattoos weren't what shocked her, of course, but the person who bore them. That she was really, truly here.

Natti backed up, then rubbed her neck.

"Look, I know this is a long time coming," she started, "and you have every right to not —"

Natti gasped with the force of Phae's arms around her middle.

"Oh," Natti wheezed. Phae had already pulled away, and Natti had been too stunned to hug her back, anyway.

Jet was tugging on Natti's jacket. "We're getting the old team back together, aren't we?"

Phae pursed her lips, tried not to get queasy with nostalgia.

Natti cut in before that could happen. "Why? What's up?"

"Saskia's missing," Phae said as she glanced about the hallway. Ella's aunt's place was remarkably silent. The ETG might have been here recently to haul her away to some therapy facility or another. They might still be around. "She, um, went to work yesterday but didn't come home . . ." She was going to say more, give more context, but how could she with Natti, after so many —

"All right," Natti nodded. "Let's go."

Phae startled. "You don't have to. It's . . . it's my fault, and you're probably busy —"

"Why do you think I came over here?" Natti asked, the hint of a grin coming up. "Did I really do that much of a number on you?"

"There's no *time*!" Jet stomped. He slapped a pair of goggles over his eyes, with all the seriousness such a costume-addition could afford. "If you guys won't get moving, I'll find her on my own." He beelined for the stairs and Phae exhaled sharply.

Then a hand was clenching her shoulder, the force behind it saying all the things Phae really needed to hear.

"We've got our marching orders," Natti said. "We can make awkward small talk on the way."

As Saskia followed Ella down and down, she stared into the flame cupped in Ella's outstretched hand and thought of Jet.

"So the Cluster is bad?" he'd asked Saskia.

Saskia frowned over the metal plate she'd just screwed into place. It was when she was working on the ETG disruptor as a kind of calm-down hobby, not yet engaging her skills in military espionage. Jet was digging through Saskia's milk crates.

She'd wanted to get her point across in a way he'd understand, but she didn't want to lie to him, either. "Do you know the difference between good and bad, Brain?"

He shrugged, yanking a motherboard and a spark plug free from a wire tangle. He was about to launch into a game of pirate ships on the sea of her bedroom carpet.

"Bad people hurt people," Saskia said slowly. "The Cluster hasn't hurt anyone yet, as far as we know. They just believe that the Darkling Moon speaks to them, and that what it has to say is important."

The little spark plug stopped pre-collision with a keyboard iceberg. "But the Darklings are bad. *They* hurt people."

Saskia was about to agree — she had direct experience with them, after all — but she stopped herself. The Darklings had destroyed things, but it was, after all, Denizens who put their own people directly in Zabor's path. Then again, Seela had swept the continents with forests of victims — kind of hard to push *that* aside . . . except that some of those motivations were guided by Killian's own beliefs, and he was a Denizen, too . . .

Saskia didn't have the answers, but she didn't say any of

this to Jet, and she'd kept it firmly behind her mental wall. He'd already moved on, anyway. "And the Task Guard?" he asked.

"Bad," Saskia said immediately. "Super bad." Though now she thought of Cam. Nothing was black and white after all, just ETG grey . . .

Jet had moved on from pirate ships, building a little 2D sculpture on the floor out of coloured wire bits. "They hurt people. They hurt Barton."

"Yes." The picture on the carpet took the shape of a rabbit with lopsided ears.

"Barton tried to help people. When there were trees all over, he set lots of people free. He was a hero."

Saskia had turned away, body itching with a feeling that might never go away. "Yes," she said. Barton had been born a Denizen but had to walk a hard road to reclaim his power. He'd only ever used it to help people. To Saskia, he'd seemed unbreakable.

Then Jet had swept his hand through his picture of wire, scattering the pieces and the conversation, announcing he was hungry. Life went on, but the grief stayed put.

Maybe, if she just had a little more time, she could connect with Barton again. Maybe, at the end of all this, she could stab grief in the face.

Saskia wished she still lived in a world where things were simple, where light fought dark and always conquered it. But how could Saskia fight the dark if she was part of it? Someone down here better have some answers. Or, even better, a way through the mess she'd done a pretty great job of getting into.

"Am I about to become some ritual sacrifice, or what?" Saskia quipped, counting the stairs to keep her mind focused on something other than how close Ella was. She'd been holding on to her shoulder, since the stairs curved down and were unevenly spaced, as if they'd been carved out of the earth. She resented needing her help.

Ella snorted. "Sorry. Bloodletting is on weekends."

Ella glanced over her shoulder and stopped them just as they reached level ground. "It's broken between us, isn't it?" she asked softly.

There was so much Saskia wanted to say, to do, but ahead of them, the chamber glowed with electric light, and it was full of strange, hungry faces. Now was not the time. It probably never would be.

"I'm sorry," Saskia said, though she was pretty sure it wasn't her fault this time.

Saskia left Ella behind and stepped into the room, feeling raw as an infected tooth. The man standing in the centre of the room was not Solomon Rathgar; he was off to the side, seated. Nearby, Saskia was surprised to see Amanda, Josh, and Dannika, who was shivering, looking worse for wear after that river hunter bite. Miraculously she still looked semi-human, though she crouched just out of the light, avoiding it. Maybe not long now.

Amongst the familiar faces were many strangers. Grown adults, some as old or older than Solomon. Because she didn't recognize them, Saskia couldn't tell if they were Denizen or Mundane, but then she remembered that *the Cluster welcomes all*. She did know, then, that they couldn't be trusted, whoever they were.

Saskia would've stepped closer to the man standing in the centre of the room, but rubbed into the black granite of the floor around him were red rings Saskia wanted nothing to do with, when it came down to it.

"Thank you for coming," the man said. His voice was soft, almost meek.

Saskia's jaw clenched. "Like I had a choice. You kidnapped me."

The man glanced sideways to Solomon, who sighed. "You passed out," he said. "We weren't about to leave you under a bridge."

"You *made me* pass out!" she shouted back. The strangers in the room seemed to tense at her outburst. She turned again to the man in the centre of the room, scrutinizing him. "You must be the famous priest, then? What do you want from me?"

He shut his eyes, seeming to collect himself. Was he a Denizen? Or just a Mundane heretic? The other people crowded in the chamber seemed keen on listening and waiting. The priest's followers. But this was Cecelia Bettincourt's summoning chamber. The place where Roan Harken learned what was ahead of her, even if she didn't know what she'd have to give up to get there. What right did any of them have to occupy such a sacred place?

Saskia's eyes darted to those red rings at the priest's feet. They weren't glowing. They couldn't call the Darklings down. Could they? She'd been joking about the sacrifice thing, but now she wasn't so sure. Ella took her place at the wall with the others, to watch. Saskia started to sweat.

"You've been blessed," said the priest with the soft voice. His hands spread. "The Darklings spoke to you, long before they went on the move. Solomon saw a fragment of your past with them, and the burden you now bear, and was concerned for your well-being."

"Concerned?" Saskia snorted, pointing at Solomon. "That man's only concern is self-preservation. He's head of the Owl Unit, but he's also working with the Cluster? None of you know anything about the Darklings. What they're like. Not one of you *knows* anything." She made sure to address the whole room with that. "Whatever you want me for, I'm not doing it. You can kill me first."

"We didn't invite you here to kill you." The man's eyes flickered about the room, as if expecting someone else to interject. "You're young, but you know more than the rest of us. We want to learn from your blessings. Your gifts. The song that is inside you."

Saskia was still. So, not execution, then. She had to try reason, even if just for herself. "I don't know what I've been hearing," she started. "How is it connected to the signal the Task Guard is making us work on?"

Solomon stood up, all eyes of the room following his painful movements. But he, too, did not seem interested in crossing over the red threshold surrounding the priest. "The transmission was picked up via the Apex, through one of its many tests. Whatever it is, the powers that be believe it's the missing piece. If they can interpret it, lock onto its location across dimensions, they can apply it to Project Crossover —"

"And they can open their Bloodgate," Saskia finished. "I know. I work there."

"The old-fashioned way no longer works, you see," the priest added, interrupting her with quick flicks of his hands, movements that Barton had shown Saskia once, when he told her what was involved for a Rabbit neutralizer to open these infernal doorways.

Saskia cocked an eyebrow at him. "You're a Rabbit, then?"

The priest's hands stilled, falling slow as snow to his sides. "Not anymore."

Saskia squinted, but she needed more to go on. "So what? I already knew all that. About Project Crossover. But what I can't get past is *why* Grant wants to open a Bloodgate at all. What's he expect to get out of that?"

Solomon sneered. "What do most people dig holes for? To *bury* something."

The sweat at the back of Saskia's neck froze. "He wants to send Denizens . . . to the other side?"

"The moon!" Dannika was still shaking all over, as Amanda tried to keep her from thrashing. "The moon will stop all of this!"

The priest turned away, troubled. "The Darkling Moon's movement means something. It wills the Bloodgate to open. The Narrative demands it. The Cluster exists to observe the consequences Denizens and Mundanes have wrought."

"Observe and do nothing?" Saskia flared, absolutely done with the empty rhetoric. "Then what do you want with me?"

The priest opened his hand. "Step into the circle and find out."

~≈~

The trek from Osborne Village to Wellington Crescent was not a long one, but long enough. Silence stretched between Phae and Natti, and once Jet's little legs got tired from parkouring heroically, he, too, was focused on the task ahead of them.

Natti's tattoos, her very presence, drew stares from pedestrians, and from Task Guard soldiers. She hadn't been stopped — yet. Natti just grinned beatifically at them all.

"Don't provoke them," Phae muttered, eyes on the pavement. Natti ignored her as they went past the all-girls' school on the corner, waiting at the Maryland Bridge intersection to cross directly onto the crescent.

"Phew. Still ritzy." Natti blew out her cheeks as they came towards the mansions, immaculately kept even in times like these. Phae noticed that, somehow, the iron fences around them all had climbed higher. "Shame about the property value. I hear it's gone down due to, you know . . . monsters."

Phae stared straight ahead, but the corner of her lip quirked. "The river was a hazard before we knew there were monsters in it." Then, before they could progress farther, her arm shot out, and Natti walked into it, grunting.

"Jet," Phae said, calling him away from looking into one of the grand yards. He hurried over, his usually dour face flushed with excitement beneath a toque that was too big for him. Gods, he looked *happy* for once.

She tweaked his nose. "Remember what Jordan taught you? About hiding?"

Jet's face brightened tenfold. "Are we going to hide together?"

Phae nodded, straightening. "You said you felt that Saskia was nearby . . . I have an idea where." She threw a long look down the winding street. "But we wouldn't want to be spotted on the way there."

"You're right. I've seen how many Owl Units are just on the streets. Better to cover our tracks anyway." Natti scowled, hands on her hips. "Never pictured Winnipeg to be regime-central, honestly, but best to work around it."

Phae looked to her friend . . . former friend. She wasn't sure which. It had been a long trek, and Jet had provided an ample buffer in the awkward silences, but they stretched on when he became preoccupied. Seven years had made Natti harder, tougher. Stronger. Phae wished she could draw some of that strength for herself.

"Saskia is always on my case for not doing enough," Phae said suddenly, her internal conversation spilling out. "She wants me to be the hero I used to be. But she barely knew me then, and by the time she did, all the heroic stuff was Barton's area, not mine." She pressed her arms into her body. "I'm afraid it's too late to do anything now that'll matter."

Natti turned, a surprised look on her face. "Saskia is just a kid . . ." she started, then backpedalled, as if remembering exactly how Saskia had crossed all their paths. "Well. I guess we all were kids, once. Now look where we are."

Phae just sighed. "Remember when things were . . . not this?"

Natti shrugged. "I remember that when two polar bears showed up in my living room, you were there like a shot."

Phae was slightly appalled at how quickly the tears gathered. "We'd been through a lot. You needed me. That's what friends do."

"You're right." The hand on the shoulder, squeezing. "We've also lost a lot. I'm not interested in losing anything else today, are you?"

Phae swiped her hand over her eyes. "No. Never again."

"And as far as it being too late, c'mon. Even when all the brickwork is coming down around us, we'll still have at least a few seconds. Then we can talk about too late."

Natti opened her arms, hesitantly, but Phae went into them like there was nowhere else to go.

"I'm sorry for being such an asshole," Natti said gruffly.

"I'm sorry for not being brave enough to call you on it."

"That's really nice," Jet was saying, sitting on a bench and twirling a dry stick in front of his face, "but can we get to the rescuing part?"

Phae and Natti shyly disengaged, laughed, and let out a collective sigh. "So where exactly are we headed?" Natti asked.

Phae looked long up the street. Behind her was her old high school, where Saskia went now, transformed into a bizarro nightmare with its high walls and Task Guard brainwashing. So much had changed. But the regime couldn't reach inside of them and change what had made them. Roan had reclaimed her family's legacy up this street. She'd found the dead girl. She'd been followed home by a fox and marked by a moth. It seemed like things were replaying themselves, and Phae was more than willing to pick up those threads, to actively choose to see this through. Phae, after all, had made a choice to become a Deer, and to confront Fia in the Glen. Doing nothing in the intervening years hadn't exactly worked out for her.

It was time to do it Roan's way.

"We're going back to where it all started," Phae said. "Then you can get creative. After all, the river's nearby. And you've flooded that house before."

Recognition made Natti's body visibly relax, and she cracked her knuckles. "I was fairly certain we'd be skirting around old times," she said, "not recreating them. But I'm game if you are."

Phae revelled, for the first time in a long time, as her hair undid itself from its braid, snaking up her head, forming its antlers, sparking blue. Jet made them all invisible, and they were off.

At least the old standards were always reliable.

A Risk Worth Taking

Saskia backed up, then stopped, looking to Solomon Rathgar. In that white room underneath the Old Leg, he'd had his crown, his limitations. Here, in the summoning chamber underneath Cecelia's reclaimed house, he could do whatever he wanted with his powerful mind. The priest stood in the middle of the circle, waiting for Saskia to join him. They all waited for her to decide.

"Even if I say no, are you going to make me?"

The priest considered her, then let out a breath. "No. If it is willed, then it will happen."

"That's not how any of this works!" Saskia, despite logic, was moving towards the priest now. "It was never about pre-destiny. Don't you get it? It's about making a choice. It's about doing *something* and accepting what happens after. No one controls me. No one tells me what to do!" She stopped, without looking down, at the edge of the red mark.

The priest had been perfectly still. "But the Moth Queen does."

Saskia sucked in a breath, turned and looked for Ella, then to Solomon, then back to the priest. "Death just wants back what was hers. She wants to help Denizens. What do *you* want?" She chewed her lip, not wanting to let slip her own reasons for opening that door, to save the one person on the other side whose cry for help she couldn't get out of her head. "I just want things to go back to the way they were before."

Solomon stood close by and Saskia couldn't really parse the look on his face with everything swimming there, but his expression was determined. "We want the Bloodgate open, yes. But we have our own reasons. We want to save Denizens, too. We can't stop the Darklings from exacting their purpose. But Ancient can."

"What?" Saskia blurted.

The priest went on. "We believe that the signal came as a response to the Darkling Moon *moving*, not from the moon itself. We believe it came from the Brilliant Dark."

Saskia's throat tingled with something like — she couldn't tell. Relief? Hope? "So Roan and Eli succeeded. They woke Ancient?"

So many years, believing they had done all of this, changed the world and everyone in it just so they could see how ugly it really could be. But it wasn't for nothing.

"There's more to it than that, to making it work." Something in Solomon's eyes changed. "But the signal is the key to finishing this, on our terms. We just need the right receiver."

"And you think," Saskia came to it slowly, then all at once, "*I'm* that receiver?"

Solomon just dipped his head. "We know that you have

a plan, an inherent part to play. I didn't see it all, but you let some of it come through during your assessment." His face showed amusement, and Saskia flushed.

"Sorry for my weak Mundane mind," she grumbled.

He was quick to defend her. "Much, much stronger than some Denizen minds, I assure you. And just know that it caused me pain to see it, to know it, that red song in your head. Maybe that will make you feel better." Solomon scrubbed his face as if he was in a great deal of pain now. "Whatever your plan is with making the Apex work using the signal and that broken Quartz, we want to help you succeed."

Help. The word was built out of barbed wire. Saskia wanted to reach for it very badly, but she knew what would happen if she put her fingers around it.

Saskia turned to the priest, who looked down at his feet, at the red rings. He stepped out of it suddenly, moving around her.

"You're right about risks," he said, tipping his head up at the chamber's ceiling, searching it. "I've taken my share of them, and I've had to live with the consequences." He looked back down at Saskia. "But we can't move forward if we don't take that step. The game will move on with or without us."

The gathering murmured, "The moon wills it."

Saskia bristled, trying to ignore them. "If you open the Bloodgate, and Ancient comes out, it'll destroy your precious moon. What about *that*?" There had to be something else here, something they were holding back.

More muttering from the peanut gallery, disconcerted hissing from the spectators. The priest raised a hand and they were silent. "The Cluster doesn't worship the Darkling Moon, Saskia," he said. "But that moon is a means to an end."

"The Cluster," Solomon continued, "is just another name for resistance." The other spectators lining the wall watched her, and she turned back, dumbfounded, to the empty red circle as Solomon went on. "The Cluster believes that, with the Darklings released, once and for all, Ancient will rise. When it does, Denizens will be more powerful than ever before, and the Task Guard, and any Mundanes who see fit to do us harm, will no longer be able to erase us. There are Mundanes who stand with us, too, who believe the old order was best. We are all invested in seeing that there is a world to fight for, before the end."

A race. That's all this was. Whoever opens the door first takes the spoils. And here was Saskia, apparently caught in the trample zone.

"What about me?" she said again, having said it so many times to everyone who had tried to use her for her brain, for having been touched by death or the dark or for just being in the wrong little Scottish town at the wrong time. They all looked at her like she was the answer, but she had none. "I'm a Mundane. What can I do, really?"

"I was *made* into a Mundane, and I've done plenty," the priest said, after breaking away from a woman with short blunt hair who had spoken something quietly in his ear. "All that matters is preventing us *all* from being erased. The Task Guard simply built our way forward. You can get us onto that road."

Solomon leaned heavily on his cane. "I don't pretend I can make up for all the things I've done while feeding the resistance from the inside. But when I saw your thoughts, saw you had some kind of plan, some kind of connection to the Darklings . . ." Solomon gathered himself. "We wanted you to know that you aren't alone."

He was right — it didn't make up for the things he'd done. But it was what Saskia had wanted, all along. To be of use. To be *chosen*. So why did she feel so sick?

She asked, "How long do we have?"

Solomon pointed skyward. "When that moon reaches the path of the sun, there will be only the dark. If we're going to move on this, we need to do it within the next day or so. Before Grant returns from his briefings." He addressed the room. "We all have choices to make. We just have to decide why we're making them."

As if on cue, the chamber rocked and rumbled, and someone screamed.

⋆⋙⋘⋆

Natti, of course, loved the irony of the river being on Cecelia Bettincourt's doorstep — and that she could use it to smash her way through. But she had to think like Phae and be practical. She could feel the water moving through the ground, deep in the pipes. Jet kept them disguised, though he was straining with the effort by now. He was, after all, way younger than they had been on their first break-in.

Phae was ready with a shield around them all.

"Step one, plumbing," Natti said, her wrists twitching as she pulled forward, as if she were dragging a great rope, and the water running beneath the house swelled like a wave. She shut her eyes and focused, listening. First she went for the water tank. It crumpled the steel and burst through, and even from the house's front yard, it was still a trial, bringing the water up, blowing the other pipes, and collecting every source as it sluiced through.

The soldiers inside, who were more like glorified paper-pushing camera-watchers, were already yelling. The water spread. The front door burst open as the personnel, soaked, flooded onto the sidewalk.

"Now!" Natti said, and the three ran through the door, still cloaked, but knowing Jet wouldn't be able to hold it much longer, or that the house's surveillance would pick them up. Natti scooped him up as they dashed.

"Jet, can you —"

His face was scrunched, turning red from the effort of maintaining their invisibility and searching for Saskia. "Down. Far down. Hidden in the dark . . ."

"The summoning chamber," Phae said, pointing them towards the basement door. She didn't have time to process how weird it was being in this house, which had been so changed, and yet still looked like the place she'd visited to help Roan with her physics homework . . .

They came to the door — or at least, where it should have been, and met with a completely solid concrete wall.

"No," Phae said as Natti put Jet back down again. "The door, the stairs . . ."

"They may have sealed it up, or at least the main way in," said Natti. She pulled a huge torrent of water from upstairs, down the front hall towards her, and it wrapped around both of her arms like sleeves. "Stand back."

She reeled and smashed both fists in a one-two at the wall, but it didn't break like it should have.

It flickered.

"What —"

Coming around the corner, panic-stricken, was just another man in grey, the white wings plain across his breast.

The three stood absolutely still, but their invisibility fell with Jet's exhaustion mixed with excitement.

"Jordan!" he cried, but Natti scooped the kid up again, slapping a hand over his mouth, while bringing the water up behind the stunned Owl in a whip.

He dodged, grunting, cutting a hard breeze across Natti's eyes, but Phae got in the middle of the next blow, sending it back on the man with her shield.

"Jordan, stop!" Phae barked, and recognition was an alarm in his eyes.

"Phae? Jet? Why are you —" He looked from Natti to the water slowly filling up the house and sighed. "You're here for Saskia, right?"

He seemed as exhausted as Jet had been, all of a sudden, but he held up his hands. "Don't worry," he said, and with a flick of his fingers towards them, he revealed that the concrete wall was a door, and he opened it. "Parts of this house are an Owl illusion. It's a safe place for —"

"He's in a uniform, I'm not taking any chances," Natti said, pulling Jet and Phae close. "Bubble us," she said gruffly to Phae, who brought the shield clasping around the three like a prayer.

Natti brought the water, and suddenly they were screaming and careening down the stairs and through the back basement wall.

※※

"What is it?" Solomon turned to the priest, then squinted, as if trying to send his mind back above ground. "Water. So much —"

Shouts above, muffled by the earth hemming them in. Ella was at Saskia's side, grabbing her sleeve.

"Go out through the back!" the priest shouted. Amanda and Josh pulled Dannika out of the hearth, and someone opened a hidden door there. Saskia and Ella went to these three, while the others fled.

"She can barely walk." Josh turned his face from Dannika and the state she was in.

"Don't leave me, you idiots," Dannika coughed, dried black flakes at the corners of her mouth. She was being taken over by a monster-parasite and still lobbing insults. Saskia looked between Ella and Amanda and Josh, but they still seemed keen on saving her.

Damn. "Okay," Saskia said, "We'll get her out and take her to —"

The water came sluicing down the stairs in a torrent, knocking the priest aside. Something bright and blue bounced down it, and the water, smashing its way around the room like a sonic clap, resolved around the sparking orb. Then it came down like an curtain, and inside the ball was Phae, back to back with Nattiq Fontaine.

"Well," Saskia said to Dannika, "I guess help came to you."

"Saskia!" Bursting out from behind Natti and Phae, unlikeliest of all, was Jet, who nearly knocked her over.

"What are *you* doing here?" she cried, then pulled him off in time to see Solomon and the priest, soaked but subdued, before Phae and Natti. Saskia cried out, "Phae!"

"I can't believe no one's killed either of you yet, especially you, Harken," Natti's hands peeled the water back to her fists, ready to use it again.

What the priest had said earlier, about being made into

a Mundane, made sense now. The priest was Arnas Harken, the neutralizer who'd severed Barton. And Roan's step-uncle.

"Saskia," Phae said, holding her hands in front of her face. "Are you okay?"

Saskia stood, Jet clinging to her, and she held tightly to him. *To reassure him*, she lied to herself. Phae looked like a live wire, ready to spark. "I'm fine. Please. You don't have to —"

"So what kinda lies you telling everyone today, Rathgar?" Natti hazarded. She was in a mood, apparently. "I hear a lot of Denizens are going missing, and your unit's keeping busy. Are the Seals next on the list? And you're snatching Mundanes now? How about the kid going mouldy in the corner?"

Solomon ignored Natti, looking only at Phae, whose hair was still in signature antlers, sharp and pointed forward. Saskia always wondered if Phae could gore people with them, and she looked about ready to find out now.

"Phae, please," Solomon started. "I know your inherent bias —"

"It was your idea," Phae said through gritted teeth, "to have Barton try the Apex. A brilliant one, because it worked. Now you're trying to get Saskia on your salvation train?" A bolt snapped off Phae's shield and flew across Solomon's face, leaving a long red mark, and he let out a strangled noise. "How many more of my family are you going to take?"

Saskia was between them like a shot, and Phae flinched.

"Stop," she said. "Just stop. Both of you."

Phae's eyes, brilliant and shocking blue, were concentrated fury. "Get out of the way, Saskia."

She raised her hands. "Look, we just need to talk. All of us. Like civilized —"

"Civilized? Don't you remember the day they took him?" Phae said, and her voice hardened, something newly woken in her and ready to charge. "*You've helped the world before*, they said to him. *Help it again. Help your family*. And he did. Solomon was the one who talked Barton into it, for weeks. Convinced that it could save everyone. Get our friends back."

Saskia remembered. Of course she did. Phae and Barton had argued about it so much, and the walls were thin. Barton had spent so much time repairing the damage of the Hope Trees all over the world that Denizens looked to him as much as they did to Phae. He wanted to act, again and always. He wanted to do something.

Then the Task Guard came, and Saskia didn't even get to say goodbye. Not really. He said he'd be back soon. He promised. But it was one rabbit hole he couldn't return from.

"I'm trying to help make it right," Saskia said, attempting to be as fierce as Phae. "What if we can get him back? What if we can get all of them back? Don't you want to at least listen?"

"I'm done listening," Phae said, and her shield began to expand until Natti pressed a hand to her shoulder and pointed.

"Hey," she said calmly, "let's not blow *everyone* up here." Saskia turned to where she'd been pointing, to Ella and Dannika in the corner. Dannika was writhing, screaming savagely.

"That's Dannika Cole. She was bitten by a river hunter," Saskia said hastily. "Please Phae. Help her. You remember when it was Barton, when he was bitten. You know how to fix this. Then I can explain everything."

Phae's eyes looked dangerous. Then the bright shield came down, and her eyes faded back to brown. The antlers, however, still pulsed.

She stared hard at Saskia for a long time, then brushed past her to do the one thing she could never refuse: help.

Footsteps pounded down the summoning chamber's earthen stairs, and Saskia, Natti, Solomon, and Arnas jerked towards it. The owner slipped, caught himself, his face pale and anxious.

"Jordan." Solomon raised an eyebrow. "Are you managing?"

"Barely," he admitted. "The whole house is flooding, and as it is there'll be more ETG techs coming in to assess the surveillance equipment. And the water tank is *in the main basement* which is cloaked to look like a storage room over a pretty obvious hideout." He stared accusingly at Natti.

Natti rolled her eyes. "Look, man, it's survival of the fittest. It's not personal. But I am the fittest." She took a quick survey of the room then, her hard stare falling on Solomon. "I'll clear the water up, and you get your little illusions back running, then I'll come back. I want to hear this, too."

Natti's gaze fell on Saskia, softening slightly. "She would've ripped this house off its foundation to get you home safe, you know."

Saskia only nodded, looking to Phae in the corner, glowing with purpose and, Saskia imagined, love — even though it hurt her badly to feel it.

Saskia hoped she was worthy of it.

It was about as calm as everyone was going to get. Natti had cleared the water away from every inch of the house before the ETG clean-up crew arrived. After some convincing from Jordan, they'd ruled it out as faulty maintenance and left. In the meantime, Jet had fallen asleep in Phae's lap. Dannika had been moved upstairs to a bed to rest, and Ella had gone with her.

Saskia sat next to Phae now, still in the summoning chamber, wishing again that she could read minds. Arnas and Solomon sat before her and made their case. Natti leaned against a far wall, in the dark, listening and likely reliving the last time she'd been down here. It was familiar territory for them all. *Let us make you an offer in a dark place, you're the only ones who can save us . . .*

After they'd gone through it all, Phae just sat there, as if she had been slapped repeatedly and now was numb to every blow. Her previous fury seemed banked up now, and Saskia wondered if it was the result of holding it in for so many years, and if it would come out again harsher than before. She hadn't moved when Solomon told her Roan was likely alive down there, wherever she was. It wouldn't be easy for Phae to trust any of this, not with what had been taken from her already.

Saskia paced as she ran through it all like she was testing a formula. "So say you open the door. You go through. Then what? It won't be so easy — it never is. If it was, Ancient would've burst through by now on its own and this conversation would be moot." She surveyed the others, arms folded, but no one offered any further insight. "You'll have to get out again from the other side, too. There'll be work to do down there. If you survive getting through in the first place."

The priest and Solomon exchanged a look. "Whoever goes in may not come out," Solomon said. "We've made peace with that."

"And who will you send?" Phae asked, looking pointedly at Saskia, who wasn't fast enough to look away.

She was caught out — at least the longing on her face was. *It has to be me*, Saskia thought, and she thought it so strongly that it somehow became a wish, and with no stars bright enough in the sky, she sent it up to the dark moon, begging.

"I will go," Solomon said evenly. "I will find my son, and Roan Harken, if need be," he seemed nonplussed, that Roan was a mere afterthought. "But I've the experience, and the power at the very least. Whatever is down there, I will manage it, and I will finish this."

Saskia felt like she was about to leap out of her skin, but Phae's cool expression nailed her in place.

"Good," Phae said curtly. "It should be you, anyway. Call it retribution." She jerked her chin at Saskia questioningly. "As for this device, signal, receiver, whatever. Why does it have to be Saskia making it work? Why can't she tell you her method, and we leave her out of it?"

Saskia didn't dare touch the pocket of her wrinkled uniform jacket where the Quartz was. Phae was trying to protect someone who had already betrayed her.

"Saskia has integrated herself into Project Crossover," said Solomon, "and she will have access to the equipment to implement her patch into the system. Think of her like an unseen mouse in the maze. If it were me doing it all, I would be stopped immediately. At least this way, I can keep her hidden while she does what is needed, act as though I'm out to stop her, and go through before anyone can get in my way."

His eyes skated to Saskia. She pushed everything down. She was blank. Even without the mind-reading, she feared that age and experience made him accustomed to teenage recklessness. Saskia was already formulating how she was going to get past *him*.

His eyes closed; he suddenly looked much older. Phae had moved on, addressing Arnas now. "And you? While everyone's inside risking their lives, what will you be doing?"

He lowered his head, rubbing a finger in the red circle which, upon closer inspection, was simply drawn on in pastel. Saskia had been so afraid of it, but it had just been symbolic. Arnas Harken didn't belong anywhere, like her, and whatever it was he believed — that the Darklings would somehow lead to their salvation, that Ancient could rise and turn the tide of war, or that he, just a Mundane man now, might be reconnected with his god by doing this service — she felt sorry for him.

"I'll be gathering the others," Arnas said, his meek voice more assertive. "And offering protection, sanctuary, for those who need it. We don't know how long Solomon will be on the other side. The Task Guard will act quickly when they realize what we've done. There will be reparations. Those of us left behind will have to fight, and those who can't fight will have to protect each other."

"Everyone's scared." Natti came forward into the light, unfolding her arms. "Mundanes and Denizens both. We can't fight each other if there isn't a world to fight over, I guess." She seemed to be working something out in her head, her jaw moving. "My people are safe for now, but the fight will come to them, and every corner of the globe, I'm sure. But they'll fight back. And so will I. If you're looking to gather an army, you can count me in."

Phae sucked on her teeth. "So much for keeping our heads on straight."

"Better crooked than off," Natti shot back, but she smiled.

Phae looked back at Saskia and exhaled. "Listen, Saskia. You know how dangerous this is. I hope you do by now, anyway."

Saskia nodded, bright hope blooming in her stomach.

Phae shook her head. "I can't deny that you're strong," Phae said quietly. "Strong in all kinds of ways that I'm not. I want to help, if I can. If that means supporting you in doing this, using your gifts —"

"Or curses," Saskia cut in.

Phae scoffed, shaking her head. "Best to not let them go to waste."

Phae knew full well the weight of giving Saskia such permission. Saskia had been through a hell none of them could comprehend and had come out the other side into a life she had to rebuild from the scraps she'd found, surprised that, in the heaps of the leftover world, Phae and Barton had been there to claim her. That kind of love didn't just come along. Not anymore. But it was worth risking everything for. Natti understood that. Maybe Phae did now, too.

"It will have to be tomorrow." Solomon's words floated in the room like a threat. "The element of surprise is required to make this work."

Saskia nodded. She had a rudimentary rigging built for the Quartz in the lab already. It wasn't perfect, but it would have to be now.

"Is it okay if I . . . stay here tonight?" Saskia directed this question to Phae, but also to Arnas, to Solomon. They'd offered her their help, and she'd pushed that to its limits.

Phae opened her mouth as if to argue but stopped short. "Fine. We can stay, too, I presume?"

Arnas nodded. "Of course."

"Beats a sofa," Natti sighed. "Any food around here?"

They all emptied out from the chamber towards the stairs. Saskia lingered, staring at that red ring that, crudely drawn as it was, spoke of a promise.

One she was going to have to break.

The ADAMANT ONYX

Chancellor Grant startled awake the moment the plane landed back in Winnipeg. He wasn't one to sleep through a night — it was when he was most productive. He had been writing feverishly in his journals. *I feel like I have to get back. Back to the Apex. I feel like we're close now. And once the door is open and Denizens are gone, the moon will be stopped, and I'll be the hero now and forever.*

It was childish but the notion had put its hooks into him. The clarity to his thoughts was overwhelming, sonic, like he'd been delivered a shot of adrenaline straight to his brain. It was a message. Today, Project Crossover was going to work. All he had to do was turn it on. All he had to do was walk through. And it would be his great legacy.

The U.N. meeting had been just an impression of order in a world thrown, as usual, into chaos. But Grant had their unyielding support now. *Do what you can to get rid of this damn moon*, they'd said. He'd smiled his promise. All his work had been for something. He'd known that before they did.

In his airplane seat, he stretched, thumbs digging into his eyes. He'd had a dream, and he was trying to grab hold of it before it slipped away. He'd turned on the reactor. It had worked. Before him shone another land, one he was destined to conquer.

There had been . . . someone else, and a black stone. The door had shut . . .

No. The dream was gone. An aide came by with today's briefing on a tablet. He flicked through. The sun had barely risen. Grant stood, pushing his way through the private plane as he bundled his coat on, tucking the tablet into his breast pocket.

Mi-ja was there, holding an umbrella at the bottom of the movable stairs as they walked together to the car.

"I want to see Rathgar as soon as we arrive," he said. "I want to test the Apex within the next two hours."

Mi-ja didn't blink, but faint uncertainty creased her brow. "Sir? The team hasn't yet completed the receiver —"

"I don't care," he said, waving a hand, though of course it was all he cared about. "Make it happen."

They got into the car and didn't speak again as it moved across the city towards downtown, towards HQ, and towards the blessed future.

⚜

Solomon stood at the back of his testing facility, the white room where he had spent many years screening for potential traitors.

The door was to his back. He had to be ready to do this, but, most of all, he had to prepare to face his son, if he was still alive. Or face the reality that he wasn't. He hoped at least Eli had managed to wake Ancient, wherever he was now. All Solomon had to do was hold the door open for Ancient, and their hopes, to rise.

Solomon brought a hand around and opened his fingers, looking down at a pocket watch whose opposing face held a faded photograph of Demelza. Bright, lovely, unforgettable. She had done everything to push Solomon and his ambitions away. She'd been correct. If he'd never gone after the Moonstone, or thought that imbalance could be corrected by the forces that had caused it in the first place, they would have been a family, the three of them. That should have been enough. Eli would have known how much he was loved, and it would have kept him safe. And Solomon could have destroyed the stone and protected Demelza from the madness it caused in her. All the choices he'd made had been the wrong ones. He would pay for them forever.

Solomon slid the watch into his pocket. This time, things could be different. The choice was his.

He sent his mind out across the roving labyrinth that was the Old Leg. He found her quickly; Saskia's presence vibrated with a monochrome melody, edged in scarlet, but much more balanced than the last time he'd been in her head. He didn't question this change.

Are you ready? he asked her, but he knew that she would be.

She seemed to flinch, but he felt her nod. *I'm just going to my lab. I need to run a few diagnostics against the Quartz. Meet me there in an hour, and we'll use your clearance to get to the Apex.*

Solomon chuckled. The girl had seemed so fragile at first, but she had put herself right in the thick of things. He knew why she was risking so much. Love was a powerful motivator. Solomon knew that without having to read anything in her head.

"Sergeant Rathgar." The voice was coming from the communication panel in front of him, the image of Mi-ja blooming there abruptly.

His heart skipped. "Yes, Lieutenant?"

"You're requested upstairs immediately," she said. "We'd like to run the Apex this morning. Please bring your reactor key, and we will all go down together."

Upstairs? To the parliamentary offices? Solomon wanted to reach out through that communication, but if Mi-ja was already in those offices, they would pick up his prodding frequency. He'd need to go and to see what this was about.

"Yes, all right." The comm went dark, and he snatched up his cane, moving as quickly as he could.

Saskia, he sent out quickly as he went up the corridor, *something has changed. I will still see you in an hour. Please be ready*.

She sent a feeling of alarm back to him but added, *Okay*.

As Solomon ascended from the labs and into the parliamentary space, he cursed inwardly. Nothing could ever be simple. At least this created the opportunity to see Mi-ja, who had *Grant's* reactor key. He'd only have a moment to slip into her mind, suggest she give it to him, and be on his way to Saskia's lab, then the reactor. Time might still be on their side.

The guards outside the last door at the end of the hall nodded and muttered "In unity," as Solomon passed. He raised a hand at them. That there was a guard contingent meant someone important was inside. Someone Solomon dreaded seeing, though he wasn't set to be back for another day, couldn't —

Mi-ja admitted him into the room, her trademark welcoming expression thin as she turned, and standing at the window was the chancellor, his jacket slung over the desk as he buttoned up a fresh shirt. Beneath his shirt was the reactor key, its twin hanging heavy around Solomon's neck.

A snag if ever Solomon dreamed it, and he should have.

"Rathgar, good. A pleasure as always."

The furthest thing from a pleasure, but Solomon inclined his head. "You're back early." He kept the tartness out, but barely.

"No rest for the wicked," Grant replied, slinging his tie around his neck and knotting it neatly. "I've read the engineering reports. I imagine you have, too. My ingenue has been hard at work."

Saskia.

"Indeed," Solomon said, unable to search for her up here with his mind. If she did as she was told, she was still in the labs. Time ticked away. "No results yet, though."

"Oh, I have a feeling there are some," Grant said, and Solomon's guts twisted. "Anecdotally, the rest of the staff have reported her working industriously on her own. Many are bitter about it. Which means she's onto something. I want the both of us to meet with her, and I'm giving you full access to pull whatever you can out of her if she's non-compliant."

Solomon felt like he was going to snap the top of his cane off. "Are you sure that's wise? Is there proof she has made any kind of remarkable breakthrough?"

The chancellor slung his jacket on, grey and black with

a white starburst, winking with its many medals and patches of service. "We'll find out soon enough, won't we? After we meet with her, the three of us will go to the Apex. I have a feeling today things are about to change. The world, after all, is depending on us."

The world. Of course. Solomon bowed again. "For the greater good."

They made their way down. Solomon wouldn't have another chance to warn her until they were in the lab corridor, barely outside of where Saskia currently was.

He realized, suddenly, that either he or Grant would have to die today to make this work.

᷼

Saskia ran the diagnostic as quickly as she could. Solomon's urgency had scared her, but luckily she had been here early enough to get everything set up. To get started on what might either be an abrupt end to her involvement, or just the beginning.

The plan was simple, and the group had gone over it before parting ways from Cecelia's house this morning. Saskia said a tense goodbye to Phae, Natti, and Jet, all of them promising to see each other later. "I'll even bake a cake," Phae had said, somewhat desperately, and Saskia had laughed, knowing the cake was a stretch; Phae was a terrible baker.

"Take care of everyone while I'm gone, Jet," Saskia had said to him, ruffling his hair. Ella had tried to say her own kind of goodbye, but Saskia wanted to get away quickly and hardly relished the quick hug before running off.

Phae hadn't given her any last advice, but she'd told Saskia enough through the years she'd been in her care. So as Saskia looked the device over, preparing to add the Quartz to its prescribed notch, she thought of all the times Phae had talked of her journey to the Glen.

"It was important that I remembered myself," she always said. "What made me, what brought me there. It was seductive on the other side. It made you forget home. It made you want to stay."

Remember yourself, Saskia repeated in her mind, in Phae's voice, and it steeled her for the work. Solomon promised that things would be all right. Saskia knew everyone would be breaking at least one of these promises by day's end.

She was already breaking a fundamental one, right now, in this lab, as she adjusted the stone in the device she'd built.

She had piggybacked on the principles of the Fractal, the crown that Solomon had used to manage his psychic ability, or his "Owl frequency." Based on that, then the signal and Denizen powers were all frequencies, which would run through the harmonizing Quartz, could be quantified, read, and managed. Like any line of code.

She would run the recorded signal that the Apex provided through the Quartz, and hope the result opened that terrible Bloodgate. She could do all this with the tablet she'd been running all her work through, patched against the ETG network so they couldn't pull any of her work from it. They'd notice that soon, though. Luckily it was all about to be brought to bear.

She checked her watch again, as she had frantically the last hour. The final diagnostic was running — it would later time the release of the signal into the stone, which was wired and strapped into the Fractal, still a crown, but easier to manage this way. Part of the signal, or the song, or whatever it was, was inside of Saskia. Maybe her mind, maybe her soul. The stone would resonate against that fragment of sound, the last piece of the puzzle, and when Solomon, with the stolen second reactor key, turned it all on, she would jump headlong into that void, because she was the only one who could.

He probably knew she'd try this. Hell, so did Phae, probably. Both of them were trusting her either way. Saskia had already broken Phae's trust, and badly. She'd be discovering, any time now, that the Quartz was missing, but it'd be too late.

Saskia was glad Phae wasn't going to see her doing the exact same thing Barton had, but she was going to succeed. And she'd bring him back. She had to.

In any case, the Quartz, shining black inside the sock she'd wrapped it in, was not the Quartz anymore. It was something else. Saskia had done that, too. The crack that once divided it had been made whole. It didn't shine; it sucked the light in and appeared flat and strange. Less a quartz now, more an onyx.

The diagnostic blipped and Saskia stared into it, thinking back to last night.

⁂

Saskia had spent too long, after everyone else had fallen asleep in the Owl-protected dorm, trying to figure out how she was going to get through the fire door.

Ella had opened it earlier. After that, Natti had blasted her way through, and a Rabbit from the Cluster gathering had repaired it. Saskia didn't have any means of opening it, and she wasn't about to involve Ella, who slept soundly now on the other side of the room. She had to do this herself. She was already getting used to that.

She had to trust that whatever was inside of her would help her now.

Saskia touched the basement's back wall, and it glowed red. The sigils asserted themselves in the cold mud brick, but she didn't read them. The door opened, and she went down alone.

The ring in the floor had been pastel, a crude sketch. Only a shadow of the potential. She knew what would happen if she crossed it — one ring turning into three, interlocking. Unmoving. So far.

At Saskia's back, the Moth Queen sat. Her little moths flickered towards Saskia, then banked away, uncertain.

"You were offered help from your human companions," she said. "What kind of help do you seek here?"

Saskia didn't turn, just faced the rings. "Yours. Theirs."

The Moth Queen's thorax crunched as she shifted. "You wish to repair the Quartz. But you can't. It must become something else."

"How?" Saskia did turn, then, holding the stone between them. That it could help was only a theory. It was, after all, broken.

The Moth Queen's many hands passed over the Quartz in a swerving pattern, like they were weaving, but the stone resisted. "It is the heart of a god. That god is still inside there, but they cannot come forward. *They* need help." Death's eyes flicked up, and the sound was a thousand lights going out at once. "You know that Fia made the Darklings."

Saskia nodded slowly. "And Fia's heart, the Quartz, is the key to the Brilliant Dark." All of it was falling into place, but there was still a knot, a question unanswered, and no god alive to speak about it. *Why did Fia make them at all?*

There were three others who might be open to chatting.

"If I call down the Darklings" — Saskia couldn't believe her own words, the plan forming grain by grain — "can they repair the stone?"

The Moth Queen picked up the Quartz, then, tenderly, as if it were one of her larvae. "I can put part of myself into the stone. You can have the blessing of Death, which you will need, in a place where the dead rule." She passed the stone to Saskia, and it was ice cold. "The Darklings do have a power that may help you. And since their mark slumbers inside you alongside mine, they may provide it. You pour all of their influence into the stone, too. It becomes a part of you no matter how separate you keep it. Just know that such a thing cannot be undone. Just know that there is a cost."

There always was. "But helping me might assure their destruction. How can I convince them?"

All of those devastating eyes neither offered guidance nor tried to stop her. "It is your choice."

Going back would help no one. So Saskia stepped forward, across that drawn red threshold.

At first, the room was still. Then all at once it felt like a magnetic field was blooming. The floor vibrated and the red rubbed markings disintegrated on the black stone, which flashed and shone as if it were new, a blank slate.

Then, crimson light, and surrounding Saskia's feet now were the three rings, interlocked and rotating around her, the intersection. The Moth Queen hadn't stirred. Saskia lowered herself slowly to the floor, Death at her back, and possibility at her front.

She placed the Quartz down on the ground before her and waited.

The piercing wail was in her head, and she covered her ears as if that would help. She flicked her gaze on the Quartz and saw it shiver. Then, in the shadow accumulating before her, something separated from the dark. Something . . . alive.

"I call . . . you to my name," she stammered, unsure how exactly to address this thing that had come when she'd called — and come so easily. "I call you down to speak with you. To ask your help. Under the watch of Death and by the mark you've given me."

The figure before Saskia resolved. She was afraid of what, or who, it might be, and what they might do to her. But, as she'd seen when watching Seela speak with his infernal parents from across the void in his summoning chamber, the Darklings couldn't harm you if you called them. They weren't corporeal. They were the dark moon in the sky. It was basically FaceTiming . . . with the void.

This Darkling looked like a horse, its neck stretching up and out, body reposed sideways on its haunches at rest. It held its forelegs before it, ending in hooves that glistened like metal. Hair hung lank from its face and body, and it had no mouth, but its green eyes were striking.

Zabor was the snake. Kirkald had many human hands and a wicked grin. Balaghast, surely the one before her now, was the most mysterious and, Saskia always fathomed, the least harmless because they couldn't speak.

There was an edge to those green eyes that said otherwise as they swallowed her whole. But she didn't move.

"Thank you for coming," she croaked.

The Darkling tilted its head.

Saskia held out the cracked Quartz. "Do you recognize this?"

Balaghast stared at the stone, then reached for it, their hoof passing through the stone like vapour. They made a sound like longing for the god that made them.

"What do you wish to ask?" the Moth Queen intoned. "Ask it now, and lay out your terms clearly."

Right. A deal. Saskia cleared her throat. "There are no gods left. Their hearts are broken. You came tonight because you recognize me, don't you? Or something in me."

Balaghast inclined their head respectfully. The red rings seemed to pulsate, strobing a heartbeat.

Saskia made sure to catalogue every detail in the Quartz as it was. It was a broken thing, and beautiful, but of use to no one as it was. It, like Saskia, needed to change.

"Your monsters recognize me, too. There are more monsters like them, in the Realms of Ancient, aren't there?"

Balaghast seemed to be looking past Saskia, towards the Moth Queen. They nodded.

"If I'm to go there, I'll need something. More than a broken stone. Something that can sing. Fia made this stone as they made you. Can you help me fix it?"

Stillness. Then Balaghast held out their hooves, stretching for Saskia. This was her answer. She reached for them, and let the hooves touch her, now somehow solid and tangible. She suddenly felt fever-hot, and she watched as her skin was incised with the language of the message that had been screaming in her head, even now. Symbols, words, a story carved in her flesh. Then she cooled, and the sigils turned to gold. The screeching resolved into a song, a perfect harmony, and behind her, Death reached around for the stone. She held it over Saskia's head.

"You have the protection of Death," she whispered, "and the blessing of the dark. You will need both to reset the balance on the other side."

Balaghast held on for a moment longer, and Saskia saw herself filling up those green eyes. It was hard to look, harder to look away. They were saying something, giving their own warning. She heard a word: *Creator*.

Then, all at once, the red rings and the Darkling alike went out like a tallow candle, greasy smoke the only evidence either had been there at all.

﹏

Now, in the lab, Saskia took the stone from the sock. It sang when she touched it. She figured that by installing it in the receiver, she could control the stone, keep its whispers from getting inside her head the way the other Calamity Stones had with their hosts. It would be different this time. She wouldn't take it into her body, or allow it to become a part of her. It was a tool and it likely had a mind of its own, like the Darkling who'd blessed it. It would see her through the underworld — and, hopefully, out the other side.

"This is the heart of the darkness," the Moth Queen had said before departing, her version of well-wishing. "With my blessing, the dead will recognize you as one of their own. Any creature corrupted by the Darklings will yield to you as well. But as for the stone, *you* must give it a new name."

"The Adamant Onyx," Saskia whispered over it. Names had power. She slid the stone into its casing in the receiver crown and hoped that her name could have power, too.

PLUNGE *into* SHADOW

The diagnostic never finished running — suddenly the tablet let out a screeching noise, and the spooling review fragmented, shivering. The text became red.

S

A

S

K

I

A

The message. It was happening again. "Barton?" she hissed. "Listen, I'm coming. Right now. Just hold on."

IT IS DARK HERE, the message flickered, *THERE IS ONLY THE DARK*.

Then more panic scratched across her mind, overlapping — *Saskia, get out of there now. Head to the next floor down as quickly as you can. The chancellor is here. He is coming for you. RUN.*

Saskia's head whipped towards the door, as if the chancellor were out there right now. Her bag was under her desk, packed with the basics — some provisions, a canteen. She'd wanted to be prepared on the other side. She grabbed the Fractal and the bag and went for the door, thrusting her head through the pneumatic entryway. No one in the hall, so she took off down it, away from the bank of private elevators that admitted those coming from the official offices upstairs.

She leapt into a stairwell and went down as far as she could, rushing through that door, and down another series of hallways, searching for a place to hide. *Are you going to the reactor?*

Not without you, came Solomon's answer, tight, hurried. *I can't speak for much longer. If he crosses paths with you, he'll kill you the second you've served your purpose —*

I'll get there myself, then.

No! You need to —

Solomon's message cut off, which was just as well; she needed to focus now. Saskia was on the Theory floor, and she ducked into a classroom, empty now, but through the glass she saw a group of ETG trainees approaching. Today was their educational briefing day, and in the throng of those marching in their combat fatigues, Saskia picked out a familiar face that made her heart leap and trust in kismet.

As the trainees passed the room, Saskia yanked him out of line, which he was mercifully in the back of, and into the room with her.

"What the good goddamn?" Cam sniped at her, and she slapped a hand over his mouth.

"Cam, you have clearance to use the back security elevators, right?"

He narrowed his eyes at her, then licked her hand, and she pulled it away, disgusted. It was an old standby of his.

"Why did you have to do that?" she snapped, wiping her palm on her jacket.

"What the hell's the matter with you?" Cam rounded on her. "Aren't you, like, on the engineering team? Why can't you use those elevators by yourself?"

Saskia dug the heels of her hands into her eyes. "My clearance is too basic. They don't want me sniffing around the Apex without supervision."

"And are they wrong?"

She grabbed him by the arms, which were a bit tighter than they had been since Cam had been in boot camp these two weeks. His floppy hair was cropped short, but he didn't look ready to fight her.

"I need your help," she said. "And I need it right now. We're still friends, aren't we?"

Cam swallowed, looking like a pot of boiled-over soup. "Am I going to get in trouble for this?"

"No," Saskia lied quickly. "It's Project Crossover. It's what I was hired for. I've made a breakthrough, but I need to test it before showing the chancellor. It's all on me, but I need to get there. Now."

Cam was already trying to work it out, trying to believe her. "How are we not going to look conspicuous? This place is crawling with soldiers right now at the chancellor's orders. Something big's going down. Are you a part of it?"

She kept her gaze steady on Cam. "No. I'm the solution. And we get past them if you treat me like a prisoner. It's the same lift to the reactor as it is to the prison cells. All you have to do is get me in there. No one will stop us." She took off her uniform jacket, crumpled it and threw it in the corner, pulled her denim jacket out of her pack, and slipped it on instead. "Forget it, I'll do it on my —"

Cam threw out a hand to stop her. "No, I —" His body might have been changing from training, but he was still the same, soft, sentimental boy who'd picked Saskia for a friend somehow, many years ago. "I want to help. If helping you means helping the Task Guard, then okay."

Saskia wasn't sure how she felt about that, but she smiled, and it hurt. "Thanks, Cam."

She popped her head out the door and saw armed guards coming down the hall. It was now or never. She nodded at him, and he grabbed her by the scruff of her jacket. He was strong. But he was being strong for her.

❦

"I should have expected this," the chancellor said, when they'd come upon the empty lab, strewn with cut wires and the screens of the computer unit flashing *ERROR — ERROR — ERROR*.

Mi-ja was already calling security. "We'll find her," Solomon reassured him. "The Owl unit has been deployed. It will only be a matter of time before she's caught."

Solomon had already lost track of her. He hoped he'd warned her quickly enough.

"I make the time around here," Grant snapped. He could've done a deeper sweep for what Saskia had been doing in this room, but Grant, too, was in a hurry. "I want to get to the Apex. Now. Have the Owl unit bring her to us there."

Mi-ja nodded curtly, and they all went back out into the hall, to the lifts. She and Solomon exchanged a glance, which surprised him. There was worry on her face. But why?

"What will you do with the girl, once she's served her purpose?" Solomon dared ask. Mi-ja seemed like she'd wanted to know, too.

"Put her where I should've in the first place," Grant scowled, "but we'll burn that bridge once we cross it."

Won't we indeed, Solomon thought.

⁓❦⁓

"This is a terrible plan," Cam hissed.

"I know."

"Can I offer you a better one?"

"Shh."

Saskia tensed as another paired ETG contingent came round the corner for them. She nudged Cam, and he hesitated only for a second that time, before slamming her into the wall.

"I said shut it, Denizen trash!" he shouted, digging his knee into her back. The contingent eyed them both, nodded at Cam, and passed by. He yanked Saskia off the wall and hauled her forward.

"The better plan is to not do this," Cam said after a while. "Please, Saskatchewan, whatever you're doing —"

"Don't call me that," Saskia grunted, wiggling a loose tooth with her tongue. "We're nearly there."

Cam's eyes darted. "All of these hallways look the same."

"I memorized the floor plan. Another left, and there'll be a service elevator. Single cabin, down only."

They took the left. Cameron looked terribly disappointed that she'd been correct. "What if I don't let you do this? I bet whatever you're doing is virtually suicide. That seems like it'd be your style. It's always the quiet ones."

When they got to the elevator, the coast was clear for a blessed second. Cam swallowed hard, then let Saskia go. He trusted her, even when what she'd asked him to do had been crazy and would likely get him in a lot of trouble. Mundane or not, he'd risked something, same as her.

Saskia's hands had been behind her back, but they weren't bound. She smiled at him after he scanned his security clearance card, a bit sadly, then pulled him into a one-armed hug.

"You're one of the good guys, Cam," she said, biting back yet more tears she didn't have time for. "Don't let go of that."

Then she shoved him away and stepped into the elevator.

She pulled the Fractal out of her bag to inspect it, the stone at its centre. Cam was right, this was crazy. But what did it matter? Crazy was how this was going to get done. She slipped the crown over her brow. The farther the elevator plummeted, the stronger the signal on the output grew, blinking on the tablet in Saskia's trembling hands after she'd pulled it from her bag.

S A S K I A, the output flickered.

"I'm coming," she whispered.

✥

Phae had taken Jet home and put him into his own bed, but she and Natti weren't interested in resting. They took a walk instead to the river, and now they stood on the Osborne Bridge, looking out at the Leg, to the Golden Boy, unchanged while everything below him had radically transformed.

Phae squinted as a chill crept up her ribs. "Something isn't right," she said.

"Ya think?" Natti retorted. They both turned towards two black military vehicles rushing over the bridge towards the Old Leg. But given the state of the city, this might have been routine.

"I came here a lot, after Barton disappeared," said Phae. The river waters below were murky as ever, the morning sun casting pale colours down on the brown water. The dark moon slipped in and out between the clouds. Phae didn't bother looking up. "It's happening all over again, and I'm just allowing it."

Natti leaned forward on her arms, watching the water. "You could've stopped both of them. But then again, I doubt it." She turned over, leaning against the rail, and pointed to the street. "Everyone wants to do their part. You can't blame them for that. You did once, too. We all did. We just didn't expect it to turn out like this." Her hands were spread over Winnipeg, a city radicalized and brimming with terror. "All because of a bunch of rocks and *believing in ourselves*."

"Rocks . . ." Phae frowned, then it hit her. She slapped a hand to her chest, where the locket that held the Quartz hung. She yanked it out of her shirt, fumbled with the clasp, and bit back a horrified laugh as the bit of concrete rubble fell into her palm.

"That," Natti said, "is *definitely* not right."

"She took it," Phae heard herself say. "She took it and she's going to go through. I knew, *I knew* —" Back when they were fighting Seela, the five of them were aiming for Ancient, for the Brilliant Dark, and Fia themselves had told Phae that the Quartz was the key to that final realm, after all . . .

Natti steadied Phae, held her on her feet, but forced her to look into her eyes, creased at the corners with their intensity. "Tell me what you want to do, and I'll do it."

Phae whipped her head to look across the river, as sure now as she had been seven years ago on that bank, when they'd all joined together.

"Fight," she said. "We need to fight."

Natti smirked. "I was hoping you'd say that."

The shield came up with the snap of Phae's antlers. Natti was already stretching herself, and her will, towards the river that started it all, ready to bring it smashing into the Old Leg.

❦

The building rocked, and Mi-ja staggered into the corridor wall before she could press the lift button. The chancellor, bless his black heart, caught Solomon before he crumpled to the ground.

The klaxon overhead blazed to life, a mechanical voice advising personnel where to exit. "What is it?"

Solomon couldn't believe he'd be saying this twice in as many days, but he relished it. "Water," he said. "A lot of it."

Mi-ja's eyes and fingers were already flying across her tablet's report. "The river, sir. It's rising. Too fast. We need to evacuate —"

The chancellor grabbed her and almost tossed her down

the hall. "Contain this. We're not going anywhere. We're getting to that reactor, and now." He slammed his clearance key against the elevator panel and shoved Solomon through the sliding steel doors ahead of him. "Lock this place down and everyone inside it. Put every unit out, from trainee to vet, and make a wall of bodies. Protect this building. Protect the Apex. We're going in. You're in charge now."

They left Mi-ja stunned in the hall, and the building rocked again, hard, to the point where Solomon didn't imagine they'd get down there in time, if at all. The cables of the lift made a terrible, straining lurch.

Then it began its descent.

The chancellor was still holding Solomon's forearm in an iron grip. Despite the chaos, he was grinning as the floors flicked past them. "The more they fight us, the closer we come," he was saying. "But we're going to win this, Rathgar. We're meant to."

"Yes," Solomon said, the lack of circulation making his arm sear. "Together."

With security on lockdown, and the distraction ample, Solomon dared to throw his mind out into the churning din of the compound.

Saskia was down there already, waiting for them. He knew what she was going to do. *Hurry*, he thought, with the last of his will.

⋙⋘

Saskia had winged it down here, and the Apex's team was a flurry of panicked activity as they prepared to turn the machine on, to do as they were told. They barely noticed

Saskia passing by, though some eyed her jean jacket skeptically. Something slightly more dire was happening — beyond doing what the crazed chancellor ordered — and Saskia was the least of everyone's worries.

"An attack," someone said. "There's a Seal out there, and — and something else, they don't know. It has antlers —"

"I thought there weren't any Deer."

"Other Denizens from the streets joined in. It's like a flash mob —"

"They're through the gate!"

"The chancellor is en route."

Saskia slipped into the control room at the base of the reactor and tucked herself under a desk, while a crowd of techs had their backs to her. After confirming a readout on the panel in front of them, they hurried out, joining the clusters of people running for the exit.

The reactor was in its first phase of function, loading its software. Saskia dragged herself out of hiding and ripped off a panel beneath the main screens with the small crowbar she'd packed. She yanked wires out, a whole motherboard. She calibrated the control of the Onyx Fractal with her tablet, fingers racing as she hacked past the control's digital firewalls with the same urgency as whatever fight was going on outside.

She couldn't help grinning, despite how her pulse seemed ready to make her veins burst. Natti and Phae and anyone willing were out there, and they were all fighting. They were all, in their defiance, *helping* Saskia.

The tablet confirmed that the Fractal and control were in sync. Then the commotion outside stalled abruptly, and Saskia lifted her head to look through the glass. The chancellor and Solomon had arrived, some remaining technicians approaching them as the pair drew closer to the ramps that led to the Apex's control bridge above.

Grant shouted for an update, and an engineer came to his side. The tech looked nervous and was quickly dismissed, but Saskia didn't understand what, exactly, Grant wanted engineering to do that was any different from before —

"Everyone, out!" the chancellor roared, spitting. "Get to the lock-in areas and seal yourselves in."

Hushed glances. It didn't take much convincing for the remaining people to obey. Saskia hastily slammed the metal panel back in place and dashed out the door, using the rush for cover as the techs hurried to the emergency lifts. As for her, she still needed to hide and get ready, so she ducked around a steel pillar just in time to avoid the chancellor. He had a crazed look on his face, eyes bright, cheeks mottled, and he was towing Solomon upward.

Solomon shot her a look over his shoulder. He, too, looked fevered in his own way, pale and sweating. But he somehow managed to smile at her. Saskia wondered if it was an apology or a goodbye.

"They won't get far," the chancellor was saying. Saskia needed to get higher, too, but she'd have to go another way. She watched them curve up to the right, so she would have to go left, get to the other side of the core. She saw a scaffold there above her, hanging over the empty void. She hoped the chancellor was too distracted to notice her, and judging by the rant pouring out of him, he was.

"Disloyalty on every side. Don't any of them *understand*? You do, Rathgar. You've always understood."

The sirens abruptly shut off, but Grant didn't seem to notice. "Lochlan," Solomon said, carefully using the name.

"You seem to know something more. The gate hasn't changed. What do you —"

"But *I've* changed," Grant said abruptly, as they were getting closer to the control bridge. "I'm going to go through and prepare the way. It's what I was built for, what this machine was built for."

He let go of Solomon and slammed his key in, and Solomon did the same. Their hands were poised to turn the Apex on as the readout panel told them the system was at eighty-five percent.

"I can't let you do that," Solomon said, though there wasn't concern in his voice. Only defiance.

They just needed to turn the keys. *C'mon*, she thought at Solomon, *just do it!*

Suddenly Solomon backed away from Grant, towards the railing that looped around the Apex, his head blocking Grant's view of Saskia. Even with this block, Saskia could see that Grant had drawn a weapon. Saskia ran, full tilt, the last few metres that led to the scaffold directly across from them.

"You are rather predictable, Grant. I don't need to be a mind reader to anticipate that," Solomon said, voice raised against the rising noise of the turbine at his back.

In a handful of strides, Grant had the muzzle of his gun pressed into Solomon's cheekbone. "I should have lobotomized you when you offered yourself to me seven years ago." He smiled. "But you did serve your purpose well. I don't think you needed to be a mind reader to know I was going to kill you today, either."

Solomon shrugged, as if his brain wasn't seconds from being outside his skull. "I don't intend to convince you otherwise. If you really want to leap over and see if your precious machine will do what it's built for, be my guest."

"I think I'd rather test it first with you. Hindsight being what it is."

Grant backed up a step, the gun still trained on Solomon. A cold mechanical voice spoke: "Apex ready to engage."

"You creatures with your fraught attempts at self-sacrifice," said Grant. "You can't even go to your precious afterlife. I suppose I'm in the mood to know why, then, before I tie up this loose end. Why you didn't try to save your own skin."

Solomon let his cane go, and it clattered to the metal grate. "Skin is just an illusion when the spirit is willing." The grin was evident in his words. "And you're right. I will get no rest in death. But I'd rather go now, knowing the one thing that you could never rip out of my head."

Grant pulled the safety free, the gun charging noisily. "And what's that?"

"That you'll finally get everything you wanted. And then some."

The trigger pulled abruptly, and Saskia saw surprise flare on Grant's face, as if he hadn't pulled it. Solomon's body tipped over the railing, and Grant lunged for the panel, engaging the keys with both hands. The machine was on.

She watched Solomon sail quietly down into the void, but she hadn't done her part yet. Of course he wouldn't go through. But now, standing on the precipice, her hands moved on their own as she placed the Fractal, heavy with the Onyx, back on her head.

The chamber sang.

Grant, leaning over the railing, watched Solomon disappear into the black. The sparking noise and electricity turned bloody and were resolving into a crimson circle. His sharp face split wide with horrible glee. "Yes!"

Then he looked up to the scaffold across from him and saw Saskia, staring at him, mouth open, the crown about her head making a song that was a searing, matching red to the portal that had just unfurled below.

"No," she saw Grant mouth. "*No!*"

Saskia glanced down, one foot poised to push herself off, like from a diving board. She felt a shiver at her back. Engulfing her were thousands of moths, unified and ready, even if she wasn't.

The Onyx crackled. The noise was a powder keg going off in her head, and Saskia jumped.

Part III
CORONA

WINGS *and* REUNION

Time is much more savage in small increments. The nights are wrong. The days hold too many opportunities. But inside the mind, consumed by memory, there is no time. And that was the only blessing.

In the margins of the work he and his mother undertook — sorting trauma, zigzagging into each other's lives in a faraway world — Eli wondered, even if the realms were in harmony, did time in the Roost matter? Phyr's duty was to make sure the trains ran, but no one said anything about such a god keeping any time for herself.

Finally, one day — which could have been the next day or a year later, for the devastating scope of retracing the wreckage of his entire life — Eli opened his eyes.

He felt his heart. Felt his blood. Touched his face and felt hair there — a beard, something he'd never fathomed

— and it was thick, and the fingers that sorted it were bony but strong. He was still alive, still in his body, still himself.

"I'm proud of you."

Demelza shimmered before him, a filmstrip with a few frames cut out. Her bright piercing gaze was full.

Eli rubbed his eyes, sensitive to the light as if he hadn't ever opened them. The migraine was so magnificent he was certain he'd been lobotomized. Then it was wiped away, and he inhaled sharply. "How long . . . ?"

He felt his mother's shade move beside him, but he was transfixed by the sky above, the dark ring of Owl shades revolving above them as if on a wheel.

"Without Phyr to manage time, I can't say." Demelza's voice was threaded with concern. "But a long while. The realms below are different. And your friend is different in them."

Eli jerked to see what she meant. "Different how?"

The landscape was still speckled like a spilled-over map, dozens more dark obelisks peppering the distant treetops, the steppes beyond the trees . . . had the forest canopy thickened?

Different didn't matter. Roan did. She was still alive.

Eli stood. "Then it has to be time. It has to be now."

As it hadn't in so long, the wind touched Eli's skin, but it felt papery, unreal. He'd take what he could get, though, letting the gust curl around his wrist, over his fingers, holding it gently.

Demelza reached for him, and he let her. "Grief is never truly gone, though, only managed. It's my fault you had so much of it to carry. I'm sorry, Eli."

Her hand cradled his face. He shut his eyes and felt lighter. "You won't remain, will you? You're . . . fading."

He had seen it, when they'd shared a mindscape, how she'd waited here for him, watching his progress, brought to pain by it, but determined to help him. Before the stones broke, she could have been reincarnated — whatever that meant to Denizens — but she'd stayed here. Now her intentions had run their course.

She smiled all the same. "The dead can rest idly for only so long. But my time, as this" — she ran a flickering hand over her stretched shadow form — "is done. A spirit is only energy, after all. What made me can be redistributed across the universe. Perhaps not now. Perhaps when the imbalance is corrected."

Eli turned for the edge. She moved behind him like a whisper, and her fading hands grasped his shoulders.

"And what if it isn't corrected?"

Above, the swarm of shades had stilled.

Nothing can last, Demelza said, into his mind this time. *But energy can't be destroyed. Neither can love.*

Her tone became more urgent. *Find your friend, and do so unburdened,* she said. *You have too much life left to spend it with the dead.*

The blood-crusted claw tracks down Eli's back felt fresh and burning as Demelza's fingers plunged into the old wounds. He grunted, vision spotting.

Shades came down in a torrent from above and behind, and her voice was in his head again. *You are ready to let go.*

Eli's foot slipped, and he tipped over the edge of the Roost, a thousand dark wings blooming as he hurtled down.

He fell long enough to see, to plan. The air rushed by and the realms below came up so slowly, as if he were falling for decades.

Eli's mind was open, and it felt a new kind of sore, like something only just born and raw, open to the whistling air.

It hurt. It was freedom.

The dead would not carry him for long, though. There'd be time to revel later, he hoped. Demelza was using the last of her power, her energy, to make him these wings, and the other Owl shades had helped accomplish this, too. But it was a Cinderella curse with a countdown.

Find Roan. It was the only plan.

Eli was a missile, a shard of atmosphere slicing. *Please still be alive*, he begged. He was a freight train, a nosedive, falling fast, falling forever. *Fall faster, dammit.*

He broke a sound barrier. The incoming canopy shuddered, splitting. An obelisk sang by him like a skyscraper. The wings of the Owl shades, a part of him but not him, flapped like a hummingbird mid-decibel shift.

The ground soared towards him.

"Faster!" he screamed at the Owl shades on his back.

A falling star. A roar — distant. Too close.

Brace for impact. TKO in the ground.

Eli forgot to gasp.

She cocked her head, fingers tangled in the undergrowth as the quake rocked the sediment. Shades scattered, but not hers, not those that followed her loyally and had made themselves almost a part of her shadow.

They were Foxes. They waited.

This wasn't the usual quake. An impact wave raced visibly for them, and she stood as it crashed into her, never faltering. It made her laugh.

Once the ground stilled, the echo of the blast left in her hardened flesh, she pointed her body west, to a wall of dust in the distance rising higher above the wilderness where the black streak from the sky had made landfall.

From the trees between her and the thing that had hit the ground came the same blood-curdling howl she'd been tracking since morning.

"Looks like you have competition, Mistress," said the Rabbit shade at her ankles.

Lowering her helm over her eyes, all that could be seen of her face was the grin. "You know how I love a race."

She took off across and into the trees like fresh-fired buckshot. The shades bounded after her.

❦

Eli stared up at the lip of the crater he'd made.

"I'd appreciate some new material," he grunted, mostly to make sure his voice was working.

The Owl shades were long gone. *You're on your own*, their absence said. With any luck, he wouldn't be for long.

The air down here was hotter than it had been in the Roost, light above blaring from a red-cloaked sun. Eli imagined a newly terraformed planet waiting for him beyond the crater as he raised his arm to shield his eyes. Dark blotches above circled then vanished from sight. The powerful scent of resin, rotting leaves, and the cones of Jurassic-looking evergreens clogged the back of his nose.

Eli rolled slowly to his feet in one piece. "And that's three points from the Russian judge . . ." He must have really gone loopy if Harken's jokes were coming out of his mouth.

He flexed his fingers, rotated his shoulders. He felt . . . remarkably fine. Likely the time spent meditating in his mindscape had allowed old injuries to rest, allowed his body to heal — but he could still break anew at any given time. There would be more threats down here than above.

He gave one last look skyward and raised his hand, wondering if Demelza could see him. He cast his mind out, but it was too far to reach. He just had to believe she could hear him, wherever she'd gone, whatever she'd become. *Thank you, Mum.*

Enough of that now. He exhaled and took stock. Luckily, the crater was only slightly taller than him. He held out his fist, pumping it like a blood donor with shy veins.

"Come on . . ."

The air shifted slightly. It threaded around his limbs, weaker than a breath but better than nothing. Feet sliding apart, focus sharpening, he tensed his back. All he needed was a boost —

"Yes!"

The wind pushed him up and he went clumsily over the lip of the crater, scrambling through a somersault on level ground.

With a grunt he staggered upright. "Phyr on a flamingo," he snarled. He felt flabby, out of shape, like he had been as a novice squaring off against the Owl-raised children at the Rookery.

Square one was not a good place to be again, but it was all he had.

"Fine," he said, dusting himself off and surveying the terrain beyond his landing's wreckage. "Let's see what we have to work with."

He was indeed in the woods. The trees were enormous, a cathedral of trunks reminiscent of redwoods, sequoia. Trees that, on Earth, worlds away, would be a thousand years old. For all that they blocked the light above, the ground steamed from buried vents. A ripe stench came up with each burp of vapour, and Eli covered his face. Some other nasty smell lurked deeper in the woods, downwind.

He took a step aside, slow, trying to move into the shrubs for cover. There were animal sounds around him and chirping above, but he couldn't take the chance of staying in the open. The farther he walked, the deeper cold doubt burrowed in. He truly had no idea where he was, or where he was going, or if there were environmental mechanics he could depend on.

A newly terraformed planet, indeed.

He plucked his shredded clothes away from his skin to try to keep cool, the sweater clinging to him with the oppressive heat, his bare toes grinding into layers of stabbing pine needles. He didn't get much farther, though, because close by, in the thick conifer growth, something roared.

Bare feet be damned, Eli remembered how to run.

Ducking low under twisting branches, crashing through brambles, Eli chanced a look over his shoulder and saw trees bowing and breaking in half as he was pursued. He couldn't see what was coming for him — all the better. The sound alone, a choked gutter-shriek through a mouth like a whistling hole, was enough to make him surge ahead, legs burning.

Luckily for his legs, but not for the rest of him, Eli stepped directly off a steep hill and the world tipped over.

He came down hard on his bad shoulder, sky and ground a spinning cavalcade, coming to a pitiful crumpled stop covered in new scratches, debris, and half of his body submerged in foul, too-warm muck. He lifted his head, and spread behind him was a bubbling, reeking bog.

Get up! he screamed inside. He tried, untangling his long legs out from under him, caught in a net of mud and panic. He made it midway onto shore, then he went still. He canted his head to the crest above him to see that black and bearing down on him was a huge garbling shade. A Rabbit.

But barely — its body writhed like an anemone flicking in a current. A wave of red dots opened, hundreds of eyes and puckered mouths in the sludgy body. A king rat–Rabbit amalgam all tangled together. Its many ears, huge like trees themselves, shivered, sloughing back, stirring ground matter around ten razored paws.

Eli tensed once before he got back up, the mud sucking at his feet, unable to take his eyes off the abomination. Crooked trees above circled the creature's head like an unholy diadem.

The bog was at Eli's back, the hill in front of him, and no way around, either. He'd been down in this horror show five seconds, and he was about to die? Really?

He pulled himself up in one swift, defiant movement, then held his arms out and howled. "What are you waiting for?" he shouted, giving the last of his fucks. "Come and get me!"

The beast opened its many lamprey mouths and screamed again. Eli planted himself stolidly in the filth as the monster leapt.

Then something split its head clean in half, like an axe through the face.

Eli gaped.

Whatever had done the job had come at great speed from behind, a mass made pointed spear-sharp by a long blade held in front of it. The black muck misted from the impact. Then the point of the blade ripped up, and a body behind it unfolded, sending a hand out to grab at the beast's tumbling body before it, swinging backward onto the head and clenching the ears like reins. Two legs stretched, standing tall on the neck as it fell faster, and Eli dove out of the way when it landed clean in the bog where he'd lately been standing.

He caught himself on a fallen log, turning to see the beast's killer still taut and ready, their back to him. He tensed as the creature popped under the hunter's boots, screeching waves of shadow streaming out of the mouths. There was nothing left of it but loose, sagging skin, still enough to use as a raft in the wallowing muck, sinking slowly.

All of this, and the hunter themselves hadn't moved.

Eli let the air out of his lungs, a mix of gratitude and shock. The hunter, drenched head to toe in steaming black blood, turned their head towards him at last.

No eyes, just dark holes. The head was misshapen, too; then he realized it was a mask, or a helmet of some kind. Their body seemed human, and in one hand, at the ready, was a sword, dripping.

Then the black burned away from the blade: *garnet*.

The hunter swept the helm off, releasing a curtain of matted, dark red hair, a pale face drawn in a tight scowl, amber and hazel eyes sharper than her blade.

Eli's face cracked into an enormous grin. "Roan bloody Harken, you brilliant, bloody bastard!" he roared, finding his feet. "Nothing changes, does it?"

The bog was silent.

Roan stared at him, mouth flat. Her fingers twitched around the sword held hip-high. He'd found her, all right. Eli's smile died, the sweat on his forehead slick.

She leapt off the monster skin before it sank completely, and Eli dodged a downward slash. The log split in two behind him.

"Hell!" he sputtered, jerking backward, another beautiful swipe coming across his belly and slicing his sweater clean open. He staggered back. "Wait, stop!"

Her face was menacingly impassive as she rounded and spun, her knuckles and the heavy hilt clenched in them connecting across his jaw. He went flying, but he put his leg and fist out, the wind he'd summoned catching him before impact and whirling away so uselessly it barely ruffled Roan's hair. Eli spat blood but he didn't look away from her. "Harken, what —"

Suddenly she was in front of him, but before she could come down for another swing, Eli brought his arms down in a windmill slash, and the wind-blast slapped her off her nimble feet.

She caught herself in a crouch, eyes narrowed, sword across herself protectively.

"Just stay down there and listen to me, dammit," Eli panted, hands out in front of him, as if they could save him. He didn't have much left in the tank, and the tunnel vision closing in reminded him of that. "I don't know what I did to deserve that kind of welcome. Lately, I mean."

Roan straightened slowly. This wasn't the clumsy creature he'd scoffed at when they'd first fought on a bridge far away. Nor was it the emotional basket case he'd comforted in his childhood home.

Her silence cut him down the most. It was her incessant babbling, Eli realized, that he'd missed most of all. "Say something!" he shouted desperately.

This girl, this creature, was not Roan. But it was enough of her that he would keep taking the risk. His arms lowered. "You don't recognize me, do you?" He remembered, then, giant sucking worms, the way the Bloodlands tried to take who they were before — maybe things *didn't* change.

She took a step, and without thinking, he pulled his sleeve up. The white chain scar seemed to glow in the dark of the woods and Roan pulled up short. "You recognize this, though." He swallowed. "I came here *for you*, you tremendous moron. To . . . to save you."

She stared at his arm, mouth parting. She was close enough he could see her pulse at her throat, but it was steady, mind already made up. Without looking away, without putting the sword down, she swiped the black muck from her arm with two fingers, revealing the twin scar there. Tangible proof — for both of them.

Eli felt something like relief. A fool's feeling. "You see? We're the same."

That was when her eyes jerked to his, and her grin pierced his chest. "No," she said, "we're not."

The arm with the scar came up and across in an artful swing, and Eli's head rang scarlet with the blow. He toppled, dead weight, at her feet.

The EXILED ARCHIVIST

Saskia was not born a Denizen. Even with the Moth Queen's warning and protections, even with the Adamant Onyx, given freely and invested with more of the darkness that had always been inside Saskia, and even with the devices her own hands had built to keep that darkness in check . . .

Nothing would have prepared her for falling down the rabbit hole like this.

Her entire body felt like pulp, slowly hardening as blood went back into her limbs when she flew over the threshold, falling, always falling, but wide awake. She'd been afraid that she'd pass out, that she'd miss it, but no. All of the sensations were into her skin like songs into a vinyl record. She fell forever through that song and signal, and it directed her exactly where she needed to go.

There were voices, overlapping, screaming in different tongues in the darkness. Were they telling her to go back?

Were they trying to eat her alive? *You shouldn't be here*, they said. They were right. No one should. And if even Death couldn't walk this path, then what business did Saskia have trying to do it?

But she was the only person for the job. No one else could've survived this.

The shivering tornado of moths squeezed her tightly, her protective shield. All Saskia felt, all she knew, was the dark. Small comfort against the chaos. Then the moths burned away, like meteors entering the atmosphere, and she was careening alone.

Saskia broke through into air, hazy light, and a searing painful burning haze like the remnant of a forest fire. She hit the ground, stumbling before her legs remembered to do what they were made for.

She went flying down a steep incline, then she was tossed end over end, and with each slam of her body she knew she was alive. When she finally came to a stop, she wondered how she'd survived at all.

When she sat up, groaning, she pulled the pack off and around and pulled out the tablet. Keys flicked. Then she touched the weird crown she'd built, nearly brushing the Onyx with her bare hand. It was all in one piece. So was she. Barely.

She exhaled. She'd wanted to touch the stone, she admitted that much. *Touch with your eyes*, she warned herself, taking off the crown and bringing it closer in the dim light. The stone was still sharp and whole, and the output signal button was still green. All of the apparatus had survived. There was a switch that could essentially wake or deactivate the Onyx whenever she wanted, and it, too, still held. Even though the stone's power was being managed, Saskia still had the odd feeling the stone had protected her down this dark road. She'd take what she could get.

Saskia wiped her face, put the Fractal back on, and tried to blink the stars out of her vision. Then her breath caught in the cage of her ribs and she threw herself to her feet when the haze cleared.

She was in the middle of a grove of Hope Trees.

Here they were huge. Enormous. Grown wild with bark so contorted there was no sign they'd once been human or had spirits inside them. Without the Gardener to cut them down and replant them, they'd twisted towards what little light filtered through their black canopies. And there was light above. Clouds. She could even taste the air. This place was real, and she was in it.

Saskia was on the other side, probably in the Bloodlands, given the trees. What she thought was going to be a hard step in itself had been achieved with less than a stumble. She saw a flash of the chancellor's face, red and white with rage, and shook it out of her mind, along with Solomon's body, which she'd watched fall into the Apex before she had. Poor Solomon. Without him, she wouldn't have made it. Not really.

All that was elsewhen — elsewhere. *Now what?*

Something whistled past her face, close and sharp enough to snag her hair but not take her with it. It *thocked* home in the Hope Tree behind her, and when she turned, she saw blood pouring from the place in the bark where the barb had struck.

She took off just in time to miss the next one that hit the ground where her shoe slipped and nearly took her down.

Saskia picked a direction at random, zigzagging. *That was quick.* She'd just arrived and someone was after her already. Or some*thing*. The little darts kept whistling past her as she ran.

Saskia dove behind a shape, unable to tell what it was in the spiralling fog, and flattened herself behind it. More hiding. It was how she was going to survive this. She saw, shuffling past, some kind of monster, all rude angles and skittering legs, a broken spider with horns writhing over its head, jibbering hysterically that it had lost its prey. Saskia thought she was going to pass out, behind this rock, just from the sight. There had been Bloodbeasts in her world but they'd always been contained by Denizens or the ETG. She had neither to help her here, and she suddenly felt like a prime idiot for not taking Cam's gun when she'd had the chance.

The creature let out a chitinous yowl, head snapping towards a voice. "Not the book!"

The Bloodbeast galloped off towards the cry, shaking its horns. Saskia shut her eyes, legs tingling as she kept them folded tight under her.

"Please, somebody — *no!*" the voice cried, then was choked off. The monster had arrived.

Saskia wanted to fumble with the tablet, to check the receiver's output and see if she'd had any new messages. But what if *this* was her message? What if it was Barton?

She tightened her pack straps and took off from her hiding place, breaking out into the grey.

Moans and howls — beast and prey intermingling. What was she going to do to once she got there? *One step at a time.* The landscape changed abruptly, though she hadn't run far. Those Hope Trees grew thinner, giving way to trees and flora that looked almost . . . like home. Her pack bounced wildly on her shoulders, heavy with supplies.

Saskia pulled up short from a curious figure, like a bundle of sticks and bark, that landed heavily in front of her.

Saskia backed up, hand at the ready on the switch at her head. She had a weapon. She needed to survive the first ten seconds of being in the Bloodlands if she was going to make any headway, anyway.

Then the bundle of sticks shivered, as if it were one body — and somehow, it was — and Saskia picked out a pair of bright little eyes staring miserably up at her.

"Are you beast or shade?" the creature whispered. The voice was neither male or female. Unsure what, or who, she was addressing, Saskia's words wouldn't come.

Then those flat steel pupils flicked to the stone on her head, and the creature jittered to their feet — hind legs? It was Saskia's height, bent over and awkward, and it was built as if someone had made a puppet from whatever had been to hand: mud, boughs, leaves. It was convincing, yet moved with the terrifyingly erratic steps that had always made her afraid of dolls.

It wasn't Barton. But it had long ear-ish sticks on its head, and the haunches were proud and strong, and Saskia immediately recognized this creature as a Rabbit. She'd take it as a sign, especially right now.

"A god-stone," the creature gushed, pointing. "Are you —"

"I'm human, a Mundane," Saskia blurted, backing up farther and searching the woods around them for the monster that had just chased this creature here. "Where did —"

The ground shuddered with a burst of trampling. The Rabbit leapt away and behind her, rounding a thicket and narrowly missing a dart headed for the base of its head.

Saskia didn't know what made her cry out, "No! Stop it!"

just as the beast was about to let fly another shot, but it turned, coming for Saskia.

"Get out of the way!" the Rabbit screamed from behind her. "You cannot reason with it!"

Saskia stood her ground, remembering the river hunter, and hoped as hard as was logically possible that lightning could strike twice.

She flicked the switch on the Onyx crown for that added bit of leverage.

The darkness inside the stone welled up when she touched it, answering the one inside her. She felt it mixing with the human part of her, and it was tempting to let the power flow into her, wash away what made her Saskia. But she had to time it and stay alert, and she reached for the switch again to cut off the power.

Then the darkness was pulled out of the monster looking to tear her apart, pulled into the stone. The monster changed shape, crying out sharply before it hunkered down to the ground, skittering legs pulling into its body as it reformed.

Saskia gasped, felt the sweat at her throat as the stone went quiet again, and she fell to her knees. She heard rustling in the undergrowth as the Rabbit poppet crawled towards her, and she tried to catch her breath. The Rabbit reached for her —

They both jerked towards the creature that had attacked them, because it was getting up. It rose to shivering hooves, white eyes regarding her beneath a rack of short antlers. It was like Phae had told her — a soul, a *shade*, of a Denizen that had passed.

The Deer sniffed the Onyx at her forehead, looked between Saskia and the Rabbit, and took off into the ashy mist.

Saskia sighed, a heaviness keeping her on the ground.

"Where have you come from?" said the Rabbit, still watching the place where the Deer's spirit had fled. "And what have you done?"

"What I'm told." Saskia got up then, appraising the Rabbit wearily. "So you're not a monster, I take it. And maybe not a shade, like that." She jutted her chin towards the Deer's exit route. "So what are you?"

The Rabbit's gnarled hands at their knees clenched and unclenched. Then they, too, got up, joints crackling. "I'm an archivist. A keeper of story." Something changed, body language suddenly just as frantic as when the beast had come for them. "My book! Please, help me find it!"

"Book?" Saskia parroted. Using the stone like that — not to mention the death chase — had taken its toll. She barely had the energy to blink, let alone go with this creature on a mad search. "Why? What's it look like?"

"Pages. Some writing. A *book*." The Rabbit pressed its bark-mask nose to the ground, tearing through moss and undergrowth. "I had it only a moment ago, before that Bloodbeast came. Those demons have been managed in the Emberdom, and I am not accustomed to the wilderness. Not since my mistress . . ."

They trailed off, going still, then stood again. "I have been exiled, you see. Whatever fate befalls me out here is of my own doing." The tall ears drooped.

Saskia had tripped into the middle of a story already being told, but she had her own story to worry about. "I . . . I don't know if I can help you. I have to find someone myself."

The creature seemed to smile. She didn't see it, but she certainly felt it. "Perhaps we can help each other, then," they said, holding out a nervous hand. "I am Baskar."

The head tilted, expectant. The hand was just wood, mismatched pieces that somehow interlocked. She took it gingerly. "I'm Saskia."

Baskar yanked her to their side, taking her in the direction from which they'd come. Saskia was too weak to argue.

"Have you come from the Uplands, Saskia?" they asked as they towed her along.

The Uplands . . . Urka had used that term to describe the living world. Saskia's world. There was no sense in lying; it was obvious she wasn't a shade. "Yes. Like I said, I'm looking for someone. Three someones, actually."

Baskar shook their head, parting ferns and brambles but disappointed when the book wasn't revealed underneath. "You flesh-dwellers are hardly a novelty. Though it has been a hundred years since the last of you came."

Saskia pulled free and stopped dead.

"A . . . hundred years?" No. It couldn't . . . but everyone did say time didn't run the same down here . . .

No. This Baskar thing simply had to be wrong. "I'm looking for Roan Harken and Eli Rathgar. They came down here to —"

Baskar leapt close to Saskia and clapped a hand over her mouth. "Do not speak of it, if you know it."

She was just about to say *wake Ancient*. She shook the hand off, which had looked so frail but clearly wasn't. "What the hell do you mean?"

Baskar ignored this question. "Just tell me: are you like them? The way the General of Ash and Flame and the Owl King used to be?"

Used to be? General? Owl King? "Look" — Saskia clenched the straps of her pack — "all I want to do is get my friends and get out of here. Things have gone to crap since they left and —"

The archivist lunged and Saskia stumbled as she dodged. "The stone you carry. It is like my mistress's. Perhaps if I bring you to her, she will forgive me, and welcome me back at her side. I can take you there right now!"

"Your mistress?"

"Come!" Baskar grabbed Saskia's hand again and ran, leading her criss-crossing through the undergrowth. "The General will receive you fairly, unlike the Owl King. He is not our ally. He would rip you apart."

Riddles. Of course. Baskar had already forgotten about the book, and Saskia wasn't about to remind them. Best to just go along with this, if it meant finding Roan or Eli, or anyone at least remotely saner than this possessed poppet.

"Gods' sakes," Saskia huffed. As Baskar dragged her, Saskia took in the shattered wilderness and saw fire in the distance.

❧

In the Court of the Owl King, memory was tended and guarded as carefully as any treasured resource. And resources were few and far between, in the high cliffs of the Once-Roost, where he had staked his claim.

Here he waited, often in silence, eyes shut. Those who attended him, his own restless dead, those of whom he had become caretaker, had long ago lost memory. Or the need for it. But the Owl King knew it was the only thing keeping him alive. Keeping him himself.

When his eyes, golden with pain, did open with the new

grey dawn, he knew. Knew that soon memory might not be enough.

The cracked stone in his chest offered no guidance. But it flickered once with its own broken knowledge — its sister was near.

"Yes?" the Owl King stated as his creature crossed the Limitless Ledge, Phyr's former seat, where the old god was said to have watched and curated the Narrative from the top of the universe. Managing time.

Time. Another resource running dry.

The creature was a shade, newly put into its shell body. The Owl King rose and went to it, because it had a hard time walking. It wasn't accustomed to its new form, and so he knelt before it, breathing the wind into the mask that made its face. It quickened, the body made of leaves and feather locking tighter, and it rose to its full height, a head shorter than him.

The king nodded. "You have a message for me."

The Owl soldier straightened, back iron-straight. "It is as it was when the Pilgrim arrived." The quiet voice was grave. "A gate has opened. An unnatural one. I saw it open, bright and crimson, and then it shut just as quickly. I saw a girl pass through it, but I could not chase."

The Owl King rose, body weary from disuse. How long had he been lost in the past this time? "Does the General know?"

The soldier did not answer right away. Then, "She will know soon enough. The girl seeks the General most ardently. The archivist is taking her there. She believes the General will help her."

"A girl," the Owl King repeated. This was a story he'd

known, doomed, it seemed, to be repeated. "I would see this visitor is not harmed. But if she goes near the Heartwood —"

The Owl soldier bent its head, mask of feather around black eyes twitching and interrupted. "There is something else."

The Owl King looked up sharply, great wings rising from the marble floor marked with broken, meaningless symbols.

"The visitor. The girl. She carries a stone with her. A new sister of the old stones. I do not know what it means; but before the gate closed, I heard it sing."

The king squeezed his talons until they bit into the flesh he had always taken for granted. He felt himself smile. "The story is trying to end itself, I see."

The soldier was quiet. When it turned, the Owl King noted that its wings were short, like the wings of a glider. It took off from the platform to join the other sentinels, watching, waiting, for the world below to change.

Alone on the broken throne, along the top of the universe, the Owl King smiled. "My love," he said. "Let us see if you allow yourself to be saved this time."

❧

The closer they got to their destination, the quieter Baskar became, wringing their hands, jumping at every sound.

"You're sure this is the way to Roan . . . ?"

The Rabbit only nodded. "What if she is still angry with me?" they said, their steps stammering as much as their voice. "What if she burns up my body and I become a Bloodbeast like so many others?"

So, Saskia realized, Bloodbeasts were corrupted shades. Is that why there were monsters in her world, the Denizen dead, unable to go to their rest, turning into something else?

"What exactly did you do to deserve exile?" she asked.

The Rabbit looked over at her quizzically, as though just remembering she was there at all.

"I am the keeper of the story," Baskar said slowly. "But I found a part of the story that the General did not like. She did not want to have it recorded, let alone heard. I often can't help myself, especially when it comes to expanding our world's knowledge. I thought I was . . . helping." They gestured towards the weird, twisted landscape, and Saskia wondered what kinds of stories this place could really tell — especially if it'd been left like this for a hundred years by their reckoning.

They moved downhill into fog that thickened, smoke choking her, intermittent heat steaming off rock. This place couldn't be the Bloodlands, but it was, at the same time. There were Hope Trees, there were monsters. But the grass gave way to sand and canyon walls. Here and there, caught between boulders, there was vegetation, the sounds of howling. It was an alien planet. The underside of everything she knew.

Maybe rescuing this strange Rabbit hadn't been the best idea. The smoke started to clear the farther she went, yet fires still burned. She figured, at least, she might be going to the right place.

Ahead, at twin gates made of twisting flames snaking over a stone archway, stood two figures wearing masks similar to Baskar's. Except these, carved from burnt wood, had much shorter ears, fanned whiskers. The eyes were completely covered. They were armed with flaming spears, branches that never seemed to burn away.

"Oh my," Baskar said, backing away. "I don't believe I can do this."

Saskia shook her head. "We're going to have to. I didn't come all this way for nothing." She didn't know what she was expecting. But approaching a flaming palace was not up there in her realm of possibilities.

She swallowed and approached the guards, not waiting for Baskar. "I'm here to see Roan Harken."

The guards looked to one another, then to Baskar, whose head was bowed in supplication. "You brought back the exile?" one grunted. "We'd only just sent them away, you know."

Saskia grimaced. "Okay, well, sorry for the excessive paperwork, but I —"

The flaming spears rose. "Are you beast or shade?"

Saskia raised her hands and took a step back. "Neither. I'm human, like Roan. Please, I just need to talk to her."

The spears lowered slightly, the guards looking between the two intruders, then they huddled together, whispering. When they moved, their joints clattered like teeth. They were encased with hard-glazed mud and clad in stitched leather armour and furry moss. Saskia's head throbbed. The air in this place was hot. Beyond the gate, and the guards, was a flame like a pyre, guttering into the shadowy dusk light.

"Hello?" she tried again. "Listen, I just —"

Baskar came forward then, stepping in front of her.

"If I may be so bold as to suggest looking closely at the stone she bears," they urged. The guards edged forward, leaning over her, and Saskia got the distinct impression she was being *sniffed*.

The guards drew back, exchanged a look, and one jerked their head. Rough thorn-tipped hands grabbed her, but at least they'd put away the fiery spears. The flames of the gate parted, and the guards steered her through it, down a rocky path that led down into a cavern, towards the burning light. Saskia heard Baskar squawk behind her, and she was glad that she wouldn't really have to do this alone after all.

Phae had been an excellent lore teacher, even though she was the first to admit it wasn't her strong suit. Saskia knew that Phae's need to relay all the stories and information about Ancient and its many realms — and the people who came from them — sprang from a devotion to Barton, to preserving him, too, in some small way.

Saskia had been expecting a land of wandering ghosts and spirits, but the guards hauling her deeper into the burning canyon were corporeal. Maybe they were the dead, but they seemed driven with purpose. Could the dead evolve?

And the Bloodlands being so near to what was likely the Den, the realm of the fox warrior god Deon, was also as upsetting as it was curious. These places were supposed to be metaphysical. But this place was real. Which made the threats bad, of course — but also the dawning realization that the longer Saskia was down here, the faster time was running out.

When they finally brought Saskia to the base of the great climbing flame, the only other word she could muster to describe her situation was *screwed*.

Standing before the flame on a stone dais as if the pyre wasn't hot enough to melt the flesh off a living body was a broad figure. Baskar's "mistress." Her mask and armour looked like those of the warriors surrounding her. Some were extremely still, barely tilting their heads to watch Saskia pass, others paced, yipping like the Foxes they were dressed as.

The figure on the dais leaned into a great sword that, in the guttering flame light, was purple as a bruise and translucent as crystal. Saskia had seen that blade before. Had trusted the person wielding it.

But the figure wore a full mask like the others, so Saskia couldn't be sure this wasn't some ruse. Not yet. This must be the General of Ash and Flame, the one Baskar had mentioned. She certainly looked the part.

"The intruder, Mother," said one of the guards, shunting Saskia forward and melting back into the throng. "She has brought the exile back with her."

Mother? Saskia didn't move nor say a word. The great masked head tilted, then swung to Baskar, who crumpled beside Saskia, shivering pitifully despite the intense heat of the fire.

"Why have you come back?" came the General's voice, sharp and demanding. "Is my word so abhorrent to you that you would disobey it outright?"

Chattering erupted around the fire, and Saskia couldn't be sure it *wasn't* the fire itself speaking.

Baskar cowered. "The v-visitor wanted to see you, my l-lady. I brought her here t-to you, as a sign . . . a sign of my p-penitence."

Saskia swung to the Rabbit as it threw her under the bus. "You *what?*"

Baskar flinched but stepped closer to the dais, hands clasped above their head. "She asked for you by the old name! She has come for your help. I will leave again, if it is your will, but I swear, Mistress, that I will never tell another story that you cannot bear to hear."

The garnet blade came up in a wide, executioner's arc, and Saskia stiffened, expecting Baskar's nutshell-head to slam into her, but the blade tip hung at Baskar's shoulder, unmoving.

"Go to your place," the General said quietly. "And I will consider mercy."

Baskar nodded frantically, took one last apologetic look at Saskia, and scampered off in a bundle of clinking sticks.

Great, thanks.

"Now. You." The General's gaze swung to Saskia, the blade coming down against the stone so quickly that sparks flew up, the length of it landing across the masked stranger's broad shoulders. "What is that rock you've got on your head?"

Saskia had definitely pictured this conversation going differently. At best, she figured Roan had been imprisoned somewhere, and she'd be greeted with gratitude when Saskia came to rescue her. At worst, Roan was infected by a Bloodbeast and the Onyx could save her. That she was some kind of . . . revered warrior god-queen was really not compelling her to speak her mind.

Saskia took a sharp breath. "You only saw it the one time," she said, "brought into your world to save it by a Deer you once knew — Phaedrapramit Das."

So much for keeping things close to the chest. But she was in a hurry to get this over with, hoping that the Moth Queen's promise that Death protected her would hold.

The General came closer. She was impassive, arms and shins covered with dark leather bracers incised with patterns.

She dropped the blade and dragged it across the stone floor as she circled Saskia.

"The Deadlands spit out more fascinating creatures each day," the General remarked, coming to a stop with the blade clapping into her open palm. The assembly chittered with something like laughter. "I've already turned one shade out for telling falsehoods. I suppose these things happen in pairs."

If this *was* Roan Harken, it definitely didn't sound like her. Saskia remembered her time with Roan clearly, despite how short it had been: she had been sharp-tongued and vibrant, with a sense of humour. That's what Saskia had liked about her in the story she often told herself.

The sword rose and the tip rested on the Onyx in Saskia's forehead. She felt the advancing pressure of the blade, but she didn't move away.

"So this used to be the Horned Quartz. The Opal recognizes its sister." Saskia glanced down to the General's leather-clad chest. Something red and purple gleamed there. A flash of green. And she felt the Onyx hum in answer to it — a question.

"And me?" Saskia tried, desperately trying to see through that mask. "Do you remember me at all?"

The sword didn't move for a good while, the observing Foxes, whatever or whoever they were, shifting and murmuring. Then the blade went down, sliding home into a sheath at the General's side. She reached up and pulled the mask away.

Saskia took a step back.

"Someone came to me once, claiming to know me. He turned out to be the greatest of traitors. Are you sure you recognize *me?*" Roan Harken's mouth twisted into a half sneer, and Saskia felt the virus of doubt spread in her gut.

A ragged scar went up the left side of Roan's face, three slashes like claw marks, all the way across her eyebrow. The scar had sealed that eye shut, the remaining area now a puckered ruin. Her remaining eye, the good one, was amber. The spirit eye that Death had given her, and that Death could see through. Obviously Death hadn't liked what she'd seen, which is why Saskia was here in the first place. Death hadn't been wrong.

This eye watched Saskia closely, then Roan scoffed, turning. "Whoever you are," she said, voice rough, "you're a stranger. I only keep from gutting you because you returned my archivist, and I am sometimes sentimental. Why have you come?"

This was Roan. It had to be. Baskar had said it'd been a hundred years, but how? Nothing made sense, especially the picture Phae had shown Saskia, bright now in her memory, of a bunch of smiling kids who barely knew what they were doing. Roan should only be, what? Twenty-five? Phae's age.

The tall warrior before her looked so much older, her wrecked face tight and corded with grief. Her dark auburn hair was cut short to her skull, spiked over her forehead with sweat. Roan Harken, the myth, the legend. Saskia desperately wanted to know what had happened even more than she wanted to tell Roan why she was here.

Then she asked the question she knew, the moment she uttered it, was the wrong one to ask. "Where's Eli?"

A hiss from the gathering. "She knows of the Owl King," whispered one of the fox-masked guards. "Perhaps *he* has sent her here."

A laugh cut through that, and Roan pivoted towards the guard, arms folded. "The Owl King does not have my mercy. He would have killed her as soon as he saw her, had he been focused on anything other than trying to keep the Heartwood from us. Or wiping us out entirely." But the idea seemed to be taking hold behind Roan's amber eye, and she spoke to Saskia now. "Are you indeed a spy of some kind?"

Saskia went cold, despite all the flames around her. "What do you mean? You and Eli — you're *friends*." *Sort of*, she self-corrected. But they'd come down here hand in hand, after all.

In the flickering firelight, Saskia saw Roan's jaw tighten. *"Why have you come?"*

Saskia opened her mouth. Closed it. Looked around the room for support, but Baskar had already fled, leaving only these Foxes, burnt at the edges, prowling, curious but ready to strike should their leader — their *mother* — ask it.

"I came down here to *get you*!" Saskia yelled, arms stretched wide. She spat an incredulous laugh of her own, as the anguish and adrenaline of the last hour started pouring out. "All this time, you and Eli were down here, playing at — I don't know what this even is! *You were our last hope!*"

The great flame crackled and Roan's one eye narrowed.

"We *are* trying to save everyone," she said. "Save them from the Owl King. The roving beasts. Our land is our legacy. We are keeping it alive."

"What? *This* place?" Saskia's heart was a hammer. "I meant *our* world! The one you came from! Don't you even know why you came down here in the first place?"

A gauntleted fist snatched Saskia's shirt up and lifted her from the ground, Roan's canines evident as she scowled.

"You've been speaking to the archivist, I see." Her words were a snarl. "Listen well: I am not a victim to be saved. Not by you. Not by *him*. The Owl King started this war. I will finish it."

Roan let go and Saskia crumpled to the ground beneath her. "There are no Uplands and there never were," Roan went on. "That stone in your head. The fell words on your tongue. More lies. The Owl King's lies, perhaps. Only the fire can save us from the wind. From the dark. And you — whoever you are, will not stand in my way."

Hands gripped Saskia roughly, hauling her up. "No! Wait, please, Roan —"

Roan was sliding her fox mask back on. For the briefest moment, Saskia saw the Dragon Opal pulse at Roan's breast before it was covered once again, and Roan unsheathed the garnet blade.

"If she is his creature, we will draw him out with her." Roan turned to the gathering, raising the blade. "My children, it is time for a merry hunt!" The Foxes howled, savage and beating drums Saskia couldn't see. Roan strode up the cavern path, and two soldiers grabbed Saksia to drag her back up and out of the canyon.

"Let me go!" she yelled, thrashing. "Please, Roan, you have to remember!"

Saskia felt something flicker in her forehead — the Onyx, struggling against the confines of the receiver she'd built to contain it. It was reaching.

Roan staggered, clutched her chest. The parade faltered as she whirled with the blade flickering in the firelight. "What is this?"

The Opal recognizes its sisters. Saskia remembered listening to Eli and Roan talk about the stones they both bore. The stones could connect to each other. Communicate, like siblings.

Saskia jerked, ripped free of the two stunned soldiers holding her back and dove, hand out, and when she touched the Dragon Opal a fire with a kickback shuddered up her arm, but she clung on.

Saskia saw and heard too much to understand it all. Voices crying out in warning. Flashes and snatches of Roan herself, of the people in her life. She saw black wings but couldn't be certain who they were attached to — if they were attached at all. She saw a floating rock against stars that did not move. She saw a cave where two shadows danced in harmony. She saw feathers and fire and felt a deep, terrible longing inter-mingled with blood.

Suddenly Saskia was beaten away, and something hard came down on her head. Wincing and looking up, she saw, in the ashy strange light of many fires, the hilt of the garnet blade.

And something else in Roan's remaining eye behind that mask — a flash of awareness.

"Saskia?"

Then Roan, and all of the assembled Fox soldiers, turned as one to a guttering shriek coming right for them from the sky. A shriek that split into many.

"The Owl King has brought his Eyes, my Hounds!" Roan cried, sword high and leading the tight charge of soldiers. She let out a howl, and the soldiers poured forth in formation. This obviously wasn't the first time.

Shrill barking battle cries filled the air. Saskia used the opportunity to get up, to try to get away, but one of the sol-diers grabbed her and held tight.

"Spy of the Owl King," it snarled, "you will pay with your shade."

Saskia didn't even have time to argue, because something that was all claws and wings swooped down and smashed the Hound aside, sending her careening back.

The rest of the Hounds weren't interested in her any longer, though, because the canyon was a blur of black shapes with tattered wings meeting with claw and teeth. The Foxes held their own with shots of fire from outstretched hands. The winged figures sent buffeting wind that stole the breath out of Saskia, cut her exposed flesh like paper. She fled backward until she was on the periphery of the battle. Roan battered off the screeching enemies, then whirled on the figure that had landed softly in front of her, catching the arc of her blade before it could meet the grinning, sharp-eyed mask she'd aimed for.

"General," the voice seethed. "My Eyes said you were agitated. As usual."

Roan pulled the sword free and swung it at the figure's long legs. He leapt up, swooping and laughing.

"Go back to your shattered sky, buzzard," Roan snarled, body shimmering with heat. "Or can I at last put you under the ground where you belong?"

The new figure merely went on smiling, flourishing its enormous taloned hand. "Remove your mask, my love, so that I may look upon my handiwork. You know I only deign to come down here to see you."

Saskia faltered behind a finger of rock. *My love?*

Roan sneered, but, in a surprising turn, did as the figure bade. At first, Saskia thought the black at his back was a cloak, but when it snapped open she saw they were wings, bigger than the man, who was taller than Roan. Expansive.

"Ah," he said, clasping his hands. "There she is."

Then he, too, removed his mask. Across his forehead was a burn, his golden eyes so bright they sizzled. What she could see of his cheekbones, rimmed in a black beard, were that they were hollow, the circles beneath his eyes smudged like permanent stains.

Eli Rathgar. He was still smiling.

"Easier to rip that smirk off now that I see it," Roan said, and in a rage of fire and wind she and Eli, and their combined forces, came at each other again.

This is not happening, Saskia lurched out of the way, nearly being taken down for a Hound throwing itself on what must have been an Owl soldier, an Eye. Then talons caught her by her backpack, pulling her into the fray.

She didn't register turning and digging into greasy feathers. In her mind, she felt that the Onyx was alive and hungry, pulling the darkness away like it had with the Deer when she'd saved Baskar. But it wasn't darkness it was pulling at — it was the shade itself. Its spirit.

Saskia tripped to her feet. The fighting had stopped on all sides, and they were all staring at her — at the pile of sticks and feathers beneath her, because the Owl shade inside the shell was gone, sucked inside the Onyx.

Eli's voice: "No."

Eli stared right at her, and Saskia was close enough to see the cracked Tradewind Moonstone in his chest, pulsing.

"She is my prisoner," Roan snarled at him. "She is *mine*."

"She is fair game," Eli said, his pupils so small they had disappeared.

"I came here for you," Saskia said to both of them, voice small. "I came here for your help." But she knew there was

333

no pleading with either of them. This had all been a terrible mistake.

Saskia's hand flew to the device, flicked the switch to full power, and the red song poured out of the Onyx. The shade poppets from both sides scattered, the Owls fleeing to the sky and the Foxes going to ground into the canyon. Both Roan and Eli clutched their chests.

"No!" Eli roared, rounding back on Saskia, wings wide and talons reaching. Roan slammed the flat of the blade into him like a home run, sending him careening backward.

It was too much, even for Saskia. There was a roar like an overloaded generator coming from the Onyx. Saskia couldn't take it and fumbled to shut off the switch. She collapsed in the middle of the impromptu battlefield, feeling her hopes dissolving around her with her blackening vision. She thought she saw rabbit ears, felt sharp wooden hands catch her, but couldn't be sure of anything.

Don't ever confront your heroes, she thought before familiar darkness came.

SPARK *of the* NEW GODS

Phae had sat so long with her head in her hands that Natti thought she'd finally snapped.

The fight had done significant damage to the Old Leg, even though the Denizens ultimately had to retreat. They'd gone to One Evergreen, but they'd soon have to find somewhere else to hide. Jordan Seneca was there, speaking in hushed tones in the living room to Ella and her aunt Cassandra, while a few other shaken Denizen fighters milled about the tight quarters, trying to make sense of things. Jordan and a handful of Owl Unit soldiers, who had gladly betrayed the ETG at the mere suggestion, were keeping the apartment protected by making it look deserted, but that would last only so long.

Natti flopped on the sofa beside Phae, exhausted. She'd just sent word to her mother and Aivik that she'd found the fight and they'd need to come quick before the ETG struck them first. It would be quickest to take the Cold Road and bring them all here but looking at Phae now, she couldn't bear to leave her alone. Things were bad and likely only to get worse.

These new rebels, even those who had been waiting for this day as the Cluster, she knew had all looked to Solomon as the leader. That position was woefully vacant now with no one ready to fill it. As the priest, Arnas Harken had been a beacon to Mundanes whose faith had been shattered, but they needed someone who would be strong enough to hold what precious ground they'd gained today by storming the Old Leg and allowing Saskia through the Bloodgate.

Something must have happened within the ETG, too, because Grant's personnel had fallen back after an initial retaliation and hadn't yet come for the rebel Denizens. Information about the attack on the Old Leg was not being widely broadcast — in fact, most major networks were on blackout standby. But the gate must have worked. The ETG were just deciding how they were going to spin it.

Phae suddenly let out a strangled noise and lifted her head. Natti was not relieved when she saw the smile on her friend's devastated face.

"She's gone," she said. "I basically raised her, and she *still* turned into Roan, no matter what I did."

Natti, unsure what to do, but figuring this was likely what was called for, bundled Phae close and held her tightly while she cried.

"I hear ya," she muttered, patting her back. "I'm sorry all your friends are mule-stubborn and stupid besides that."

Phae pulled away, rubbing her face hard. "No, I can't. I've cried enough. There's too much to do now." Her hands rested on her thighs as she took a look around the room. There was scant food, but everyone was too hyped up to eat anything. They were all coming down from the high. "If Saskia was smart enough to get through," Phae went on, "she can get back out. That's the whole point, isn't it?"

"And we have our own problems up here. If Roan and Eli are down there, and Barton, too, they'll help her." Natti didn't know that for sure, of course, but she also didn't want to entertain the notion Saskia had leapt full bore into a death trap.

In Winnipeg, the remaining Denizens certainly had, anyway.

"It's only a matter of time." Phae shook her head. "Word will get out about Project Crossover. The rest of the world will militarize against Denizens and they'll call it justice, or claim getting rid of us will get rid of the Darkling Moon problem."

She looked like she'd wanted to pace, but there wasn't any room to do it. Jet was pressed against the kitchen wall, listening to everything, clutching one of Saskia's old keyboards close. There'd be so many Denizens who couldn't fight, who would be picked off first. Jet reminded Natti of that all too easily.

"There are a lot of us," Natti said. "Denizens complied with Restoration only to show we meant Mundanes no harm. About time we backpedalled on that and got the message out to the others."

"How? The ETG controls all the networks, and they'll be sweeping hard for internal traitors, if they all haven't gone underground already. When their own message goes out about this, it'll become holy writ."

"Hmph," Natti grunted. "I'm not much for the planning part of a war. I'm here as the brute force." She threw Phae a glance. "You noticed how we're all a bit lacking in the leadership department, I assume?"

Phae's pale, brown face lifted a little, and she sighed. "Don't worry. It's coming."

As if on cue, Jordan turned to look at both Natti and Phae. So did a few of the others in the room, and it went quiet. Without looking at one another, the women stood as one, surveying everyone who watched them.

"We started this," Phae spoke clearly, confidently. "We will finish it one way or another." She looked to Jet. Smiled. He nodded, and Natti took in his mix of childlike wonder and brave determination.

Natti folded her arms. "We can't exactly tell the rest of the world what we're doing, but we can show them. We start here, with Winnipeg, where it all began. We take the city. We hold it. And in doing so, we show everyone else that we're stronger together."

Phae blinked at Natti, who shrugged, her neck reddening as if to say, *I really have no idea where that came from, but it seemed like something a leader would say* . . .

Jordan nodded. "I'm with you." The rest of the room echoed the sentiment.

For now, they'd rest and plan. But soon they'd be back on the streets. Streets that were theirs now. Natti remembered the image of Roan, spray-painted on a statue by the river.

"We are the flame," Natti said.

"Join the fire fight!" Jet howled, and the room cheered with him.

Run, run, *run run* . . .

Saskia kept repeating it to herself. Running had always helped. It would help now. Monsters. Fire. Darkness. *Run.*

She ran headlong into the past.

They had been walking home from Saskia's new school. She'd walked apart from Barton and Phae, who were ahead, talking quietly, with Saskia pretending she couldn't hear every word.

"She's just scared," Barton said. "This is all new to her. New country, new life. It's going to take adjusting to. We're *all* adjusting. Let's just try to make the most of what we get every day, okay?"

Phae sucked on her teeth. "I wish we knew more about her. I mean . . . what happened with that monster, Urka? I remember what Roan told me about it. But Saskia destroyed it with some power we can't even look up."

Barton glanced over his shoulder at Saskia, who had quickly dipped her face back to the ground, hiding her flushed cheeks behind her hair.

Barton turned back to Phae. "She's just a regular kid. The entire Coalition, the Family leaders, they all agreed. She's harmless. She's Mundane." He lifted a shoulder. "I'm kind of jealous, if I'm being honest."

Phae sighed, laughing partially. "Same."

Suddenly Saskia stopped, two thick black running blades now in her line of sight. Startled, she looked up, Barton standing over her, hands on his hips.

"How about we go to the track, Saskia?" he asked.

She blinked, looked from him to Phae. "I thought I was in trouble."

Phae laid a hand on Saskia's head. "You two should go. Burn off some steam. There'll be time to discuss what to do about your temper when we get home."

Home. Saskia bit her lip. "Okay," she said, reluctant to let go of how mad she'd been at the other kids in her school, the things they'd said about Denizens, how mad she'd been at Phae and Barton for not getting it. How mad she'd been at *herself* for liking that she'd put those kids in their place with just her fists.

Then Barton had gathered Phae to him, kissing her on the cheek, and Saskia let all the anger go, remembering what family could be. She realized then that the thing she'd been most scared of was that Phae and Barton would give up on her, or send her back to Scotland, to the dark place that she saw in her worst dreams peopled with the Cinder Kids who'd convinced her *they* were her only family.

Phae walked up towards the Maryland Bridge, waving goodbye as she took the corner. Barton led Saskia to the park behind the high school on Stafford, where the running track shone in the diminishing daylight.

"You used to go to this school, right?" Saskia had asked him, gazing around in awe as she clutched her backpack straps.

Barton took off his jacket, put it with his own bag by the bleachers. He nodded, his gaze a little inward. "Phae and I used to go here, with Roan. It's weird, seeing it now. After everything." He'd graduated from this high school almost two years ago, and now he and Phae were parenting a ten-year-old.

Whatever the bemusement meant on his face, he wasn't going to skirt the more pressing issue. "You can't just go after people if they say something you don't agree with. Violence just makes space for more violence, mostly inside you." He pointed to her chest, where her heart hammered.

She kicked the grass. "You all fought. For what you believed in."

Barton sighed with more than an air of drama. "There were sort of world-destroying monsters in the way, Sask. Not loud-mouthed kids." He nudged her and her eyes darted at him. "I know what it's like. To feel powerless. But you're not power-less. You're a bright kid. You're going to do amazing things." He bent down, face to face with her. "But you have to be smart. The world is changing very quickly right now. Before, Denizens blended in. We don't anymore. People are scared. We all are. Best to just keep some things to ourselves. And when it gets hard to take, you talk to me or Phae first, okay?"

She hated that her eyes stung. "But what if you guys aren't here anymore? What if something happens to you?" The kids she'd gotten into the fight with had said that all Denizens should just be killed, with the braying, stupid, know-nothing tone that most kids had. It wasn't anger Saskia had acted on, but fear.

Barton shook his head. "When I'm alone, and I'm feeling like that, I run. It makes me feel in control of my own body at least. After a run, things are a bit clearer. Do you want me to show you?"

Saskia nodded. He handed her his stopwatch. "Okay, kiddo," he said. "I'll go first. Then we'll go together."

They'd stayed at the track for hours. Barton was so fast, like a hare. He looked free. Saskia whooped and hollered, louder still when he raced straight for her, scooping her up in his arms. And when they ran together, side by side, that was the first time Saskia began to believe things would be okay.

❦

Saskia jolted awake with such a start that her chest hurt, choking on air. She felt like she'd been squeezed between solid walls of rock, paralyzed, unable to wake.

Hands on her forearms. "It's all right."

At first, she'd thought it was Ella again, in a hidden dormitory beneath Cecelia's house. Then she jerked backward, a dark mask face angling down at her with bright eyes. "What —"

A huge rabbit, made of sticks and rubble, tilted its head at her. The name swam up — Baskar. The archivist. She touched her head, which smarted and then panic set in as she ran her fingers through her tangled hair.

"It's not lost," Baskar said, pulling the Fractal crown from a shadowy corner and holding it out to her reverently. "Here."

Saskia snatched it from the long fingerbranches, then turned it over, checking for damage. It seemed intact, but she'd have to run a diagnostic —

She whipped around, searching the tight space. It was warm in here, but not as stifling as it had been when . . . it came back to her in stutters: the huge pyre, Roan towering over her with a blade, one-eyed and raging. Eli had been there, too, and . . .

She shut her eyes and pressed her knuckles into them.

"Are you all right?" Baskar was close, hovering over her and uncertain. "You do not look well."

"Should I be well?" Saskia snapped, and Baskar leapt back so quickly they rattled when they struck the smooth wall behind them.

Saskia sighed. "I'm sorry. It's just been a lot." She pulled her legs to her chest. The walls around the two of them were close — though not as close as the crushing stone in her nightmare, and not made of the same material, either. She reached out and touched smooth wood. Beneath her were star-shaped fresh leaves, and just a few feet from her shoulder, a large opening into the overcast world beyond.

Something rumbled above. The air felt warm and smelled earthy. It was raining outside. She and Baskar were inside a tree, she realized, or at least underneath it, in a burrow, a bit of daylight filtering in. Saskia reached out and ran a hand over a network of gnarled roots in the smooth, dug-out soil.

Baskar's finger extended to the Onyx but did not touch it. "This device you wear. It muzzles the stone. It is very clever. If you made it, you must be very clever, as well."

Saskia ran her dry tongue over her lips as the finger drew away, flushing under the compliment. "I've seen what these stones do to people who let them in. Didn't want to chance it."

Baskar nodded. "Yes. Clever." Then they cocked their head at Saskia and pulled their own legs up, mimicking her.

"Is this your home?" Saskia asked. Her throat was parched, and she tried to clear it. She'd had a canteen in her pack, along with her tablet. Seeming to sense this need, Baskar pulled the bag from a nook hewn into the trunk and handed it over. They had kept everything neatly for her. They must have brought her here, too, after the battle, and kept her safe. She didn't have the mindspace to question why.

"It is a retreat," they said. "I spend most of my time in

the archives below my mistress's pyre. All of my books, my stories, are there. Save the one I have been missing."

That detail came back to her as she rummaged in the pack for the canteen. "You still haven't found it, huh?"

Baskar shook their head in dismay. "It is just as well. It contained the story my lady did not want. The wilderness can have it, I suppose." Then the mask lifted in something like a smile. "You may stay here as long as you like, though. I have taken care of my mistress before, so I know how to take care of you. You need rest in the way the dead do not."

Too much to unpack there, Saskia thought, taking one long pull of her water before stopping herself. She'd have to ration. She glanced at the Rabbit. "Is there somewhere I can get fresh water? Or do you all just, like, not need to eat or drink either?" How Roan and Eli had survived this long was another question she'd add to the list . . .

Baskar looked from Saskia to the hole of the burrow. "Do you not have rain in the Uplands?"

"Well I don't know how any of this works!" She threw up her hands. "There wasn't exactly a walkthrough available."

Baskar snatched the canteen from her before she could stop them, holding it out of the opening in the tree's trunk. "You will be fine. My mistress and the Owl King used to have needs such as yours, but you'll find as you are here longer, hunger and thirst fade. Then you will become undying, as they have. Especially with that curious stone of yours. The stones keep you safe."

Saskia frowned, fingers tightening around the Fractal in her lap. The Calamity Stones weren't called the *Happy Joy Protecting Stones* for a reason. It sounded like Roan and Eli had become myths themselves. Saskia definitely had no intention of staying down here long enough to see if she would turn into one, too.

She hoped she'd have a choice about that.

After a while, the canteen was full again, and Baskar handed it back. Saskia slid it back into the bag and put it aside. "This isn't exactly going the way I planned."

Baskar shivered, and their shell-body crackled. "Perhaps if you spoke to my mistress again, you might find a newer, better plan."

Saskia huffed. "She was pretty ready to feed me to the birds. I doubt she's interested in anything I have to say." She looked outside into the rain. Weather, vegetation, an ecosystem. The sky even appeared darker, like they were coming onto night. This was a real, tangible world. As far as she knew, it hadn't always been like that. And the things that she once aimed for — all that hero nonsense — seemed empty now, after the confrontation with the "General" and the "Owl King." Everything was wrong.

She turned to Baskar. "What happened to them? They're both so . . ."

"Omnipotent?" Baskar finished, leaning back, considering the hollowed roof above them. "So much has changed. It only follows that they would, too. They haven't changed *lately*. They have been fighting a very long time."

"And I don't have a lot of time to spare, myself." Baskar seemed as though they knew enough to be helpful. "What was the story, the one that Roan didn't want to hear? That got you exiled?"

Baskar went from partially relaxed to all nerves again, stick-bones chattering. "I promised her. I promised I would not tell it again, and I intend to keep my word this time."

Okay, Sask, back it up. "Never mind then. Can you tell me *your* story?"

Baskar swung towards her, then became still. So still she worried the shade had vacated the shell till they spoke. "My story?"

"Sure." She thought of the Deer shade she'd seen when she arrived in this wasteland, put her finger in the dirt and leaves beneath her, and started absently moving them around as she talked. "You were alive once. Do you remember it?"

Baskar twitched then lifted a lopsided shoulder. "I have been dead a very, very long time. Most dead return to the place they came from, eventually, or change into something else. A spirit is just a sort of energy, after all. That is what the Owl King said, though his word cannot be trusted.

"All I know is my story as it has changed here. For a very long time, the Deadlands were all separate — the forest of the Warren, the canyon steppes of the Den, all of them had clear boundaries that could not be crossed. Then, all at once, the gods we knew were gone, and the ways back up were closed, and everything was . . . new." They leaned down, inspecting Saskia's leaf patterns as if there was a message there. "The Bloodlands, too, and all the damned parts of it, became a part of this new world. The dead were all looking for a purpose again. The General of Ash and Flame provided us with one. Some joined the Owl King instead. They are the new gods." Baskar pointed to the crown in Saskia's hands. "The stones are their rights to power. My mistress may have seen yours as a threat, at first, but now she sees an opportunity."

"For what?" Saskia dared.

Baskar put a finger to the place their mouth should be. "Are you sure you're not a god?"

Saskia was going to say no immediately, but she glanced down at the Onyx. Filled with the power of death, of Darklings, and maybe of Fia. Part of her was in it, too. It listened to her. She realized a part of her wanted Baskar's guess to be true.

"No," she did say, eventually. "I'm just a regular person. Just me."

Baskar nodded. "That's as may be. There are many stories here. Many missing. But there is room for yours."

Missing stories? Saskia sighed. "The only missing thing I'm after is Ancient."

The twig hand slapped over her mouth as it had when she'd first met Baskar, as though her low-toned lament could be heard for miles. "Don't. *Do not* say that name if you want to survive."

The hand drew away slowly, and Saskia was utterly still. "Why?"

But Baskar was shaking their head again. "Mustn't say. It is not a story to tell."

Saskia was about to let herself have a well-deserved meltdown, when movement in the middle distance outside the burrow caught her eye and she ducked. "Something's coming!"

Baskar was quickly pressed into her shoulder, but after a squint, and a pause, their body loosened slightly. "My mistress is come."

Saskia pulled herself back into the tree, flattening against the smooth grain, feeling a horrible mix of panic and extremely naïve high hopes. "What does she want with the Onyx?"

Baskar did not seem intent on leaving the open bole, wanting to be seen by Roan. They were reverent of her. "She saw what your stone can do to the dead, and how it sent the Owl King and his Eyes into retreat. She will feel she owes you a debt. She will try to win you to her side."

"And whose side are you on?" Saskia asked quickly. It should have been obvious, but how Baskar spoke about both Roan and Eli, perhaps exile had made them rethink things.

The way Baskar's face was made, there was no mouth for them to speak from. Just flat planes and black, ghostly translucence. But the white eyes seemed to smile. "I am on the story's side, until it is ended." They shook their head. "But I made a promise to protect my mistress. That is the point of *my* story."

Saskia peeked around the edge. Roan was closer, but she had stopped twenty feet off, rain hissing into mist when it touched her, her spiky hair seeming to spark with each droplet. The scar over her missing eye stood out like a hot coal.

She pulled the long blade from its sheath at her hip and slammed it into the ground with one even thrust. She did not take her eyes away from the tree.

"She does not want a fight," Baskar interpreted. Then, eagerly, they asked, "Will you go to her?"

Saskia stiffened. "Will she listen to me this time, do you think?" Saskia's mind rushed, filling with probabilities. "Can I change her back?"

Baskar placed a hand on Saskia's shoulder. "My mistress does not need changing. You just need to know her as the dead do." Then, a slight sniff, a jerk of their head. "You have a touch of death about you as well. Maybe even stronger than hers. It is most becoming."

Saskia grimaced. "Uh, where I'm from, that's not really a good thing."

Baskar grabbed Saskia by her jacket, shoving her through the hole. "I won't let her kill you," they said.

"Somehow I don't think that'll be enough," Saskia grunted, sorely tempted to dive back into the hole at her feet.

Roan was still standing there, hands on her hips, rooted as if she'd sprouted out of the ground. Saskia could hide in Baskar's tree all day, but what would that do? Much the same as she couldn't sit in her tech-crowded bedroom while the world went by, while her friends and family were in danger.

She still held the Onyx, contained in its crown, and for now it was all she had. She slipped it over her forehead, the familiar weight settling. She swallowed a hard pit of discomfort as she straightened, dropped her shoulders, and walked forward.

Roan appraised her the whole way, and when Saskia stopped short a couple feet off, the General nodded. "Saskia."

Her heart sped up, and she fought the urge to swipe her suddenly soaked hair out of her face. "Do you really remember me?"

An eyebrow tilt. "I have spoken with the archivist after witnessing your . . . performance. I know your name. That is all I know of you." She folded her armoured arms. "What I do know is that you defied the Owl King. You came here looking for me. I think we are in need of each other."

Saskia's teeth clamped down, and her ears popped. Words were only as good as the intentions of their speaker. Roan's temper was as hot as the flame flickering inside her. Just as Saskia had made a deal with a Darkling to repair the Onyx, and a promise to Death, she'd have to make another deal if she was going to beat them all at their own game.

She turned back to the tree where Baskar was clearly watching. They waved at her encouragingly, and it reminded her of Cam's faraway birthday thumbs-up. Everything was blending.

"If I go with you," Saskia said, turning back to Roan, "you have to hear me out. The Moth Queen sent me. Do you remember *her*?"

Roan's smile was tight, but her eyes gleamed with something that looked like hunger. "Oh yes," she said. "But this place no longer belongs to Death. Or the former gods. I will show you, a fellow stonebearer, why this place is worth saving."

Saskia hesitated. Everything was so twisted. If Saskia couldn't convince Roan to help her, what were Saskia's chances of going home at all?

This was the only chance she had. "Okay." She nodded. "Let's go."

Roan plucked the blade free of the ground, lifted her eye to the tree, and whistled. Baskar slunk out and past Saskia, as if she weren't there at all. Roan afforded Baskar a *hmm*, before patting them on the head, turning on her heel, and leading the way.

Saskia wasn't a sycophant like the Rabbit, but she'd have to pretend to be. All she could do was follow.

〜〜

The Owl King paced along the Limitless Ledge. "How many were lost?"

His Eyes looked just as battle-worn as Eli felt. "Many on both sides. That stone . . . it devoured them."

"We heard it sing, my lord. We all wanted to go to it. It felt like home —"

"Enough," the Owl King flared. "This stone's presence changes too much of the game, too quickly. Is the Heartwood still secure?"

The shades turned to one another, then nodded, perfectly in sync. "Yes, my lord."

"Good." He dismissed them with a flick of his wing, then pulled it back in tight, dragging a talon through his long, dark beard. Hidden beneath it was something he tried not to think about, the memory of something along the skin of his cheek. Something that wouldn't fade.

He cast his mind out past the Roost, into the Emberdom and Cinder Town at its centre. Roan was there, as she often was, and so was the girl. Saskia. His mind cast backward, memory sparked by the girl. He remembered a time, so long ago, when both of them were tucked under his arms as they flew over a wide and endless ocean.

Then he lifted the book the sentinels had found in a thicket.

"I'm not ready for this to end," he said to the empty room. He opened the book and read the story he knew to be true but still couldn't face.

The HEARTWOOD

Mi-ja hadn't the time to embrace the harshness of her new reality. There was only action, and she was still unsure where her place was in it. *You're in charge now*, the chancellor had said before hurtling into oblivion. If that's where he went. Both Grant and Rathgar had gone into that reactor room and not come out, and they'd left a mess Mi-ja could never hope to clean up. The responsibility had been thrown over her so carelessly, a suffocating plastic body bag, and she'd forgotten how to breathe.

But there it was. This was her circus now. From lieutenant to aide to . . .

Chancellor by proxy.

"Madam?" The door to the office opened to Mi-ja's aide, Trey, also struggling with his new role. She had already been training him the last few weeks to assist her, ever since the chancellor had come to rely on her for everything. At least before Mi-ja was thrust into this office she'd been its unwitting understudy.

"Are they ready?" she asked, straightening her jacket, the badges against the breast heavier than she'd imagined. She'd thrown the question at Trey, but it had been meant for herself.

Trey nodded, his bobbing turban the same grey as his flawless uniform. "It will be live to all networks. Strike forces are also mobilizing, but they are on standby, awaiting your word."

Mi-ja came around the desk and followed him out. It seemed like she was walking in a haze. "One thing at a time," she heard herself say. She wasn't about to bomb Winnipeg. *Just to help those that would*, a voice inside gnawed.

She took her seat behind another desk in a room that was lit so brightly it made her teeth hurt. There were many cameras, and nervous people operating them, and government and Task Guard officials. A backdrop of flags. She had already debriefed the prime minister, who was standing in this very room now and had already said his piece. How Mi-ja wished they could just handle it without her. How she wished so many things could reverse, and she could get off this freight train.

The light on the cameras flickered, the teleprompter loading with the speech she had written only a few hours ago, and she spoke. "Citizens of Canada, and these united nations. My name is Song Mi-ja, direct aide to Chancellor Lochlan Grant, coming to you from the Elemental Task Guard headquarters in Winnipeg. As Prime Minister Orison said only moments ago, we must be vigilant and unified in this time of crisis. We feel your fear and we recognize it, but this government, and the Elemental Task Guard, will not bend to it."

Mi-ja had penned the speech by imagining all of Grant's gravitas in the language, but it sounded so jagged in her voice. She'd have to become someone else, then, just for this moment, to convince everyone, including herself.

"Chancellor Lochlan Grant, shortly after his internal meetings at the United Nations, returned to Winnipeg as his Project Crossover reached a breakthrough." She had edited out Saskia Allen Das's part in that, for surely it had been pivotal, and Solomon Rathgar's presumed end, because his key had been found, but he, along with the chancellor, had not. "The chancellor saw his work complete and has passed into the place known as the Realms of Ancient in the hopes that what he finds there will put an end to the Darkling Moon that Denizen-kind unleashed upon us all seven years ago."

The security footage was burned into her eyes. She'd watched it so much it was trapped there, and always would be, which made destroying the footage futile though necessary. Saskia jumping. Grant lunging after her. A cloud of electricity bursting, and they were gone. Both of them. Maybe forever. Mi-ja had to believe otherwise. She needed the promise of an out to get through this.

She cleared her throat, took a drink of water from the glass at her wrist, and willed herself not to spill a drop. She continued. "We are confident that the chancellor will return —" *No we aren't.* "— and when he does, the Denizen agenda will be put to rest, as will the differences between us." *Not if they are rising up now, ready to strike.* "To those Denizens out there in the world — we implore you to move forward peacefully and in unity with the Elemental Task Guard. In this crucial time, we do not wish any further casualties, Denizen or human. Despite our good intentions, there were those Denizens who saw an opportunity as the chancellor went ahead with his noble work, Denizens who attacked our headquarters here in Winnipeg, hoping to stop us. We withdrew, but we will not hesitate to strike back should they test us again. We stand on guard for this country, for this world, for those who cannot defend themselves, and will do so until the Darkling Moon has left our skies at last, and we can rebuild this planet to the glory that it once was."

The speech went on, the fervour rising. Mi-ja went elsewhere, separate from it all as the words came out of her with a passion she'd never had for this regime or any of what it stood for. But now rules and authority made her feel safe.

She was not in control, though. None of them were. She announced herself as the chancellor by proxy, but it was just another made-up title. They were all kids playing at war.

At one point, the words stopped, and so did the cameras, and her desk was swarmed, and she smiled up at the prime minister and the people who grasped her, congratulating her, telling her they stood with her. She smiled and smiled and smiled.

She should have run out onto Broadway when the Denizens had attacked and lost herself in the horde that had blasted their way through the gate.

It was going to be a long war.

࿔

Saskia kept her questions to herself. She wanted to know more about Roan, and she'd get there by hanging back, observing. Baskar followed more like an obedient dog than a Rabbit, and at first it made Saskia cringe, but then she recalled what they'd said: *the dead were looking for something to believe in.* Disgust turned to pity. Everyone just wanted to belong, and she didn't blame Baskar for clinging to whatever acceptance they could get.

Roan led Saskia through the deep-cut channels of the canyon. Cinder Town, they called it. Saskia discovered quickly that Roan's soldiers, the Hounds of Deon, were all Fox shades, and Roan took her down to the barracks first.

"The shades come to me," Roan said. "I welcome them and I give them a bit of the light they crave." Huddled in a corner of a long room, dug out of the earth, were maybe three Fox shades, crouching. Roan beckoned one forward, and Baskar assisted in grabbing parts from various nooks — branches, stones, layers of bark — laying it all down on the ground in a way that made Saskia think of Jet and his floor paintings with her tech garbage.

The Fox shade stepped into the pile of wilderness debris, and Roan stretched out a finger, at the tip of which was a flame. All at once, almost too quickly to see, the debris shivered into crackling, broken-jointed angles, and the shade went inside of it, pulling the body on like a coat. Roan really might be some kind of god, making her own followers in her image. Judging by Eli's forces, he'd learned how to do the same thing.

Maybe with the Onyx, and how it could fix corrupted shades, or pull them into it, Saskia was doing it, too.

"Tell me," Roan asked, without turning to Saskia. "Where did the shades go when you turned on your clever stone?"

She needed to answer very, very carefully in order to proceed. "I don't know how it works," she admitted, which was only partly a lie. "Only that the Moth Queen wished to see the dead to rights, and I promised to help her. Maybe they want to rest. Maybe they're resting inside the stone."

Roan turned halfway, assessing. "Do you mean to release them on me, as your own army?"

Saskia felt the blood leave her face. "No! I just escaped one war, I'm not looking to get involved in another one."

"Hm." Roan seemed to accept that for now. She turned fully and led both Saskia and Baskar back out into the main thoroughfare of Cinder Town. "Either way, it is a clever trick. It would be useful against the Owl King. Without his soldiers protecting him, he will be weakened, and we can rest easy knowing he's given up the Heartwood."

There was that word again. Saskia glanced at Baskar, but they just shook their head at her. She hadn't wanted to ask any questions but did anyway. "What is the Heartwood?"

Roan was in a generous mood. "It is a tree. A very valuable tree. It appeared long after the Owl King and I arrived. It is guarding something terrible. It should never be disturbed. Whoever controls it, controls this world. The Owl King currently keeps me from it — I'm concerned he will use it against us all."

A tree that had appeared after Roan and Eli had . . . the only trees she'd seen so far were Hope Trees. Which made her think of Barton, which made her wildly guess — and desperately hope, this tree had something to do with him.

Eli was protecting it. Roan was trying to take control of it. Saskia needed to get to it and figure out the truth first.

Roan stopped then, hands on her hips, letting out a very deep sigh. "There is much, I'm sure, you don't understand." She pivoted on her heel, an elegant flourish, and Saskia was surprised — the Roan she knew was clumsy. "Before I take you farther, there is something about this world I wish you to know."

Saskia folded her hands before her to keep them from shaking. She nodded.

"Grief cannot survive here." Roan opened her arms, like a preacher. "This is heaven. Heaven is worth protecting, worth eliminating any threat for. Don't you agree?"

Of course, Saskia had heard this all before, from the Task Guard, and so hearing it almost verbatim from Roan chilled her to her Keds. "It depends on how far you want to take it. I'm too young to know anything about heaven." *So were you*, she wanted to tell Roan, but she didn't. "I'm not here to eliminate anyone, either. Or be eliminated."

Roan smiled. "I'm not really sure what you're here for. But I intend for you to see it my way before either of us finds out." The smile dropped like it hadn't even been there, when Roan turned to Baskar. "Take her to the archive and tell her our purpose. Hopefully I can trust you to do that much."

Baskar bowed their head and seemed to trill with excitement instead of flinching in fear. "Of course, Mistress."

Roan appraised Saskia one last time and nodded curtly. "Perhaps once you've heard it all objectively, you will come to me as an ally." She didn't say what would happen if Saskia didn't, but Saskia could guess that, too.

With that, Roan turned abruptly and left them behind.

Saskia dropped her face into her hands, running them through her hair and getting it knotted in the Fractal's framework. "Okay. This is getting way too intense. Is she going to kill me or isn't she?"

"Not today!" Baskar cried, looping a gangling arm through Saskia's. "Did you hear that? She trusts me! Oh, lovely day."

"Great for you," Saskia groaned, and Baskar led her down a steep and narrow causeway, further into the canyon.

"All the stories I have collected and sorted are in the archive," Baskar buzzed, and Saskia couldn't help but catch on to their excitement. "Soon you'll know all. Soon you'll understand. There is no greater power than understanding."

Saskia would've agreed once, but she didn't know what it was going to take to understand what was going on down here.

They took a few corners and went farther down into a deeper labyrinth. Here and there were shades, in both poppet bodies and without, their eyes flashing at her as they passed. Saskia noted there were many Rabbits down here, intermingling with fewer Foxes than she'd seen above ground. Most of the Foxes seemed pressed into soldier service. There were even a few Deer, though Baskar explained that the Deer were the most likely to become Bloodbeasts, as their Realm was the first to shatter. There was definitely one other Family missing. "And the Seals?" she asked.

Baskar sucked in something like a breath, then she remembered that the dead couldn't breathe. "We do not go to the Abyss. It surrounds us on all sides. They are protected by a Bloodbeast in the depths, and they are allies to no one."

Things just got better and better. "This really is too much."

Baskar swung around so quickly that Saskia bumped into them. Their hands steadied her, head tucked in concern. "I will help you through this," Baskar said. "When you hear the story, you won't feel so alone."

Saskia blinked, not sure what to say to that. Baskar went ahead, beckoning. "Come and you'll see."

Baskar had gone through a doorway, and Saskia noted that scratched above it was a shape — no, a symbol. One she recognized from the many sigils that had shown themselves to her. *Story* came the interpretation from a place in her mind she didn't know was there.

And a different word came up beneath it, a synonym — *Narrative*.

Saskia stepped over the threshold into an enormous room whose end she couldn't find. Stacked neatly, from stone floor to stone ceiling, were strips of bark. Books handcrafted carefully. There were many of them. Baskar raced between the pillars gleefully.

"Oh my stories," they said, making a good show of leaping into the air and spinning. "Oh, I am *home*."

Saskia let out a nervous laugh and bit her lip. For a moment, she let go of what had brought her here, taking it all in and spinning, too, except much slower. "This is really something." She bent to examine a slip under her foot and realized that the text written on the bark was made up of the sigils she'd seen. They hadn't been some ill omen, then. Just a different language. The language of Ancient, of the gods that came from it . . .

Baskar snatched the sheet she'd been looking at, examined it, then raced off to categorize it. "Did you build this place?" she called after them.

Baskar seemed to swell with pride. "I collected these stories as they happened, yes," they said, rickety hands wide. "It has been a glorious task. I could not stand for any of it to be lost. That is why my mistress kept me close. She does value the story, too — where she came from, where the Owl King came from. It helps her to look ahead."

To Saskia, it seemed like all Roan was interested in was her war with Eli. But convincing Baskar of that might take longer than she had. "Can you tell me how it all started between them . . . down here?"

"By heart," Baskar said, laying a hand across their narrow chest as if they were a thespian finally arrived to their stage. "Once upon a time, a fox followed a girl home. The girl was marked by Death. Death gave the girl to the fox, on one condition: she must banish a snake . . ."

Saskia sat still and listened. She had heard this story before. Ella had told it to her. Saskia had told it to herself. Everything was folding in on itself. She sat, cross-legged, as the edge in Baskar's usually uncertain voice smoothed out. The way they told it, it did sound like something beautiful, something worth believing.

"I lived this story," Saskia said when Baskar had paused, and they came down slowly on their knees before Saskia.

"So you know," they said, "that Roan and Eli came down here together, as one."

Saskia nodded. "They were looking for something. Like I am."

Earlier, she had checked her tablet, and though the battery on it was reading fine, there had been no messages. Not from Barton, not from anyone. Saskia was out of her depth, and she needed something, someone, to cling on to. Heartwood. New gods. Baskar was casting a spell, and she was getting too tired to refuse it. She wanted to take a moment to not be hurtling forward. She needed to learn how things had gotten this way before she could untangle it all and do what she came here to do.

Remember yourself and what brought you to the other side, Phae had warned. Saskia repeated it again.

"Roan came first," Baskar said, weaving their hands as they weaved their words, mesmerizing. "The shades did not respect her then. They blamed her for the loss of their god, Deon, and of the fire. But Roan carried the fire with her all along, and when she reclaimed it they followed her. It is how I met her, that first time." Baskar's voice overflowed with devotion. "She showed me kindness when the wilderness had shown only cruelty. I will forever be grateful to her for that. She gave me the first story and inspired me to collect these."

Saskia nodded at the impressive collection they were immersed in now. "And Eli?"

Baskar raised one hand high, then let it drop, fingers angled downward like a paper airplane crashing. "One day, when Roan had accepted the fire fully into herself and turned away the grief she had felt in the Uplands, she and her shades watched as a strange winged creature fell from the sky." Baskar's fingers spread like wings. "It was the Owl King, but he was then called Eli, and he told Roan he was there to save her."

Saskia shivered, remembering the brief encounter when Eli, himself incredibly changed, had shown himself. "Then what happened?"

Baskar landed a finger gently on Saskia's nose. An affectionate gesture that reminded her of Ella, but not exactly — it made her remember how Ella used to make her feel when they traded stories of their heroes. It made her feel something in her chest, fluttering.

Baskar's mask rose a little, which Saskia took for a smile. "They disagreed. They were always very good at that."

As Baskar told her this story, Saskia fell into it.

HOLLOW TALK

Dark and heat and light. A tightness across his chest, growing tighter. The dark withdrew as the light grew, his closed eyelids turning red as a sun in . . . a place he couldn't recall, slipping away by inches.

Remember, warned his mother, weaving her thoughts into his in a cross-stitch, clarifying years of gaps, of things he had purposefully cut out, building emptiness to convince himself he wasn't already empty. *Remember to always keep yourself close. You are alive in the land of the dead. The very air will try to take what makes you, claim it, and wipe it out. You've only just taken back what you lost. Remember how. Remember why. Remembering is what will rebuild the door back to living. Not just for you, but for* —

Eli opened his heavy eyes, nostrils flaring with the burning. "Christ!" He tried to pull back from the fire in his face but couldn't get far. The flame banked with his exhale, and when the white dots cleared from his vision, Eli saw the flickering blaze was held in an outstretched palm, and above it an impatient, twisted mouth.

Roan's mouth.

"What the hell are you doing?" Eli croaked. There were other things he'd wanted to say to her now that he'd found her, but best to deal with the immediate threats.

He was lying on his side, shoulders tight to his ears. His knees were bent under him, stiff, locked. He tried to move his hands, wrists grinding at the small of his back, ankles much the same behind him.

Confusion turned into panic. "A little much, Harken, don't you think?"

She kneeled next to him, face blank, head cocked. "What's that word you keep calling me, demon?"

Demon? This was . . . less than ideal. "Your name, you Lost Boy reprobate." Eli struggled against the knots, tried to pull his arms up, but realized more bonds were tight around his chest and waist, binding him in a full harness. *Thorough.* Eli scowled internally.

"This is ludicrous! You have eyes in your head — I can barely stand let alone do you any harm. Let me *go*." He tried to master his face, at least, but he still had a right to be pissed.

Roan twisted her wrist and the flame seeped back into her skin. "And how else was I supposed to carry you back here?" She stood with a snap of her thighs, moving away behind Eli so he couldn't see what she was doing. "Besides, I had to sleep, and I don't know what *kind* of demon you are." He heard her laugh once, oddly ominous. "Not yet, anyway."

His heart slammed into his chest like a spooked horse against its stall. "What are you doing?" Eli tried again to pull himself up, dragging his body forward by inches; there was heat at his back, though the ground under him was sharp and cool. He needed to rein in the ever-rising panic and catch his breath, turn it into a piece of wind in his loose, flexing fingers . . .

A boot came down hard on his hands and he screeched.

"Best keep your tricks to yourself," Roan said above him. The smirk was gone from her voice.

"Nng," Eli grunted. "This really isn't necessary, Harken. I don't know what you think I'm going to —"

The boot heel crushed his knuckles into the ground and he cried out.

"You said we were the same. I'll admit, you're the first demon I've seen to mimic living flesh, but this world gets smarter each day. I won't allow it to outsmart *me*."

Suddenly the pressure was gone, and Eli finally breathed, shaking as Roan stalked away across the dark shale. Cold sweat ran down the back of his neck, and he managed to turn his head just enough to see her over his shoulder, but she was measuring him, arms folded, deciding what to do next.

A blaze wound around her body like a loyal dog. Eli's jaw tightened.

I could always reach into her mind, he thought. *But with that look, she'd likely finish me for it.*

Instead, Eli tried to get back to basics and figure out where they were. Put simply, by the look and smell of it, they were in a cavern — cold, earthy. Beyond the entrance, ten feet from where Roan stood, inkier darkness. Night. What struck Eli the most, however, were the floating ambient flames scattered around them in the air, casting dancing shadows from blades of damp rock. A constant dripping echoed somewhere in the distance, but from where Eli had been tied up, he couldn't tell how deep the cavern went; into the dark at the back of it were pinprick lights, more little flames.

How deep it went didn't matter just then. This was Roan's domain, and he wasn't going anywhere until she allowed it.

Or until he bested her. And if not through a contest of strength, then it'd have to be wits and will. Two areas where Foxes and Owls were evenly matched. *Damn.*

Eli tightened his abdomen and pulled himself to sitting, easing against the far wall. She watched him do this and didn't move to stop him, the fire at her back banking with a shift of her shoulder, the tilt of her inquisitive head. She seemed taller somehow, though Eli realized that as long as he'd known her, Roan had been prone to hunching her shoulders. *Living like a wild animal improved her posture, at least.* Eli failed to stifle a snicker.

Roan bared her teeth. "I could kill you now, demon, if that's what you came here for."

Eli coughed, trying to prevent himself from falling into a hysterical spasm. "It's just too much, honestly." He shook his greasy hair from his eyes. "I only wish you could see the irony. You'd be the first to point it out."

He scrutinized her clothing, handmade, far from the jeans and hoodie he'd seen her in last, her feet and hands wrapped in fabric, forearms and calves armoured. Her garnet blade was lashed in a belt. Who had outfitted her? Who had *trained* her? Gods knew she was barely battle-blooded, even after Zabor. Now she was a one-woman army. She even seemed . . . older.

How had she changed *so much* in so little time? How had she surpassed Eli?

And why did it annoy him so much?

There was a spark quick as flash paper. Roan slid in front of him then, the flame she'd snatched from mid-air engulfing her hand and hurtling towards Eli's face. His body tensed.

"You act like you know me," Roan said. The light seemed to be pulsing beneath her skin. Her eyes were bright. "*How?*"

The very air will try to take what makes you, claim it, and wipe it out. No hungry worms this time, but Roan definitely did not recognize him.

Eli didn't know if he had the patience to remind her, let alone the language to bring her back. At least they both spoke snark rather fluently.

"You think you can threaten me with that?" Eli deflected, grinning, though he was really testing the limits here. "Look at the scar on my forehead. Whose handiwork do you think that is?"

Her sharp stare flicked to where he'd indicated. He hated to admit that having her not look him directly in the eye, even for a second, was a great relief. The flame got closer as she surveyed his face, pushing his hair out of the way and pressing her thumb into the knotted blemish.

"Easy!" he snapped. Her hands were rough, warm. His chest tensed.

The flame lowered — so did her hand. "We are enemies, then."

Eli ran his tongue over his teeth, picking the words carefully. "At the start we were. That was my fault." She leaned back on her haunches, listening; sweat gathered on his jaw. "But you and I, we've been through some . . . things. World-altering things. Things that made us allies." He wanted to say *friends* but felt that'd be pushing it. There was nothing friendly about *this* Roan.

For a second, her face lost some of its tight suspicion, and the words rushed out of him: "We fought *together*. We came to this world *together*. You've forgotten, but I can make you remember. All of it. If you let me."

Roan stood slowly. She came around to Eli's right side, hands on her hips. She sighed, and he felt foolish with hope.

She kicked him over onto his stupid face.

"If I don't remember you," she said, almost bored, "it's likely because I chose not to."

Eli felt the rope across his chest tighten, squeezing the argument out of him. She had gripped his bonds from behind. "I'll admit there's something familiar about you. A bad taste in my mouth, you could say." Suddenly Eli was being dragged backward, on his side across the ground. He struggled but got nowhere. "You talk of things long past, but how can that be? I've always been here. There was no before the Deadlands for me. As for you, well. You're an interloper. I watched you fall from the sky myself. As far as I'm concerned, you're just another beast to be gutted, though you're more talkative than the others before you."

"Wait," Eli huffed. "Wait, stop —"

She dropped him back onto his stomach. He jerked as his bare feet touched fire over an empty ledge.

Then Eli was hauled upward and above the smoking fire-pit Roan had nearly dumped him into. He lurched to a stop, twisting as he spun slowly like a rotisserie chicken over a bonfire while Roan tied the line off at a spike of rock in the wall. The harness around his trunk dug through his sweater, cutting into flesh where she'd sliced the wool away, back at the bog. He could barely breathe.

"Now," she went on, businesslike and dusting off her

hands smartly. "Talkative works to my benefit. Information has its rewards. Shades are chatty, too, but when they've become corrupted, they become Bloodbeasts, so you can see my predicament. Are you either of the two? Are you both? Are you something new entirely come to rip my throat out? I'm very torn."

Eli tried to swallow, dragging air through his nose as he stared down into the deep, flaming hole less than three feet below him. The cuffs of his pants singed. His flesh would blacken before the ropes would.

"Pretty speech. I can't see you being torn about this, though, no." His throat was dry, strained as a hanged man. "You're enjoying this. I don't blame you."

Roan smiled, lifting her shoulders in an airy shrug. "I could have killed you while you slept. But you're right. Where's the fun in that?"

Eli didn't have the breath to snipe further, icy dread creeping. Roan may not remember him, but she certainly *sounded* like him, the Eli who would have done the same thing to her were the tables turned, once upon a time.

"You're still you," he hazarded. "You won't kill me. You can't. You're not like this."

She flicked invisible dirt from her shoulder, ignoring him. "Killing you wouldn't help either of us, you're right. But when a beast is desperate enough, that's when you learn the most about them."

Her finger pointed above him like a gun. The floating flames near the line suspending him moved nearer to the rope.

His face whipped to hers. "I was good and desperate *before you planned to roast me*," he shouted.

"Desperation is survival, demon. And at least with desperation comes the truth. That's all I'm after."

Eli's face contorted. "I've already told you the truth!" he said, voice cracking. "I came here for you! To save you! I can see what a bloody mistake that was."

"Save me from what?" she asked almost sweetly. Eli cranked his head to watch the line above coming apart strand by strand. "How can you save me if you can't save yourself?"

"Let him burn," came another voice from the dark. Eli tensed, looking beyond Roan to the white pinpricks he'd seen earlier. *Not* more floating flames in that hollow black — eyes, advancing. White-coin eyes in Fox-shade heads, at least ten of them coming into the light.

"Whatever he is," said another shade, thrusting its snout towards him, "he will try to tear you down with his intentions."

Oh good, a peanut gallery. He'd had his fair share of brushes with Owl shades, and Roan, like Demelza, seemed aligned with them.

Eli's eyes stung suddenly, which surprised him more than Roan. "You're going to make me beg, aren't you?" He grimaced, jerking his head at the shades. "The dead have nothing to lose. Burn me, and *you* lose everything."

The shades yipped. "Demon," they hissed, "enemy."

Eli stared steadily at Roan, only at Roan, the fire dancing wickedly over her impassive face. Would she listen to him over the souls clinging to her heels?

He hadn't wanted to do this, but it was the only tactic he had left.

Please, Eli sent the thought out at her like an offering, penitent. He saw her eyes widen, and he reached further. *Please, Roan.*

The images flooded out of him and over her — Winnipeg. The two of them locked together as they plummeted through the Pool of the Black Star. The Golden Boy in a deluge. The pressure of his arm around her over a wide open sea. A golden tether, tighter than the one she'd bound him with now, pulling her free from poison darkness. *Remember me*, he repeated into her head with all the desperation she demanded of him. *Remember yourself*.

Eli felt all the force of her rage as she shoved him out of her mind, heard the furious roar from her mouth as she launched a volley of flame at him. The line above him snapped, and his heart lurched as the pit raced up to meet him.

As he exhaled, the wind rose.

The torrent of air pushed out of Eli's lungs and leapt into his crushed hands, then burst outward again like cannon shot, slicing the lines holding him, and throwing him into the nearest wall.

He crumpled, groaned.

Hands were clenched into his sweater, hauling him over and holding him up. The hands were shaking.

"What did you just *do* to me?" Roan snarled into his face.

"You wanted the truth," he croaked. "I tried to . . . show you."

"You put things in my head! Against my will!" She shook him as if trying to keep him from blacking out. "I should kill you now!"

He put a weak hand to the centre of her chest and she went still. "Do what you want," he said, "just kindly stop rattling me around."

She breathed unevenly under his palm, like an animal in a trap. He let his hand drop. "I'm sorry," he said. "I know doing that . . . always creeped you out. But I didn't put any-thing in your mind. I just showed you my *own* memories. "He winced. "Yours are deeply buried. Locked away." By what, he couldn't guess. An outside force, or something she'd done to herself?

Roan's face struggled between rage and confusion. He expected her to roast him there and then, but instead she loosened her grip, let go.

Her mouth was a hard line. "It took you long enough to free yourself," she said.

Eli stiffly rubbed his wrists. "So that was a test, then? To see what I could do?"

She shrugged. "As I expected, you can't do much. I don't know how much use you'll be to me, after all."

Use?

Strange air *whuffed* through the back of Eli's head, and he caught sight of a Fox shade's pinprick eyes hovering over him. "You would've been better off to burn him, lady," the shade advised. "This one will trouble you until the end with its hollow talk."

Eli jerked up and the shade danced away into a cluster of the others that stood by the cavern entrance. He thought he saw the tall, floppy ears of a Rabbit amongst them, but it shim-mered away into the night before he could get a closer look.

Eli coughed awkwardly. "You going to give me back my personal space, Harken?"

She blinked then stood, slapping the dust off herself. "I'm not going to kill you, but I don't trust you." She moved away, as if she'd made up her mind. "You can't stay here."

Dumbstruck, Eli watched as the bulbous flames in the air around Roan made contact with her body, sliding back into her and leaving Eli in the advancing dark like an afterthought.

"You're kicking me out?" he said. "You beat me within an inch of my life then toss me to the metaphysical curb?"

She was quiet for a while, looking past Eli and at the shades fidgeting behind him. With a jerk of her head, they bounded out of the cavern, their fox-yips sounding like taunting laughter in the echoing night.

Roan squinted at Eli. "Where did you come from? When you fell."

The only light left in the cavern was the blazing pit between them. Eli pointed upward. "The Roost. What's left of it, anyway. Before that, somewhere in the Atlantic." He stretched his legs out in front of him. "We came here intentionally, together. But things haven't exactly been going to plan since we were separated."

"What plan? Came through where?" Her flames licked upward, and for a second it looked like they wound through her hair like a child's fingers.

Eli just groaned, shaking his head. "Somewhere that gets farther away the more we bicker about it. I told you. I can show you everything and we can be on our way to —"

"Enough," she snapped. Her hand was around her own throat. "I'm not going anywhere. Least of all with you. You can rest here, and in the morning you'll go. To where, I can't say I care. You're nothing to me."

Eli was, for the first time in a long time, speechless. Roan had always been a pigheaded, stubborn brat, but going further with her like this was obviously dangerous. Part of his power had been restored to him, but it wouldn't be near enough. If she came at him again, that'd be it.

He tilted his head in momentary submission, then looked back up. "You said you were expecting to get some use out of me. May I ask what for?"

She stopped mid-turn. "You may, but don't expect me to supply the answer."

She'd needed him for something. Eli clung to the opportunity. "Why don't we make a deal, then? You're a Fox, yes? Foxes *love* deals, I hear."

Her mismatched eyes ranged over him, calculating. Either way, he didn't have much to lose.

She walked around the fire pit then, running her hand and arm through it thoughtfully. "What sort of deal?"

Eli got to his feet, even managed to straighten despite how his back protested. He opened his arms. "I show you how useful I can be. You allow me that one chance, and if I don't prove worthy to you, then I walk out of this hole and the considerably busy life of ne'er-do-welling you've got going here."

She didn't look at him. A gob of fire bounced between her hands in lazy arcs.

"Roan Harken." She spoke the name mockingly, as if he'd made it up to insult her. "What kind of a name is that, anyway?"

Eli was out of gambits. "The name of my friend."

The flame disappeared and one hand went to Roan's side, brushing over the sword hilt.

He swallowed. "Perhaps you could use a friend, too, but I won't presume. Since we're starting from scratch again. It was hard enough the first time."

"Hard for who?"

Eli realized he'd been clutching the edge of his sweater in his hands. He wiped the moisture from them, jaw relaxing. "I'll let you guess."

The one hand left the hilt. The other stretched out towards him.

"One night and one chance," she said. "Then you're gone."

He hesitated, wondering if he'd be burned for his own trust, but he clasped her hand in his. Her skin was still somehow cool — everything about her was control. No more girl burning up from the inside with unchecked power and unflagging uncertainty. He was hers to destroy if she decided.

She pulled away half a second after contact, whirled, and stalked to her dark cavern corner.

"I'm Eli, in case you were wondering," he called after her dumbly.

"I wasn't," she said, crouching and watching him unblinkingly.

Eli scoffed, then shook his head. "You'd find this all funny if you were in your right mind, Harken." He pushed his fingers into his eyes, muttering, "You'd find it funnier because you never were."

She continued staring. Evidentially, she wasn't going to shut her eyes until he did.

Eli returned to his own designated rock wall. The fire in the pit went down like a curtain but didn't extinguish all the way. He didn't relish lying down on the hard floor, but it was better than staying upright for any longer. Growing heavier with each breath, he splayed out like a star, shut his eyes, then placed a hand over his chest, where he had every night, reassured and haunted by the Moonstone.

"Friend," Roan muttered suddenly, hand to her chest, rubbing absently. When she caught him looking, she frowned, so he rolled away, facing the wall.

It took hours before Eli fell asleep, his heartbeat finally slowing beneath his hand.

"So what did Roan need Eli for?"

It was the next day — if days could be called that here — and Saskia had laid awake all night in Baskar's tree, replaying this information. She wanted more of the story. She knew it was the key to bringing Roan and Eli back and helping them do what they'd come here for.

Baskar had met Saskia outside of the open bole, dipping their characteristically tilted head at her as she climbed awkwardly out.

"Good day to you, too," Baskar sniffed, avoiding the question with one of their own. "What have you got there?"

Under Saskia's arm was the tablet — she'd been testing the Onyx's receiver to see if she could get any messages through. Still nothing. "Before I came here, I received a message from . . . someone else who came through. You wouldn't happen to know Barton Allen, would you?"

She'd waited till now to ask, especially knowing what little she'd discovered about this mysterious Heartwood tree she had yet to investigate.

Baskar shrugged. The odds and bobs of their shell reminded her of all the things she used to collect on walks as a child, disparate bits completely at home when put together. "I know no one else living but Roan and Eli. And you. Saskia."

They spoke her name carefully, tipping their lopsided, lop-eared head down at her. "You are very interested in Roan and Eli," they continued. They couldn't exactly frown, but it came across in their high voice. "They're enemies, if you did not already gather that."

She clicked her tongue, and they walked together around Cinder Town's epicentre. "Uh huh. But I think they can become allies again."

"But they were enemies *before* even that," Baskar recounted with the air of the lecturer, as it had been yesterday. "So you see, it is inevitable that the story repeats itself."

Saskia shook her head. "If they break the cycle, they can accomplish their original goal of —"

"Shh!" Baskar pressed a twiggy finger to where their mouth would be beneath the mask. They passed by a few Hounds, who had their heads pointed towards them, semi-sneering with their burning eyes.

"I have only just returned to my mistress's good graces," Baskar reminded her. "Keep your machinations to yourself, thank you."

Saskia was agog. Baskar really didn't want to talk about Ancient. Already a bad sign. "If you didn't want to help me, why bother telling me any of this at all?" She prodded Baskar's side, but they only peered over at her. "You love stories. Theirs is central to this entire world. And if I'm going to know the General's enemy, then . . . I need to know it all."

Now she was taking a page out of Chancellor Grant and the ETG's playbook. Study them so you can conquer them. *Or get them back in their right minds*. That Saskia had to do this at all was unfair, to say the least. She'd already done the work to get down here. Surely they could stop moving the goal posts.

"A story for a story," the archivist intoned. Saskia wondered what Baskar had been like in life; if they'd been this insufferable, for instance. "Tell me a story of you now. Who is Barton Allen?"

Saskia was keenly aware that the Rabbit getting close to her was probably Roan's ploy. To make Saskia one of her Hounds and make the Onyx her own. But she wanted to trust Baskar.

Saskia looked around, then yanked Baskar into an alcove. They clattered but didn't come apart, pressed shoulder to shoulder with Saskia as she booted up the tablet and tapped away.

She swiped. "I like to build things." A few photos were all she'd had at hand to show Baskar, but they leaned in eagerly to look. "I initially got into this mess because of *this*."

In the photo gallery, the first thing to show up was the original, terrible sketch Saskia had made of the Deon VR illusion, cribbed from the lore book lying around the apartment and Phae and Barton's descriptions. "This is the fox warrior, Deon. Roan could change into her, because she had the Calamity Stone. Did you know *that*?"

Baskar looked from Saskia, to the screen, back and forth. "Roan is Deon now, though. Because she has the Opal."

Saskia sighed. "It's not the same." Nothing was. She swiped through some of the 3D models, and the next thing that came up was a photo of Saskia and Ella.

"Who is that?" Baskar pointed, finger hovering over the screen, then tapping it experimentally. Saskia brushed it away.

"She is someone you love," Baskar said. "I may have been dead a long while, but I remember that look."

Saskia bit her tongue with some surprise. Being surrounded by these weird, puppet-bodied shades, she'd completely forgotten that they'd been alive once.

"You said you didn't remember much of your life," Saskia recalled.

Baskar took the tablet, bringing it closer to their face, and ultimately bonking it against the wooden mask for bringing it a tad too close. "I remember love. I remember it was a bit difficult, finding any for myself when I did not ascribe to any available gender." Baskar dipped their head at Saskia, giving the tablet back. "Would it be different for me now, in your Uplands?"

Saskia hadn't been expecting that question. "People fear what they don't understand," she answered. Baskar lifted a shoulder, then swiped across the screen to another picture. A picture of a picture, really. The original had been ripped in half and thrown in the trash, but Saskia pulled it out, carefully taped it up, and taken a digital photo to make sure it couldn't get lost again.

"That's him," she said, coming back around to Baskar's first question. "Barton Allen."

In the picture were her and Barton. She had a medal around her neck from the track meet. This was the year Barton went to the Old Leg, thinking he was helping, and hadn't come home. But before that, all of his running influence had rubbed off on Saskia, and she'd competed at school for the first time. Saskia was on Barton's back, and Phae had her arms around him.

Saskia shut the tablet off, remembering what Barton had said to her that same night, before she went to bed. They'd both been wired from the excitement, and in a rare moment of quiet, he'd blurted, "I told you, like, a million times about the Battle of Zabor, right?"

She'd shrugged, half-grinning. "A hundred million, yeah."

"We all came together. All five of us, in that moment where we put Zabor away. It was a weird experience, invading everyone else's thoughts, being in sort of, like, one mind. I dunno." He was smiling to himself, trying to find the words. "We all had these little flashes, these visions. I thought I saw . . ." He glanced at Saskia, suddenly sheepish. "Well, I thought I saw a kid. *My* kid. And I was watching him run a track, and I was so proud of him."

"Him?" Saskia felt disappointment wash over her, and he saw it.

"Wait, wait," he said, "let me finish. What I saw was an impression. Son. Daughter. Sibling. It didn't matter. It was that proud feeling. That feeling that, whoever that kid was, we'd built something precious together. Blood or not."

He'd taken Saskia's hand then. "I felt that again today. The exact same feeling. That's not something I could ever mistake. It was like I was fighting that giant snake, and all my friends were there, and we had done something good and beautiful. Thank you for reminding me of that, Saskia."

She shut her eyes and swallowed hard. Then something clumsy and slightly pointy took Saskia's hand. She blinked in surprise to realize it was Baskar.

"Even this far from life, the dead do not forget love," they said. Then they leaned over Saskia, peering out for any passing Hounds, but the coast was clear. When they came back to her, their strange eyes sparkled. "Roan and Eli hadn't forgotten, either."

A Prison of Memory

No sooner had Eli shut his eyes than they were open again, and Roan was gone.

He sat up. His stomach felt tight with the pounding need of hunger, something he could manage for a little while longer, but only just. Daylight, or the simulacrum of it, streamed through the opening in the cavern. Despite being tortured and tossed around like a ragdoll, this body was still a needful thing. He had to piss.

As he got to his feet, he nearly buckled into the firepit. Eli edged towards the hole in the rock, catching himself on the doorway as he looked out. A steep, trodden, dirt track wound downward, closed in by familiar enormous trees and bush. He picked his way down to somewhat level ground and took a few minutes to test whether or not he could stand long enough to relieve himself. He staggered, but he managed.

The trees behind him rustled. Eli tensed and whipped his head up, expecting to find Roan there, gawping at him like the murderous pervert she probably had become, but there was no one there. He readjusted his filthy clothes and rubbed a hand down his face.

This was, slightly, a disaster. Though Eli's life had been one disaster after another, this one felt scarily permanent. He thought he could just jump back into the fray and solve this how he always had — using logic. But this would be tedious work, and his patience was thin.

He shielded his light-starved eyes from the sun filtering through towering trees, past rock. The cave was in the base of the cliffside, framed by hills. It was hidden, secure. Below was a valley, where the light caught on the surface of running water. Eli wasn't about to wait around for Roan to come back, and with a time limit on his presence at her dwelling, he'd have to be efficient.

He went towards the water, carefully. He still felt weak. It would take months to recover, at this rate, time neither of them had. His powers were still mostly dormant. How had Roan tapped into hers? There had to be a rudiment he could suss out. The Realms of Ancient were all about their rules. Their caveats. Their costs.

Whatever he was experiencing, likely Roan had, too — just down on level ground, and maybe with the bonus of extra time. With Phyr gone, time was out of whack, and perhaps time down on the ground was not the same as time up in the sky. Eli didn't want to imagine how truly long Roan had been trapped in these woods, all alone, imagining he'd abandoned her. *Luckily she doesn't remember you at all.* Still, he suddenly burned with guilt. Empathy cut deeper than apathy. Maybe there was an upside to her forgetting him, after all.

Eli whirled at the merest snap of a branch. He needed to rebuild his most basic defenses. This place was riddled with monsters, and worse, the lost dead, scattered by the cataclysm he and Roan had initiated. There were no allies here. But the Fox dead seemed to rally around Roan like she was the god they were looking for. He didn't blame them, either.

Eli shook his head, continued moving gingerly towards the water, through the trees.

When he reached the brook he bent down, which hurt in every way, and drank until he fell back, gasping. If the water was cursed, he didn't rightly care. He thought, *This is the water the gods drank from. This is the place where everything began.*

It's probably exactly where it's all going to end.

Eli wanted to lie down, close his eyes, and not wake up. Waste his chance. Call it off. Or leave Roan here and do it all himself. He'd already done enough to her. This could be the rest Roan deserved.

But he got back to his feet like a shot the second he heard the drums.

Eli fell into the first form that he'd been taught: legs spread, left foot in front of him, head and body leaning into sound. As an acolyte in the remote Rookery, he was taught to hear the wind. Not to manipulate it or harness it, right away, but to listen — it always carried some message, some lesson. He'd rolled his eyes at that. But here he heard the wind, which everyone up to this point had said had died, and the wind had brought him the drums.

The second form was to thank the wind and grasp the tail of it as it pulled you to the answer of the question you hadn't realized you'd asked.

Eli followed the sound, feeling more restored already — whether it was mad adrenaline or magic, he didn't care. Where the wind took him wasn't exactly the answer he was seeking, but it was, at least, a distracting spectacle.

The drums were not loud, but persistent, and seemed to be everywhere, surround sound. Eli discovered the sound was *inside* him. A heartbeat. Following it with her body, beat by beat, in the clearing he'd just stumbled out of, was Roan.

Of course it was.

Eli was out in the open, and when she turned she'd clearly see him, but he didn't bother hiding himself.

She moved fluidly, with an elegance she'd never had as long as he'd known her. The Foxes had their forms, too. All the Families did. The Rabbits used hand gestures. The Seals had swimming strokes. The Deer's forms were all metaphysical, meditative. A form was a movement of the body, a way of speaking to a First Matriarch, to channel their element into you. A Denizen asked for that power to be put to their name.

Roan was doing something else entirely. Here, she *was* the flame.

And she was dancing.

"Isn't it something?"

Eli felt a mass brush against his ankle, and when he looked down, he saw a shade, gem-nose searching the air. It was a Rabbit, the size of a large hare, leaning up on its powerful hind legs.

Eli's jaw worked as he looked from the Rabbit to Roan.

"Something. Yes." Now Eli felt like he was intruding on whatever it was she was doing. "I should go."

"No, no!" the little shade twisted, then bonked itself into the back of Eli's knees, making him step awkwardly forward. "It is a wonder to behold. It is something precious. You are meant to see, I think."

Now he *really* didn't want to be here. "I . . . who are you?"

The Rabbit jostled, flowing like a little patch of liquid, curious and bright. "I am Baskar," the shade said, seeming to preen. "And you are the mistress's new friend, aren't you?"

Eli sighed, folding his arms. "Uh huh. 'New' friend." He turned his attention back to Roan. "And you are what, to her, exactly?"

The large upright ears flickered. "I am her old friend."

Par for the course. "Right."

Up to this point, it had seemed like Roan was moving through repetitive motion, like a singer warming up through their scales. Now Eli felt the drums grow faster, slightly, and she shifted from stance to fluid movement, improvising.

"What is she doing?" Eli muttered under his breath.

Baskar shivered. "She is calling back the fire, and the fire is calling her."

The drums seemed to lead Roan through, her arms spiralling, her steps pulling around and through like a needle in skin. Ribbons of fire, too many to count, consumed her, twin dragons, leaping from flesh to ground and back again. She sprang. This was a very old technique, one Eli had seen when leafing through old manuscripts in the Rookery's libraries, but no longer put into practice (not that the Families shared their training modes these days). It was a holdover from the first Denizens, those who had transformed from their animal counterparts into humans, bridging the gap.

This was how they were going to get out of here.

"And who taught her that?" Because, surely, it wasn't something anyone just *picked up*. Not now. Not here. Not her. Roan was a lot of things but a spirit-deep practitioner wasn't one of them.

"The fire did!" Baskar cried joyfully.

Suddenly the drums stopped, and Eli's nostrils flared. Roan had her back to him, arms winged out, palms facing away from her, like she was keeping two walls from crushing her. The fire was a tide at her feet, then in a flash, it was back inside her. The Rabbit surged for her, jumping and rolling around her in what seemed like exaltation. The shade itself was strange — that Fox shades had rallied around Roan was one thing, but this lost Rabbit was something curious.

Roan seemed to be relaxing, smiling, as she bent a hand down to the shade, which scampered off moments after, leaving the two of them alone.

Eli tensed, thinking it best to lead with a compliment. "That was very impressive."

Roan's shoulders rolled, arms dropped to her sides as she spun. "I know."

He bristled. "Your grandmother was a dancer. Did you *know* that?"

Roan's hands cupped her hips, head cocked. She wasn't wearing the garnet blade. Weaponless, maybe he stood a chance against her if this went south.

"Anyway," Eli coughed. "I was wondering if we could get started. Or if you had any food first."

Her grin ricocheted off him, and Eli was mortified by how good it made him feel to see it.

"So you crash-land in my territory, then expect a meal out of it?" she taunted. "If you can't survive on your own, then why am I bothering?"

Eli bit his lip hard. "Fine. I'll leave you to your roasted ballet and go forage."

A rush of footsteps, and Eli only just flipped Roan off him and cleanly into the tree ahead of him, her legs dangling over the branch. She was laughing, probably at how strained his face looked.

"Not that useless, then," she said, smirking like an imp. She seemed much more laid-back now than she had last night, but Eli decided it was a trap.

Back to basics. To forms. Eli slid quickly through one, a jackknife of his palm and a twist of his torso, snatching a shard of the wind and expanding it between his hands. He shot it past her head, and when she relaxed, thinking he'd missed, she yelped when the branch beneath her gave way.

That landing was not so graceful.

"Less useless than others," he said, examining his fingernails.

Roan leapt back up, and the two fell into their fighting stances. Her eyes swept over him. "You have strange gifts. Channelling air. Breaking into people's minds." She snorted. "If you're not a demon, then what are you?"

Eli's hand was a blade before his face. Then he squared back up, and brought both his hands together, fingers splayed like wings. "I'm an Owl." At least, he was starting to feel like one again.

Roan eased up. "I've seen flying shades in the sky. Are they Owls, too?"

Eli looked up, half expecting to catch one wheeling overhead to screech into him, but he saw only flickering leaves and the Deadland sunlight. "They are. But like the Fox shades, they are the dead. The spirits of those who have come here to rest. My shade is still inside me. For now, anyway."

Roan looked down herself, as if she could see her own shade through her body. "I see." Her face wrinkled. "But I *don't* see. How can we be here, amongst the dead?"

"Oh, they haven't been so forthright in supplying you with that information?" He shook his head. "We came through a doorway, and we took our bodies with us. Though I don't think there's a precedent for such a thing. Everything we do here is charting new territory."

She huffed, then pointed at him. "Just remember that *this* territory is mine. I know it better than you do. Anything you tell me could be a lie to take it from me."

Eli's eyes widened. "Why would I want to take *this* from you? It's not exactly luxe living. We also were never meant to stay here. We had a mission. And I've come to remind you of it, because we can't finish it any way but together."

She readjusted her footing. Her expression closed. Then her arm lit up like it'd been elbow-deep in kerosene.

Eli pointed, deadpan. "It's a firearm. Get it?"

Roan blinked. "What?"

Eli shook his head, then kneeled before her painfully. He glanced up at her confused expression. "I can't keep fighting you. It won't get us any closer to where we need to be. We've done all this before. I know you feel it, too."

Roan's mouth clamped shut and she flushed. "Stop doing that, demon."

Eli grinned. "Nothing changes."

Roan's flaming fist tightened, and he caught her about to reel back, but he held his hands up. "These strange gifts of mine. I used to be better at using them than you, but I've forgotten how. Just like you did."

"I told you to stop doing that!"

"It was just a guess, that time." Eli ground his teeth. "Your power is different now than it was when I first knew you. It's raw but controlled. As close to the original manifestation of it that even I know of. The truth is I want to . . . learn from you." The admission felt bitter, but it was, at least, true. "I want to be of *use* to you as well. You know I can be, whatever it is you're looking for. Maybe we can help each other."

It took her a second, but Roan lowered her arm, and the flame flicked out. "Fine," she said. "Perhaps, once, the fire wasn't mine to command. But I was shown my way back. With the help of the shades, and the drums."

Eli narrowed his eyes. "Shades trained you?"

Roan knelt before him on one knee, arm slung over it as she chewed the inside of her mouth. Eli repressed the urge to tell her she always did that, too.

"I'm the only living thing here," she started, looking down at the ground as she picked her words. "Aside from you, anyway. I've been here a long time, though I stopped counting. I feel like I'm a part of this place, but while the shades showed me the fire, and the drums led me through it, I always felt like something was . . . wrong. Something was missing."

Eli sat still, hands on his knees, trying to control his

stupid pulse, his rising guilt for having left her here, alone, feeling so lost. "I see."

She shrugged. "The shades call me Deon, sometimes, which is why I feel like you've mistaken me someone else, for this friend of yours. Roan."

Eli's nostrils flared. "There's really no mistaking you for anyone else, but sure."

The girl before him was so far from the girl he'd jumped down here with. Time had definitely passed. Her hair was so much longer now than before, the same way he now had this ridiculous new beard. Her tactical skill was without loophole — anytime she let him in, it was with its own finely honed purpose. Being alone had made her strong in a way it had made Eli weak.

For a second, terrible moment, her logic made sense. This wasn't *his* Roan. But of course she was never "his" to begin with.

Her mismatched eyes wavered, only slightly. Then she picked up his arm, pushed his sleeve back to show his most elegant scar. "We're the same, you said."

The veins at his wrist tensed as her thumb pressed hard into them. "And you said we weren't."

"Not the same. But alike. Somehow. An Owl can fly, but a Fox must stay on the ground." She let his arm go, then undid the leather bracer covering her scar. "Where does your power come from?"

Eli groaned like a busted pipe organ as reality crushed him. "You don't even know who Deon *is*, do you?"

A pause. She shook her head.

"What about the Calamity Stones? Ancient? The Five Families? The Matriarchs? The Darklings? Winnipeg? Anything?"

She didn't blink.

Eli swung from shining empathy to ridiculously pissy. "Harken, do you realize how trying it was to blast your impenetrable skull with expository *the first time around*? Stupidly hard. I don't think I could stomach it a second time."

Roan's open expression slammed closed like a fallout bunker, and she smashed her fist into the mossy ground. A massive ring of fire flashed around them, and Eli froze.

Her anger settled into a wicked smile — from his expression or the display, he couldn't tell. "I know power," she said, settling back. "I know I can control mine. I need to know more about you before I throw you to the wilderness, because knowledge is another kind of power. And I want it."

"And you feel bad."

She balked. "What?"

He tried to ignore the heat snapping at his heels. "For, you know, all the beatings and whatnot."

"I don't feel bad about that." Her eyes darted away from him. "I'm still evaluating the benefit of keeping you alive, anyway."

Eli felt himself going a tad crazy, but here it went, voice rising. "You far surpass me in power, but here's my offer: I'll provide you with every bit of knowledge I have, about this world, and about your powers and mine. You hereby have access to it all, and I'll allow you to mould me to your backwoods intentions. I'm all in."

Roan's body language affected boredom, but a subtle wave of something other than her heat came off her. Something like a thrill, or at least, the barest interest, leapt in her gaze.

"And what's the catch for such . . . voluntary submission?" she drawled, rolling her hand. Quid pro quo.

Eli grabbed tight to it with both of his, grinning some-what manically. "I don't *tell* you what I know," he said, "I get to show you."

And in that second that Roan let her guard down, Eli pulled her mind into his with bright golden barbs and didn't let go.

It was a trick — a mean one, at that — he'd honed at the Rookery. He'd only returned to it recently, when Demelza's shade had gone with him into his splintered memory to force him to repair it. Eli had had to face all the things he'd snipped away so he could manage every terrible choice that led him to value power over people.

The game was this, and it was highly frowned upon by his instructors: distract your fellow Owl long enough to get through their mind barrier, change one of their less import-ant memories, and have them try to guess which one it was. It was cruel, ultimately, and there was more than one inci-dent of a student having to undergo psychic reconstruction therapy afterwards. That wasn't Eli's intention with Roan, though she was annoying the absolute hell out of him, and it was tempting.

He wanted to show Roan *his* memories of her, hopefully resurrecting her own memories which she — or something else — had suppressed.

He was still holding on to her when she finally opened her eyes in the blank mindscape he'd pulled them into, and, just as he suspected, she had a hard time struggling against this mental projection of him. Her physical body was strong, but her mind was as splintered as Eli's had been. Roan had learned the trick of keeping an Owl's psychic spear to her surface thoughts — likely her grandmother, Cecelia, had taught her that — and as a protective measure, her mind had obviously maintained that memory.

But ego-stroking was usually the best way to find that one razor-thin entryway into someone's waking subconscious. Roan's own projection of herself here, meanwhile, was panicking, but Eli held tight. "What have you done to me? Where am I?" she asked.

"Relax," he said. "We're inside *my* mind." The projection of his self let go of hers, and she staggered in the nothingness. "I can't change these memories. I worked hard to rebuild and to ground them. And also, well, I don't let just anyone in here. So consider it a gesture of trust. Something that didn't come easy for either of us."

Eli felt his own panic ping through his mind like sonar, and when it struck her on the reverb, she sounded less startled and more curious. "Why did you let me into your mind?"

Eli rocked backward on his heels, sorting himself. There was no way to avoid talk of the stones. At their chests, at the same time, two lights bloomed. His was golden white. Hers was crimson-green.

"Because it'd take too long to explain," he said, "how we are the same. We've made the same mistakes too many times. I'd barely earned your trust before, but I had it. I'm confident I can earn it again." *As fast as possible*, he quipped, before realizing that Roan could hear his thoughts.

She folded her arms. "And what if I'm not interested in being shown any of it?"

Eli lifted his shoulder. "That's fair. How about you let me show you one thing? A regret I will always carry, but one I can't erase. Then you can decide if you want to know more. Or if you can trust me to show you more."

She moved closer to him. "A regret?"

The light flooded outward from Eli's feet with bright and blazing memory, and they were suddenly standing on the Osborne Street Bridge.

"We only became friends because I was convinced you were my enemy," he said. "Stupid, really." He hoped it could work again.

They were standing on the concrete traffic partition separating north- from southbound. The two of them were spectators in these events that, because of how much had happened, seemed decades ago. Eli was surprised at how young he looked, despite his painfully obvious snark-smirk and fashion choices. Roan looked even younger — her forearm ablaze as she stood atop an accident-ravaged car. Eli's wings were huge and gaping. It was a comic book panel, the action trapped in a freeze-frame. Unreal and ridiculous. But it had happened. And not that long ago, either.

The Roan of the wilderness beside him now was in awe. "Wow," she said, "I didn't think you could look *more* pretentious."

Eli cleared his throat, revelling in her insult. "Villainy requires a whole look, you see."

Roan pointed. "That's . . . me?"

Eli looked at her and his chest swelled with something like victory. "Yes."

"And you're trying to kill me."

"Ah. Yes."

Around them, time switched back on, though it moved at a slow pace. Each punch thrown or blocked, each ragged flame hurled, every snapping whip of the wind was fluidly drawn out. Sparks and sharp words and the insistence that, from each side, they were in the right. Unstoppable fool meeting immovable moron.

Then the bridge exploded, and suddenly memory-Eli seized memory-Roan around the neck, dangling her over the frozen river.

Time stopped again, and now-Roan was walking into the destruction of the past to stand beside her defeated imprint.

Eli followed at a grudging, guilty distance.

"Is this how you remember me, then?" Roan frowned.

Eli looked between the two Roans. "Yes, why?"

She sneered. "You like to remember me as pretty and weak, a thing I'm not now."

Luckily, he was able to keep his psychic projection from flushing. "No. That's not . . . you're entirely missing my point here." Eli stared at his past-self: golden eyes pinprick-sharp and consumed in a different kind of victory than the one he'd just felt. A terrible, dark one he never wanted to feel again.

"I hurt you," Eli said. "I hurt many people on the road to you. I blamed the Moonstone, at first. It had its influences. But the truth of it is, I wanted you, and everyone else in my way, to feel the abject emptiness I'd always been made to feel. Killing you was justification for my own pain. It was wrong."

The humour died from Roan's face then. He hadn't wanted that; Eli had missed her humour, too, so he smiled.

"You were never weak. You were always stronger in a way I couldn't be. I tried to rewrite this encounter a lot."

Roan cocked her head. "You wanted it to go differently?"

"It did go differently — than I wanted it to. Which is *exactly* how it should have gone. If I'd gotten what I wanted, you'd be dead, and I'd still be a prisoner of my own mistakes."

Roan considered the scene one last time, then turned to go back over the wrecked bridge, the sequence of the fight moving in slow, careful rewind. Explosions were sucked back into their detonations. The wind put Eli's Therion back together. Roan stopped and watched herself strolling down that sidewalk, backward, as twilight fell, amongst her friends, a fox at her feet — a living one. Her memory's smile was blithe, momentary. The ruined Roan of now looked at that scene a long while.

Then it faded back into a blackness beneath them.

"We've done this before," she said after a while, walking endlessly into nothing.

Eli followed close beside her. "The fighting? Oh yes. From bickering to brawling, we've fairly done it all."

"Not that," she said, stopping so short that Eli stumbled over her. She was gesturing in the space around them. "We've walked in these types of places before. In memories. The sensation is . . . familiar." She looked hard at him. "I remember how things felt more than the things themselves."

She touched her chest, and the crimson light there flared again. At Eli's sternum, the white gold glowed in answer.

"All of it's a long story," he promised. "But I'm willing to tell it a second time."

She was quiet. Then, "I want to be back in my own mind now."

Eli snapped his fingers, and they were back in the ring of fire like they'd never left. The ring flashed outward once, like a ray, then went out.

Roan, and the woodland around them, was quiet.

"Are you . . . okay?" Eli prompted. Maybe this, like every other attempt of his so far to get through to her, had backfired utterly.

"We were dancing," she blurted.

"When?"

"On that bridge," Roan insisted, waving her hand around her head. "Back then, I mean. You were stronger, like you said. So much was different. If it was true." She touched her chest in the place where the Dragon Opal once hung, ruining her life.

Eli suddenly regretted this. Did he really want to make Roan relive all the pain that had brought her here? Her parents. Her grandmother. Zabor. Her father turned darkling. The darkness that had consumed her, too. Forgetting it all could mean a fresh start.

She got up and turned away from him. Her body was rigid. "I'm not convinced," she said. "Not yet."

Eli opened his hand, spread the fingers, closed it. "I see."

She shot him a look over her shoulder. "Eat something. And bathe, you're making my eyes water." Then she started out into the trees, towards a ridge. "I need to think."

Eli nodded even though she wasn't looking at him at all. His skin itched from the inside out. This felt like a mistake, but it also felt like something Eli couldn't turn away from now. Instead, he turned back towards the cavern.

The Osborne Bridge had been the beginning. He couldn't see how it would end. But something he'd already known was creeping to the surface, something he couldn't keep shoving down: he cared about Roan Harken, and he was about to hurt her again.

WIND DANCER

Another day, another story, the pieces coming together. But Saskia was far too aware of time. Seven years, a hundred years. How many would pass by the time she got back — if she ever did?

Roan had begun to trust her, and as much as she liked, and looked forward to, spending time with Baskar, Saskia needed to be alone sometimes. Hounds watched her closely but didn't stop her when she walked around the edges of the Emberdom, the borders between it and the wild, Bloodbeast-plagued country beyond. Roan went out into it often, and apparently so did Eli, but of course they could. They didn't have limits. They were *undying gods*. Saskia scoffed.

They were still humans. *My love*, Eli had called Roan. Obviously there was still something between them, some-thing eternal, or they would've killed each other by now. She imagined Roan dancing. Is that all this was to her, a dance? Why were they keeping it going? And why was any talk of Ancient, their reason for being here, forbidden?

Saskia had to see it for herself, this thing that was keeping Roan and Eli apart. The Heartwood.

She walked up and out of the canyon where Cinder Town lay. Baskar said that she would come upon a cliff where she could see the Heartwood clearly. They'd said she'd know it when she saw it. Baskar had looked worried, offered to go with her, but demurred when she'd refused.

"I will be here when you return," they said shyly, going back to their work in the archive. Saskia smiled, remembering it.

The Heartwood was, of course, beyond the Emberdom. It was in contested territory, closer to the cliffs of the Roost.

The tremors of Roan and Eli's arrival had sent up obelisks, a few of which Saskia had noted on her walks. There hadn't been so many tremors lately, but there had been a great one when the Heartwood appeared. It had to coincide with Barton's appearance. She'd brought her tablet, and the Onyx was already on her head. She was willing to turn it on to find out.

Roan and Eli had lost themselves to this place, that was all. Eli had, truly, tried to bring Roan back. It obviously hadn't worked. Both Roan and Eli had their Calamity Stones again, but Saskia's understanding was they had to find them and purposefully use them . . . Baskar hadn't gotten to that part of the story yet. Saskia guessed it wasn't a happy part. But Roan and Eli were connected. That couldn't be erased. Saskia could work with that.

Baskar had noticed the black obelisks, too, spent many

long hours staring at them and wondering where they came from, but not daring to find out.

Or, considering the forbidden story, maybe Baskar *had* found out.

"The Heartwood is like these spikes, I think," Baskar had posited, telling her of the day the tree appeared. "One day, there was a quake that made me fear the realms were going to shatter apart again. Many other Rabbits would tell me later they were sure it was Heen. A few went to find out but did not come back. Or they did, perhaps as Bloodbeasts."

"Maybe the Emerald is there," Saskia puzzled. That's all this situation was, a puzzle, and most times when she thought she found a missing piece, it didn't fit right.

She climbed a rise, getting closer to the cliff Baskar had mentioned then stopped. All at once, the horizon was filled with branches, taller than anything, reaching into the wide open sky.

It looked like a Hope Tree, but even from this distance Saskia could see it was a gnarled amalgam of cords. It looked like it was wide as a mountain. Beyond it was the Abyss, the dark and fathomless sea that belonged to Ryk. The Sapphire was out there somewhere. Saskia didn't want to think about having to go looking for it. The stones all coming together had forced the *realms* back together, creating a new order. Imagine what they could do if they came together again, down here, and with the Onyx so changed.

Maybe it could unbind Ancient from whatever was holding it back.

Maybe that's what this tree was trying to prevent. Too many gods-damned *maybes* for her liking.

A foreign sound came from the inside of her jacket, and her hand shot into it and pulled out the tablet, its screen scrolling with code. She flicked on the Onyx, and every sensation she hated about it filled her head.

She pointed the tablet at the Heartwood, and the screen cracked.

YOU ARE CLOSE NOW. The message was inside her blood. *YOU HAVE COME AND I AM AWAKE AND THE DARK HAS COME WITH YOU.*

She dropped the tablet. This was a new voice. It made her lose her footing. "Barton?"

For a moment, she saw his face pushing through a knot of black roots. She looked into his eyes, which were bright. He was there. He was alive.

She slammed the Onyx's switch off and threw up. Bile, berries, what little she'd been eating. She curled up on the ground and Baskar's words came back to her.

"Before the tree, a gate opened. Then came the great quake, and all of the dead held their breath. It felt like something was going to change, but instead there was only the tree, growing very slowly up. Like a —"

"Hope Tree," Saskia finished. The Rabbit dead had thought it was Heen, mover of the earth, whose ears were roots, and whose divine connection turned Barton's arms into them . . .

Saskia got back up, running, even though she had no stomach for it. She was running headlong for the archive, blowing past Hounds who looked up but didn't follow her.

She burst into the archive, startling Baskar as she grabbed hold of them. "The Heartwood," Saskia said. "We have to go there. You're going to help me."

"I will not!" Baskar hissed, pushing her away, and she staggered. "My mistress will think you are betraying her — and you are! And the Owl King will stop us! I mean . . . you!"

Saskia didn't bother pushing down her grin. "They can try," she said. "They both can." Barton was calling out to her. The idea bloomed with what she knew. The Owl Court was close to the Heartwood . . . Saskia knew part of Roan's story. It was time to get Eli's.

"Eli lost his connection to the wind," Saskia started. "Did Roan show him how to get it back?"

Baskar was shaking their head, turning away from her and wrapping their twiggy arms around their body. "You are telling yourself a different story than the one that is here."

"You promised," Saskia reminded them. "You promised you'd help me understand. I'm trying to. Please."

Baskar gave her another unreadable, unknowable look, and their shoulders drooped. "I keep my promises," they said. "I will keep it for you, Saskia. Just do not harm yourself with the understanding I provide."

Saskia nodded, trying to calm down as she sat down like a kid at storytime.

Baskar sighed. "Eli. I did quite like him as he was before," they admitted. "He was willing to do what it took for Roan to trust him. He was willing to change . . ."

Eli returned to the cavern, which was deserted. It was fitting that she would make him wait, her judgment hanging over him. It had been too much, showing her what he had. He hadn't asked. He'd tricked her. *Same old Eli, doing harm with the veneer of good intentions.* Why did he always have to take everything too far? And what in gods' names was he going to do when she decided she wanted nothing to do with him?

"You don't look well," a familiar voice chirped from the dark recess of the cavern, and Eli froze. A shade manifested into the bare light where the firepit would be, its long ears twitching.

"Ah," Eli said. "Baskar, was it?"

The shade crept closer, scenting the air, assessing. Then it gave a strange cry when two Fox shades burst out from behind it, yipping and snapping as the Rabbit cowered.

One of the Foxes circled the firepit, the strange glow from it lighting its inky, wavering coat from underneath. They both approached Eli's sides like pincers.

"You will soon be weighed and measured, demon," said the first Fox. "Maybe you should run, get a head start before our mistress comes back."

Eli held his ground. "That's between her and me." His eyes narrowed. "You are the dead, and you've been here all along. And yet you call Roan 'Deon.' Surely you know she isn't your god."

The second Fox let out a curdling noise. "She is living but she carries death on her. She sees with Death's eye. She is our way back to the fire. Stay out of her way, and ours."

That gave him pause. Death's eye. Her spirit eye, then? Had that been what drew these disparate shades to her, including the Rabbit? Had it been what protected her from the shades' assaults in the way it hadn't protected Eli?

Now they'd chosen her as their god. She had become . . . something else entirely.

Eli held his hands up, moving towards the pit. "I'm not here to harm her. I'm here to help her."

"Help?" cried one of the Fox shades with a yowling cackle. "And where were *you* when she was alone? We were there for her. Even the pathetic Rabbit was here, at the start of this new world's beginning."

The thread of a sneer pulled at Eli's lips, but he loosened it, trying for humility. He looked to the Rabbit shade they were mocking, but it hadn't moved, flattened to the ground in submission. Eli felt how that shade looked. "I failed her," he said. "I know I did. I won't do that again."

"Words," the Foxes said together, surveying him. "Meaningless sounds that the living bleat when they don't know what waits for them. You'll get your due, soon enough." Then they looked at one another and padded out of the cavern, to make mischief or whisper more oddities to the landscape — Eli didn't care.

"Don't blame them," said Baskar, who had come to Eli's ankle. When the shade stood up, their head was past Eli's knee. "We all thought eternity was a guarantee. They are just looking for something to believe in. Change is hard for the dead."

Eli considered this strange shade and realized it was the first creature here to make any sense to him — Roan included.

"It's hard for the living, too." He peered down into the firepit and saw the source of the glow: a low flame, burning almost blue and strobing like a heartbeat. When he took stock of the way the pit had been dug, the room arranged, and certain markings incised in the rock, Eli smiled. "This is a summoning chamber." She must have built it herself. Which meant she might not be an entirely lost cause.

"The fire always burns. The mistress told us tales of the Uplands before she put them away. And when she did, the flame burned brighter."

For a moment, Eli didn't breathe. "She put her stories away? Her memories?"

The Rabbit moved steadily around the three circles incised in the stone, reciting. "Once upon a time, a girl was followed home by a fox, who gave her a great task she didn't feel she could manage. But she did. And everything went wrong. She found a room beneath her grandmother's house, with an empty hearth. She never had a room like that of her own, but when she could, she swore her own hearth would always be burning."

A chill shot through Eli's blood as he exhaled. "Of course." But Roan had put that history away. Pushed it aside, and became stronger for it. Was it because of grief? It stood to reason that Roan was only trying to edit out the things holding her back . . . but she'd gone too far. Eli wasn't sure he'd convinced her the value of accepting, let alone reliving, the victories and the failures that made her Roan Harken.

"I believe you're the mistress's friend. In your own way. But if you think you might hurt her, then you should leave. No matter what you feel."

Eli bristled. "And what, you're her security detail now?"

The Rabbit stared at him with expressionless, white eyes.

"I'm doing this for her own good. Not mine." Eli turned his back to the well-meaning shade. "I'll let her decide if it's so."

He waited until the bare scampering of shadow steps went across and out of the cavern, then strode to the other side of the pit. He considered the smooth granite beneath his blistered feet. Pain was in the mind, and he had a strong one. He could manage it. What he couldn't manage was the Rabbit's warning, or his own. They were in a godless country of ghosts looking for an idol — or else shaping Roan to become one for them. That was as unfair as Eli coming here, trying to turn her back into something she didn't want. It had to be her choice. And whatever that was, he'd have to respect it.

And find another way to save the world. Whatever.

He tried to strengthen his resolve. He skinned out of his ruined sweater, the warmth inviting on his bare flesh. The cave faded around him, his mind opening like an aperture to replay the wilderness, and Roan in it, dancing.

Eli's foot extended as hers had, swept back, and leaned his body over it. He faltered, waking up abruptly, scowling. *This is stupid. I'm not a dancer. Neither was she. She was awkward and stupid and grasping and too tender-hearted and we both deserve better than me noodling around here like a moron —*

He was in the thicket again, Roan just a wavering outline in the air. She squared her shoulders, hands pressing outward, and Eli couldn't help but raise his, becoming her mirror. He was in the memory, and in the cavern, following her steps, slowing them down.

The drums emerged to meet Eli as he moved through. Step, pivot, turn. Ease backward. Step, pivot, turn — scrape his torso against rude angles. The drums were only a blueprint rhythm but still a guide. He let them lead him, and suddenly, like his cells were each inhaling, the wind rose inside him.

Moving lightly on the balls of his feet, Eli felt something shift deep inside. There was nothing stupid about it now. He felt utterly locked in to sensation. It was like he could feel new skin forming beneath scar tissue, pushing, multiplying, remaking him.

He paused, mid-movement, teetering on a precipice. Was it dangerous to want to be remade? Why, after everything he'd gone through with his mother in the Roost, was he still so terrified of letting go?

The drums were a heartbeat from the stone to his soles, and he twisted, repeating the steps again and again, speeding them up in memory and reality. His body was light as an easterly, the air filling him as it did once, when wings were a chance at utter freedom, and when power was only a consequence.

Eli's arms snapped out, and his breath came quick on the backspin. The flame in the fire pit shot upward, a meteoric, bright blade. When it came down again, Roan was there — *really* there — on the other side of the fire, staring at Eli with a stunned expression.

Eli dropped his arms as if he could hide what he'd done. Or how impossibly exalted he felt. Or maybe at least cover his chest.

"Your form is *terrible*," Roan announced.

Eli felt his face pinch. "Yes. Thank you."

She approached him and pressed her arms out. "It's less about perfect execution and more about perfect feeling."

She swayed, moved. Waited for him. When he didn't immediately mimic her, she lifted his arms for him, so he could really see. He did. This close, he saw her amber eye flare in the light beside her. *The eye of Death*.

They moved together, an exhalation, through three of the basic movements, and that same sensation came back to Eli. A syncopated cadence. A locked-in frequency.

Eli pulled away abruptly. "Well?" he said. "I need you to tell me now. I'll leave, if you wish it. I know you had your reasons for forgetting. I don't blame you." The words rushed out too quickly. He folded his arms to try to get the buzzing to leave his chest; his sweater was annoyingly far away. "It's fine. Really."

Her hand came down again on his scarred arm. "There's something binding us," Roan said. "I believe we can tap into something beyond the fire — but we have to do it together."

She pulled away. What he'd felt, moving like that, a kinetic primal spark he'd never felt, even with the Moonstone . . . he wanted desperately to feel it again. To be connected to something greater than himself, even if — especially if — it meant being connected to Roan. He'd do it, but there was always a price.

"So I can stay, then?" he pressed, perhaps a touch too moodily.

Roan cocked a brow at him. "Baskar likes you," she said. "I suppose that's enough to go on, for now."

She extended her hand to him. "I'll show you the way to get back to the wind. You show me the life I came from, on my terms. Then we can both decide if whatever you came here for in the first place is still worth pursuing."

Eli took her hand, gripped it tight. He knew it was an agreement that, if broken, would cost them more than what either of them could pay.

Still, he grinned. "Then let's begin."

﹏﹏

Saskia hadn't wanted to blackmail Baskar, but when it came down to it, she had no choice.

She was pleased with how quickly the plan had formed when motivation and need arrived. It really was like coding, every choice a line in it.

She'd really come to like Baskar, her only reliable friend here, and the trust between them was as fragile as it had been between Roan and Eli when they were trying to come back to each other.

But Saskia needed to get to that tree. And she needed to get to the Owl King to understand how she was going to get Barton out of it.

"The book that you lost," Saskia said, still ensconced in the archive, back to back with Baskar as they wove their hands to the story likely going on inside their head. "It had the forbidden story you weren't supposed to tell in it."

Baskar leapt up so quickly that Saskia fell back, nearly cracking her head on the floor. Baskar was bent away, head in their hands.

"I — I will find it. No one will know —"

Saskia was up just as fast. "But you know the story. And you wrote it down, because you couldn't bear it getting lost. Except now it is. Who do you think could've taken it?"

Baskar uncurled slowly. "It is possible . . . that one of the Owl King's Eyes found it . . ."

"Then we should both go looking for it before Roan figures that out. Shouldn't we?"

Baskar's mask somehow took on a darkly troubled expression. "You wouldn't tell her, would you, Saskia?"

Of course not. It wouldn't bode well for either of them, and Saskia didn't want Baskar to get hurt. She sighed. "No. But that means we both have reasons to go to the Roost. We just have to make Roan believe it was her idea."

Baskar paced. "She did believe you were his spy, initially." They pivoted. "Perhaps it could be a test of your loyalty, to go there and use your stone against Eli."

Then they clapped a hand over their face. "But it would be a test of my loyalty, too, and helping you do this may make us both traitors. This is far too confusing to consider."

Baskar looked ready to escape, and Saskia lunged, put her arms firmly around them before they could. "I know you want to run away. But both of us can't. All of these stories you've saved are important, and connected, and so is mine. We all have to be archivists and make sure they survive. But there are holes in this one, and I think it's up to us to fill them."

Baskar looked down at her arms around them. She hastily let go. A bony finger lifted to Saskia's hair, moving it out of her eyes. She wasn't sure why her heart skipped a beat, but she was okay with it. Love was a strange, fragile thing, it turned out.

"That was a thing Eli did for Roan once," Baskar qualified, before moving awkwardly back a step.

Saskia tried to picture it, picture Roan and Eli still dancing together, an elegant knot of flame and air, tied together forever no matter how many times they'd broken apart. Dancing, Baskar had said. It seemed unbelievable now as it would have seven years ago. Had *they* loved each other? Did they still? It seemed silly to picture them like this, but Baskar had only ever told Saskia the truth.

Saskia was grasping. "If I can confront Eli, maybe I can find out what happened between them. And then they can be . . . whatever they were again." She wanted that forbidden story, but maybe it wasn't the only one she needed.

Baskar groaned. "You are very young. But I won't try to

stop you." They interlocked their knotty fingers. "The forbidden story could undo all your plans, anyway. So I will do this thing, and we will do it together. I would not like to see you hurt, I've decided, especially for a mistake I have made."

Saskia was touched but didn't know what else to say. "Together," she repeated. Baskar nodded, holding out their hand, and Saskia took it.

The ONLY ONE WHO KNOWS

Roan was seasoned and still as Baskar laid it out, and Saskia had stood to the side, carefully silent, awaiting her judgment.

"She must leave the stone behind here," Roan had tried initially. "For safekeeping. If the Owl King gets a hold of it —"

"But it would be her only defense against him," Baskar had argued, which had, at first, made Roan bristle. "Were she to use it on him, it may even finish him. If she goes to him, feigning loyalty, his guard will be down, and she may strike. Then nothing would stand between you and the Heartwood."

Baskar had spent many hours contemplating who this lie was going to hurt if it was told, or if it was held back. They had decided it would harm Roan if they didn't go forward with this plan. Saskia knew that, either way, Baskar would be in the line of fire. They all would be.

Roan appraised them both. "Don't get too attached, Baskar," she said, eyeing Saskia and turning away sharply. "Love is a game for the living, and we have always played it terribly."

Saskia waited for Baskar's reaction. Yet Baskar, expressionless as always, inclined their head. "I love you, too, Mistress. I do not wish to see you come to harm. Please let us do this."

Something of Roan was still there, because she'd softened and agreed. "Go towards the Heartwood. I am sure the Owl King's Eyes will spot you and take you directly." She laid a precious kiss across Baskar's woody brow. "May the fire protect you."

❧

They made their way to the great tree that seemed to have grown higher since Saskia had last seen it, and Baskar stuck close to her. She felt that this time, they did it more out of protectiveness than a self-serving survival impulse. Saskia didn't mind Baskar's closeness. It reminded her that she was still human, and needed to be . . . needed.

"So Eli and Roan danced, but it wasn't happily ever after." She was trying to distract them both. "Eli wanted Roan to remember herself. Roan had put her memories away so she didn't have to face her mistakes. I'm sure both of their tempers didn't make for getting along."

"Not at all," Baskar said, but the night was falling, and they would need to take shelter soon. "Are you not tired, Saskia?"

She was. To her soul. She was surviving by moving forward, by eating the weird foods Baskar brought her that had once sustained Roan and Eli. But whatever spell was over this place was quickly making her forget the needs of her very real body.

She ached for rest, for this all to be done.

"I need to know," she said stubbornly, as they made their camp for the night, and Baskar wrapped their arms around her to keep her warm, though their stick body gave off no heat. "I need to know as much of the story as I can to make sense of it."

By now, Saskia could guess Baskar knew about that all too well.

They had been practising the movements, pulling up those precious drumbeats that Eli still hadn't figured out the source of. But from what he'd gleaned from the Dragon Opal when he and Roan went inside it together on Skye, dancing had to do with Cecelia. She'd even written to Roan about how dancing had helped her find her fire. That may have been the key to getting Roan in any shape to fight Zabor in such a short window. But Cecelia was long gone now, as were her secrets — likely fled to the same holding place where Demelza had gone.

There was something primeval about it, this dancing, and it did give Eli some hope that not all was lost. That maybe the gods weren't really dead, if the two of them could still command their power. Moving with Roan like this made him feel stronger, more hopeful. The days went on, and though they got closer and closer to articulating exactly what was between them, Eli still thought he knew better than her.

He had been showing Roan parts of herself in small increments, unlocking all those things about her before she'd found out anything about the Realms of Ancient: they walked the halls of her high school. They opened doors leading to greenhouses and looked objectively at stone statues of five animals, but Eli didn't go too far. They told each other their stories, because Eli wanted it to be fair. He wanted her to know him as he knew her. She did, too. It was a partnership of equals, growing back to who they were, together, and as they made their way through the wilderness, this shared knowing made them a stronger unit. Eli felt the wind move inside him in a way it never had. Roan made the fire something marvellous to behold.

They were the new gods. For a while, Eli allowed himself to forget what, exactly, he needed to help Roan with, because he knew that giving her back everything might truly break her.

But the more they held to one another, and the more secrets built up between them, the harder it was for Eli to keep up the lie. He decided it was time for Roan to know everything about Cecelia.

Roan didn't agree.

"But she's a part of who you are," Eli insisted, voice rising. "We are everything that's happened to us, the good and the terrible. This is how you get back to yourself. Knowing her will help you know who you are."

"I *do* know who I am!" Roan had snarled back, sharpening her dancing form like her garnet blade as they practised one night in the cavern. Eli should have known to quit then.

He stepped out of their choreography and threw a zephyr in her face. "I am the only one who knows you, because like it or not, we *are* the same. Always have been. Pigheaded and running away from the dark. But neither of us can outrun it forever."

The air had pushed her out of the circle, and she'd barely waited for him to finish before rushing back at him. They knew each other too well by then and could predict each falter and feint, every arcing fist. A different dance. They met each blow, turned each strike off, but neither gave ground.

"Roan, enough." Eli caught both of her hands and tried to speak gently despite her thrashing. "We have to be finished hurting one another. Whatever power we're sharing — we have to put it to its intended use. Protecting lives beyond just ours."

But some things were impossible to change, and she got free of him, striking him hard across the face with a hot, open palm. All at once he threw more than just Cecelia at her. He fired everything he knew about her in a hundred-mile-per-hour arrow — and made sure it struck home and stayed there.

Roan collapsed like a rag doll.

At first, he thought it was just another of her wild-thing tricks. "Roan?" A cautious step, then he threw himself down on her, lifting her up, shaking her. "Roan, come on." Her mismatched eyes stared into nothing. He sent his mind into hers, and he cried out like he'd hit an electric fence.

Eli held Roan close, all the corded strength he'd come to admire completely fled from her. She still breathed shallowly, but she felt so fragile just then. And she was. So was he.

She didn't wake for days, and he was sure he'd killed her mind.

He remained by her side. He didn't sleep. Self-flagellation became his only companion. The shades, even Baskar, kept silent vigil. They blamed him — they had every right to. Eli promised himself that if Roan did awaken, he'd leave immediately. He'd done enough damage.

One morning, he'd fallen asleep only for a second, but when he jerked fitfully awake she was sitting up beside him, staring. She could burn him to ashes, and he would gladly allow it.

Instead, she pressed his chest in the place the Moonstone had been. "I'm sorry," she said. "I'm sorry for all of it."

He took her in his arms. She was warm as hers slid up his back. They did not let go of each other for a very long time.

"I'll leave," Eli said into her hair. "I don't want to hurt you anymore."

She grasped him the tighter. "Leaving will hurt me," she whispered. "Don't let go of me."

He didn't. Who was he kidding? He *couldn't*.

Eli was certain they could move forward now. But then Roan began asking him about the Calamity Stones. She was tentative at first, wondering aloud where they could be hidden in the new world they were forging.

"What does it matter?" Eli asked, but the idea had already taken hold of her, and Roan had always been like a dog with a bone.

"We might need them again to finish what we started," she said. "After all, some things never change."

Eli was reluctant to argue with her. They had been at a stalemate in this Deadland, and the gods hadn't shown themselves. No one was coming to help them and never was. But weren't the gods part of Ancient? It did have a terrible logic.

Of course they would go looking, and they agreed to do this thing together. There was no other way to do it.

"They went out in search of the Moonstone, first." Baskar's voice had become strange with this recollection, in a way it hadn't with the others. "When they returned, Eli was different and his rage terrible. We found Roan bloody and weeping, and it only renewed her resolve to build Cinder Town and fight Eli. He made his own kingdom, and we all became a part of their never-ending dance. Whatever happened between them is a part of the story I did not want to know, and even now it frightens me. I could not fathom such pain."

The Heartwood was only a half day's walk away, on the other side of this night. It was still dark, and Saskia was too wide awake, but she kept still and let Baskar hold her tight. The closer they got to the Heartwood, the harder it was to ignore the Onyx, crying out to be reunited with its sister stones. If Calamity had to be restored, and Roan and Eli couldn't do it, how could Saskia manage it alone?

"There is one worry I wish to share with you," Baskar said very quietly. Saskia turned over, looked up at them in the dark.

"What is it?"

They still wouldn't look at her. "If we find the end to this story, will you stop needing me to tell you any others?"

Saskia pulled Baskar's mask towards her, looking them square in their coin-winking eyes. "I'm not going to leave you behind. No matter what happens or how this story ends."

Baskar held her hands to their face, and sighed, mimicking the sound of what Roan might have once called *perfect feeling*. "Are *our* stories connected now?"

Saskia closed her eyes and put her ear to the place where Baskar's heart might be. It was quiet. The Onyx hummed, and Saskia wondered if it did this because there was death rattling around inside Baskar's shell, and the stone carried death inside it, too.

"Roan may be touched by Death," Baskar spoke, as if they could read Saskia's thoughts, "but you are honoured by it." Somehow, Baskar sounded sleepy. "I am honoured by your story, Saskia, and my part in it."

She felt herself drifting off, clasping tight to her friend who, poppet or not, alive or not, had made her feel known in a way she'd always wanted to be. And in that moment, it was enough.

﹌

This close to the doomed tree on which she planted all her own hopes, Saskia dreamed within a dream.

"Saskia."

It was no longer a message bleeping red on a screen, or in her head. It wasn't a signal, either. It was a simple plea. And she knew, without a doubt, it was Barton.

She followed the roots of the tree, stabbing deep down into an oblivion. An emptiness, complete in its lack.

Below the tree, in the darkness, something was pushing up, using the tree as the weapon. The tree pushed back, blocking the way. At the heart of the tree was a green light, held close to what had been a man's body. He and the tree, together, had fought back against what tried to push them away, away from a doorway that had been opened in the world above.

The dark shone. And it moved.

"Please, Saskia," the tree, the man, said as he felt her awareness. "Please turn back. The message wasn't me —"

The thing in the dark pressed harder. The man tangled in the roots cried out and fought back. He would always fight, if it meant preventing this.

"It's too late," Saskia said, "the story is already being told."

Then she was moving up the tree at an alarming speed, and the ground was splitting, sending the tree up and piercing the land and the sky, like a spear, and Saskia was still climbing higher, unable to stop herself until she realized the spear was pointing towards a black inevitability in the sky over her home, tracking closer to the sun, slipping over it like a hood.

The ring around the moon was red. It sang into the ground and opened the way for the tree, which the man Saskia had known and loved and wanted only to save could no longer hold back. The tree would break into her world, split it apart, and bring the darkness along.

The Brilliant Dark was not a place, but a plan. A story, lying below, waiting for its chance to be told.

⋙⋘

Saskia woke feeling like she was being crushed, but it was just Baskar's arms tight around her, wood arms crackling. The nightmare was slipping away, and Saskia wanted to banish it, but it left a terrible taste in her mouth.

For a second she thought, *Damn Eli, and Roan, and all of them. I'm going to that tree, and I'm going to pull Barton out of it. I don't need them, I don't need their stories.*

Then she looked around the thicket where they'd taken refuge overnight, the trees filled with the narrow bark bodies and sharp-horned helms of the Eyes of the Owl King. His soldiers, surrounded them, pointing their primitive, sharp weapons.

They weren't getting anywhere near the Heartwood today.

"It's okay," Saskia said, low and quiet, to Baskar. "Just stick to the plan. This is how we move forward."

Baskar didn't reply, but their hands loosened.

The Owl soldiers were on them like darts, and Saskia and Baskar were separated in a flurry of wings, carried through the wild Deadland canopy, and yanked skyward and screeching to the Roost.

❧

Six months this conflict had gone on. Mi-ja didn't know how much sleep a person could miss before their heart eventually stopped, but she was certain, by now, she'd blown past the point of no return.

Two sides, the same message: We will not stand down. We will protect this world.

The rest of the world swivelled its head from side to side, unsure which to pin their hopes on.

The violence couldn't be avoided. Hard decisions were made that Mi-ja hadn't ever been prepared to make, and they were wearing her down with every executive order, every emergency council, every call for armistice that had to be put aside. Chancellor Grant had started all this and he wasn't even here to deal with the consequences. Could he have? If he did return, she'd shoot him herself.

Mi-ja's hatred for him was gradual, then at once all-consuming. She tore through his ridiculous memoirs, his treatises on his vision for the world, burned any copy she came across, and knew that if she didn't pull it together, the Task Guard would just replace her with someone as bad as Grant had been — she just had to play the long game, hold it together a little longer.

She looked to the leaders of the current Denizen incursion, to try to understand how it had begun and got so out of hand here — in Winnipeg, of all places. Of course it wasn't just happening in Winnipeg: it was everywhere else, too. But in this prairie river city threatening to flood, Mi-ja had to make a decision that no one in the world was willing to make.

There had been nothing more from "the other side." No more signals or messages. The Apex was silent. Just the dark moon in the sky like a promise, that entity that made no sense and could be seen by everyone, around the globe, at any given time. Mi-ja came to believe the moon was just punishment for what Denizens and regular folk did to one another, what humanity itself had done to the world since they'd crawled out of the primordial fire.

She read the reports every day. The Darkling Moon was on a path to the sun, to an eclipse. There was no telling what would happen and given the state of the world — overrun with element-wielding miscreants and monsters that didn't discriminate — it could be anything. It could be nothing. It could be the end of everything, and then, at least, there'd be blissful quiet.

The files on Nattiq Fontaine and Phaedrapramit Das were extensive, but what of it? These women fought for more than ideals. They fought for what had been lost, and the possibility of what could be reclaimed in the aftermath. They fought towards a hope that Mi-ja dreamed of. Too many times, she wished she could just talk to them both, wished she could just give what was left of this ragged world to them, close her eyes, and embrace the dark.

Then she would sign another executive order, address new troops, feel herself readjusting to her skin, the skin of a leader that the powerless still needed.

She would keep fighting, for now. So would the Denizens. And she would beat any attacker back until victory was assured. Project Crossover had been shelved and a new one had taken its place — Project Annihilate. If they had to, they would blast that dark moon out of the sky with whatever firepower they had to bear. The world was already getting ready for it.

And if it didn't work . . . well. Then maybe Grant had been right about something — there would be a new dawn. Just no one left to see it.

STRAINS *of* ADAMANT

They put Saskia in a cage, high above Roan's realm and the other broken ones below. She didn't know where the Owls had taken Baskar, but she'd caught a glimpse of the archivist and sent out a kind of prayer to them — *I'll be all right. Stop struggling or you'll break in half.* She wondered if the Onyx could transmit messages to the dead; after all, it could suck them into it.

The Owl soldiers were afraid of it, and even though she would never use it on them, she let them think she would.

"We have been watching you," one soldier said, the voice a grating screech. "We are the Owl King's eyes, and he will take that stone that kills the dead away from you."

Saskia stood at the back of her cell, wiping any expression from her face. "Tell him I'm here to give it to him. Because I want to help him."

The Owl shades seemed to cringe. "Even looking upon

that stone, it makes me want —" One shook its masked head. Another grasped their arm and pulled. "Come away. She is a pretender. We will tell the Owl King as we are bidden, and then we will throw her over the side."

They left her alone, and Saskia waited. She was used to jail cells by now, and though they'd taken her pack from her, she'd come prepared and slid a hand inside her beat-up denim jacket for the crowbar.

As a Cinder Kid, she'd scurried around like a rodent, able to move with the shadows and strange sounds of Seela's world. She remembered how that felt now, breaking out of her cell just as the soldiers returned to set a watch, but by then she was already going up through this compound, pressing into walls. It was only a matter of time before Eli, with his powerful mind and his own Calamity Stone, found her. She wanted to get to him first, though, on her own terms.

She had to use the Onyx.

She was scared, crouching there behind upended, cracked marble, hearing skittering footsteps coming for her. But she'd been scared a long time. Maybe fear could be a power. She flipped the switch on the Fractal, and whatever was inside her answered the stone on her head. The dark came sluicing out of the stone, and she wrapped herself in that shadow. She saw it separate into tiny little flickers, little triangular wings floating up the corridor, past guards who dashed past her without seeing.

The moths flew ahead, waiting for her at the end of one hall, up stairs, until she was back out in the open air, the wind too loud and everywhere at once.

The moths kept waiting, and she kept following them up and in.

"I always liked Phyr," Phae had said, during one of her many lessons. "Though she seemed like the god that all the others despised because she represented authority and all-knowingness."

The conversation from the past kept pace with Saskia's hurried steps. She didn't want to use the Onyx for too much longer. Whatever part of its power that had been touched by Death she sent out to find Baskar, to tell them she was safe. She kept climbing, following Phae's voice, remembering how it felt to be outside of the story instead of inside it.

"I thought I read somewhere that Phyr was the reason all the realms were separate," Saskia had said. "I guess we won't ever know, though. Can't ask her."

"That's right," Phae had agreed. "Phyr's realm, the Roost, was above the others. Some said the top of the universe, or the underside of the moon, which is the Owls' chief symbol."

This moon was in pieces, though, if this was it, floating as little connected platforms. Saskia crossed ascending bridges between them, knowing that at the top she'd find the person she was looking for.

"We can't ever know the gods, though," Saskia had said, wishing it weren't true. "I mean, maybe the Paramounts did, because of their connections to them . . . but it's like any family. If only they'd talked out whatever had happened, things could've been different."

The truth, whatever it was, had always been too hard. Across history and mythology and stories. If only everyone had been honest with each other. If only people — and gods — weren't motivated by fear. In that way they were all the same, at least. That meant that gods, like people, had flaws, and could course correct, even at the eleventh hour. Old gods *and* new ones. Saskia clung to that.

The Onyx strobed, and she felt it trying to get inside of her. That sliver of the darklings that had always scared her, teasing her heart, and she tripped, grasping for the Fractal crown, to shut it off, but her hands wouldn't work.

"No," she seethed. "We're separate. Remember our deal."

No deal, the dark answered, *only truth*.

She saw the Darklings, all three of them. Then she saw a god who must still be inside the Onyx, the old Quartz, and its triple-horned head. Saskia saw a vision of Darklings in Fia's reflection, beneath them. Fia said, "*My children*," each of their heads swivelling. "I wish I could take it back."

Saskia found the switch and collapsed with dizziness in a broken hall on the last platform before the top. She was close to ripping the crown off and hurling it over the side, but this wasn't over yet. She thought of everyone relying on her, of those she'd lost. Papa. Mama. Albert. Even Killian. Then Roan and Eli and Barton and Phae and Natti and Baskar and the Moth Queen and the gods and Ancient and — and —

The story for all of them wasn't finished and neither was Saskia.

She got her legs back under her and stood at the bottom of a great staircase. She tilted her head to look above, wondering if she stared long enough she'd see the underside of home. There were only stars, constellations she would never recognize.

She sent a prayer up there, like an arrow, to Phae. That love was stronger than Saskia's fear, and it always would be. She put a foot to the stairs and climbed.

The Owl King knew she was coming. He put the book away, having read it for a time past counting. A story he already knew. But Roan, obviously, had rejected it. She might never embrace what they'd come here for, because it meant she'd have to face herself. If that's what she wanted, he'd give it to her. Forever.

Soon the girl, Saskia, would be at the door. And he would give her the answers she sought, but he wasn't sure what good it would do her, or him.

The Heartwood was the end of it all. And this girl, walking bravely now over the threshold to the top of his domain, was keen to see the page not only turned, but to write that ending herself.

They'd all been so young.

"Saskia." Eli inclined his head, as if he wasn't the king here. "My Eyes tell me you're here to give me that curious, death-grasping stone you brought with you." His hands, tipped with their black talons, linked before him and brushed against his folded wings which covered his shoulders, his chest. Keeping the Therion shape made him feel further away from the man he'd once been, made him feel safe. "Of course, it's not true."

Eli's broken throne was on level ground. Saskia stood quite far from him, but even at this distance, he could see how tired she was. He knew that feeling well.

"I came here to remind you and Roan of your purposes and to ask why you didn't fulfill them," she said.

Eli spread his hands. "We are fulfilling our purposes," he replied, tone mocking. "Playing our parts. Just like you are."

Saskia turned red. "You're both running away! You tried to fix things once, and when it didn't work out, you *hid*. Everyone was counting on both of you! And now I have to —" Her voice caught, but she still held her ground, thrusting a finger at him. "You're both acting like children. But you're going to be made accountable. And you're going to tell me exactly what went wrong."

Eli tilted his head. "Are you done now?" He held up the book, and Saskia faltered. "If it's all just a story, then what does it matter if it never gets told or finished? Roan and I realized that, in our own ways. We put away the things that made us weak and told a different story. Now we're stronger for it."

Saskia walked towards him, fists clenched. "I wish I could put away my responsibilities, too, but I made a choice — a promise," she said. "I need your help. I need you both to remember. I need the world not to end, because there are still people in it that I care about."

She lifted her hand to the crown on her head, but there was a black rush in front of her, around her, and suddenly she was hoisted up by a hand and dragged, screaming, until she was dangling over the side of the Roost.

"This story will go on forever, as long as we allow it." Eli scowled as he held her with one hand. In the other was Baskar's book, that forbidden story, which he released over the precipice.

"We tell ourselves all kinds of stories," Saskia choked, grunting under the pressure of his squeezing fist pushing the bones of her wrist against each other. "What kind of story have you and Roan been telling each other?"

Eli's eyes flexed. "Maybe you don't deserve to know."

Then he grasped the Fractal, crushing it, and the switch that controlled it, like it was made of tinfoil.

The Onyx opened like a jaw and swallowed them both.

❧

The song this time was two melodies — the Onyx, once the Quartz, had its own unique discord. The Moonstone, though cracked, was a gentle flute. They reached for each other tentatively, swirling, recognizing that, despite their differences, they were cut, ultimately, from the same song.

The Calamity Stones, once, had been the hearts of the gods. They trusted them to their descendants. But gods and people were also cut from the same song, and hearts, whoever they belonged to, were easily broken. Easily betrayed. Eli's heart was no different, even if he tried to convince Saskia he didn't have one.

Saskia imagined that the darkness both she and Eli were in now may have been inside his Moonstone, his heart, his memory. Whatever was there, he didn't want Saskia to see it, but she sent her red song ahead of her like a javelin, then ripped the tear wider so she could see.

No, it wasn't that he didn't want to show her — *he* didn't want to see it. Not again. He had put these things away, just like Roan had, so that he could survive in his cold kingdom, always fighting her. Fighting *for* her. He did not want to reclaim himself, though he had been trying to get Roan to do this exact thing. Somewhere along the way, he let himself go so he didn't have to let her go.

They had become trapped by the past and by the uncertainty of what was ahead.

He wasn't choking Saskia. She was holding him up, and he collapsed in this dark place, head in his hands.

"When I tried to force Roan to reclaim herself, I thought I'd lost her," he said, looking at his human digits, like they were foreign now. He seemed utterly lost when he stared up at Saskia. "I was lucky she came back to me at all. I would have done anything for her."

"You still would," Saskia said, trying to get him up and moving. "Come on."

He seemed to unravel more the farther she towed him. "But tied up in all the things I'd known about her were the things I — felt — for her."

He didn't have to say it for Saskia to understand it, as she saw it happening, felt it inside her, as they went deeper. When he'd tried to force Roan to remember, it was his own perspective he'd thrown at her, not her own memories. All she'd seen was how Eli perceived her. She still hadn't opened herself back up. She still didn't really know herself.

And in all the things he'd forced her to re-learn were things about Eli. His memories. His experiences. And his own mistakes when it came to the Calamity Stones.

His grin appeared, and it was sick. "She'd seen exactly what it cost me, my mother, and my father, when it came to finding the Moonstone. That's why I can't forgive her for what she eventually made me do."

Calamity Stones ruined those who claimed them. Roan knew that. And still she made Eli do this terrible thing. She'd made him do it again. And for her sake, he'd done it. Anything to keep their charade in the underworld going, because there was no future for them, certainly, if they woke Ancient. There was no certainty they just wouldn't fail again.

What a fool he'd been, finally choosing love over power. He'd been angriest at himself.

The story unfurled before Saskia like an abandoned battlefield of broken promises.

⁓⳥

Eli and Roan made their way beneath the Roost, to the place where Eli had fallen originally. Beyond it was something of a mountain, a last vestige of the Glen, perhaps. The place seemed familiar, even though Eli had barely left their corner of the wilderness in what could have been twenty years. Time meant nothing. This was certainly how the gods must have felt.

"How do you know where you're going?" he'd asked Roan. He could have tried probing her mind, but he swore never to do it again, swore he could know what she was thinking without it. He'd nearly lost her to his pride, his imagining he knew better than her.

"Just trust me," she'd said. And he had. He thought he always would.

⁓⳥

Parts of Eli's fragmented past, those he'd reconstructed with his mother's help, snicked Saskia's spirit like shrapnel blowing by. Demelza was a cursed princess in a fable. The Moonstone was put away by Owls because it was too powerful. But the Moonstone woke one day, seeking a Paramount. Phyr needed an avatar in the Uplands and would not be ignored. Her eye went to Demelza. Demelza told no one where it was, but Solomon found out that she knew. She'd trusted him too much. He'd tried to persuade her that it was *for the greater good*. Pregnant with his child, she sent him away and told him that if he ever tried to come back to either of them for the sake of ambition, she would do something they'd both regret.

But the Moonstone wouldn't be denied. In its hiding place, it waited, and when Demelza refused it for the last time, it took her mind.

Slowly, at first. So she was still aware of everything coming apart at the seams. So she could know that her son had inherited the vision of the Moonstone's location, and that it would be found by him eventually. The logic of her madness told her that if she took her own life, maybe the vision would die with her. It hadn't. Then her spirit had waited many desperate years in the Deadlands, consumed by guilt and regret but holding it together, in case her son was stronger than she was. He wasn't, it turned out.

His father did return to the little town by the sea and took his son with him into the hidden Denizen world, made promises of power, made Eli realize potential he'd never wanted but couldn't give back. He grew up and grew hungrier, pushing anyone out of his path who would distract him. Pretending that the hole inside of him wasn't there.

We'll find the stone together, his father had said, once Eli had confessed Demelza's vision. Solomon thought that, once they found the stone, buried deep under fault lines and wind-eroded pathways in an uninhabited place, the stone would cast its eye upon Solomon. He had wanted to spare his son. He had hoped Phyr would do the right thing.

The other Owls agreed that he'd make the best Paramount. But the stone had its own will then, as it did now, and it chose Eli, smothering the last bit of the innocent boy with the demands of the long-dead. *Maintain the Narrative. Protect Ancient's story, Ancient's plan, whatever the cost. Do this and we will give you great power*, the stone's voices promised. Eli had done terrible things. Allowed terrible things to happen, just like Solomon had. In order to wake up every day, not consumed by this, Eli had put it all away. Demelza had come back to tell him he needed to take all the mistakes, all the darkness, and accept them now. Accept that they were a part of him. *Heal around your grief. Help Roan heal from hers.*

He'd tried. He'd failed.

"We'll find the stones together," Roan had said, and when they crested the top of a cliff she pointed across a chasm of mist to a slab of white that had crashed into a summit just beyond. Eli had seen it in a vision once. The top of the Roost. Phyr's former throne. Roan was already making for the narrow pass to it, and he knew then he couldn't stop her. Knew then it was too late.

The only way she'd have known was if another stone, a sister stone, was leading her there.

Eli confronted her when they climbed to the shattered platform, and she stood with her back to him.

"You have the Opal," he said, clenching his fists. "You had it all along, and you . . . you kept it from me."

Roan turned in profile, holding a bundle that had been wrapped up in shreds of what may have been the hoodie she'd worn, once upon a time, when they'd come down here together. She unspooled the pieces carefully, and the broken Opal shone, defiant.

"I think I knew I'd need it one day," she said. "With it,

we can both be made new. There are no Uplands for us, Eli. Down here is a new land. Fresh and free from our mistakes."

"This place is the *result* of our mistakes. Please, Roan, don't make them again."

She was shaking her head, holding the stone lovingly to her chest. "The fire can't live with all that pain."

"If you do this," Eli said, "then you'll break what is between us forever." And once that cord snapped, there would be nothing that could ever see them home again.

She gave him a pitying look, then slammed the Opal to her breast. She gasped, maybe in pain, maybe relief, and when a corona shot from it, it cut through the pale rock at her feet, and she fell, cleared away the rubble, and pulled the white-gold stone into her hands.

"You know it has to be like this," she was saying, cradling the Moonstone as she had cradled Eli close, convincing him that they were moving forward. "You answered it once. You can do it again. And we can become what we were always meant to be."

He couldn't believe they were back here again. "I won't. You know I won't do it."

She put the Moonstone down then and backed to the edge of the platform. "You'll have to."

Eli rushed, the wind rushed, but it was too late. Roan tipped over the side and fell to the mist. Eli had no wings to catch her and couldn't make them without the Moonstone.

She really *was* the only one who knew him, and he screamed, smashing the stone into himself before diving after her. He grabbed her out of the sky, his wings and talons ripping through him with the thrill of an addict's rush, and she pulled him to her, kissing him with everything they had left before their golden tether broke.

⇜⇝

The dark of the Onyx cradled Eli and Saskia, the two kneeling before each other in this remembering place. They were still inside the Moonstone, inside Eli's memory. He looked shaken, like he'd just been woken from a draining slumber.

"You loved her," Saskia said, "and she betrayed you."

Eli held Saskia's hands loosely. When she looked down, she saw they were the hands of a child. The Eli before her, in his mind, was so young, a child from a distant shore. Saskia's age when all of these conflicts were thrust on her so harshly.

Young Eli smiled. "Love and betrayal. It's what she and I do best."

Then he showed Saskia what he meant.

⇜⇝

When they touched ground, the two of them upright, Eli held Roan close. She was hot, almost burning in his hands with life. He was shaking — with rage, with absolute despair — and she was grinning from ear to ear. He was so relieved to see that grin, to hear her voice, that he hated himself even more.

He let her go.

"Look at you!" she crowed, triumphant. "*Now* we are the same. You can feel it, I know you can. You look every bit the god you were meant to be."

Eli stared at his taloned hands in a way that regret couldn't cover. "I didn't want this," he said. "I didn't."

"Come on," Roan said, dusting herself off, as if Eli had seen sense, finally, and all was forgiven. As if things were as they always had been, though they couldn't ever be again.

She tightened her blade belt and turned to him, holding out a hand. "Now we can do this as we were meant to. Together."

He stared at her hand, sorely, terribly tempted. His chest throbbed.

So Eli stepped closer. Then he was upon her, talons slashing. They grappled, spinning in their perfected dance, all grace and calculated symmetry. They knew each other too well, though, and she caught his wrists, holding her ground as he struggled. Eli bent over her, shivering with madness. Her feet slid wider on the ground, shuddering, but she pushed back.

Roan's grin evaporated when she saw the tears streaming down Eli's face.

"I should kill you for this," he sobbed. Something inside him cracked, in the general latitude of the Moonstone, where his heart might be. "You keep making the same choices again and again. We were so close. And you . . . you ruined *everything*."

Roan's forehead creased with the effort of holding him back. She was genuinely confused that this wasn't what he wanted. His hands wrapped around hers in a flash, squeezing so hard he felt the geometry of her bones change. She let out a high-pitched cry from the back of her throat, but she wouldn't give in. She would break first. Her hands were white hot.

Her face changed. Suddenly, she was the young girl he'd known so long ago, a girl with whom he'd felt an odd kinship in their mutual isolation.

"Then why don't you kill me?" she asked. Just as he'd asked her. And the answer was still the same: because they needed each other. Because they always would. Because they couldn't ever go back to being without each other again.

The fragile thing inside Eli broke in two, and he released her. Roan staggered back just as Eli's hand slashed across her face, ripping backward like a grappling hook.

Roan collapsed, screaming.

Eli backed away then, eyes dry, wings heavy, taloned hand dripping blood. He'd wanted to take both eyes out for how blind she was, but he'd settle for this. He wanted her to be in pain and never again see herself as whole.

"I can't kill you," he whispered hoarsely, wings a painful thunderclap as they opened. "You know why."

No matter how far Eli flew upward, back to the Roost, Roan's aching, lonely sobs would always be etched in the high cavern walls of his ringing skull.

A Cold, Cosmic Wind

Saskia faltered, her legs coming out from under her. The white marble floor would have cracked her on the head, but hands caught her. Her head swam as the darkness in the Onyx went back inside of it, finished for now. The Fractal's crown was a crumpled ruin, but the stone, loose and separate from Saskia, went quiet on the floor. She would have reached for it if her arm worked.

Another arm around her shoulder led her to the throne twisted out of cold rock. Eli lifted her into it, and for a moment Saskia felt ten years younger, and she had an aching flash of her father, smiling down at her, saying, "Careful, love." Tears welled up, spilled over, and she wiped them away with a shaking hand.

"I feel sick," Saskia said, clutching the sharp arms of the throne. It was surprisingly comfortable. Eli knelt before her, his great cloak of wings brushing the floor.

"I understand," he said. "I feel that way most days, living with this thing inside me." His face twisted. "If you call it living."

Saskia looked at him, waiting for her double vision to resolve. "Are you yourself?" she asked.

Eli sighed. His golden eyes had changed to a pale grey, and he dipped his head. "My mind is clearer, yes. But I'm . . . not sure what I can do with that."

Then a clattering rose outside the great hall, making both Saskia and Eli look up sharply. The enormous stone doors groaned open, and a lanky, somewhat dishevelled figure burst into the hall.

"Don't you touch her!" Baskar cried, wooden armour jittering. They pulled up the front of their body like someone adjusting their shirt.

Eli snorted. "I see you've made friends with the dead as well."

"I'll take any friends I can," Saskia coughed. Baskar was limping, but otherwise seemed in good shape. Saskia pulled herself stiffly out of the throne, and went to them. Baskar almost fell on her, arms wrapped around her still woozy body like a shield. They held each other up.

"Did he hurt you?" Baskar asked, voice quavering. Saskia couldn't help but laugh, albeit brokenly.

"No," she said. "But I feel like I've hurt myself." She looked over her shoulder at Eli, this Owl King, hunched and brooding and dark and sad. "You still love her despite all that." She felt crushed by his pain, just as Baskar had predicted.

Eli bunched a claw at his face, as if it could hide it. Then the claw retracted, and before them he turned more into a man. Wrecked and dark-bearded. Haunted. Old. "Love is as painful as grief. Hurting her seemed the only way to stay close to her."

Baskar leaned on her, and she could feel their body shaking. "Did he tell you then, Saskia? How he betrayed our mistress? How he started this war?"

Saskia sighed, patting Baskar and holding their hand. "They betrayed each other," Saskia said. "Roan isn't exactly innocent here." She let go of her friend and approached the throne again, nausea floating inside her. "How much longer is this dance going to go on?"

Eli had been watching her in stoic silence. Then he straightened his back, pulling his wings behind his body so he was no longer cloaked. His arms were pale, but the chain scar stood out. So did the broken Moonstone in his chest, like an heirloom whose value had long diminished. "She wanted this world. I can give it to her, give her a purpose. Maybe, with that tree, it will be coming to an end soon. Maybe we both deserve that end. She wanted this world more than she wanted me."

Saskia argued, "That's not true. She wanted to be with you. She wanted to build something with you, and it should've been the way forward, to finding Ancient —"

"Don't you know?" Eli laughed harshly, his kind, calming tone falling away again. "Ancient is a myth. A story that's not allowed to be told. So is the happy ending. Ask your archivist here. They know. You know *everything*, don't you, Baskar?" Eli pointed. "That forbidden story of yours. Tell it now, to your *friend* here. Tell her what is at the bottom of that tree."

Baskar hunched forward and turned to Saskia. "I think I was always meant to tell you," they said. "Or perhaps you already know it."

Saskia looked between Eli and the archivist. "The Heartwood is blocking the way to the Brilliant Dark. Ancient is awake beneath it." The words coming out of Saskia's mouth felt like they were spoken by someone else. But she knew. Something twigged in her memory, some dream, but everything was getting mixed up; she couldn't tell the difference between everyone else's memories, lives, and dreams, and her own. "If you do allow Ancient to rise, like you were supposed to, then you'll both have to face that this world you built together . . . it might come apart."

Eli clapped. "Very good. You were always clever." He sneered. "Roan doesn't want to leave this place. She doesn't want to face herself. I can't make her. No one can."

Saskia reached down for the Onyx, but Baskar scooped it up so she wouldn't have to touch it. It was still quiet, despite all the darkness inside it, and for all the things it had made the Moonstone show her.

"You're both scared of losing each other. There's nothing wrong with that. But please, Eli. I don't want things to end like this. I don't think you do, either. Let's go to the Heartwood. We can convince Roan it's the right thing to do. I can do it with the Onyx, I —"

His wings were already folding back over him, his expression going dull. "Some endings, whatever they are, come too late." He turned away. "I won't give Roan up, and I won't give our little war up, not for you. Not for that tree or a story, not for this world or yours."

With the last of his speech echoing in the cold hall, Saskia and Baskar looked at each other. They had no other choice. Then Baskar stepped forward, pushing Saskia behind them.

"We are going to the Heartwood," Baskar said, "to finish the story with or without you."

Eli did not move. "You know what's there, Rabbit. You can't take Saskia there."

"We have to go," Saskia said again, heartened by Baskar's courage.

Eli looked like he was coming back to himself, but this didn't last. If he didn't come on his own, Saskia would have to make him.

Eli did move then, in a terrifying striking wave of wind and body that crashed into Baskar, shattering some of their outer shell, but the Rabbit shade stood their ground despite that. Saskia leapt backward.

"Saskia," Baskar cried, "run!"

She was backing away, heart slamming. "I'm not going to leave without either of you!"

Eli's eyes, changing to crisp gold, caught her even as Baskar held him back, their shell slipping to the ground like broken pottery, revealing the shade beneath. Even with their face coming apart, Baskar seemed to grin at Saskia. "I didn't think you would."

Baskar slammed the Onyx into their bark-mask. There was a dark surge, and Eli cried out, leaping back. Most of Baskar was gone, but their mask flew into Saskia's hand. Their shade wrapped around her, and the mask slipped over her own face.

For safekeeping, Baskar said. She twisted for the great staircase she'd come up. *Now, run!*

Lunging for the stairs with Baskar's speed suddenly surging through her shaking body, Saskia leapt, fell, tumbled, and recovered, with the agility of a Rabbit she'd only dreamed of being.

The wind howled at her heels, but still Saskia ran.

She faltered when a group of Owl guards fell on her as she took a corner. She dodged a soldier down a steep curve of rubble, throwing herself over one ledge down to another one.

Baskar spoke in her mind. *I won't leave you, Saskia. In this world or the one above. If that's where you need to go.* Saskia felt an impossible warmth from the dark stone. *How are we going to get back down below?*

"I haven't thought that far ahead." But maybe she had: Roan jumped off the Roost and took the gamble that Eli would always be there to catch her.

She came to another ledge, stopped short, and felt a powerful blast of air knock her back from it and into the last staircase she'd just skidded down. She landed hard on her hip and groaned. Looking down on the other side of the crumbled steps, she saw only the dark shining waters of the Abyss below. She was on the wrong side of the Roost, she needed to get to the ledge hovering near the Heartwood —

Saskia! Baskar screamed. *Look —*

She jerked just before a screeching Owl guard was on top of her, and she narrowly rolled out of the way. On her feet now, emptiness and dead ocean at her back, Eli and a flank of guards faced her down.

"Don't," Eli hissed at her. "Dying here would not help either of us."

Saskia's heart might have been racing, but her breath was even. "Help us, then. Don't just sit up here trying to stop the ending from happening. Be a part of it!"

Eli's wings cracked open. "I will make you see your mistake."

Saskia narrowed her eyes. "No one gets to choose what I do except me."

Baskar didn't even have a chance to talk her out of it; Baskar was inside the stone. They knew that the water, and something deep below it, was calling to the Onyx in the same way the Moonstone had. Saskia was just following orders.

So Saskia leapt over the edge, her only sure landing the cold, stretching waters that rushed up to meet her. Behind her she heard wings. Below her, a great roar.

Then the dark.

❧

And the Seals? Saskia had asked Baskar.

We do not go to the Abyss. It surrounds us on all sides. They are protected by a Bloodbeast in the depths, and they are allies to no one.

But Saskia couldn't avoid it. She'd jumped and hoped and was sinking fast.

Saskia, Baskar shook her from inside the stone. *You're going to die.*

Somewhere in her head, she wondered how bad that would be. *I'm in the right place for it,* she answered. She tried to keep the precious air in her lungs contained, but she could feel it bubbling up.

As much as I'd like to spend eternity with you, Baskar said, *you still have work to do.*

As her vision clouded, Saskia saw something huge coming in the distance. Something with teeth, something that could've been a god once. Somewhere in the midst of this Bloodbeast's rippling body was a shock of blue calling out to the Onyx. Something that could've been a cracked Sapphire.

Let the darkness out, Saskia said to the stone, raising her hand to it in the middle of Baskar's mask.

Something had grabbed Saskia by the back, pulling her up sharply as the beast surged. She broke the surface and gasped. She looked up and saw Eli, his wings struggling to get them clear of the maelstrom and the leviathan in the centre of it. Saskia tried to warn him before the great tail slammed into him, knocking them both backward to dry land, and eliminating what precious breath Saskia had only just sucked in on impact.

They had little time to recover on the rocky shore. The beast loomed over them. In the light, and with maybe a little more clarity, Saskia saw its mass was shivering scales, teeth in places they didn't belong, and a head bisected by a flashing harpoon.

Saskia pulled Baskar's mask from her face, and the Onyx out of it, holding it between her and the Bloodbeast. The Sapphire at the beast's shoulder strobed and answered its sister.

As it had before with the Deer shade, the Onyx took hold of the corruption, sorting it. This Bloodbeast was not one shade, but many. Too many shades, in the shape of seals, split from the mass surrounding the Sapphire and slid back into the water. With each Seal restored, the beast shrank down to simply the Sapphire. But there was something else at the core of it that the Onyx still pulled at. Something that was not a shade. Something with hands that held that giant harpoon over its head. And when the darkness dissipated again, the figure clarified.

Eli sat up slowly as Saskia's arm dropped and she realized she was no longer holding the Onyx — it was set *inside* her hand, a part of her.

Standing before them all now, staring at her own hands, was a god.

"Ryk." Eli barked, startled.

The Sapphire was still set in Ryk's shoulder. She bore down on the two stonebearers, and the sea behind her rocked. Her hair was endless kelp and seaweed, wild and beautiful. She was broad, wide. Devastating.

"What," she said, after a cursory look around, "have you done to my sisters' realms?"

Saskia cradled her wrist, her hand heavy with the Onyx. "Baskar?" she asked, not able to look at the discarded mask beside her, because the Onyx might have dragged them into the stone.

But no — Baskar's mask rose up, the shape of their spirit beneath it somewhat like a formless body. They hung over Saskia, and she felt their pity as they looked at her hand.

"I am all right," Baskar said. Then they looked up at Ryk and tilted their head. "You are not all right."

Ryk stabbed the great harpoon into the ground next to her and turned, surveying the landscape. The fury and confusion fell away from her face. "It is like it was. In the beginning."

Saskia looked to Eli, who was getting shakily to his feet. He started to speak. "We thought all the gods were —"

"Dead?" Ryk barked a laugh. "Might as well have been, Son of the Wind." She eyed both he and Saskia skeptically. "You have my sisters' hearts. You draw power from them. They are not gone."

Eli dipped his chin down, but Saskia stepped forward,

Baskar wrapped around her like a stole, like a bit of armour. "We're looking for Ancient," she said. "Will you come with us?"

Ryk was a battle-god, and even though she wasn't a Bloodbeast anymore, she was still over six feet tall and captivating. She *was* the sea, after all. The tides behind her pulled back, and she snatched up the mighty harpoon.

"We will need my sisters first," she said. "Especially my twin, Deon."

Saskia closed her eyes, so tired. She looked over at Eli, who seemed, for the moment, not intent on harming her. He seemed awake now that he'd been sprung from his dark cycle of misery; he was a part of this now.

He stared at Ryk's Sapphire, then pointed to Saskia's hand. "Your stone," he said slowly. "It's imbued with the power of the Darklings. Darklings are able to separate Paramounts from the Calamity Stones." He touched his chest. He looked like he was daring to hope.

"Yes," Saskia said fiercely, clenching her palm and the Onyx in it. "Which means I can separate you from your stone. And Roan from hers." *And me?* She wasn't so sure. She might need the Onyx all the way to the end.

"You have many stories!" Baskar snaked towards Ryk, curious and not at all afraid. "Will you tell us what this land was, when the realms were all as one?"

More stories. Maybe these would be the last ones. And with the story of the gods on their side, she hoped, they could do this.

Ryk dipped her head, regarding Baskar with something like affection before she sighed heavily. "The memory of my sisters," she said, "has kept the gods alive all this time."

Part IV
NOVA

A SISTERHOOD *of* BONES

Ancient created everything: The realms of the living. The realms of the gods, Ancient's first children, each reflecting part of Ancient itself. Then it created a different creature altogether — humanity.

And the day that humanity came into being, Phyr immediately assumed the worst.

Deon wasn't too concerned, as was her custom. "What is there to be afraid of? We are all woven from the same thread. And while we are the same as them, they are under our dominion. We will have control over them ultimately."

The world was not new, even then. But it was a beautiful and precious place. The trees were alive with their songs, their hopes, stretching upward towards Phyr's endless sky. From high above it, at the top of the aurora-strewn universe, she had watched this world unfold, and had provided her counsel and her gifts to shape it — as her siblings had. They had built this place together as per Creation's wishes.

And even though she could see across time and possibilities, Phyr did not like this wrinkle after ages of knowing what was expected. She wished she knew what Ancient had been thinking when it brought humanity into the fold, but, as always, the gods bowed and did as they were told.

Still, Phyr frowned and turned to Heen, whose eyes were shut in demure composure beneath her enormous rabbit's ears. "Even you are concerned, Wood Wife."

Heen cocked her head, as if she'd heard something the others could not perceive vibrating in the rock beneath them. "Concern and caution, sister," Heen replied. "These shifts must be observed."

Phyr flattened her nine wings closer to her great body. Her talons on the Pendulum Rod grew tight. "Time will tell. It always does."

Ryk elbowed Deon and the two twins smirked. "If it's a fight they want, against us or amongst themselves, they will not want for spirit." The sea empress was all confidence. "We will keep them in their place."

The twins' laughter echoed throughout the Roost, where the four had met. Beneath them shone the three golden rings, and it was this silence that was loudest — the silence of their fifth sibling, present through those rings but not in being. When the humans were born, the door to the Glen swung shut, as if slammed by a small child. Even Phyr couldn't penetrate the separation, and while she didn't say it, that fact weighed heaviest against this new burden of humanity in their world.

Heen placed a rooted hand across Phyr's shoulders, as if sensing right away that something amiss. "Would that we could hear from Fia," the sage said. "For it is from them this new order has emerged."

"From Ancient," Phyr corrected. "Always Ancient."

"By the Godhead," the four gods echoed, nodding. Even the battle twins were reverent, which relieved Phyr. For if Ancient was still observed, and this was their creator's will, then all of this was surely part of the Narrative, and that could always be trusted.

Fia had given humanity their spirits, though. The last ingredient that bound them to the gods. That made them *more*, beyond the gods' influences. Fia had known Ancient's plan before the others had, and that troubled Phyr the most.

Phyr straightened her back. "We have our place in this. Deon is right. These creatures are under our dominion now, and so they are our responsibility. We will go out amongst them and pass along our divine gifts to those we choose, and see that Ancient's will is perceived. We will trust Fia's withdrawal on this matter, for whatever happens is meant to be."

～～～

The next time the sisters met, it was in the Warren. Things had been progressing as the ages did, and they watched closely, intervened as they saw fit. They were in the Realms and they were without at all times.

But they did not expect the shadows.

These shadows, the little shards of dark, were calculated and subtle. Darkness dogged the steps of the gods' new children. Greed. Ambition. Killing. None of the four gods guessed where the shadows had come from, save that these new enemies, once again, must be the will of Ancient. But

Ancient was silent on the matter — Fia, too — and the sisters had no right to ask. They were only there to guide. To inspire. To make this world grow. A difficult task when grief entered the new world. But light and shadow needed each other to exist. It was the order of all things.

As humanity grew, and those who were born under the gods' blessings manifested their powers, there were those who coveted these gifts, those who were not born with them. Foxes and Deer and Owls and Rabbits and Seals changed forms, to blend in with the other, new creatures, but it was not enough.

These Mundanes are of a different gods' domain, Ryk had said when it had come up, time and again, until the Mundanes became violent, and Seals were killed just as often as Foxes and Rabbits dwelling on land. It became quickly apparent that it was best to shield one from the other — Denizens from Mundanes. Death, always a certainty, and still a true neutral, was often sought for counsel.

"They covet and envy," the Moth Queen said, bowing her head to the gods. "These words may mean very little to eternals like us, but these creatures are not us. They are finite beings. And fragile, despite your gifts. They compete like any animal. They kill. They blink into and out of existence. They must be protected, for it is into them that Ancient has poured its will. It is through them that Creation will endure."

Heen, who had always been the calm centre of them all, paced the Warren on her long feet, and Phyr noticed then that the roots that once were just her sister's hands were growing wild amongst her hair, her ears. It seemed she was becoming more a part of her realm the more she fretted, and had Phyr addressed it then, perhaps none of this would have happened.

"Some have chosen," Heen said, "to take their animal forms permanently, and live out their lives in this way. But Denizens still must learn to protect themselves."

Deon said what the others refused to. "You speak as if we will not always be here to protect them."

Heen looked directly at her sister, face hard. "You do remember the point of us, do you not?"

Deon folded her mighty arms. The flames licking her mantle died down, and Phyr saw the great warrior question herself. "I know that we must separate ourselves from them. We all know that. But we have come to care for them. That is not something we can deny. How can we care for them if we must be separate from them?"

Heen was quiet a long while. Then she reached inside of herself and pulled out an impossible green light.

The light danced there, and after a time compressed into a shining solid surface of many facets. The sisters drew closer, considering the stone.

"Be careful, Wood Wife," Phyr warned. "Our Denizens are young yet in the world. Weakening ourselves for their benefit, when we are not assured of their endurance, is a dangerous play."

"This is not a game," Heen reminded Phyr, reminded them all. "We are gods with obligations. If we wish for them to protect themselves, we must choose one among them that will lead them from this oppressive darkness and towards the rising light. And this is how that leader will do it."

Even when the darkness made them spill blood.

Deon, never looking away from Phyr, plunged her short-clawed hand into her chest, and pulled out her soul-stone as if it had always been outside of her. The red and green and purple light folded neatly into a stone that was at once smooth and jagged, the inside of it a flaming starburst. A fierce thing of exploding love, contained, as Deon herself was.

Phyr smiled, for she loved her siblings well, and trusted them, and was content to know they were doing this together.

Once they had all performed the act, they gazed upon the things they had made and that had been inside of them. Phyr's heart, a stone like the moon where her throne was, would shield all Denizens from Mundanes. From harm.

They all knew the risk, even then, of doing this thing. But seeing what life had cost their respective children, even with the gods' gifts, they would risk whatever to keep them safe.

"Send these stones out into the world," Heen said, "and the stones will choose. It will be a burden, but what is life if not a burden of survival?"

⤙⤚

A divine body is a thing beyond reckoning. None of the gods considered such a thing as tangibility. Though they felt and loved and commanded and made things, they were — and remain — on a plane beyond anything humankind could comprehend. And it worked the other way. Time meant nothing to them. Death, while tinged with a kind of regret, always gave way to new life. Denizen spirits had a choice: remain in the realm of your god if you wished, for an age or for a blink, or be thrust into the world as something new. Nothing really ended. Not for Denizens. And especially not for the gods.

They never considered mortality would become their dominion, too.

The little shadows of dark thought, of greed and bad intentions, became stronger. And the gods learned where they had come from. The time of the Darklings arrived and cast a pall over Ancient's great creation. The Darklings meant destruction, and they were capable of it and more.

Ryk, of all the siblings, had brought up their own mortality out loud. If the Darklings could destroy Ancient's work, could they, the gods, be destroyed as well?

"We are undying!" Deon cried. She was angry — and afraid. The gods hadn't known fear, until now.

Ryk's fist tightened around her great harpoon. "We must consider it. Now more than ever before. We have seen what this conflict with the Darklings has done to Heen, and now I worry the same thing is what happened to Fia."

Heen had changed. Once so assured, she had been shaken by the new world order, by control slipping from the gods' grasp. She had not left the Warren for a time, going deeper and deeper into the realm and speaking less and less to her trusted sisters.

Deon paced across the wide and endless sea of the Abyss, the water around her bubbling and snapping with her god-heat. "Heen will recover. She is strong. We will endure. We will weather this storm." Everyone could see that the garnet blade, held tight at Deon's side, was black with the muck of Bloodbeasts, the immense monsters that the Darklings brought up from their cold nothingness and threw at Ancient's daughters, at the gods' very Denizen children. At first, both Deon and Ryk had treated it as sport, as a challenge accepted. The bracers on Deon's great arms and legs were incised with these battles that seemed endless.

But everything had an end.

"We must speak to Ancient."

They all startled at Phyr's suggestion. She could not stand idle, though, and her greatest strength had always been her ability to observe, then decide. The sisters saw her as the leader amongst them, the one who could see through infinity and make them all feel in control.

Deon and Ryk stared at her. "To speak to Ancient is to question its plan."

Phyr held the Pendulum Rod steadily in front of her, in both hands, bisecting her great face, which showed only strain. The stars vibrated in her wings. For this war, she had stopped time. But she could not do it forever.

"We already question the plan," Phyr said. "Was the destruction of this precious world, of Mundanes and Denizens alike, Ancient's plan? Is it a test for us all? Are we failing Ancient?"

Phyr's questioning seemed to shake them. Phyr was not made to question. She could see beyond infinity. And yet here was a god, one who should know all . . . not knowing.

"We will fight using faith," Deon said. "Speak to Heen, Phyr. I do not wish to see her isolated as Fia became. Ancient gave us a purpose: protect this world. Teach our descendants to protect it. Darkness cannot endure. That is not our legacy."

Ryk nodded. "There is something else to this. There cannot be creation without destruction. We know this well. And we cannot go against Ancient. But until we know more, we must keep fighting while you find out." She shook her kelp-crowned head. "We won't speak to Ancient until then."

Phyr spread her great, galactic wings, and was gone from the Abyss. Ryk swept her harpoon, and a current snatched her away. Phyr saw, in her expansive mind, that Deon lingered, beneath the crushing water, smouldering. She knew that Deon, like Phyr, loved her siblings dearly. But even Phyr was beginning to lose hope it would be enough.

CALAMITY'S RESTORATION

Roan paced under the wrathful pyre, blazing behind her, all around her. The shades watched her, like they always had. At first they had come after her. Then they worshipped her because she had the fire. Now she'd seen their doubt, especially with Saskia's appearance and the stone she carried. The dead were looking for rest, or at least considering it, and it made Roan frantic.

"What are you worried about?" the voice asked, comforting. Roan hadn't heard it in a long time and stopped dead.

With one amber glance, the pyre chamber emptied, the Hound shades fled.

She turned, left alone with a single person. One she didn't recognize.

Herself. Younger. Whole. The person she had become now was such a mockery of this nearly pristine version, despite its dead black eyes. She hated it and longed to be it all at once.

"What are you doing here?" Roan asked it.

"You know what my purpose was. To put aside the things that held you back. I did that. If I'm here, it means those things are coming to the surface. You don't want that, do you?"

For all her armour and her sword and her scars and her rage, Roan could not fight this part of her. "No. Of course not. So go back inside me and do your job."

"I'm trying," this other part of her hissed, circling her. This dark version of Roan was an impulse. A selfish need. Roan didn't want to know anything about what this part of her had put aside. Why was it leaking through now?

"The girl," Roan said, voicing her fears. "She reminds me of a time before. A time when —" She shoved her gauntleted hand through her short hair and held on tight.

"Then you have to kill her," said the other Roan, comforting, a memory from a dream. "Take the stone from her. And make sure no one ever finds out what's under that tree. Then you can stay here forever. With Eli. That's what you want, right? It's very *simple*."

Roan's arms fell to her sides, the inside of her head ringing. The thing that was causing her pain and panic was already fading, being tucked away. "Yes. Simple."

She unsheathed her garnet blade, tipping her helm over her one eye. "I am touched by Death, too. I am a god. The girl is no one."

Roan left the chamber and walked out of the canyon, alone, towards the Heartwood.

It was more than strange, walking side by side with a real, start-of-creation god. But Saskia had to be adaptable.

She swallowed and addressed Ryk, and all of them, as they walked together through the wilderness. "I had a theory about the Heartwood, when I saw it."

Out of the corner of her eye, she saw Eli nod gravely. He said, "Barton must be inside of it, along with the Emerald. It's the only thing that could make such a tree. Not even the Bloodlands could."

"Yeah," Saskia agreed, "but it feels like . . . from what the Onyx showed me. It's like he's trapped. Or fighting. I don't know." She looked up at Ryk. "If it's on top of the Brilliant Dark, and Ancient's there, we'll need to get the tree out of the way so Ancient can rise."

Ryk, for all that she was devastating, had had a playful, even jubilant expression across her brow the second they'd started off. "Ancient will repair this rift. My sister, Heen, must be *protecting* Ancient. I am certain that if we gather my other siblings' stones and awaken the others, Heen will unfold and the way will be clear."

So Saskia had been right, partially. It just seemed too one-dimensional to work. "Roan and Eli brought the stones together in the Uplands," she recounted. "The Darklings came through, yes, but it still woke Ancient. Down here, the result was that all the realms came back together again, like they were, at the beginning . . ." Saskia frowned. "What had broken them apart in the first place? I thought it was Phyr —"

"That's just something the other Families always said,

blaming the division on the Owls," Eli snapped, but Ryk held up her hand.

"I was there. It was her, my winged sister, who was Ancient's mind." She shook her great head. "Some terrible fear had consumed her. She told Deon and me, while we were fighting the Darklings, that it was the only way — separating the realms. The only way to save everything: the world of our descendants, but especially Ancient." Ryk stared Eli down, looking from his gaunt face to the Moonstone he carried. "I resented her for it. For not trusting us. Perhaps I can confront her at last, when this is all through."

Eli cloaked himself in his wings, then he stopped abruptly, as if something had cut him across the back. "Roan is coming."

A glimmer from the Moonstone shone through his feathers. Ryk's shoulder strobed blue. The Onyx let out a deep groan in Saskia's hand and she winced.

"*My twin*," Ryk grinned, striding ahead of them to meet the coming fight full on.

Baskar was still in shade form, wrapped around Saskia's arm like a slumbering python. But Baskar seized strangle-tight when Ryk's great harpoon met with Roan's garnet blade. She'd appeared suddenly like a terrible comet of fire and human limbs. Roan and Ryk smashed together and held but didn't break.

"*You*," Ryk grunted, "*are not my sister*." She shoved back and Roan leapt, sliding around the god and striking with a corona flare.

"Your sister is dead!" The blade was now all fire, and it snapped against Ryk's furious face. "*We* are the gods here! Go back to your shallows!"

Saskia didn't know what to do, how she was going to do this. Ryk beat Roan back, but Roan *was* fast, and strong, and something beyond her normal power seemed to be carrying her through these steps. Her expression was vicious and focused.

Saskia whirled on Eli, who had fallen back and frozen at the edge of the confrontation. "You have to go into her mind. You have to remove whatever it is holding her back and keeping her like this."

He looked wildly unsure. "I tried. You know I tried."

"Try again!" Saskia shouted. Baskar gasped, and one of Roan's flaming tongues came off her blade and struck Ryk's Sapphire.

"Your sister is dead, and I killed her!" Roan screeched. Ryk may have been a god, but she was, obviously, weaker than what Roan had evolved into. Ryk staggered back, blocking the blows with raised forearms. "And I will kill the rest of you, and I will endure here, alone, forever."

Roan's blade came down again and again like a bludgeon, and Ryk shrank. But a great taloned hand caught what would have been the finishing strike and held firm. Eli's arm shook with it, but he didn't let go.

"You're not alone. You know I wouldn't leave you." He grunted with effort. Roan grinned, and when she stepped back, Eli nearly fell forward onto the tip of the sword still held at hip height.

Roan laughed cruelly. "I don't need you," she said, surveying them all with the blade held out before her. "I don't need any of you. I'll cut you all out. Every last one of you, until all that's left is the fire." Then she levelled the garnet at

Eli, and Saskia saw his pained eyes reflected in the dark red glass. "I'll start with you."

Eli straightened his spine and held out his hand to Roan.

Baskar hissed, "What is he doing?"

Saskia shook her head. "He's giving up."

Roan brought the blade smashing down in a wide arc, and Eli gracefully sidestepped, his wings lifting and cracking as he spun, half-knocking Roan out of step. She didn't make a sound, but her grin was gone. One darting glance at Eli's feet, and she neatly dodged the next striking blow of his talons. Feint, repost, recover — they wove in and out, gaining ground then missing. Saskia was having a hard time keeping up as they spun faster.

The wind had risen.

"They're dancing!" Baskar cried as Saskia dove, grabbing hold of Ryk and pulling the diminished god out of the path of the flames — because they'd come up in response to Eli's power ripping the grove up from under them.

"They're going to take the underworld down with them, whatever they're doing," Ryk bellowed as Saskia helped the god back to her feet. She clasped the Sapphire at her shoulder as if it caused her great pain. The crack running through it was as a wound. Saskia met the sea empress's eyes, fathomless as a glacial bay. "She said she killed Deon."

Saskia bit her tongue and looked to the battle happening inches from them. How could a god be asking Saskia of all people for reassurance? "I don't think so. She couldn't have done that. Eli has a plan." She hoped. She prayed.

The wind fell, Roan and Eli on opposite sides of the clearing. One of Eli's wings hung off-kilter, but his stance was wide, unyielding, hip pointed as if he was readying to swoop back in at the slightest indication from his dance partner. Roan, for her part, held the garnet blade point-forward, two-handed, and it was shaking.

Her hair was the fire. Her eyes were bright with rage. "Come on," she goaded him. "Or is that it, then?"

Eli took a step.

Roan charged him.

She was a comet, he was a hurricane. They were about to collide.

"Saskia!" Baskar yelped, and Ryk stood swiftly, pulling both Saskia and Baskar into her powerful arms as she shielded them. The wood was filled with a torrent of fire, and Saskia forgot to fill her lungs.

Just as she felt the heat on her cheek, the wind came back like a hand, snatched it up, and the hurricane was filled with hot blazing flame, a vicious storm cell. In the centre of it, Eli and Roan held breakingly fast to each other's hands, locked, the ground beneath them shuddering. The garnet blade was too far away on the ground for Roan to reach.

"Now, little human!" Ryk cried, picking Saskia up and whirling her towards the spinning torrent of fire. The Onyx in her hand strobed a black flare, and she heard the Moonstone and the Opal calling it.

"No!" Roan struggled, the flame consuming her, bigger than this world, and eating up Eli's black feathers. As Saskia approached, an arm shielding her eyes, she saw Roan's face go from anger to anguish, the light of the inferno sputtering.

When Roan looked directly into Eli's eyes, she seemed to get a hundred years younger in her desperation. "Please, Eli. If you love me, you won't."

The wall of fire guttered, and Saskia leapt over it, the darkness cocooning her. She watched as Eli's hands slipped up to either side of Roan's face, and the wind tangled with the crackling fire still left. His back was being burnt for his hesitation.

"I'm doing this *because* I love you, you idiot," he said.

Then Saskia opened her palm, and the Onyx reached for Roan at the same time the Moonstone reached for the Opal.

❧

Saskia was only a conduit. They all were. And she was an observer in what was happening to Roan and Eli now, as she had been in a sea cave on Skye, where they'd made a promise to each other as friends. As more than that. Even now, all Saskia could do was watch and hope this story had the end it deserved.

They were fighting still. Eli was a body of shuddering breezes, and Roan was a lick of flames. Fighting or dancing, it was hard to tell. They twined around each other. They struggled. They came together.

"It feels safer in the dark," Roan said. "We could be safe here, together."

A sigh of every wind current. Then something bright flickered beyond the fire, beyond the wind. A golden tether fastening one to the other.

"I know we could," Eli said. "But refusing to give in is what I always admired about you."

Everything went still. Saskia held her breath.

Then, from the dark, there was another Roan, one who looked more like the one Saskia recognized, and she was growing bigger than both of them and screaming.

"You think *grief* will save you? Save *her?*" this Roan yelled, smashing into Eli like a battering ram. "I won't let it! I won't let you!"

Still Eli held onto the fire, held onto Roan, who shook her head. The tether around them was firm.

"It doesn't matter what you want," Eli said, flinching with every blow he took. But the fire that was Roan was a part of him, and they were one thing. "It matters what Roan wants."

Roan, a concentrated flame, broke away towards the version of her that had been trying to rip them apart. Dark Roan stepped back, but the Roan that was the fire put her flaming arms out and embraced the dark, shrieking, terrible core of her fear, and took it into herself.

The Onyx perceived that this was the moment, wrapped around them all, and pulled.

⁓⁂⁓

Saskia and the others woke in the grass of the underworld. Baskar, for all their lack of a body, held onto her, and Saskia felt the protection. But Baskar wasn't looking at her. She sat up and followed their gaze.

Eli was holding Roan. She was crying. He held her very tightly. But she was okay, whatever that meant. Saskia heard "I'm sorry, I'm sorry . . ." Eli just kept holding onto her, his broken wings draped around and over her sobbing back.

There was a warmth behind Saskia, and she turned to that next.

Standing beside Ryk was another god, of a height with her, with nine tails shimmering behind, a great cloak of flaming fur. Each god had a hand on the other's shoulders. They really did look like twins, somehow, despite their opposite elements. Despite that they had been separate for who knew how long. They looked into each other's eyes, and beneath Deon's great fox-helm, she smiled.

Everyone, even gods, needed someone to hold onto. Saskia slumped down with exhaustion, and Baskar held onto her gladly.

≫≺

Roan and Eli sat shoulder to shoulder on a bluff away from the others. Deadland night had fallen. Above, the unmoving stars framed the Roost. Just ahead was the Heartwood. Neither of them had ever been this close to it before.

All in all, they were heavy with saying goodbye to this place.

"I remember lots of things," Roan said. "Too much. I remember you always trying your best with me. Even up till now. Though you were still kind of a dick about it."

Eli snorted. "I like to be consistent."

She touched his beard. "You need a shave."

He put his palm on top of her close-shorn head. "You don't."

She took his hand in hers, and he laid his other over it, clasping. "I remember that we thought we were some kind of heroes, always doing the right thing. Or trying to. I didn't want to imagine we couldn't be heroes. Or that we'd let everyone down."

"I thought we had, too, to be fair," he told her. Something screeched in the distance. Something roared. "But it wasn't just you. We became a part of this place. We needed it. Letting go is always hard. So is doing the right thing."

She looked up at him, and he tipped his chin down. Eli ran a finger over the knotted scar on her face. "At least we didn't let go of each other."

"I guess I can't get rid of you that easily," she said wryly. They looked back out into the wilds. "It's not just the living depending on us. It's the dead, too."

Eli turned partway to look down the bluff behind them, where the gods rested, speaking low, maybe praying to Ancient, maybe trying to reconcile themselves. Near them, the shade Baskar held Saskia, who had stripped herself mightily after removing the Opal from Roan. She'd have to do the same, too, with the Moonstone. Later, the Emerald. He hoped it wouldn't break her.

"The Moth Queen sent down an emissary to make sure the dead would be safe," he said, nodding in Saskia's direction.

Roan's shoulders dropped. "We protect her then. To the end."

"To the end," Eli repeated. They surveyed their kingdoms. It was time to go home.

THESE ROOTS GO DEEP

During the stalemate, Phae and Natti walked between their own fighters, the former healing who she could, the latter trying to encourage those who were unsure if they were going to come out the other end of this or not.

None of them was sure, but they had to be prepared.

"We can't stay down here forever," Phae had said, meaning the underground mall that once had been City Place, but now had become a post-fight stronghold. The ETG had tried to take it, and the connected networks of tunnels and skywalks all over the downtown core, but the Denizens had been holding it. They'd been holding the rest of the city, too, this past year. And now that the Darkling Moon was tracking ever closer to the sun, they wanted to show the world they would fight until it was over.

The ETG had said similar. Their ambitious fire-everything-we-have-at-it, aptly called Project Annihilate, was also winding up. Phae felt the Denizens were just on standby, because she was convinced it wouldn't work.

"We'll have to make ourselves allies soon enough." Natti had been the one to suggest it, bitter though she'd been. Both sides had suffered losses, had dug their heels in. But what would the point of fighting be when they couldn't do a thing about the moon hanging over them like a guillotine?

They had been sitting in the abandoned food court. Phae was fairly out of it from healing so many at once. Her powers weren't limitless. None of theirs were.

Phae asked, "A week, the reports said?"

Natti nodded. "They might be lying, though. It might be even sooner."

"Well, when they fire their missiles, and they see they're wrong, then we can talk. They won't listen to us otherwise. They have to stare failure in the face like we did."

Natti grimaced. What a waste. "And Saskia?"

Phae lifted her eyes, then shook her head. "There's been no more signal from anywhere. I don't know if . . ."

Natti put her hand over Phae's. It didn't need to be said.

"We'll do what we can," Natti said. It'd be something, if not enough.

᭟᭟᭟

When the group came to the Heartwood, there was no one left to stop them.

"I can feel the Emerald inside," Deon said. "Heen is there." She turned to the humans. "And your friend."

Saskia had rested as much as she could, and she knew it still wouldn't be enough. The tree was enormous, as wide as

One Evergreen, and this close they saw it shifting, the cords throbbing with life as it grew moment by moment. It made her think of the Apex inverted; the impulse to turn around was sudden and tempting.

The ground rumbled. The roots before them were pulling free of the soil, curling backward on the tree's own folds. A curtain. A doorway. They were being invited inside.

No one moved to go in. Saskia looked at them all, because they were looking at her. Even the gods.

"Are we sure this is the way?" Baskar asked, standing beside Saskia in a shell body made from things they had gathered on the journey.

"Not at all," Roan sighed. "We're never sure about anything. We just, sort of . . . do it."

Eli folded his arms, his wings shifting as he half-shrugged. "Not like it hasn't worked out for us."

Ryk had her harpoon at the ready. Deon held the garnet blade. They walked together into the Heartwood, and the other four could do no more than follow.

The roots closed behind them. Saskia should have seen that coming.

Roan held up her hand, and the flame was still there in the palm. In the ring of the light, she seemed glad.

Deon lit a similar flame, looking down upon Roan curiously. "You were a good Paramount," the god said, and Roan looked startled.

Then Deon's whole body was fire, and she walked ahead into the darkness, which dipped downward, and led the way.

Saskia drew up beside Roan. "Are you okay?"

"Define okay," she snorted. Then she shrugged; for all that she had outwardly aged, she seemed looser, like a great tension had been released. "I'm . . . myself. I'm what I should have been." She nudged Saskia with her elbow. "What about you? You've had to put up with and take on everyone's garbage. What's going on in *your* head?"

Saskia didn't rightly know and couldn't answer. She just focused on keeping her legs under her, the farther they went down. "I'll be better when this is done. Ancient will finish it. Then we can go home."

Baskar nodded beside Saskia, holding her hand and swinging it with a blithe comfort that caught Roan's attention. She smiled, as though reliving some memory twigged by the gesture, but then her face twisted abruptly. "I hope there's a home to go back to," she muttered.

"Don't." Eli was on her other side. "There's no time left for regret."

Roan composed herself with a shake of her head. "You're next, you know. You ready to be yourself again?"

Eli stopped, looking down at the Moonstone, in the halo of Deon's light, which had also halted nearby. "We should do it now," he said. "Bring Phyr back. Then we might have a better chance of releasing Heen, too."

Roan looked skeptical, glancing down at Saskia. "That's a lot to put on one person."

"I can do it," Saskia said immediately, eager to get it done. "For Barton, for all of them. I'll do it. And it's not just on me, it's on all of us."

Ryk hadn't said anything yet. She was just watching the darkness, where something had moved.

The ground came out from under them and Saskia screamed. She heard Eli's wings snap open, heard some guttural cries, but they all landed on their feet within a few seconds' freefall. Deon glowed as she swivelled her head, trying to see. The roots around them were closing in, a woven tangle.

Then they all had the impression that the ground beneath them was a platform, slowly pulling them down on pulleys made of living wood. The roots of the Heartwood snaked them down to infinity.

It was less like going down, though, and more like the tree was stretching, higher and higher above them. There was no sense of movement, no feeling of air rushing, or closing in, no smell. It was nothing. It was darkness. The Heartwood was listening to them and taking them where they needed to go.

"Is this haunted room actually stretching," Eli intoned darkly, "*or is it just your imagination?*"

Saskia stared openly at him, and Roan covered her face. Baskar slid closer to Saskia, scrunching their shoulders. "Haunted?" they asked.

"Baskar, you're literally a ghost," Saskia retorted. She glanced at Eli, all regal and devastating, trying to look innocent as he rolled on the balls of his feet. Even after all this time, he remembered their last exchange on the Isle of Skye, with Saskia's childish wish to go to a theme park with them if the world didn't end first. She realized, now, that Eli had asked her what she wanted, knowing that things would, more than likely, not end well. His desire to do good, even for a throwaway moment, it had always been there. Saskia was feeling a lot of things, but suddenly she felt incredibly sad.

She tried to shake that off, and said to him instead, "I thought you'd never been to Disney World." The line from the Haunted Mansion hadn't been lost on her, even though she'd never been, either.

Eli lifted a shoulder. "Not in Florida, no."

Ryk, banging her harpoon on the platform floor, startled the lot of them like chastised kids on a field trip. "I would feel better if you ceased your chatter," she said, "and if Phyr was here."

Roan sighed. "Did we ever inhabit a place where our highest ambitions were going to amusement parks?"

Eli took her hand abruptly. "Yes," he said fiercely. "And we'll get back to it."

He lifted their hands as one, and the fire twined carefully around them. Eli pulled the wind from his exhale, catching the embers, and sending the light out into the darkness. Floating flames freckled the dark, and they saw there was so much more moving there than they'd feared.

Beyond them was a vast . . . chasm? Their platform stopped, the roots coiling backward. They were underneath the Heartwood. Before them shone utter darkness. Ancient was here, somewhere.

"Do it now," Eli turned to Saskia. Roan still held his hand; he looked like he needed it. Saskia nodded, and allowed the Onyx to do what it was made for.

A great hurricane. The others held on as Saskia reached for the Moonstone, letting the Onyx guide her, and she pulled.

For a moment, she saw those stars above the Roost again, but they weren't stars. They were sigils. Words. The Narrative. Something cracked. Saskia tried to turn away from this story that she was being forced to see. She felt the tree around them trying to recoil, too. The Onyx touched the Emerald, which was somewhere in those roots, clutched close. She tried to call out to Barton, but it was the Moonstone that answered.

Saskia thought her mind was going to come apart.

At the centre of the hurricane there was a light, and a god with nine wings stepped out of it, holding a golden rod whose end point was weighted, swinging. A pendulum. The Onyx fell back, and Saskia choked. Baskar caught her; she had heard someone screaming, cut off by an abrupt grunt, and Saskia saw Roan catch Eli against the root wall, holding him steady. His eyes were squeezed shut, and he buried his face in her chest but was still alive. His wings were gone. He was just a man.

Saskia closed her fist around the Onyx and commanded herself to stay conscious. It was getting harder and harder to close off the aperture that released the Onyx's hungry need for darkness.

She looked up into the golden glow at the centre of that hurricane, focusing on it. Piercing eyes, shifting like mercury, were shut with the same absolute anguish Eli had closed his with.

Phyr opened them, stared at her sharp-taloned hands. Deon and Ryk started for her but she lifted a hand and they didn't come any closer. Phyr turned her gaze on Roan and Eli. He was shaking, but he didn't look away from Phyr.

She turned and examined the vast emptiness of the Brilliant Dark. "What have you done?" she asked flatly. "What have you *all* done?"

Roan let out a noise. "Saskia?"

Saskia didn't know what to feel. What could she do now? She was staring at Phyr, and a croaking noise was coming out of her throat, as she tried to make sense of it. Phyr regarded her with utter devastation.

"The Brilliant Dark," Saskia said finally. "It's not a place. It's a plan."

The silence was a pain they all had to bear. Phyr tipped her face up, and the hurricane faded into a broken sigh as she closed her eyes again, exhausted. "Heen," she said quietly. "When you told me the first time, I should have known."

The CONCEIT *of the* GODS

O wls take comfort in the sky because they feel closer to Phyr there. And so, when Phyr descended into the Warren to speak to Heen so long ago and was compelled to go deep beneath it to find her Wood Wife sister, she rippled with tense uncertainty. Only the thought of visiting her dear sibling offered any incentive to keep going.

Phyr had come to the Warren many times before to seek Heen's counsel. Heen, though not inclined to heights, had come similarly to the Roost. They were there for one another — the setting was meaningless. After all, the realms were subjective projections. Tangible in the way that a galaxy is tangible, in the eyes of a god.

Phyr did not look forward to what she might find beneath the Warren. Namely, the truth about Ancient she had been avoiding.

Even then, the Warren, like the other realms, teemed with the spirits of the deceased. Flickering bright spots that were the dead went out of Phyr's path but were not afraid. She knelt to pass a hand over and through them. These spirits would linger for a time, then become *part* of the Warren — a tree. A rock. Something to pass an age. Then they might choose to return to the mortal realm in a new life. Or not. It was all a cycle. It was reliable. It was all about choice for them, but not for the gods.

Heen was deep, burrowed down. Phyr could tell this dug-out tunnel was her sister's handiwork; the pathway glowed as green as her heartstone. She was there, at the bottom, curled up. She had assumed the form of an enormous rabbit, ears made of roots, and growing into the earth above her head. Heen sometimes took this form in an effort to think. To feel connected again.

"Sister?" Phyr's voice was hollow in the burrow. The fear in it was soft, for she did not wish to wake Heen when she needed this time . . . but time, itself, was in sharp danger.

"I am awake," Heen said. "I am perhaps too awake. I am in pain."

Phyr knew precisely what she meant. "I am in pain also."

The great rabbit's head was a slow arc of a nod, and the earth shifted around them, but her root ears seemed to grow further, plunging deep above her. "You are right to question. And you are right in another regard. These shadows, these Darklings. They did not come from nothing. They came from one of us."

Phyr pulled her nine wings around her, but she was the North Wind itself. Strong. Heen's admission of fear and pain took the courage from her. "It cannot be true," Phyr said.

"These beings are an absolute end to Creation itself. How could one of us make such monsters?"

One of Heen's great eyes opened. "*Is* darkness a monster?" she asked. "There is no creation without destruction. There is no light without the dark. Everything comes from nothing. The darkness has its place."

These were not words that Heen might have said at the beginning of life; she was one of its sources, after all. "If we are meant to become nothing, then what is the point of living now?"

Heen's eye shut then. A sob came up from the Rabbit's body, and she opened both eyes, fierce and full of love. "I know," she said. "I know. I have asked it all. I have prayed for it not to be so. I should have done more."

Phyr's wings fell behind her, and she strode forward, laying a hand on Heen's head. "What do you mean?"

The earth shuddered. "The Darklings came to me. They came to me for guidance."

Phyr resisted every urge to plunge her talons into her sister's head. She was not a battle god. She needed to understand. "Show me."

Heen told her, and Phyr felt like she was there as she viewed her sister's recounting within the Wood Wife's mind.

It was not a betrayal. It could not be. They were all sisters, yet they had hidden things from one another. When had they become so separate? Was it when Ancient made its plans absolute and turned away? Was it when Fia went into hiding?

Perhaps this was Fia's attempt at finding her way back to them all. Or perhaps it was a different kind of response. A retaliation.

Fia had sent the Darklings. Fia had *made* them. And the

three shadow creatures had not rained blood and destruction on Creation immediately. They had come to beg counsel from a creature that gave life.

Three shining golden rings had appeared in the Warren, each occupied by one of these dark beings — Zabor, who made chaos. Kirkald, who made harm. Balaghast, who made silence.

"Are we gods, as you are?" Zabor had asked. Her snake tail was coiled beneath her tightly. Heen remarked that on the monstrous face there was actual concern. Phyr realized she had never seen these beings up close. They were concepts made manifest. Phyr had dissected their existences and their influences, their potential powers, but she had been utterly one-dimensional in appraising them. Until now.

Heen looked from each of them. Phyr imagined that her sister looked on these beings with love, and it hurt Phyr to imagine this. "I do not know," Heen said to the Darklings. "But I welcome you, as I would my sisters."

"We were made. Were you made?" Kirkald asked. He leaned forward, hands tracing symbols in the air. There was a red afterglow with each of them. Phyr knew what these symbols could be, for each represented a potential. A choice and an equation that led to a conclusion. This creature could move time in a far less sophisticated way than Phyr. This may have been why she had been struggling with her Pendulum Rod during this conflict. Kirkald was passing harm through all of time.

Heen frowned. "We are part of one whole. We are Ancient. We are outside Ancient. And also beneath it."

The one called Balaghast nodded but did not speak. They had no mouth, but only eyes. Deliberately sad ones. Silence meant utter nothingness. Silence was an unfortunate promise to bear.

"We are also part of a whole," Zabor said, chin dipped down as she considered her hands, her scales. "We have come to reset a balance. As you and your sister-gods have your purposes, so too do we. Our maker was adamant about this. But we also carry their message."

Heen's back was straight. Heen had walked many millennia at Fia's side and had taken on many of their aspects. If Deon and Ryk were twins, Fia and Heen might also have been, in spirit. Earth was delicate *because* of Spirit. Spirit had nothing unless Nature could contain it. Heen had suffered the most from Fia's leaving.

"What is Fia's message?" Heen asked.

Balaghast raised a hoofed hand, and the message passed through the golden rings, which had begun to shiver, and, suddenly, glow red.

Ancient no longer has any use for life, Balaghast said. *We have come to end it all, by Ancient's order. But we do not wish to; we are touched by Fia, we feel their distress. But still, we cannot deny our maker. We must do as we are bidden, as you do.*

The rings were once again golden. Heen was painfully still.

When Heen was done relaying this memory, Phyr staggered backward from Heen. "No," she said.

"So you see," Heen said sadly. "We have all been betrayed. Even the forces of the dark."

Phyr cradled her head, feeling more pain than she was created to bear. Inside her head was the universe. It was as if all of it was dying. It was as if it was *made* to die.

"It isn't true," Phyr wished. But Heen wouldn't be so

distressed if it wasn't true. Ancient had set out to end Creation. But why? *Why?*

Phyr felt the anger changing her as she straightened, pointing at Heen. "If there is a traitor here, it is you. You should have destroyed the Darklings when they came to you." Such a thing to say, but Phyr knew that if the roles had been reversed, if the Darklings had come to the Roost, she couldn't have killed them. That terrified her more than Heen's admission now.

If it were possible, it seemed Heen became more and more Rabbit-like before Phyr's eyes. "You know I could not harm them. You know I am sorry for it."

Phyr stabbed the Pendulum Rod down, pulling her nine wings over her. "I will stop this. I will make sure of it." Secure in her knowledge, in the recklessness of patching her broken faith, Phyr folded herself out of the Warren, knowing she would not see Heen again.

❦

Ancient only ever endured as an absolute because the sisters were always together. That bond made Ancient strong.

The bond broke when Fia left them. *Fia* had done all of this, had made these Darklings that plagued both the gods and the peoples they protected. Now returned to the Roost, Phyr was smashing the Pendulum Rod again and again into the floating rock of her white realm, having become a god made not of wind but of pain. Beneath the rod, the floating rock splintered, the gold rings there flickering but not going out.

"Why would you do this?" Phyr shouted into oblivion. "Ancient could not have willed it. Ancient needed us."

484

Spooling outward, in its endless message in a spiral that always came back to itself, was the Narrative. Constant and knowable. Phyr, or her sisters, did not read the Narrative, because they were born knowing to obey it absolutely. The gods were only to trust it. The Narrative's sigils and symbols contained the design of countless lives, layered and layered. A perfect system and a reliable equation, they'd believed. Phyr could fly to the top of the universe, and still she wouldn't find the end of the Narrative. She shouldn't be able to.

When she did look, the sigils began to bleed red, and she screamed.

She fell to her great knees. She stared into the golden rings, Fia's rings, and saw the time-stopped human world as if the circles were windows. The world Ancient had made and had given to the gods to manage. This world was young, with so much potential. The Darklings had tried to undo it in small measures, but now that dark smudge hung in the humans' sky, about to detonate it all in one swoop at Ancient's word. Beneath the Roost were the realms of Phyr's sisters, unified. Beneath those realms was Ancient itself, content to see all it had made be destroyed, not moving to stop it.

Ancient's plan or not, Phyr would not allow it. And this broken ruin inside of Phyr, in the space where her heart had been — she would not wish this pain on her other sisters, Ryk and Deon.

Fia had been right, going away. Fia had gone so as to protect the others from their sorrow. Phyr must do the same now. Ancient's strength came from the unity of Phyr and her sisters. If they were separated, then Ancient could be weakened. The sisters could manage the world. They had been doing so, all this time. Now they just had to keep doing it — apart.

Phyr looked above her at the Narrative that she'd tried to make sense of, the sigils glowing in the sky above the Roost. Then she dismissed the sigils and the golden rings below her feet with a wave of her hand. Both things meant unity. Not anymore.

"It's only a story," Phyr told herself. Then she composed her mind, wiping it clean, and called her sisters to her.

"What is this?" Ryk had demanded. Ryk felt things more intensely than the rest of them.

Deon flared when she looked closely at Phyr. "Sister? Are you well?" She tilted her flaming head. "Have you been to Heen?"

Phyr turned her back to the Battle Twins. The platform of stone beneath her feet had resolved to pure, unblemished white, as if she hadn't just been trying to break it in half. The Pendulum Rod was standing on its own, tracing out a picture of the Realms of Ancient, and her sisters' territories in them.

"I am glad you've come," Phyr said. "We have been betrayed."

Deon hissed. Phyr felt the fire jolt at her back. "How? By whom?"

Phyr did not move, hands clenched at her back, beneath her wings. The rod did not move, either. It stood straight up. The golden rings returned, framing this elegant map of everything she and her sisters had known.

"By me."

Silence. Perhaps an age went by.

Ryk moved forward with her great harpoon. "What have you done?"

Phyr took the rod and stepped into the golden circles.

"Ancient's will," she said. "This world is in peril because of the gods. Because the rest of you are weak. I am the authority now. The only authority. Believe in that." Phyr figured that, in as much pain as she was, it wouldn't hurt too much more to do this to them.

It did.

"Fia was right," Phyr went on. "We could not manage this world together. And so it is better that we do it apart."

Ryk advanced, saw the image drawn out in the white stone. "Please, sister," she begged. "We have only ever been together. We can save this world *together*."

Deon raged, racing forward, garnet blade blazing. Phyr raised the Pendulum Rod and Ryk grabbed hold of Deon, who howled.

"It's too late," Phyr said. "It is my choice to make."

"It should be all of ours!" Deon bellowed.

Through the golden rings, Phyr felt it. Felt Fia, felt Ancient. Ancient pulled the Darkling Moon to it. Fia touched Phyr with her spirit and urged her to act.

The rod came down. It did not take much force — only the force of love. And the realms were separated, and Deon and Ryk were banished from the Roost and sent to their respective planes. Time itself was still stopped.

Phyr shook with the effort of holding it all together. Of pushing Ancient, the furnace of Creation, down and down and down, though it wanted to rise and destroy. *Sleep*, Phyr thought, and it was done.

She looked down into the rings, and she was surprised to see Fia there, their triple-horned head dipped down sadly. It helped, only a little, that Phyr wasn't completely alone in this.

"It had to be done," Fia said from the rings. This connection, too, would snap shut forever, and the siblings would be parted until the end of everything. Phyr held on as long as she could, but the rings winked out, and Fia was gone.

Heen came out of the depths of the Warren, surrounded by her ancestral dead, and let them comfort her for a time.

The Realms of Ancient split to five, then, with perfect, sharp boundaries. In the dark spaces between the realms, and beneath them, was a new land built from tears and blood, a burned land that reflected the gods' pain. They called this place the Bloodlands, and into it went the Darklings and all their malicious brood.

And while the Darklings did not wish to destroy, it was still their purpose. Not even a god can deny its purpose. Heen, despite her sorrow, dug their prison in the Bloodlands, and Phyr pulled them out of the sky where they had joined together, splitting the three dark siblings apart as she had done with her own. The Darklings, weakened, were condemned to their hold. The walls of the prison were strong, but the Darklings' desire to fulfill what they were made for was stronger. It would only be a matter of time. And eternity to an eternal is as certain as the purpose they were made for.

The Darklings sang. They waited. They never forgot.

Fia provided the locks — the targes. They knew they would only remain in place for so long. They told their children that Ancient forged the locks, for Ancient loved them. They hoped that their conceit would spare the world.

And, when all of this was done, the sisters mitigated their pain by watching life continue. Time ticked onwards. The world was saved, and humanity was allowed its chance to grow. Darkness, however, couldn't be banished from the world entirely. Heen had been right; creation could not exist without destruction, a balance now to be maintained by Denizens by believing that what the gods had given up was for a greater good. The gods' hearts were on Earth, with their descendants. It was enough to love *through* them.

And as millennia passed, the longer the gods were apart from one another, the more their sister-love faded. Separation had to become strength. Their Denizen children began to believe this was also true.

Even gods make choices. Even gods make mistakes. And in the deepest dark was Ancient itself, pushed down, made to sleep, made silenced, by what Phyr had done, by the bonds that she had broken.

But nothing remains in a cage for too long. And eventually, in the way of conceits, it would be misconstrued. The lie would be undone.

But nothing can be caged forever. All Ancient had to do was wait.

"And if we are brought back together?" Phyr had asked Fia through the rings, just before the connection had closed.

"Then it will no longer be in our hands," Fia said. "Humans will have to make the last choice. Unity may save them in a way it could not save us."

The Narrative endured. This fragment of the story went unheard. But stories, like gods, don't ever really die.

Once upon a time, Creation dreamed, and called itself Ancient. It had five aspects, calling them its children. Gods. These gods managed Creation's great work — humanity and the world they inhabited. But Creation was unhappy with it, with the creatures it called Denizens and all else that had sprung from them — humanity failed Ancient's expectations, and so it wanted to see the work undone. It wanted to set it back to what it had been at the beginning.

A brilliant darkness.

WAKE *and* WONDER

FIVE YEARS AFTER
ROAN AND ELI DISAPPEARED

B arton hadn't known what to expect.

He had gone along with Solomon's plan, because he
had some foresight. He'd earned it. Sacrifices would have
to be made for the long run. Solomon had told him about
Project Crossover when it was just some throwaway notion
by some Denizen, co-opted by some world leader, when the
Task Guard was new and flourishing. Long before the Apex
was a hole in the ground, it was the hope Barton, all of them,
needed. He didn't know the specifics of how it could work,
but he knew, somehow, *he* could make it work.

Long before he'd agreed to help the Task Guard make
their Bloodgate, even when he and Phae had argued, they
would always come back to one another. Put the argument

away and remember they were together. Barton always made sure to hold her close afterwards, because he remembered what her absence felt like, when she had gone to the Glen. That separation was a chasm he never wanted to experience again, but . . . he had to make choices that were beyond what he wanted. He had Saskia to think of now. And a world full of children who had had their choices taken from them.

If he could open this gate, he could fix things. Hadn't they all thought the same, childish thing? *Even a bad decision is better than making none at all.*

So he'd hold Phae close whenever he could and memorize the sensation so that when they were separated again, it could make Barton strong.

Now it had been too long, and he was forgetting what she *felt* like.

Opening this gate had been different. The first time he'd done it, in the Pool of the Black Star, it had been like looking for a hidden seam in a curtain. Holding it open so Roan and Eli could get back out had been the hardest.

This time, Barton knew he couldn't hold it open. Once he went through, there'd be no coming out unless the people on the other side managed to do it without him. So he had to succeed.

Something pulled him in. That's the only way he could describe it. A cry for help. He'd crossed over into a world about to burst wide, and it had; it was shaking so hard that he'd felt foolish for bringing his body with him. But if Roan and Eli could do it — and, damn them, they could do anything — he'd be fine. He thought.

A sensation Barton couldn't forget was Heen. She was in his blood now, restored there by great pains when all this has started, with Roan's help. He didn't think he'd see Heen again so soon, or that this time he would be returning her favour, that *he'd* be restoring *her*. It had all happened so quickly. He hadn't landed, not precisely; it's like he was careening through the Veil, through a dark passage. There was a great quake, and the Emerald was a green flicker in the distance, and it was coming fast for him as he approached — both he and the stone desperate for help. Barton caught it, because he owed Heen, could hear her deep inside the stone when he'd touched it. *Please*, she begged. *Please don't let it through.*

There was very little left of Heen, but that little remaining sliver of the god hiding in her broken heartstone encased Barton inside a seed, a seed that became armour, and that collided with the rising dark sending out a red, terrible song. The tree around Barton stretched and thrived off the heart of him and his fool's hopes.

Heen was sorry for it. *Please, little leveret — we must hold it back a little longer, until my sisters return. For the love you bear for your world, and the people in it.*

Barton thought of Phae and Saskia, every day, every year, every age. He wouldn't stop fighting, because he knew they wouldn't, either.

The roots churned the world, but the dark was rising, pushing the tree up. If it couldn't get out, then it would push through.

Neither Phae nor Natti imagined they'd be strolling the halls of the Old Leg as they had before, a very long time ago when they'd walked through the front door to open the first Bloodgate.

But here they were.

Much of the old iconography was still prominent. The Legislature had been built as a sort of palace with pagan echoes, the heads of old gods. Phae wondered where those gods were when all of this was happening. But she learned a long time ago about the best-laid plans of humans and their makers — they never seemed to make it work on the same playing field.

They walked, side by side, up the stairs flanked by the bronze bison, watched by soldiers and government personnel alike. Outside, a Denizen force waited to back them up if need be. But everyone had been told to stand down. The eclipse would happen tomorrow, around noon. The time for fighting was done. Nothing more could be said with fists.

An ETG soldier stopped them as they rounded the alcove above the Pool of the Black Star and too many memories Phae didn't have time to confront.

She was startled to recognize the soldier. "Cam?"

Strange what a year could do to a chubby kid with a love of fantasy. Then Phae remembered what a year had done to her and her friends. Cam smiled at her. "Phae. It's nice to see you."

Between them stood a war, but she hugged him anyway, which may have startled Cam more. He pulled away and led them the rest of the way towards the proxy chancellor's office.

"You know," he said, when they reached the door, and Natti raised an eyebrow at him, "I saw Saskia. Before she, you know . . . went through to the other side."

Phae was very still. "Did you help her?"

He nodded. "You know Saskia. Usually doesn't take no for an answer."

Phae smiled past the pricking in her eyes. "Like so many other people I knew."

"She said that . . ." He was shy, but he obviously wanted to get this out. "She said I was one of the good guys. I hope she was right. I hope this can be over now."

Natti pinched his cheek. "Cute, kid."

The office door opened by the hand of a guard outside it, admitting them into Chancellor Song Mi-ja's presence and closing it behind them just as quickly.

They'd seen this woman on screens, heard her voice over broadcast. She'd loomed over the Denizens and they'd chosen her as the figurehead of their enemy. But this woman, they realized, was not much older than Phae or Natti. And she looked small in her pedestrian clothes. The desk was bare. She sat on it, legs crossed and hunched over with her eyes closed.

Natti cleared her throat. "Chancellor?"

"No," Mi-ja said. "Just Mi-ja is fine."

Phae moved tentatively forward but tried to make her voice even. "We're here to discuss the terms of the truce —"

"It's fine," Mi-ja said, as if she was annoyed. "It's done. The ETG will stand down entirely. I've already alerted the world's governments. Those not gone underground, at any rate." She opened her eyes, and they were exhausted.

"And your little weapon?" Natti asked, confused. "You haven't even fired it yet."

"I know what's going to happen all the same," Mi-ja said grimly, swinging her legs over the desk and standing. "The world's missiles are armed and aimed. They'll be going off within the hour. A waste, if you ask me." She turned to the two Denizen women before her, and her voice turned pleading. "Please tell me you've heard something from the Realms of Ancient. Is that godhead of yours coming?"

The room's silence was enough of an answer.

"I see," Mi-ja muttered.

Phae was suddenly in front of her. "We have to have faith." She took the woman's hand. "It's all we have left."

Natti went to the window and looked out on the city of Winnipeg, or what was left of it. The city had long ago been cleared, and, as Mi-ja said, anyone who could hide was doing so, somewhere, anywhere, trying to see if they could wait out the apocalypse. The only people left in the city were a group of Denizens who were backing Phae and Natti. They'd all sent the others away. Aivik. Natti's mother. Arnas. Jordan. Jet. They'd done all they could. They'd held the line and kept their promise. It was up to Saskia now to do the same, if she could.

Rather fittingly, it was snowing.

The last few Denizens were outside, on the Old Leg's lawn, white flakes accumulating on them and the many disparate bronze statues. The people milling amongst them were looking up at the Darkling Moon, wondering. Hoping. Clinging to faith.

"May it be enough," Mi-ja said.

❧

It wasn't.

The guns blazed. No matter how much ammunition the world had in its arsenal, the Darkling Moon endured. It always would.

The next day, the sun rose.

The world watched as it moved across the sky towards black inevitability.

~≈~

Now. Beneath that tree, in the darkness that was so painfully bright, all of the gods' conceit and everyone's good intentions were brought to bear.

"This can't have been for nothing." Phyr said, turning to them all. Roan, Eli, Saskia, Baskar, her sister-gods. Only Saskia understood, having learned Phyr's story as she separated Eli from the Moonstone.

"What are you talking about?" Roan finally snapped.

The Owl Matriarch swung towards her, scowling. "Bringing us all here, together. That is what Ancient wants. You've played right into it."

Eli moved Roan aside, to speak to the god from which he was descended. "We're here to free Ancient, to stop the Darklings from —"

"The Darklings," Phyr cut him off, "can only destroy if Ancient wills it. Which is what Ancient will do, if it rises."

WHEN, came another voice, separate from all of them, and they turned to a great hanging knot of writhing roots coming down overhead of them. The three gods held tight to their armaments, prepared to fight.

The roots parted, showing the Emerald. Showing part of the man attached to it, looking weak and ready to let go.

"Barton!" Saskia screamed.

His eyes were open. He stared down at them all, pityingly. "I didn't want you to come," he said quietly. "The Darklings would have passed by us. But Ancient . . ."

It wasn't me! The dream came back to her now, sickeningly, a message, a warning. "The signal was Ancient," Saskia sobbed. "It made me believe it was you."

Barton reached for her, but the roots closed over him, pulled him and the Emerald away. Then the darkness rose.

Baskar held her tight and looked away, but Saskia could do no such thing. She felt her human mind trying to work out what she was seeing. After all, it had gotten her this far, and allowed her to see and parse so much cosmic nonsense that it shouldn't have ever understood. But before them, in that vast emptiness beneath this tree that was actually the last line of defense against destruction, Saskia saw a pulsing, nightmarish mass, and she knew it was the source of everything. Of life, of death, of utter absolute nothing.

This was Ancient. And it was very much awake.

It has been so long, it spoke at them, into them, *since I have been able to see the results of my work. My first children, and my last, together with me here.*

"Silence!" Phyr howled, her wings beating a tornado at the dark. "Be silent, and sleep! Let us still manage the world you seek to destroy!"

If Creation could laugh, it did, and it made Saskia shrink into herself, bury her face into the hard, rough shell of Baskar that quivered so hard they might fall apart.

You all fight for nothing. The darkness swelled like it was taking a gulp of fresh air. *This was always the intended end to the Narrative that I gave to you. Life was a fleeting inkling, a dream. It was not meant to last. It was not made to. And those who people your realm, they wish to see it undone as much as Creation does. This plan was only postponed. My Darklings nearly succeeded once, and now they have been given a second chance. Now our great work can be realized. You have done that for me, all of you, and in return I will repay you with absolution.*

The group fell back as a tangle of roots shot to them, pulled away, and dangled something over them. A man's body — not Barton's. This man had been made *a part* of the Heartwood, the roots piercing his eyes and his brain. Saskia thought she'd pass out and staggered to her hands and knees to look away, though she'd never, ever, unsee it.

Saskia recognized the husk as Chancellor Grant, who must have fallen through the Apex behind her and paid the ultimate price for thinking he could ever rule this place.

This creature is the pinnacle of human ambition, Ancient went on, hollow voice singular, puncturing, and absolute. *I have seen what he has seen. What is in his dark heart. It is where the Darklings have always lived. It is where I live. Human beings and Denizens alike allowed themselves to be consumed by greed, avarice, apathy. The world they inhabit will die before they do. My end, my way, is clean. Wipe it all away now, end all potential future suffering. Nothing left, not even a memory. It is just. It is inevitable.*

"It's not!" This time it was Roan, and she'd pushed her way past the gods. "We fought for life. For love! Do you know anything about it? Did you ever?"

The three First Matriarchs looked paralyzed by Ancient's words, but they seemed to be animated again watching a human show no fear in the face of it. But the gods were Ancient's direct children, after all; together they *were* Ancient. And like children they wanted to be reassured. Told that Ancient had made them because it had truly wanted them, trusted them —

Love is a construct. As am I. Nothingness is a kind of peace. It is what you have all been searching for. I will give it to you. You have given it to me, by bringing to me the children I have longed for. I will bring them close to me, and we will be strong again in our unity.

There was no way they could have stopped the roots coming down like grappling hooks on all three gods at once. They touched their Calamity Stones with the barest flick, and they shattered into dust. Phyr, Deon, and Ryk all looked to the others one last time.

"Do what we could not," Phyr managed to say, and the gods were suddenly gone.

The Brilliant Dark was quiet as it went back in on itself, almost considering, pulling its roots and its cables and then shivering with excitement.

Ah. Already I feel them inside me as they were meant to be. All is close now. These realms, all as one, and I will bring this Deadland into the Uplands, there into then, and for a moment every piece of my creation will wonder at this waking, before it sleeps forever, and I will never have to dream or long again for any of it. Do you not crave the same?

Saskia was staring at the Onyx in her hand. No matter what she did, it could not reach for the other stones. They were gone now. Ancient had taken them back.

"We can't kill Creation," Saskia heard Eli said. "The gods are gone."

"They're not," Roan said, coming down beside him and Saskia. "There's still us." She clasped Saskia's wrist, where the Onyx was. "All of us. Together. Now. We're going to go home. I don't care what the odds are. Just think of the place, think of the people we love."

It was foolish and saccharine and, Saskia thought chiefly, stupid, but she felt Baskar beside her, too, felt them nod, desperate to believe.

The roots came down, aiming for Saskia, but Roan was all fire, and Eli was the wind, and they battled them back. The tree itself seemed to be warring from inside, because the roots could not reach the Emerald, either. Barton was still fighting. So would they.

The darkness roared, seeming to come to a decision. *Then I will take you all with me. I will show you. We will all do this together, whether you like it or not.*

Then, all around them, with the mightiest of quakes, they felt themselves shooting upward with the force of Creation's will to see it all undone, pulled by black plinths and pincers that Ancient had been sending out through the underworld all this time. The Deadlands rose, and so did Ancient, and the fighting tree with it.

Roan and Eli grabbed hold of Saskia and Baskar, and they pressed into the bottom of the Heartwood. They didn't have time for despair. The tree was getting higher and taking them, and the land of the dead, with it.

They held tight to one another and thought of home.

Part V
UMBRA

THIS MARVELLOUS WRECKAGE

The Darkling Moon was one thing, but it was three things first. Three beings, intricately wrapped up in one another, as they had been when Fia had made them so long ago.

In the Darkling Hold, they had been in three separate prisons, and it had been unbearable. Now they were together, as they were meant to be: three bodies, one mind, one moon, and they would be together like this until the end.

As the moon tracked over the blue world below, the three minds that were one had thought, perhaps, they could pass this world by, as they'd once dreamed. *Perhaps we can continue moving through this cold black space and find somewhere for ourselves. Perhaps we can outrun our purpose.*

But the Darklings that were the moon did not get to choose. They thought they could, once. They thought, by putting Seela into the world, they might be able to build their own domain — if not in the world below, then above it, beyond it, away from it. But they could not escape Ancient's design. They were as much children as the humans below.

They had wills that were never their own to begin with. They moved to their place, their final place, and did as they were bidden, finally fulfilling their purpose. They held on to each other, too. Ancient was singing. Ancient was calling them from the place it, too, had been made to sleep. While they did not want to do this thing, they could not deny they were pleased that everyone might be free now, including the malevolent creator of all. Despite what it meant for Creation itself.

Below, the world watched the three beings as one move into the path of the sun. As they came together, the light cast a red umbra. And all at once, absolutely everywhere on that blue, fickle, precious, doomed world, there was a red dark.

The world stopped turning. It didn't need to, any longer. It was an echo of the great battle between the Darklings and the gods, when time had been stopped. Though Phyr was gone now. If Ancient was rising, all the gods were gone.

The Darklings' position in the sky pointed the way down like an invisible pole. And Ancient, whose own design had been to pull the Darklings down to the world to cleave it in half, rose to meet this path.

Not even the Creator could slip its own design now.

～※～

Phae and Natti were together with the chancellor as they watched the eclipse. The ring around the Darkling Moon was red and unforgiving and Natti thought, *This is it, then*. She imagined it would be like this: the moon would just blink everything out of existence, in one merciful jolt, and then . . . nothing.

But of course there'd have to be some kind of spectacle first.

☙❦

The world was caving in from the inside of its matrix. Thrusting itself upward through this last Bloodgate, to which the Darkling eclipse pointed the path below, Ancient pushed the Heartwood through. Ancient had spent so much of its own time sending little barbs throughout the Deadlands, and it pulled the underworld up with it. The dead and the living would share an equal playing field, and they would all go out together.

But what Ancient did not count on were the humans inside of the Heartwood, carving their own path. *Think of home*, Roan had said. They all did. And they thought of Winnipeg.

Saskia thought of One Evergreen and her bedroom of inventions. She thought of Jet and all his questions, of Phae, and her compact, fierce devotion, and Saskia wondered if her last thoughts could go to them, carried by Ancient's deadly trajectory.

Barton had heard Saskia's prayer, even though he was losing his battle, the tree consuming him. The Emerald let out a sigh, crushed to dust, but even with it gone, Barton held on. He thought of Phae, too, of running again, of breathing the air of his world, of watching Saskia grow up.

Eli thought of his mother, and his father, of the possibility they could all get some peace after this, whatever happened.

Roan thought of Cecelia.

Ancient thought of nothing at all.

❧

The entire world shook when the Heartwood came through, but not even the people trapped within the tree knew, exactly, where this enormous destructive tree was going to come out the other end. Like a heavy drill it churned through concrete, up and under Portage Avenue and Main Street, in a Canadian city that had become the epicentre of the last war.

And the Heartwood was not a delicate instrument. The downtown core, and all its empty skyscrapers, asphalt, and abandoned cars, were sucked into the chasm at the Heartwood's base. The tree, and Ancient underneath it, intertwined within it, didn't care. It just reached for the Darkling Moon like a mother beckoning its lost children.

Then something inside the Heartwood made it lurch to a stop. A sickening, horrible hope, a girl with one last stone, at first a Quartz, and now an Onyx, screaming with every inch of her spirit, gathering her friends to her, sending out a beacon for the one being left in any of the realms who had been watching and waiting, for her moment.

The Moth Queen gathered Roan, Eli, Saskia, and Baskar into her thousand arms and pulled them free of the Heartwood.

❧

Many of the military drones that had been hovering above Winnipeg didn't make it out unscathed. A few did, and their coverage was transmitted back to where Phae had been watching, from the Old Leg, with the others.

Phae had only run once, full tilt, and it had been when she was in the Glen, that forgotten realm, alongside the Deer shades with whom she'd felt a brand new kinship. Now there was the tangible, living kinship that she had with her family, and that's what drove her out of that parliamentary office and into the street.

Even with the world coming down around her, and the smoke of wreckage wreathing the city, Phae ran for Portage and Main, knowing this was what her legs were made for. Air screamed through her.

Deer were fast as Rabbits. Phae was *fleet*. She felt like she was one of them, four long legs pulling her and her spirit, in tatters as it was, through deserted streets. Bodies were just shells, after all. Hers could do anything if her spirit was willing enough — Fia had taught her that. So Phae ran for that horrific tree in the middle of downtown. *I'm coming*, she said in her heart, always ready to rescue that gods-damned boy she loved. Always.

❦

Natti was a bit more practical. She leapt into a heavy artillery ETG vehicle. Mi-ja stayed behind to guide the last ETG units on standby, to send them in, with Natti bringing up the charge, to retrieve the survivors. If there were any.

Natti would make sure there were.

❦

The Moth Queen could only get them so far. She'd pulled them out, yes, but after that, they were on their own. She had her thousand hands full, it seemed, since the dead had come back to this world, and there was already so many new dead to manage.

But Eli was happy to take over for her.

A great wind came up in the shuddering intersection, the aftershocks of the tree fierce and terrible, and swept the smoke out of the way of the torpedo of flame that brought up the rear. The one-eyed woman controlling the fire pumped her legs as fast as possible and carried a dark-haired girl in her arms.

Eli ran by Roan's side, the ground heaving as spikes — roots — shot up and tried to bar their path or send them flying. Eli pulled up a zephyr that was as powerful as Roan's garnet blade had been, cracking these intrusions aside and clearing the way.

Ahead, on the empty, shuddering avenue, someone was running towards them. Behind the runner, a vehicle attempted to navigate the splitting, bursting chasms in the road.

"Phae!" Roan called, and even Eli couldn't help but grin.

She was coming fast. Her arms were out, and even in the dark, all of her pulsed with that blue, effervescent light that encircled her antlers, her flickering shield, and she sent it to them just as a wall of singing roots was coming down on top of them.

When Phae reached them, they all pushed their way through just as the military truck pulled up. The *rat-tat-tat* and surging of an armed cavalcade — guns, shouts of soldiers, machines in the air — drew the ire of the tree with a gunfire assault. The woman driving the vehicle was shouting something, maybe obscenities, but loudest of all, "I don't have the same death wish you do! Get in!"

The roots clutching their shield retracted and flew upward, swatting at the Mundane men and women who had put themselves at the front line even though they might not come back from it, because the impulse to fight for something was still there. The *world* was still there.

The vehicle swung back around as soon as it was loaded with its precious cargo, throwing itself down side streets and crashing through parking meters that wouldn't charge anyone anything again, back towards the Old Leg, back to a place where they could celebrate whatever small victory this was.

Phae watched from the back window as the Heartwood went in and out of view behind the wrecked, burning remains of the buildings that hadn't come down yet. She stared at that tree and promised it she would be back, because she'd felt something. A pull on a thread that she thought broken. Barton.

For now she held tight to Saskia, unconscious in someone else's arms, and looked up into the drawn face of Roan Harken — a tear-streaked, eye-gouged, soot-stained pale face of a no-longer-a-teenager, a hero. And, most of all, her best friend.

"It's you," Phae said dumbly. Roan's expression was fevered, but she managed to just shrug. Sitting pressed into Roan's shoulder, rolling his eyes behind her, was Eli. Phae didn't believe her eyes at the sight of them both.

"You all really waited till the last fucking second to show up," griped Natti from the front seat, flooring it and smashing over a barricade. For an instant, everyone in the back left their seats, especially Eli, whose head actually smashed into the roof. He cringed, and Roan burst out laughing, and then Phae laughed, and somehow it was really happening. They were really here.

Roan's smile fell when she leaned forwards, pushing Saskia's hair out of her eyes. Clutched in the girl's stiff hands was a mask made of bark crudely shaped like a rabbit's face.

"Is she . . ." Phae couldn't help asking.

"She's the person this has been the hardest on," Eli said, rubbing his head as Natti brought the truck to the Old Leg. "She's the one it's all for."

⁂

Saskia was inside the Onyx. She didn't want to come out. She felt safer in the dark.

She curled in on her own spirit. It was too much. Too much for one person. Too much for one world. Imagine finding out the Creator had only one purpose, and that was to correct its mistake. You. Everyone.

What could you do against that? What could anyone do? No matter what Saskia had chosen, this is where it had brought her. Choice seemed, then, like it was just an illusion, overseen by a bitter cosmos that could take it away from you at any moment. What did any of it matter?

"The spirit is matter," something else said. Something inside the stone with Saskia.

She unfolded a little to look. It was a small, golden moth. But it had silvery eyes, like the shades had, and it unfolded, too. It was a Fox shade.

"Love matters," said another moth, another shade, an Owl

this time. "You who have been touched by Death, you know you are not alone."

"Even when the last living person is just made back into matter," said a much more familiar voice, one keeping her close, still protective, a Rabbit shade who loved a good story, "the dead will still be there. And the dead will stand with you, for the sake of the lives they lived. For the possibility of the lives ahead."

Saskia still couldn't do it. It was a pretty speech and a pretty notion, but it wouldn't be enough. It couldn't be.

"How can we even think of winning this?" she asked them, asked herself, asked any god left to listen.

"We can't think," said the dead as a chorus. "We can just hope. When you have breath, you use it. We will be with you. Until there is nothing. Making the wrong choice, when there are none left, is better than making none at all."

Saskia's own words, thrown back at her. She needed to remember what the risks had been for.

For Barton, Phae, Roan, Eli, Natti, Jet, Baskar, Ella.

For tomorrow.

Saskia didn't have to be worried that the stone would take her over and exact its will on her. That's not what its purpose was; after all, she'd poured her will into it first. It would follow her lead. It may have been the last Calamity Stone left, but it was the only one that could do this.

She had always wanted to be chosen.

Now she had to choose.

She woke up.

". . . a year?"

Saskia woke all at once, staring up into lights in a ceiling above her. It was strange to look at a light bulb and think, *I haven't seen one of those in a while.*

Baskar had come out of the Onyx with her. "Hello," they said. The voice was smiling, even if the bark-face couldn't.

She turned her head, even though it ached to do so. The lights in the room flickered. They were in a large office filled with fancy furniture and bookcases that seemed more like a movie set than a real place. The shattered Realms of Ancient, even the expansive nothing of the Brilliant Dark, had seemed less extreme than this office.

A Korean woman — *Mi-ja*, Saskia's memory said — sat with her hands between her knees. Behind the huge desk, arms folded like the general she once was, stood Roan, squinting her single amber eye down at a screen in her hand. Eli was at the window with Natti, speaking quietly. Scraps of the conversation floated towards Saskia, but she didn't want to draw any attention to herself. She just wanted to rest here a while before she had to stand up again and do what she'd woken up to do.

". . . so that makes eight since we . . ." Roan sighed, putting the tablet screen down and sliding it back towards anyone else who wanted it. "I'm sorry."

"Stop saying that," Phae snapped. "You did exactly what you aimed to do. None of us expected this outcome. We were all too trusting when we should've known better."

Natti had turned towards the argument that seemed to be escalating too quickly. "Hey, this was the hand we dealt ourselves. We still have a bit of wiggle room, I think. If you guys could come crawling out of the underworld without being totally annihilated, then we can take this to the finish line."

Then Natti patted Eli's shoulder. "*I'm* sorry, about your dad."

Saskia winced, remembering the last time she'd seen Solomon. What he'd done to make sure she got through the Bloodgate. Someone must have told Eli while she was unconscious. She was glad it hadn't fallen to her.

Eli did something that seemed to surprise Natti. He smiled. "I'm sure Solomon isn't sorry. And my . . . views on death have rather changed somewhat in these intervening years."

"That's all well and good," Mi-ja said, picking up the tablet Roan had abandoned. "But communications with, well, the rest of the world, are down." She threw it aside. "We're all we've got. If there's a plan, best we mobilize it now. My troops, what's left of them, have fallen back, but our firepower is grossly limited. These back-up generators will blow soon — I'm surprised they haven't already." She dug her fingers into her eyes. "We can try to blow the thing to kingdom come, but if we couldn't do it to the Darkling Moon, then I doubt we can bring down the, uh, Creator, with a gun."

"We can't blow the tree up. Not with Barton inside it."

The group swung as one to Saskia, and Phae was up and at her side in a rush, pulling her in uncomfortably hard.

"Agh," Saskia grunted, feeling Phae's power go into her and reset bones she hadn't known were actually out of whack.

"You've seen him," Phae said, pulling away but not letting go. "You know he's in there? How can he still be alive?"

"Because he's stubborn," Saskia half-smiled, "like you and me."

"I don't know if we can —" Mi-ja started.

"Oh, no," said Roan. "We're going to get him out of there. Barton is the only thing preventing that tree from getting any closer to reaching its goal, I think. Once we pull him out, we're going to finish this thing." She slammed a flaming fist into her open palm. "We shouldn't still have our powers if the gods are gone. But we do. And I'll use them up to the last to stop this thing." Her face brooked no argument. "None of us are getting left behind."

Saskia uncurled her fingers to reveal the Onyx, turned it over, saw that it was coming out both sides of her hand. Phae sucked in a breath at the sight of it.

"The dead will help us, too," Saskia said. The Moth Queen had disappeared since she'd helped them, but Saskia still trusted Death's earlier blessing. She looked to the others. "After that, if it doesn't work, at least we can say we tried."

She put her feet under her and stood up. Baskar rose alongside, tipping their mask down in a bow.

"We have to be the last thing we believe in," Saskia said to them all. "Whatever the ending is, it'll be ours. Our choice."

"Our choice," Roan repeated. And that was it.

STRAIGHT *to* YOU

The Darkling Moon did not move. Red light, and the immovable night, covered the world.

In Winnipeg, Heart of the Continent, a famous intersection split in half, there was a tree. There had been malignant trees like it before, but this wasn't a tree that could be healed. The Darkling Moon stopped above this tree. And the tree, its roots going as far down as the underworld that it had brought up with it, only had one purpose.

Pull the moon down into its broken, twisted branches, break this world apart, and cast everything in its Brilliant Dark.

The world sharply took a breath.

But there were still those, at ground zero, who were willing to fight.

〰

"We should have left. With the others."

"No," she said, standing in the living room, looking out onto the dark, deserted street, as if watching for guests to arrive. Or for a wayward niece to finally find her way home before curfew.

They'd returned to the house on Wellington Crescent as though magnetized there. The three of them hadn't lived there long; most of their life as a family, hodgepodge as it was, was spent in Wolseley, after all. They'd only spent a year here. But that year had changed everything. It had been the beginning of the end. And when it came time to get as many people out of Winnipeg as possible — people the priest had become responsible for, had thrown his life towards helping — it made a strange kind of sense to send them off and go back to a place that had been home.

He slid his arm around her waist. She leaned her head on his shoulder.

"You did everything you could for the Cluster. For the resistance. For us." Deedee let out a sigh. "But you'll still never forgive yourself, will you?"

Arnas didn't turn his head. He stared out into the red-tinged dark with her. The aftershock reached their neighbourhood, a wretched, grinding tremor. Still, they didn't go.

"We can't outrun our choices," Arnas said quietly. "But at least . . ."

"We made them," Deedee finished. It was too late to go anywhere now. The sky, in the eastern distance towards downtown, flickered. A band of lightning crackled, but there was no thunder. Only silence.

"*You* didn't have to stay," Arnas said wryly, after a while.

"Believe me. I wasn't going to." Deedee tipped her head

up at him, and no matter how many years had passed, or what had transpired between them since she found out the miserable secrets of Arnas's life, she still smiled like a troublesome teen herself. "But you were too interesting to dump, I guess."

Arnas laughed under his breath. He kissed the top of her head. "I hope it was interesting enough. While it lasted."

They held on to each other as the sky changed. They thought of Roan. They shouldn't still believe that she was out there, given everything, but they *were* the ones who'd known Roan the most, after all. They'd had to go through the parent-teacher meetings, the tantrums, puberty, everything that came with raising a child. Even one that wasn't really theirs by blood — but she had been theirs. She was still part of the matrix of their family. They'd raised her the best they could, and she had done so many wondrous things they'd never imagined.

They didn't have much else to believe in, right in this moment. And so it made sense, now, to believe in Roan.

⁂

They'd been picked up from the deserted parliamentary offices of the Old Leg via helicopter. Sliding through the crumbling remains of the downtown core, they would land on a relatively intact skyscraper and head down to ground level from there.

The wreckage below was almost peaceful, Saskia thought. Saskia had asked, earlier, about Jet. She imagined he would have loved this view. Phae told her that he'd gone with Jordan, that he'd taken to honing his powers with him, and that, despite the distractions of the war going on around him, he asked about Saskia every day. She wondered if she'd ever see him again.

Saskia looked up from the window to Roan and Eli, the two of them pressed to the glass like they were memorizing every broken thing against what was broken inside of them, too.

Roan pointed, the frigid wind tossing her short hair about her one eye. "At least we finally opened up Portage and Main."

Natti laughed, at least. Eli leaned his head back into the wall of the helicopter, smiling. Phae, belted in beside Saskia, was eyeing Baskar, wrapped about Saskia's neck and shoulder like a harness and still wearing their little bark Rabbit mask.

"Your world," Baskar said, taking it all in, "is beautiful."

Natti sucked on her teeth. "It's still here. Has that going for it."

When they landed on the roof of an abandoned bank's high rise, they headed immediately for a door that Natti kicked in without hesitation. They'd then head down to street level, then below even that, to meet up with members of the ETG unit stationed in the partially uncovered trench that had been the underground mall near the intersection. Miraculously, much of it was still intact, though the roots were close enough to the structure that it likely wouldn't last too much longer. Mi-ja would be stationed there in the cobbled-together control, and Saskia was glad the proxy chancellor was here with them, proof that things *could* change, especially at the eleventh hour.

The group went down the stairwell, all thirty storeys, and Saskia revelled in this last, bitter respite they all had together. She really couldn't guess what would happen after this.

She opened her right palm to the Onyx. Even after

everything, even knowing what the state of death was, knowing that the Moth Queen was watching them all, she didn't know if she was ready to die.

Baskar pressed themselves close to her but offered no comforting words.

"Drones have identified a heat signature at the east side of the Heartwood." Mi-ja had a tablet out, pointing to the reading to show Phae and Natti. Roan and Eli took off and were several floors down by now. They were preparing themselves for the fight. Maybe even excited for it to start. Saskia shivered.

"It has to be Barton," Saskia said. "He has to still be alive."

Mi-ja glanced back up to Saskia as they passed the nineteenth floor, then back at her screen. "You'll have ground support, and we have two air strike teams ready to deploy. You have a plan for extracting him, I take it?"

Phae spoke first. "We go in, guns blazing, and blast that thing to hell."

Natti shook her head. "I rely on you for composure, you know. But I guess we've run out." She jerked her head at Mi-ja. "We have to weaken it with whatever we have. Barton is the priority, but once he's out . . . that thing will have nothing holding it back. We clear a path ahead for Saskia."

Saskia tripped on the next stair, and everyone saw, but she didn't care.

When they got to ground level, the doorway to the stairwell had caved in. Roan's arm lit up, and she punched her way through like it annoyed her. One last thing in her way. She bowed, holding out her arm, and Eli went through before her, straight-faced but bowing in return. They looked older, but they were still, somehow, kids.

Natti clapped Roan on the back in passing. Phae paused in front of her former best friend, touched her ruined eye, then pressed her forehead into hers. Roan clasped Phae's hand warmly and pulled her along through the doorway. Mi-ja, Saskia, and Baskar followed a little farther behind.

The room opened up into disaster, though it was in much better shape than a lot of the buildings near the Heartwood's epicentre. The windows were blasted out, and errant snow had blown in. They had a good view of the Heartwood, wide as any skyscraper, the viral topography of its bark of twisting, throbbing cords that stretched slowly towards the Darkling Moon. Lightning crackled in the sky but no thunder followed.

They couldn't let the tree reach all the way into the sky; Barton was out of time.

"We're watching its progression, and the tree's past the stratosphere now." Mi-ja had turned to Saskia, because the other four were all ahead, staring out into the empty avenue, the overturned cars, the utter dark silence lit only by red.

"We get Barton out first," Saskia said quietly, repeating the plan to herself, "then we destroy the tree. However we can."

Standing before her were the four heroes she'd worshipped. She'd brought them all here together. They all still had the will to fight and to see it through to the bitter end.

"It'll be enough," Roan said. She kissed Phae on the cheek, hugging her one-armed, before turning for Saskia. "One thing at a time."

Saskia came forward, and Roan surveyed her, hands on her hips. She was still wearing the armour she had built out of what she'd found in the wilderness of the shattered realms. Her amber eye squinted.

"Don't look at me like that, the both of you," Roan said. Saskia glanced at Baskar, who slid from Saskia to the ground, pulling concrete debris to them and building themselves a new body from rebar and broken glass. They still made themselves Saskia's height, maybe an inch or so taller, but they stooped, trying not to meet anyone's eyes.

"They're worried about you," Saskia said, meaning Baskar, but maybe also meaning everyone in this room.

Roan sighed. "Enough of that. Let us worry about you for a change." She tipped her face to the ruin outside. "It's time we finished what we started."

"Scion of the Fox," Saskia said, and Roan turned to her, surprised. Then she laughed as she dropped her hands around Saskia's shoulders, squeezing.

"Enough of the fancy titles, too. General this. King that. We're just us. And we're family."

They were all looking out into the middle distance, considering what was out there for each of them. *Family*.

Roan seemed bright, suddenly, with fire from inside. Perhaps Roan's grief wasn't gone completely. It never could be. That smile, at least, wasn't sad any longer. There was only pride there. Maybe even hope. It felt too much like a goodbye.

"I *was* the scion of the Fox," Roan said to Saskia, to herself. "But I'm not the last. When I'm gone, the story will keep going. That was always the point. We are all a part of it. We are all tellers of it. And there was never one story. It can't end. But you knew that already, didn't you?"

Saskia's throat was thick. "You're going to come back," she said, looking from Roan to Eli, to Phae and Natti, and feeling so young again under the weight of what was ahead. "You have to. You all have to."

Eli had been watching Baskar thoughtfully, then looked back out into the great open, damaged intersection, the ash mingling with the fresh snow around the silent Heartwood pike Ancient had thrust into the living world. Eli's hands were folded before him, body weight on his back leg. He was ready, waiting to spring, and the corner of his mouth twitched.

Then he turned and extended a hand to Roan. "If we don't come back," he said, facing Roan only, "it's so you can, Saskia."

Eli had said *if*. Roan had said *when*.

Saskia glanced at Baskar, their shade rippling under the pane of glass from which they'd made a new chest, looking out, still, in childlike wonder. She missed that feeling.

Roan went to Eli's side. Their shoulders were low, bodies calm. Despite their tangible differences, they were a single unit in two, a duet, the wind stoking the fire, the fire bolstering the updraft. She held his hand. They stood like that a while, as if no one else was there to look. The sight of it made Saskia's tears dry.

Then Roan and Eli let go of one another, the link between them invisible but still golden. They fell into step and went out first.

Phae's arm came around Saskia, holding her close, and Saskia fell into her embrace so she had something, anything, to hold onto.

"Go with Mi-ja," Phae said into Saskia's hair. "We'll see you soon."

"Don't make promises none of us can keep," Saskia said, pulling away. "We made this choice. We just have to remember why."

Phae's smile seemed to bloom, and Natti appeared at her

side. "You were always miles ahead of us, Saskia," Phae said. "But for now, please stay behind. We'll do our best."

Saskia nodded, trying to be brave. "Bring him home."

Phae turned to Natti. Natti slapped her on the back, then yanked her into a fierce hug. They followed Roan and Eli, and Saskia lingered, watching. Hoping. Baskar peeled themselves from the window, knotting their shadow hands in front of them as their cobbled hare ears twitched.

The ground shook.

Ahead, Roan and Eli broke into a run like two horses reckless with joyful abandon. Phae and Natti went after them.

They all leapt into the grey, like they were kids again.

And then they were gone.

～❦～

Ancient would feel them coming. The group wouldn't get a chance at surprise, but they had to fight, all the same.

Phae covered them all with a protective shield. Natti used the river, the Red this time, a power she recognized. She smashed it into the Heartwood, bathed in the red light of the eclipse, willing to hover there in the sky until this work was done.

The ground shook. Ancient's many roots, bespoke for one purpose, had already pulled down buildings, mountains of glass and steel, and it would use them to rend these much more fragile beings that thought themselves better than Creation. A root pulled up a huge steel beam from the debris, slashing it through the four of them.

They broke rank and scattered in four directions, trying to make for the base of the tree. Natti guessed it was at least fifty feet ahead as she pulled herself and Phae out of the way of another root, swinging at their backs.

"Where are Roan and Eli?" Phae shouted over the rumbling. Natti pointed, and a flare fanned out, smashing through a tangle far ahead.

"We have to go!" Natti said, pulling her and Phae back into the fray, the wall they'd crouched behind exploding as a dark spear pierced it.

The Heartwood was just a twisting mass of these writhing roots, and each of them had a will of its own. A need to destroy and tear. There was a great knot at the base of it, and Natti begged Barton, if he was still alive inside of it, to *hold on*.

⤙⚘⤚

Eli and Roan separated. Everything was slow. They fell into their steps easily.

Perfect movement, perfect feeling. Roan was the flame, Eli was the wind. She flipped over him, her leg a torch, her body a flare gun. They lit up the Heartwood's onslaught of branches, beat it back. This was the dance they had long practised. This is what it had been for. At least they could know the time they thought they'd wasted was worth something. They clasped each other's arms and became a shivering inferno, tangled up in one another, making wreckage of their own.

A root ripped free of the concrete and came down between them. They split apart, whirling, but each mirrored the other's steps. Always a unit. Above, the top of the Heartwood sang out as the Task Guard air support rained down their rockets to distract the tree. Roan swore she heard the tree scream. She and Eli tightened their connection as shrapnel came down on their heads, and they fought on.

❧

The river sluiced over the back of the tree, over Natti and Phae's shield, and when the smoke cleared they saw a gaping wound in the Heartwood's bole, where the knot had been. Half a person hung out of it, up to the chest. Phae shot forward for Barton, and Natti took his other side, hauling him free of concrete and rebar and roots still twisting, burnt at the base, like blown-off tentacles.

"We've got him!" Natti yelled into the mouthpiece Mi-Ja had given her. "We're getting clear of the blast zone!"

They held Barton between them, and Phae was hyper-ventilating as they ran, missiles of writhing branches raining down on them and smashing, cracking the shield she could barely hold as they went.

"What about —"

Another explosion from the road in front of them, and Natti faltered, nearly dropping Barton, the roots exploding up in a jet of black.

The fire consumed the next root attack before it could land on top of them, and a hurricane pulled the other corded cables that were seeking to pincer the three from the other side.

Roan and Eli circled one another, arms outstretched, beating Ancient back.

Phae and Natti were frozen for only a moment. Phae felt, harshly, that they were maybe looking at the pair for the last time. Then Natti turned the three of them around, and they limped back the way they'd come.

≈≈

"There!" Saskia pointed to the screen, one of the street cameras still operating near 201 Portage. "I see them!"

Natti's comm had cut out, and in the control room, Mi-ja was barking orders to the airstrike team. "Bank around, prepare for the second assault. Ground support, meet the rescue team at Portage and Garry." Natti and Phae, and the figure they carted between them, disappeared behind a bank of smoke.

"Roan and Eli are still down there," Baskar rustled in Saskia's ear. They seemed too afraid to watch what was unfolding on the wall of screens before them.

"I know," Saskia said, unwilling to look away even for a second. "They'll get clear. They will."

She'd watched them closely. Up to that point, their strange dance had only been something from Baskar's stories. But the story was unfolding there, and all Saskia saw, as Roan and Eli wove in and out of the Heartwood's striking distance, was love. She would hold onto that forever.

She glanced up at a drone that was circling in the camera feed. Her heart squeezed, and for a second it looked like the Heartwood was losing ground, recoiling on itself, trying to protect the rest of its bole as its growth towards the Darkling Moon slowed.

"They're winning," Saskia breathed.

She called it too early.

≈≈

Eli bent backward as a black root sang by him, twisted to avoid another coming for his arm, but another came roaring forward to smash his legs out from under him.

The fire took it out, and the ground where he landed was hot, but it didn't matter.

He saw Roan laughing, saw that she couldn't help but allow herself joy, to take what little she could in this moment. She was beautiful. Her face was bright with it, and Eli caught that look, sent it back with joy of his own. He loved her so much.

His face fell, suddenly, and neither he nor Roan were fast enough.

❧

I don't think I ever had the time for love. To think about it. To imagine myself in it. I was too young. Love was corny. I didn't have the room for it. I didn't understand it. I figured I would, someday. Then a few things got in the way.

I look over at Eli. I feel so much, right now. I feel young, and I feel old. And I feel him, there. Fighting beside him. I feel seen, and known. And I see and know him. I realize that that's enough. I'm laughing. It feels good to look at him, that miserable grouch, his stupid face splitting as he laughs back at me across a hellscape, both of us asking ourselves, *How did we get here?* and not having enough time to form the answer. So we don't say anything. We just move together. We just look at each other.

I see him. My chest is alive with that thing, that love. It's enough. *It's enough.*

I —

꙳

Eli watched Roan look down at her chest, the place where the Opal once nested, the place where her heart was contained between her fragile ribcage. Watched her face contort in confusion, like she couldn't understand how such a sharp, devastating spike of black could be there now. He couldn't tell if she felt the pain of it yet.

She choked, and something hot that wasn't the fire dripped down her chin. Her feet weren't on the ground anymore. Eli screamed with every step as he flew towards her.

꙳

The Task Guard support met Phae, Natti, and their prize with a MEDVAC. Barton was taken out of Phae's hands, but she followed doggedly, getting in their way when they put the oxygen mask over his face, the blood pressure cuff around his arm. She touched him. He was real. Someone said he wasn't breathing. Someone tried to move her away, but she was vaguely aware of sending them back with a blue electric wave, and no one tried to remove her again.

Rushing feet, soldiers everywhere down here, in the abandoned section of the City Walk that had been hollowed out then shored up like a bunker. The entire place shook with every blast above. Yet for all that, Phae didn't look away from Barton, her hands covering him and throwing every bit of the Grace she'd been given, the Deer powers she had chosen, into him.

Don't you remember when I saved you the first time? she begged and pleaded with any god left alive to listen. She would blast the Moth Queen back, too, if she came. *Come back to me. Come back.*

She held tight to him, and he was still.

Barton's chest swelled and his eyes shot open, and Phae was already far beyond crying. She just breathed, fast, like she could breathe for him, like she was still running.

Barton stared at her. Seemed to stare beyond her. He was shaking. She held him close, feeling the stuttering twitches of his arms before they came around her. More shouts. Explosions and earthquakes. But they held onto each other.

"No," Barton said.

Phae pulled away, dust settling in her hair. "What? What is it?"

Barton was still looking past Phae to Saskia, who stood in front of the bank of screens near the ruined stairwell of their impromptu bunker. The room was quiet, then, and yet everything inside Saskia was noise. A calm that was nothing more than the windup.

Saskia fell to her knees.

⁂

The hurricane was high. Thunderbolts and sparks collided and came down, and all of the branches that had come for Eli exploded backward with his anguished howl. Infernal splinters rained down but didn't stop him. He went running straight to Roan, as he always would. The tree pulled away from him, retreating as it defended from a new Mundane onslaught. The world was still for Eli, at least, for that last moment.

He staggered to a halt in front of her, not knowing where to put his hands. The root had pierced Roan through her chest, her blood pouring out down her stomach and pooling at her feet.

"No, no," he said to her, disagreeing, in every way, with what he saw. "No, you can't."

Roan reached out, shaking with the effort, and grabbed Eli's forearms and pulled him gently to her, careful that he wouldn't be pierced, too.

"Good thing you're here — to —" Every word was an effort, so was the smile. "— to tell me what to do."

Eli was crying like a child. Roan had seen him cry before, and it had always been over her.

"We still have too much to do together," he said. "Snap out of it." His hands passed over hers, then up her arms. He would pull her free, and take her to Phae, and —

Her fingers dug into his skin. "Get out of here now. Help the others. Help Saskia."

She'd asked him to do this before, and he'd obeyed. But not this time.

He could feel the ground beneath them moving again. Eli watched those evil cables shoot up, slapping the next air-strike team clean out of the sky and sending them hurtling as far as St. Boniface. Their explosions just became part of the scenery. Eli didn't hear them at all.

As if the Heartwood's roots could *see* both Roan and Eli, the cables turned towards them, rising like a tidal wave about to smother them both.

Eli looked at Roan through the screen of his tears. "I'm not leaving you. When will you get that through your thick skull?"

Roan showed her teeth, the blood foaming pink at the back of her jaw as she laughed. "We always have to do every-thing together."

He could see the light going out of her eyes. The fire, the last of it, flickering out. He pulled her very close, pressing her head to his. He whispered, "Don't let go of me."

Without the Moonstone, he had no wings to carry her away. Without the Opal, she wasn't the Fox warrior that could cut them a path out of here. It didn't matter. They were, at least, themselves. Roan brought up the last of the fire, and it consumed them both. Eli sent it higher, higher, the updraft of his last scream building the inferno tall as their ambitions had been once. The twisting column of it was as big as their love had become.

The ground heaved. The Heartwood crashed down and there was a shockwave.

There was nothing left of Roan and Eli when the smoke cleared.

LAST STAND *of the* DEAD

Before the screens had cut out, before that last, devastating crash that they'd all believed would bring the concourse down on their heads, they'd seen it.

Natti had been the one to scream. Roan had only looked away for a second, cavalier, and that's all it took. It didn't seem real, or possible. Eli had gone to her. They had both gone down together.

All was silent. Saskia still hadn't looked away from the black, cracked screen, even though it only showed her face, winced tight and streaming with tears. No one there, none of the soldiers or Mi-Ja or anyone who'd survived this wave, had to look outside to know that the tree was still there, but it had stalled. Roan and Eli had seen to that. It wouldn't stall for long, though, even with an attack like that. An attack that had finally stopped Roan and Eli, two immovable forces, larger than any realm.

Roan and Eli had only made way for the last stand.

Saskia went to Barton, and he put his arms around both her and Phae, Natti covering the other side. They were numb. It was barely a comfort to feel each other breathing. They held on as long as they could before Saskia peeled herself off, willing herself to move.

Phae wanted to reach for her, but she knew it was time to let go. She just watched, unable to speak, loss cresting over her again and again, the sensation of Roan's kiss on her forehead still fresh.

"Keep holding on to each other," Saskia said to them all. Baskar went with her, past Mi-ja, whose face was blank as she sank to the floor, tucking her legs under her.

The hall, filled with what was left of the Task Guard soldiers, echoed with the clatter of weapons being placed on the ground as they all watched Saskia leave. One by one the soldiers went down to the floor, some of them kneeling, some of them closing their eyes, all of them quiet, waiting for the end to come over them all. Saskia went up the frozen escalators, and found her way back out into the street, as if she was going out to meet a friend in the Exchange District.

The darkness outside was almost complete, the Heartwood still intent, despite its damage, in going up, touching space, because Saskia could see it reaching still, trying to get back to the way things had been before Ancient had dreamed up humanity.

Above what was left of the city skyline, there was heat lightning. There was wind. Clouds gathered and thunder finally rumbled and soon there would be rain. The tree shivered. One last element remained. Saskia pressed the Onyx in her hand to her heart, and Baskar's shell collapsed beside her as their shade went into the stone.

Where Baskar had just been, the Moth Queen now hovered.

Saskia couldn't look anywhere but ahead. "Roan and Eli —"

The Moth Queen shivered her papery wings. "With the others."

The air snapped and the wind whipped around the Heartwood. Bolts slithered around the tree. The eclipse above seemed to burn.

Saskia let the Onyx inside her, let the song pulse through it, through her. Let it amplify in the centre of the cataclysm happening right in front of her, and she felt Baskar with her, at least. *I'll finish it for you*, she sent out into the ether, imagining that Roan and Eli were somewhere close by, and still able to hear it.

Saskia walked forward and told herself one more story.

"Once upon a time, the dead were no longer able to cross over, and so they remained in the world, restless."

The Onyx strobed out at the Heartwood, lashing a whip into its bark. Bloodbeasts, the world over, shivered and the corrupted shades vacated their husks, and the dead went marching.

"The Moth Queen, Death itself, wanted to repair this rift. And the dead wanted this, too. They wanted peace for themselves. For the living. For the future." She was running now, the tree crackling in front of her as the stone inside her hand shot hot spears of energy ahead of her, into it. The eclipse was growing brighter as the tree began to reach again, pulling the moon down towards the earth. The dark expanded.

"The heart of Spirit had made the Darklings, but the dark was not the enemy. The dark was not the end."

The bark split open and Saskia passed into Ancient's great, infinite mind.

❦

The dead came when the Onyx called them. The dead that had been brought up from the underworld when Ancient had dragged them here. The Denizen dead who couldn't cross over into their promised afterworld when the realms shattered. The Moth Queen expanded, big as the world, and called them to her. To Saskia.

Above, the Darkling Moon shivered. Then, like an apple, it fell towards the world, towards the Heartwood that was Ancient.

And the dead, a thunderhead of manifold souls, rose up to meet it.

❦

Chaos. Harm.

Then Silence.

Saskia was inside the Onyx. No, the Quartz. No, she was standing before a creature with three swivelling faces crowned with triple horns. Their reflection beneath them was another triple creature, a snake woman, a beautiful man, a horse with no mouth. Saskia wasn't in her body. She didn't need it holding her down. Baskar was behind her, holding her up, holding her together. Ancient was above, spreading, and there was something bright piercing it. A golden tether. An Owl, a Fox, holding tight to the line.

Saskia was inside of the moment and outside of it.

This is what is meant to be, Ancient said. *This is the Narrative. This is the end.*

"For you, maybe," Saskia said. Fia opened their hands, and Saskia put the Onyx into them. Death rose from the black stone and put her arms around the universe's consciousness. Ancient tried to expand.

"The dead are more invested in life than Creation is," the Moth Queen said. Saskia said. Fia said. All at once.

"In the beginning," Fia intoned, and Saskia felt the red sigils beneath her firing off in a wave. Going backward. Turning gold. Then, as soon as the wave came, slowly fading into nothing, it was gone. "There was darkness."

"But that was only the beginning," Roan and Eli said together, and the other dead echoed.

Saskia felt their golden tether slipping around her spirit. The Moth Queen held on to them all.

You cannot undo me, Ancient bellowed. *I am where this world comes from, I am where it goes to end!*

"You gave this world to us, and it is ours, and we will protect it," they all said. "The end may be inevitable, but it's not coming today."

Together — even the Darkling reflections beneath Fia — they pushed at the writhing godhead, no different from any of them, pushed it back to the dark from whence it'd come beneath the horizon of the light.

"You slept. You turned away. And the world still turned," Saskia intoned.

The last of the sigils dissolved. The Narrative was gone.

The Darkling Moon and the Heartwood tree collided, folded in on themselves, and were gone, too.

🙚🙘

The world, whose axis had been halted, let out a breath.

It turned.

🙚🙘

"Saskia."

She'd had her arms over her face. She lowered them now, and standing before her was a person. Not a shade. Their eyes were keen and kind. Everything around them both was humming, golden light.

"Baskar?"

They smiled. Their features were hazy, imperfect, the forehead high, shoulders narrow. Saskia glanced past them, into infinity, and there were others. Weaving in and out of these many faces, all gazing into the flickering gold, were little moths. Some smiled as the little wings tickled cheeks, brushed past eyes, closing slowly. Saskia knew, without having to guess, that these were the dead that had only just helped her. And they were going home.

Each of them was a star in a constellation she couldn't recognize when she had been in the Deadlands, but she didn't need to. There were hundreds of thousands of billions of them. When a moth touched them, they winked out of the gold zeroscape.

Saskia reached for Baskar suddenly, and they held on to her, surprised. "Are you . . . are you going?" she asked. It wasn't her right to beg them to stay. Baskar needed peace. They both did. "If you are —"

"Do not say you'll come with me." Baskar shook their head. "Besides, I promised to be a part of your story until the end. I hope you remember that."

Baskar slid an arm around her, and she felt utterly calm. They watched, together, as each of the trapped Denizen spirits went ahead into another realm, or back into the world, or just made their own choice of where their energy might go next. Flickering fireflies, each choosing their own peace.

Saskia glanced away from this procession, thinking she saw a man with black hair and a redheaded girl, moving together and away, but it was only for an instant, and they were gone, too.

"What will happen? To the dead? To the realms?"

Baskar smiled beside her. "They'll make their own stories. I imagine it will be a new realm. A new country. Perhaps some new gods will emerge. To manage it."

Saskia felt her spirit warming. "I think I've heard that story before."

Soon the golden light was getting dimmer, as each spirit went away. The moths remained behind, and came together, and the Moth Queen was a singing gold as Saskia had never seen her before.

When the Moth Queen turned, Saskia knew that she, too, had changed. Colour radiated at her chest — the memory of five matriachs, whatever shards were left of them. All of the mothers, one being.

Death smiled, and this strange in-between place began dissolving, Saskia and Baskar along with it.

The soldiers went tentatively into the road, many hours later. They had all fallen asleep, it seemed, and woken to absolute wreckage, but somehow they were glad about it. Some of them didn't understand why. The sun shone above, the last of a snowstorm moving away as the light dipped into the west. The sky was clear. Clear as it hadn't been in seven years. Bright with possibility.

There would be a tomorrow.

Barton, Phae, and Natti looked out into the sunset, more than surprised they'd lived to see it.

Somewhere in the crater at Portage Avenue and Main Street, Saskia woke back in her body, by herself, though she didn't feel alone. She raised her right hand to her face, the palm clear but for a fading mark that looked like it'd always been there. Somehow, it made her think of rabbit ears. She closed her hand and put it to her heart, shut her eyes.

And breathed.

The FOX *and the* OWL

Myth and memory are as changeable as the world. They must be, and some stories survive cataclysms. People told them and told them again, and they changed, and it was good.

Dreams are the miracles that take us back to those places, those first, uncharted landscapes, deep beneath the reality we've been taught can be felt only with empirical evidence. Interpreted by five senses. Or five elements.

But there must be something on the other side of the twilight. Such things have been dreamed of before even Creation dreamed. Energy can never be destroyed. Only changed, like the story.

A myth is only a dream that has been recorded and retold. A narrative is not a plan, but an expression. The last dream is this — that darkness is not an enemy. It is the start of all things. It is the end of all things. It is the wheel, flashing, telling us something. Something that can be retold while we are still here to tell it.

There is a splinter of gold there, in the depths of that brilliant darkness. Someday, slipping through that crack may be as easy as dreaming for you. On the other side of that last dream is a rich place where grief can do us no harm when we take it into us. It is a place beyond what we know.

Here is a story, but it won't be the last: in this great beyond there is a fox, and she is accompanied by an owl, minding the infinite threads of the story that came before, and the story to come, and the possibility that the story is not over, even when it is. Saskia always imagined they'd be there together, in that wild new country, minding those who passed through or sought to return to the world again. She couldn't imagine it any other way.

Nothing is certain. Nothing is meant to be known. The gods, what little was left of them, dreamed. The Darklings, the promise of the other side of day, dreamed. Saskia dreams now, many years after, at the end of her long life, well-lived for all its jagged edges. What mattered was the love she had, the people she knew, the stories she was a part of. And it was good.

At the end, Saskia saw clearly the golden splinter in the dark and went home to it — and whatever was on the other side of it — to begin her story anew.

ACKNOWLEDGEMENTS

A nd so, we come to the end.

Writing a trilogy is a tricky thing, as I have learned through the process of completing this one. From a development standpoint, there are many moving parts, questions to be answered, and a constant looping-back to make sure your original intent is not only clear, but still there. I started writing *Scion of the Fox* on a whim in 2014, without a plan, after encountering the titular animal on a snowy night walk, and I've followed that fox down deep into places I never fathomed. I came out blinking on the other side, exhausted but, as a writer, altered for the better. I hope as a reader you came out with something that will hold meaning long after these covers are shut.

The series itself was always focused on a wished-for horizon, on endings, on the fallibility of even the most infallible, on inverting the tropes that I, as a reader, always relied on, on making difficult choices, on found family, on mistakes, and the emotional toll of grief heaped on those far too young to deserve it. I built a mythology, a world, an underworld, and creatures that seemed to erupt fully formed and heedless of my creative energies, and though their stories are now over, they will always exist in these three volumes, and I'm content with that.

But I didn't do it alone. Writing a series requires support, in actual fact. Thanks, first, to ECW Press for taking on this series mostly sight unseen and trusting me to deliver. To my editor, Jen Hale, who has always been forever my strongest, loudest advocate, without whom I would not be a published author. To my copy editor, Jen Knoch, who went through every book with such meticulous fervour and caught so many things, offered such incredible insights, and left her amazing reaction comments throughout the manuscripts — the latter of which kept me going through those heavy editing phases. And to the entire team at ECW — the designers, publicists, marketers, sales folks. You have all been fabulous. I still don't feel worthy.

Thank you to my poor blurbers, also, who gave the earliest review of these embarrassingly large books, and did so with aplomb and grace.

To my family, for encouraging my desire to create stories, to pursue art, no matter the cost. I say without any irony that making art has saved my life, and continues to, so I am grateful that my parents bought me every book I asked for and never demeaned my delusions of grandeur when it came to writing at a young age.

Warmest thanks to my dear husband who, while not in the arts himself, holds them, and my work, in high esteem and has been nothing if not my champion, reminding me how difficult this work is and how I am lucky I can not only pursue it as a career but that I have the drive for it.

And, finally, and with the tenderest affection, to the readers I say: Thank you, thank you, *thank you*. You are seen for seeing me and my work, for buying it, taking it out of the library, talking about it with your friends at school, for your kind personal messages, your Tweets, your thoughtful reviews, and your general wonderfulness. It has been a privilege to share this trilogy with you, and I hope to see you again at the dawn of the next adventure.

And should you be an aspiring writer yourself, person still sticking around at the end of this, take heart. If you write, you are a writer. Passion and discipline and a desire to tell a tale are all you need to get started, plus a little bit of courage to keep going. Just know that I believe in you, whoever you are.

Keep reading, keep dreaming.

~S

At ECW Press, we want you to enjoy this book in whatever format you like, whenever you like. Leave your print book at home and take the eBook to go! Purchase the print edition and receive the eBook free. Just send an email to ebook@ecwpress.com and include:

Get the eBook free!*
*proof of purchase required

- the book title
- the name of the store where you purchased it
- your receipt number
- your preference of file type: PDF or ePub

A real person will respond to your email with your eBook attached. And thanks for supporting an independently owned Canadian publisher with your purchase!